CRITICAL ACCLAIM FOR THE NOVELS OF BARBARA MICHAELS

D1012073

THE DANCING FLOOR

"Everything a romance reader can ask for."
—*Publishers Weekly*

"Yum, all the ingredients needed to mix one of Michaels's Gothic concoctions."
—*Poisoned Pen*

HOUSES OF STONE

"I wouldn't have missed this for anything. . . . Barbara Michaels has surpassed herself."
—*Phyllis Whitney*

"Vivid descriptive writing and convincing dialogue."
—*Publishers Weekly*

"Eerie supernatural events . . . a refreshingly intelligent and unstereotyped heroine."
—*Kirkus Reviews*

VANISH WITH THE ROSE

"I leapt on [this] as if it were chocolate. . . . This book and this writer are addictive."
—*Alexandra Ripley*

"Involving . . . a cleverly spun mystery."
—*Booklist*

"Barbara Michaels can always be counted on for a darned good mystery with fascinating characters and a chilling tale. . . . Magnificent!"
—*Ocala Star-Banner*

Books by Barbara Michaels

HarperChoice

BARBARA MICHAELS

THE DANCING FLOOR

HarperPaperbacks
A Division of HarperCollinsPublishers

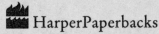

HarperPaperbacks

A Division of HarperCollins*Publishers*
10 East 53rd Street, New York, N.Y. 10022-5299

This is a work of fiction. The characters, incidents, and
dialogues are products of the author's imagination and are not to
be construed as real. Any resemblance to actual events or
persons, living or dead, is entirely coincidental.

ISBN 0-06-109254-1

HarperCollins®, ®, HarperChoice®,
and HarperPaperbacks are trademarks of
HarperCollins*Publishers*, Inc.

Cover illustration © 1997 by Donna Diamond
Handlettering by Michael Sabanosh

A hardcover edition of this book was published
in 1997 by HarperCollins*Publishers*.

First HarperPaperbacks printing: February 1998

Printed in the United States of America

Visit HarperPaperbacks on the World Wide Web at
http://www.harpercollins.com

❖ 10 9 8 7 6 5 4 3

To Rosie—Eleanora Elizabeth Brown Mertz
September 23, 1995
With love from Ammie

AUTHOR'S NOTE

The fictional liberties I have taken with the famous
Pendle witch case are clearly designated as such.
Aside from "Old Demdike" and the other victims of
that case, all the characters are figments of the
author's deranged imagination and bear no resemblance to real persons living or dead.

ONE

They have no definite approaches,
but wander about in circular side-tracks,
and most savage monsters are concealed
in their labyrinth of deception.

HENRY, ABBOT OF CLAIRVAUX

It was still dark outside when I woke, sweat-soaked and shaking after another of those awful dreams. The plot changed nightly, the danger differed, but the theme was always the same; a desperate attempt to reach him, through fire or flood or some other monstrous menace, before it happened. Sometimes I saw him, smiling and unaware, deaf to my screams of warning, just before the wave broke or the flames engulfed him. Sometimes he had seen the danger and turned a tormented face toward me, crying out for help, as I beat vainly at the barrier that separated us.

Sometimes she was there, sometimes she wasn't. But I could always feel her presence, watching and waiting.

My groping hand found the light switch. It took me a while to remember where I was— what hotel, what town, what country. There had been so many different rooms. They were all more or less alike, whether the furniture was imitation Chippendale or imitation Danish modern. This one was imitation Elizabethan, with fake beams across the ceiling and a bed draped with imitation hangings that didn't actually open and close.

I had learned how to fight the lingering horror of the dream by concentrating fiercely on prosaic details like those, and by playing back, like a recorded tape, the memories of how I had got to . . . the Witches' Roost Inn, in the village of Malkin in the county of Lancashire in the country of England. It was getting harder and harder to place myself. I had covered a lot of territory in the past three weeks.

We had planned to start from London, and that was where I began, in the quiet church in Lambeth. It was a museum now, and part of the churchyard had been laid out as a garden. We always assume the sun will be shining when we're on vacation, but it was raining that day, not hard, just a slow gray drizzle like tears. The little garden had a softer kind of beauty in that misty air. The bulbs made a brave show, crimson tulips and blue scilla, narcissi yellow as sunshine. The gray stone sarcophagus looked less incongruous in that setting than one might have supposed. It was carved with designs as exotic as any that ever graced the coffin of an Egyptian pharaoh—crocodiles, dragons, temples. I sat on the edge of the fountain for quite some time while the rain straightened my hair and darkened the shoulders of my raincoat. There was no one else there. No one at all.

Hampton Court, Winchester Castle, Hatfield House; London to Surrey to Sussex, Hampshire and Somerset and Wilts, and then east, into Suffolk and Norfolk before heading north to my present location. Not from stately home to stately home, though I had seen a few; it was the gardens I sought, the old gardens. I had followed with dogged persistence the route we had planned, driving long miles every day and falling exhausted into bed every night, each time in a different hotel. (Not tired enough to sleep without dreaming, though.) I had avoided the smaller inns and the bed and breakfasts. They were too cozy. I didn't want to be welcomed like a friend, or chatted up by ye hoste and hostesse.

This "inne" was smaller than I would have liked, but I had had no choice; it was the only hotel in town. The town was smaller than I would have preferred too; I had planned to spend the night in Manchester, but the events of the afternoon had left me too shaken to go on— first the disappointment of being refused admittance to the place I had come so far to see, and then the accident and its unpleasant consequences.

The accident wasn't my fault. Admittedly I was in a bad mood because I had been turned away from the gates of Troytan House so unceremoniously—not even by a person, but by a brusque electronic voice. I had known the place wasn't open to the public, but the anonymous voice hadn't even given me a chance to explain what I wanted and why. It roused all my worst instincts, which were in the ascendant anyhow, so I headed for the nearest village, thinking I would have tea and try to decide whether to give it up or make another attempt the following day.

It was a small town, and the narrow High Street was congested. As I later learned, it was market day. This, and the fact that I was an American, convinced despite all evidence to the contrary that I was driving on the wrong side of the road, made me proceed with caution. When the boy darted out in front of me I slammed on the brakes, and was thrown forward against the wheel when the car behind rear-ended me.

I hardly felt the jolt; I was too busy looking for the kid, praying I hadn't hit him. When I saw him standing safe on the sidewalk, conspicuous in his bright blue sweater, I was so relieved I felt sick. Then I saw his face. He wasn't hurt or frightened. He was grinning broadly, and he was looking straight at me.

He appeared to be about twelve, or, if he was small for his age, thirteen. His sweater, of a particularly garish shade of bright, electric blue, and his gray wool pants might have been a school uniform. He was a nice-looking boy, with a shock of fair hair and features that were probably regular and attractive when they weren't distorted by that ugly smile. It fattened his cheeks and narrowed his eyes, and I knew, as surely as if I had read his mind, that he had deliberately run out in front of the car—playing chicken, or trying to scare me.

Traffic had stopped and people were gathering around my car and the other vehicle whose bumper appeared to be attached to mine. Ignoring the profane shouts of the other driver, I headed for the boy.

I suppose he had expected sympathy and apologies. The expression on my face must have told him he wasn't going to get either, but he was slow to react, and I had had a lot of practice dealing with smart-ass twelve year olds. I grabbed him by the shoulder.

He struggled and swore. I had expected that, and had no trouble holding on. I only meant to lecture him, and maybe shake him a little, until he bent his head and sank his teeth into my hand.

My reaction was pure reflex. It was just a slap, it couldn't have hurt him as much as those sharp white teeth were hurting me, but he screamed as if I had stabbed him.

A nasty scene ensued, as they say. The first to arrive was his mum. I deduced as much from the fact that the boy, still screaming, flung himself into her outstretched arms, though she looked awfully young to be the mother of a child that old. She was a tiny woman, not much taller than the boy, with a fashionably emaciated figure set off by tight pants and fitted jacket. Her smooth, fair-skinned face would have been pretty if it hadn't been distorted by rage. She added her screams to his, accusing me of everything from child abuse to assault and battery.

I tried to apologize. I wasn't exactly proud of what I had done, and the crowd that had gathered made me uneasy. Mum finally ran out of breath, but the broken ejaculations that succeeded her shouts made it clear that she wasn't buying my excuses.

Then a man in the front row of the spectators cleared his throat. "It ain't the first time he done that, Miz Betancourt. Who's gonna pay for my fender I'd like to know?"

He was a big man, who would have made two of her, but when she looked directly at him his eyes shifted and he said no more. The spectators began to drift away and mum, with a last blistering glance at me, put a protective arm around the boy and walked off. He glanced over his shoulder and smirked at me.

The owner of the dented fender remained. I lost the ensuing argument. No witnesses stepped forward to support my suggestion that maybe he had been following me too closely. After I offered to exchange insurance information, or whatever the procedure might be, he gave me a squinty-eyed look, and realization dawned. He wanted money. Call it settling out of court, call it a bribe, by that time I didn't care. I had a splitting headache and a sick sensation of isolation, the way a new kid in school feels, surrounded by indifferent or mocking strangers. I handed over fifty pounds, and checked into the hotel.

The Witches' Roost. I'd seen Queen's Heads and Boar's Heads and Green Men and other quaint names, but never a witch's anything. It must refer to some local legend, since several shops had similar names—The Witches' Cauldron (a restaurant?) and The Witch House. I wasn't moved to investigate; I was too anxious to get under cover, away from the unfriendly faces and hostile looks.

I couldn't get away from my accusing conscience so easily. I had never laid a hand on any of my students. I had never even been tempted to do so. I prided myself on my ability to handle troublemakers, and small-town Midwest schools are still pretty safe. I ought to have been able to control myself.

A boy that age shouldn't be biting people, though. He was no street kid, scratching for survival; mum's accent had been refined, if her vocabulary had not. I inspected my hand. His teeth had broken the skin in a couple of places, so I washed and sprayed the abrasions with antiseptic. Some people would say it served me right if they got infected.

Since I didn't want to go out I was pleased to discover that the hotel had room service. I ordered a club sandwich and a glass of milk, and checked my chocolate supply—adequate, since I had stocked up the day before. It wasn't until after the waiter had come and gone that I realized I had nothing to read. I had intended to pick up a thriller or a romance, something light and distracting, but the near-accident made me forget. Too late now; the shops would be closed. That was probably true, even if it wasn't my real reason for not wanting to leave the room. The mounting loneliness of the past weeks had come to a climax. Loneliness has nothing to do with being alone. Sometimes you're more aware of it in a crowd than when you're by yourself.

I watched television for a while and then got ready for bed. By then I wanted a book the way some people want a drink, or a chocolate bar— the latter of which I had. For years I had been accustomed to reading myself to sleep. TV was not an acceptable substitute. Looking through a pile of brochures and local magazines the hotel had thoughtfully provided, I found a slim paperback book.

The Pendle Witches.

So there *was* a local legend. The book had been privately printed; flipping through it I saw photographs of houses in various stages of decay, and a woodcut that showed several people hanging from a gibbet. Not pleasant fare, but it was the printed word. I propped the pillows behind me and opened the book.

"By this devilish Art of Witchcraft his head is drawne awrie, his Eyes and face deformed, His speech not well to be understood, his Thighes and Legges starke lame, his Armes lame especially the left side, his handes lame and turned out of their course, his Bodie able to induce no travell."

The victim was one John Law, an itinerant peddler. On March 18, 1612, he encountered a girl named Alizon Device, who asked him for some pins. When he refused, "there came to her a black dog which asked, 'What wouldst thou have me to do unto yonder man?' 'Lame him!'" she said; and before the unfortunate Law had gone a hundred yards he fell to the ground speechless and paralyzed.

So began the infamous Lancashire Witch Craze, which was to end in the death of a dozen innocent people. The victims included Alizon's brother, mother and aged grandmother.

To a modern reader with the most casual knowledge of medicine it is clear that the unfortunate peddler had suffered a stroke. In the early seventeenth century the cause of his affliction was equally obvious. Witchcraft! As everyone in Pendle Forest knew, Alizon came from a family of witches.

Elizabeth Southerns, known as Old Demdike,

was the matriarch of the clan. "She was a very olde woman, about the age of Fourescore years, and had been a witch for fiftie yeares." In 1609 under her guidance her son James and her daughter Elizabeth had sold themselves to the Powers of Evil. A year or so later young Alizon, her teenage granddaughter, had sworn allegiance to the Devil and received a "familiar"— the Black Dog with whose aid she had cursed John Law.

The Devices were not the only family of witches in Pendle. In fact, as some of them pointed out, they had resorted to black magic in order to defend themselves against their rivals— Anne Whittle, familiarly known as Chattox, her daughter Alice and the latter's husband. Ironically the two aged women—for Chattox was also in her eighties—may have shared the same cell in Lancaster Castle. . . .

It was at that point that I had stopped reading. The story was new to me, but I had read about the Salem witches and other cases, and I could anticipate how this one would end—the trial, the wild accusations, the unjust, inhuman sentence. I wasn't even thinking about it when I fell asleep. However, I guess it isn't surprising that the dream should have taken the form it did: the stake, the faggots piled high around him, the gloating smile on the face of the woman who held a torch, ready to light the pyre.

One of the worst ones yet, that dream. I wiped the cold sweat off my face and looked at the clock on the bedside table. Twenty minutes past five. I rolled over and tried to get back to sleep, but I kept seeing faces—the highway robber's inimical glare, the kid's grin, the mother's distorted mouth and wild eyes. Ugly faces, ugly people.

My own ugly mind, rather. It had warped and spoiled everything I had seen since I arrived.

We had planned the trip together, poring over maps and guidebooks, discussing the best route from Sussex to Scotland, locating each stately home and historic garden. Now even the memories of those hours together were tainted. I had been a sentimental fool to suppose that this would be a way of sharing. You can't share life with the dead.

Sleep was impossible. I got out of bed, plugged in the electric kettle and dumped a packet of instant coffee into a cup. No restaurant would be open at this hour, but coffee and the tasteless biscuits the hotel had supplied would get me moving—not farther north, toward the next stop on the long dreamed-of itinerary, but back to London. It was time to abandon this pathetic pilgrimage and go . . . home? There was no such place, not any longer. It didn't matter where I went, so long as it was someplace he had never been or dreamed of seeing. Money was no problem. I had been spending it hand over fist, but there was plenty left.

A drowsy receptionist checked me out and unlocked the front door. The young woman obviously didn't give a damn where I was going or why I was checking out at such a peculiar hour. She didn't offer to help with my luggage either. There are some advantages to being husky and big-boned; one is not dependent on the kindness of strangers, a commodity that appears to be in short supply these days. The suitcases weren't heavy. I saw no one abroad as I walked down the dark street toward the town lot, where I had left my car.

As I drove out of town the spire of the church showed black against the graying sky, like a giant's arm raised to strike. The sun would be up shortly. Perfect timing. It was light enough for me to see where I was going but the occupants of Troytan House wouldn't be stirring for another hour or so.

I had decided not to risk another rebuff from the gateman, but there was nothing to prevent me from walking around the perimeter of the estate and maybe, if I was lucky, getting a glimpse of the grounds through a back gate or a gap in the high metal fence. I just wanted to say I had seen it. It was the culmination of the trip we had planned, and it would be my last stop— a final gesture to memory before I turned my back on it and on the past.

The dawn light darkened again when I turned into a sunken lane lined with high hedges. I encountered no other vehicles, but I had to swerve to avoid an animal that darted across the road. I hadn't identified the creature; it had been only a blur of brownish-orange, and a flash of glowing eyes. A badger? A cat? If so, it had been a very large cat.

I passed the gate without stopping; paired lanterns on the stone gateposts shone brightly, but there was no other sign of life. A quarter of a mile farther on, I turned off the road onto the track I had spotted the previous day. Unpaved and stubbly with weeds, it followed the line of the fence that enclosed the estate. It was a formidable structure, close-set steel bars topped with spikes, and it looked new. From what I had heard about the present owner he liked his privacy and could afford to ensure it.

I had no intention of trying to climb that fence. Mind you, I could have. It wouldn't have been easy, but it could have been done. All I wanted was a look inside.

After I was far enough from the road so that the car could not be seen, I stopped. I was wearing jeans and heavy walking shoes, and a denim jacket with big pockets. Stowing my camera in one pocket, and my keys in another, I locked the car and started off along the track. The sun was still below the horizon but there was enough light for me to see where I was going. Unfortunately I couldn't see anything inside the fence; shrubs and/or the walls of various buildings blocked my view.

It must have rained during the night, though I

hadn't been aware of it. The ground was soft under my feet and the breeze carried the delicate scent of wet green leaves and clean air, and something I couldn't identify—a faint flower fragrance, like blackberry blossoms. The wild roses would be blooming now back—back in Missouri. Not roses, this fragrance, not from any species with which I was familiar, and I knew many of the old ones. Something wilder, uncultivated— hawthorn? Mist rose from the matted grass of the track and hung like a translucent linen shroud over the hedge on my right. Only an occasional sleepy ripple of birdsong broke the stillness.

I had not been alone for weeks except in the sterile stuffy confinement of a hotel room, not even in the gardens I had visited. They were all open to the public, and if the public had not been present a gardener or custodian had. I stopped looking for a gate or a gap in the shrubbery. I walked, head up, sniffing the air, until a ray of sunlight crossed my path and brought me to a stop.

A rim of red showed over the horizon and the sunlight struck straight as a sword into the tangled greenery at my right. The fence had disappeared, swallowed up by a tangle of brush higher than my head. It was not an ordinary hedge of boxwood or yew or any other garden shrub; brambles and vines and trees were interwoven, almost as if by design, into a matted wall. One vine boasted a particularly vicious-looking set of thorns.

I turned and looked back. I had come farther than I had realized. The track I had followed, now no wider than a footpath, wandered off to the left, across a pasture and over a narrow bridge before it vanished into a grove of trees. Some distance ahead the ground rose, culminating in a long ridge whose steep sides showed no sign of cultivation or habitation. On the right side, blocking my view and stretching as far as I could see, was that brambly jungle.

I knew I ought to turn back. My original idea, of walking around the perimeter of the grounds, was looking more and more impractical. Yet the hedge fascinated me. I had never seen anything like it. How far did it extend? Had it been deliberately designed as a barricade?

After I had gone a few more steps I saw a break in the jungly growth. Not a natural break—this opening was man-made, by a chain saw or machete, and beyond lay a narrow passage—a tunnel rather, since it was roofed with the same tangle of vines and brambles that formed the walls.

It was as anomalous as the hedge itself, too narrow for the passage of a machine or a horse and cart, just the right size to admit a single human being—a short one, for when I stepped cautiously into the opening the viny ceiling was not far above the top of my head. I measured it with my hand, cautiously, for the thing was studded with thorns. I am five feet six inches tall. A six-footer would have had to stoop, or get a painful haircut.

I resisted temptation, but not for long. This might be the back entrance I had hoped to find—an unorthodox, unconventional entrance, but that only made it more intriguing. It couldn't do any harm to have a look.

I pulled on a pair of heavy gloves and walked into a green, wet shade. Under an uneven layer of fallen branches and clippings the ground was soggy. Except for an occasional, startling snap of a twig under my feet the place was deadly quiet; the thorny walls muffled even the sound of birdsong.

I hadn't gone far before I realized my original assumption had been mistaken. The mass of vegetation couldn't be a hedge; it was obviously much more extensive. The tunnel curved and angled, sometimes turning back on itself, and it wasn't long before I had lost all sense of direction. The tortuous path reminded me of a maze like the one at Hampton Court, but such mazes had been deliberately designed, the shrubs planted to form a pattern of open paths. Here the path had been cut through a pre-existing jumble of mixed brush. But for what purpose? It couldn't have a practical function, it was too narrow and too indirect. An adventurous child might have relished exploring such a labyrinth, but this was no child's playground. The rotting vegetation underfoot was slippery, the thorns that plucked at my sleeve were sharp enough to tear bare skin.

Outside the sun had risen; a faint greenish light filtered down through the leafy roof. The strange place had a dreamlike atmosphere, as if it had led out of the real world into another dimension or another century. By that time I was so confused I doubted I could retrace my steps. There was nothing for it but to go on. It had to end somewhere.

Another abrupt right-angled turn in the path left me confronting a wall of foliage thicker and darker than any I had seen thus far. The underlying structure might have been an evergreen of some variety, but the branches were interwoven with ropelike strands of honeysuckle and Convolvulus. Through them I saw a glimmer of white.

My gloved hands moved without conscious direction from my brain, tugging at the vines. They resisted with sullen strength and I pulled harder. Then the curtain gave way and a face looked out at me.

Brown streaks ran down its bearded cheeks like the tracks of acid tears. A green stain smeared the leprous white of the horned brow.

I knew what it was, but that knowledge was the last remnant of rational thought. Mindless, overwhelming terror buried my brain like a dark avalanche. I ran, blinded and deafened by panic, slipping and falling, scrambling up and running again. Claws ripped my cheek, ropey arms grasped me. I covered my face with my hands and tore free, feeling the walls close in, the roof subsiding. I knew it was coming, moving ponderously and inexorably on its broken marble feet, its cold stone hands reaching out to grasp me. I knew there was no way out, only a coil of paths that led to a place where something awaited me—something even worse than the crumbling, dead stone thing that followed, herding me back toward the heart of the maze.

Blinded by tears of terror, arms shielding my face, I went on running until I tripped and fell facedown on the grass.

Grass. I had lost one of my gloves. My fingers caressed the soft carpet, stroked it, dug deep into it. When I raised my head I saw sunlight lying bright along a stretch of clipped, mowed green—a lawn, the triumph of civilization over the jungle. I was out, and the panic was gone. Even the memory of it was remote, like something I had read about but never experienced.

The emotion that replaced it was not relief but pure solid embarrassment. I had seen something else besides grass. They were feet—not stony, broken hoofs, but human feet, neatly shod in expensive brogues and silk socks.

I was tempted to stay where I was and pretend I had fainted or knocked myself out. The feet were obviously those of a man, and they probably belonged to the owner of the estate. Not only had I invaded his property and his privacy, but I had made a spectacular fool of myself. A polite apology and quick withdrawal weren't going to get me out of this debacle. Slowly and reluctantly I rolled over and sat up.

I found myself staring into the big, brown, astonished eyes of a man who had obviously come out of the house to enjoy a leisurely breakfast al fresco; he was seated beside a table spread with food, and he was as neat and tidy as if he had been tended by a trained valet—black hair smooth, brown cheeks freshly shaved, shirt spotless, jacket pressed, shoes shined. He held a book in one hand and a piece of toast in the other. His mouth was open.

I cleared my throat and croaked, "Good morning."

"Good morning."

The man continued to stare. His lips had not moved. Was he a ventriloquist? An animated android like the ones at Disney World, his recorded voice out of sync with his programmed movements?

I got a grip on myself. The voice had come from behind me.

The man who had returned my greeting was tall and stout and some years older than the seated man; a fringe of gray hair circled his balding head and the wrinkles in his cheeks deepened as he went on, "Good morning, she says. Who the devil are you, young woman, and where the devil did you come from? This is private property. You are trespassing. Grab her, Jordan, I'm going to call the police."

"For God's sake, Dad, calm yourself." The

younger man closed his book and put on a pair of horn-rimmed glasses, through which he studied me with disgust. "I don't want to grab her. She's covered with mud and blood and muck. At least let her answer your questions before you call the cops. What is your name, miss?"

His cool stare and supercilious tone had a surprisingly therapeutic effect. I still felt like an idiot, but I react poorly to being sneered at. Suppressing an insane urge to throw myself into his arms, wrinkling his neatly creased slacks and smearing mud and blood and muck all over his nice white shirt, I glowered back at him. "I'm sorry. I had no idea I was trespassing. My name is Heather Tradescant and I—"

"What?" The older man's bellow hurt my ears.

"I said I was sorry. I didn't know—"

"No, no. Your name?"

"Tradescant." I spelled it. "I'm an American. The name is English."

"I know." The older man's frown had been replaced by another expression, one I found less easy to interpret.

"I'll go, all right? You don't have to call the police, I'm just a dumb tourist who got lost."

I started to get to my feet. A stab of pain shot up my left calf, and I would have fallen again if the older man hadn't grabbed hold of me. He let out a grunt as his arm took my full weight. "You are a big girl, aren't you? Sit down." He emphasized the suggestion by pushing me into a chair. "Give her some coffee, Jordan, she looks as if she could use it."

"This is ridiculous," Jordan snapped. "Let her go. There's no need for the police."

"Police?" His father gave him a reproachful look. "I'm surprised at you, Jordan. Does not the Koran tell us to welcome the stranger and tend the wounded? Here's a poor young woman, injured and lost, and you let her kneel bleeding at your feet, without offering her sympathy or assistance. Have some breakfast, Miss—Miss Tradescant. Have mine. I'll be right back."

The look Jordan directed at his father's rapidly retreating form should have raised blisters on his neck. "Kneel bleeding at my feet," he muttered. "Damn him and his purple prose."

I couldn't imagine what had changed the old man's attitude, from hostility to effusive hospitality, but I was not about to object. Jordan's description of my condition had been rude but only too accurate. My clothes were filthy, my ungloved hand was striped with scratches and my ankle wasn't the only part of me that hurt. In fact, almost every part of me hurt, including my face. I raised my hand to my left cheek. The stickiness was blood, all right.

My unwilling host continued to stare at me with mild revulsion. Avoiding his gaze I took note of my surroundings. I was where I had wanted to be, and I might as well take advantage of the old man's unexpected amiability before he changed his mind and had me hauled off to jail.

The table and chairs were garden furniture, fashioned of cast iron in ornate patterns of fat flowers and intertwining leaves. They had been placed under the biggest tree I had ever seen except in photographs. It wasn't a cedar or a sequoia; some variety of oak, I thought, turning for a better look. Though I sat in the shade of the branches the massive trunk was a good ten feet away.

The grounds, if you could call them that, were completely lacking in distinction. No fountains, no paths, no elaborately planted knot gardens or parterres, only a large expanse of clipped grass with clumps of rhododendron and azalea here and there. There was not a trace of the fabled lost gardens of Troytan. Nothing I could see, except the huge oak tree, was more than half a century old, including the house. Its roofline bristled with chimneys and towers, but the back part, which was what I saw, consisted of a kitchen wing, a cement paved patio, and a typical Victorian porch or veranda. It appeared to be an architectural hodgepodge.

I fished my camera out of my pocket and took a few pictures; in for a penny, in for a pound, I figured. I think Jordan was too outraged to react at first. When I pointed the camera in his direction he grabbed it away from me.

"I wasn't going to take your picture," I protested. "I just wanted a general—"

"You're pushing your luck, lady. Do you want this coffee or not?"

The coffee smelled wonderful. Sipping, I studied Jordan out of the corner of my eye. Like his father he had dark eyes and black hair, and his skin was the shade of brown dedicated sun-worshippers acquire after a summer of tanning. High cheekbones, a narrow nose, and a long, thin-lipped mouth made up a countenance as forbidding as that of a Grand Inquisitor.

Silently he lifted a silver cover to expose the breakfast I had been ordered to eat. I was pleased to see that the old gentleman liked his eggs scrambled and his bacon crisp.

"I thought Muslims didn't eat pork," I said, without thinking.

His eyes narrowed into a squint. "Aha. You know who he is."

"Uh—they told me his name. At the hotel. When I asked who owned the place."

It wasn't a bad explanation, considering that I had invented it on the spur of the moment. I took a bite of scrambled eggs.

"I see," said Jordan, watching me. "As for your implied question, there hasn't been a practicing Muslim in the family since my great-grandfather emigrated to America. My father doesn't practice anything. He doesn't know any more about the Koran than he does about the Book of Mormon, he only throws it at me when he's trying to get me mad. Not," he added, "that his religious convictions are any of your business."

"Right. I apologize."

"Eat. When my father tells people to do something, he expects them to do it."

"He's very kind."

"No, he's not."

"Then why is he being so nice?"

"Because he's up to something," Jordan said grimly. "I've no idea what, but if you knew my father like I know my father, you'd be running for the nearest exit."

"I don't think I could run."

"That's right, you sprained your ankle, didn't you?" Raised eyebrows and skeptical expression strongly suggested he did not believe in the sprained ankle. Before I could reply, he went on, "I don't think my father saw your dramatic appearance on the scene. Before he gets back, perhaps you'd be good enough to explain how you got in here, and what sent you into screaming flight. If there is a rabid wolf or a rapist on the premises I probably ought to know about it."

I was tempted to snatch at the excuses he had suggested—a threatening man, a dangerous animal. He'd never believe what had really happened. I had a hard time believing it myself.

"I don't think I screamed," I said, stalling for time.

"It was a silent scream. Do you know the Munch painting? Good God, woman, I almost had a heart attack! I was sitting here peacefully reading and enjoying the morning air when you came at me, streaming blood like the survivor of a massacre. Then you fell flat, and for a few horrible moments I thought you were . . . What the hell happened?"

There was nothing for it but the truth. Part of the truth, anyhow. I didn't want to explain my real reasons for being there. The world has gone fitness-crazy; an early morning jog sounded convincing. He accepted that without audible or visible signs of skepticism, but by the time I had finished the story his mouth had curled and his eyebrows were raised.

"It was a statue?"

"I suppose so."

"A nasty, scary statue?"

The sarcasm was unmistakable. I glared at him. "It was ugly as sin. I'm not usually a nervous person, though. I don't know what came over me."

"No? Sounds like a classic case of panic." He leaned back, fingertips together. The pose, the horn-rimmed glasses, the dry impersonal tone were professorial, but there was a lively gleam in his brown eyes. "It would be interesting," he continued, "if the statue you saw was a representation of Pan. That's the derivation of the word panic, you know."

"Yes, I do know."

"What did it look like?"

"I didn't hang around long enough to take notes. Look, I really am sorry about—about everything. I'd go back the way I came, only, to be honest, I don't want to very much. If you'll direct me to a more conventional exit, I'll take myself off."

"Oh, no, you don't." He removed the glasses, tossed them onto the table, and fixed me with a hard stare. "That was a very impressive performance you put on, Miss Whoever You Are, but there's one small flaw in your story."

"It was true!"

"Like hell it was. Lady, there is no way through that jungle. No tunnel, no opening, no labyrinthine path."

"But—"

"The gardener keeps it trimmed. More or less. That's it. No tunnel."

"Then how do you think I got here?" I demanded, flourishing a bloody hand under his nose. "How did I get these scratches?"

"Oh, I admit you've gone to considerable lengths for the sake of verisimilitude. I don't know how you climbed the fence, but there's no other way in, so that's how you must have done it. Then you gritted your teeth, swiped your face and hands with a brambly branch, and ran shrieking—silently shrieking—at me."

"I tell you, there is a tunnel."

"Show me." He jumped up and grabbed me by the shoulder, trying to lift me to my feet. I let out an involuntary yell. Jordan let out an involuntary expletive, or maybe it was voluntary, and released his grip. He had seen his father coming.

Mr. Karim came trotting across the lawn smiling like a heavily tanned Santa Claus. Another man was with him. "Now what are you doing, Jordan? You have the manners of a pig. Did you enjoy your breakfast, Miss Tradescant? Good, good! Your room is ready; Sean will take you there."

"Room? What room? I checked out of the hotel this morning."

"I know. You don't want to go back there, it is not very nice, and anyhow you can't drive with a sprained ankle. Where did you leave your car? Are the keys in it? No? Give them to Sean, he will bring the car after he has taken you to your room."

It was an order, not an offer, and I knew it would be a waste of time to argue. If he wanted to detain me there wasn't anything I could do about it, not when they were three to one and my legal position was, to say the least, shaky. Had I entertained any lingering notions of making a break for it, one look at the man called Sean would have ended them.

He was under six feet tall and his build wasn't especially impressive, but there was something about him—the way he stood, the tilt of his head—that made him look formidable. Oddly familiar, too. He had a big black beard, like a pirate's, and heavy matching eyebrows. The beard and the mustache that curved around to meet it hid his mouth, but I was reasonably certain he was not smiling.

The keys were in my pocket. Meekly I offered them to Sean. He definitely was not smiling.

With a nod he accepted the keys and, at a gesture from his boss, scooped me up into his arms.

"Hey," I said, stiffening.

The beard quivered. "Afraid I'll drop you?"

His voice was higher than I had expected, tenor instead of baritone—generalized American, with no identifiable regional accent.

"I can walk."

"Sure you can. Relax, why don't you?"

"Quite right," said his employer, nodding. "I'll see you later, Miss Tradescant."

Jordan said nothing.

I was not accustomed to being carried like a baby. To be honest, none of the men I knew could have carried me very far. Sean wasn't even breathing hard when he reached the room that had been assigned to me, though he had hauled my solid frame along a lengthy corridor and up a flight of stairs. After depositing me in an armchair he left, closing the door behind him. Neither of us had uttered a word.

It was a big room, comfortably but not lavishly furnished. An open door led to an adjoining bathroom. I was trying to summon enough energy to make use of it when there was a brisk rap at the door.

The woman who entered made me stare. She was dressed like a housekeeper out of a Victorian novel, in a prim dark dress with a high collar and long sleeves. The mop of fashionably tangled bright red curls and the heavy makeup were jarring notes, however. Seeing my stupefied expression, she grinned. "Tatty dress, isn't it? The old boy is a Puritan, he doesn't like us to show our skin. Or maybe he's trying to protect his precious son. It's a bloody nuisance, dressing like this, but for what he pays me I'd wear a ruff and corsets."

She was the first person I had seen who didn't make me nervous. I grinned back at her. "Have you been with him long?"

"Just a few months, since he bought the house. He's a funny old chap, but nice enough." She studied me curiously. "He said you'd had an accident. The car, was it? You are a right mess. Get those filthy clothes off while I run you a bath."

She trotted into the bathroom. An explosion of water drowned out my reply.

I took off my jacket, wincing as my shoulder protested. How many times had I fallen? I couldn't remember. When the housekeeper reappeared I began, "It's very kind of you to do this, Mrs.—Miss—"

"You can call me Doreen. Here, give me that jacket."

"Now just a minute! I am not going to take a bath! I know I need one," I added, feeling the film of dried blood on my cheek crack as I smiled. "But if I can just wash my face and hands and make myself look a little more presentable, I'll be on my way."

"Mr. Karim said you'd be staying for lunch."

"Oh, did he? He might have had the courtesy to ask me."

"That's not his way." Doreen yanked the jacket away from me. "What are you going on about? He's not got a harem upstairs, if that's what you're thinking."

I let out a gasp of outraged laughter. "I wasn't."

"So what's your problem?" She brushed my cheek with a gentle finger and shook her head. "That's a nasty gash. How did it happen?"

"I went for a walk early this morning, and by mistake I—uh—I wandered into the hedge, I suppose you'd call it. There was a kind of path, like a tunnel; I got lost and ended up inside."

"Inside?" Her eyes widened.

Jordan hadn't believed me either. His skepticism had annoyed me. Doreen's put me on the defensive.

"I know I shouldn't have gone as far as I did, but I was curious, and I expected it would end or turn back, but it didn't, it kept turning and twisting, and—"

"You mean you were *in* it? Right *in*?" She put an odd emphasis on the prepositions.

"In and through. I didn't mean to, I lost my way."

"In and through," Doreen repeated.

She was gaping at me as if I had sprouted a pair of horns. I went back to being annoyed. "I've already apologized to Mr. Karim. Hadn't you better turn off the water?"

"What? Oh." She started backing away from me. "You go ahead and have a nice soak, all right? Take all the time you want. I'll—uh—I'll be back."

She was out of the room before I could reply.

She had left the water running. I limped into the bathroom and turned off the taps. A glance in the mirror over the washbasin informed me that I did look a right mess. The cut on my left cheek had stained half my face rusty brown, and other cuts and scratches crisscrossed forehead and chin. My hair was a bird's nest of twigs and dried leaves, my left hand was swollen and itching, and my ankle had started to puff up.

I stripped and maneuvered myself into the tub, favoring ankle, shoulder and assorted bruises. The hot water felt wonderful. I was reclining, with only my head and foot protruding, when I heard the bedroom door open. "It's just me," Doreen called. "Got everything you want?"

"Yes, thanks."

Footsteps retreated and the door closed again. I reached for the soap. I had to peel the wrapping off with my fingernail; it was a brand I had never seen, pale yellow and delicately scented. Everything had been supplied—shampoo, big fluffy white towels. It wasn't until I had finished drying my bruised body and my hair that I realized something was missing. My clothes.

I had piled them on a stool by the bathroom

door. Wrapped in a towel, I searched both rooms without result.

Harems.

"Oh, don't be ridiculous," I said aloud. The very thought was racist and prejudiced. Mr. Karim was an American, not a medieval sultan—and anyhow, if a man were looking for candidates for his harem he could do a lot better. Deliberately I dropped the towel and turned to look at myself in the mirrored wardrobe door.

According to the most recent "ideal weight" charts, I was off, in the wrong direction, by a good twenty pounds. I had always suspected those charts were drawn up by companies that manufactured diet foods and exercise equipment, but the additional weight I had gained over the past six months wasn't healthy; it came mostly from chocolate and fast foods. The only thing that had kept me from blowing up like a blimp was the fact that I couldn't sit still. I walked miles every day, returning to the empty house only to sleep—and eat.

Even without the extra weight my figure was nothing to brag about. My shoulders were broad and square, not gently sloping, and my hands were as big as a man's. I ran my fingers through my damp hair. It was short and straight and dull brown; my eyes were an equally undistinguished brown. Prominent chin, high forehead, thick unshaped brows—there wasn't a feature of face or body that held any promise of beauty. "A padded bra might help, though the good Lord knows it would take plastic surgery to do enough to that shape of yours . . ."

I spun away from the mirror. There was a terry robe hanging on the hook behind the bathroom door. I put it on. It was a man's robe, clean but obviously worn; the hem brushed the floor. Assuming it was ankle length on the original owner, he would be five or six inches taller than I—about six feet tall. One of the Karims, presumably. Jordan had never bothered to stand up (his mama obviously hadn't taught him right), but he had seemed to be as tall or taller than his father.

Resolutely avoiding mirrors (just like a vampire, I thought wryly) I used the comb that had been supplied. I didn't need a mirror to know what I looked like. That voice had told me often enough. It would probably echo in my mind for the rest of my life. Homely, fat, flat-chested . . .

Not a suitable candidate for a harem, I thought with a sour smile.

Time dragged on. I prowled the room, opening the wardrobe (empty except for hangers), and the drawers of the bedside table and dresser. (Not even a hanger.) This was obviously a guest room, normally unoccupied. I went to the door. It wasn't locked; I had half expected it would be.

Which was ridiculous. He didn't have to lock me in, I couldn't leave the house attired in somebody else's bathrobe, and on foot—one foot, to be precise. Harems aside, the situation had distinct

Gothic overtones. I had checked out of the hotel that morning leaving no forwarding address and no mention of my destination. I had met no one on the road. If I disappeared . . .

"Ridiculous!" I said it out loud this time. Karim was the sort of man who probably had no scruples about disposing of inconvenient enemies, but he wouldn't go about it this way. Anyhow, his son and his servant and his housekeeper knew I was here. And besides, I wasn't an enemy, just a stupid, innocent tourist.

I went to the window. There were two in the room. This one looked out over the lawn and the big tree, and the dark mass of the wilderness beyond.

Vines wove the structural skeleton of trees and fallen branches and vegetation gone wild into an impenetrable tangle, from which brambly branches stuck up like bony arms. It extended as far as I could see, stretching up to the sky.

Illusion, of course. The wilderness was large but not endless. The path had twisted and turned like the windings of a labyrinth and I hadn't been inside that long.

Inside. Funny, how Doreen had stressed that word *in*.

I went to the other window. A few feet below was a shingled roof, that of a one-story extension or a porch. On the right was another wall, with a window in it. Having exhausted all the possible sources of entertainment, I went back to the chair and sat down. I had been sitting for a long time before I heard voices approaching. One was unmistakable; Mr. Karim's normal speaking voice was audible at a distance even when he wasn't angry. The other voice was that of a woman.

High time, I thought, and called, "Come in!"

The woman was almost my height, but thinner and older. A second, longer look made me question the first appraisal of her age; her skin was smooth and unlined, her coal black hair untouched by gray. High cheekbones and eyes of vivid emerald green were the only remarkable features in a face few people would have considered beautiful; her chin was long, her nose large. But I'd have rather looked like her than the plastic-faced lovelies in the women's magazines. She wore a long-sleeved tunic of green that matched her eyes, brown corduroy pants and a profusion of jewelry; chains and bracelets, dangling earrings, a belt of gold links tinkled musically as she walked.

Mr. Karim followed her into the room. Hands clasped behind him, he bounced up and down on his toes and gave me a big smile. "Ah, good, you are washed. How is the ankle? Jennet will have a look at it, and take care of your other injuries."

"I don't need a doctor. If you will be good enough to return my clothes, I'll go."

Jennet knelt and lifted my foot, stroking my ankle with long spatulate fingers. "It's not sprained or broken, but you've wrenched it badly. A few nasty scratches and a bad case of nettle rash on that hand. Didn't you know better than to handle nettles?" Reaching into the pouch at her belt she took out a small bottle, which she shook vigorously before opening it and pouring a quantity of viscous milky liquid into her palm. She smoothed it over the cuts on my face and massaged the remainder into my hand. It felt cool and a little sticky.

There was no label on the bottle. "What is it?" I asked suspiciously.

"A mixture of various herbs. Mostly aloe. Feel better?"

"Yes. Thank you." I had used aloe for bee stings and rashes. It was perfectly harmless.

I tried to free my hand, but she held on, turning it so that the palm was exposed. She stared fixedly at it for several seconds before releasing her grip, then stood up and looked at Karim. The movement of her head was slight; I might have imagined it.

"Ah," said Karim.

The cuts had stopped stinging. Aloe is effective stuff, but I had never known it to work that fast. Even my ankle tingled pleasantly, as if a mild electric shock had passed through it.

"I appreciate your hospitality, Mr. Karim, but I want my clothes and the keys to my car, and I want to get the hell out of here."

Karim gave me the same look of pious reproach he had given Jordan when he quoted the Koran. "My dear Miss Tradescant, you sound as if you are accusing me of holding you prisoner. You can leave whenever you like, of course, but I had hoped you would join us for luncheon. You'll stay, won't you, Jennet?"

The other woman nodded. Karim went on, "My housekeeper tells me your clothes are still in the dryer. Sean has brought your car around; he will fetch your suitcases."

"And my purse," I said.

"Your purse? Oh, of course." He had been holding it behind him, like a jovial uncle teasing a child by hiding its present. "No doubt you'll want to examine the contents to make sure I haven't stolen your money or your traveller's checks." His open amusement made my cheeks burn. "Ah, here is Sean with your bags. Call when you are dressed—the telephone is there, on the table, and the kitchen extension is three—and Doreen will come for you. *À bientôt*, Miss Tradescant."

"See you later," Jennet said.

"Thank you, Doctor," I said.

"I'm not a doctor, dear."

The village witch, no doubt. I didn't say it, but I thought it.

Karim bowed her out but he was in a hurry; the latch didn't catch, and when he spoke I heard the words clearly. "Are you sure?"

I got to the door in a limping rush and eased it open another couple of inches. Jennet's reply was equally distinct, but not particularly informative. "Of course not. How can I be certain at this stage? But all the signs are there."

The turn in the stairs cut off the remainder of her speech.

Signs of what? Congenital stupidity? Homicidal mania? Leprosy? Maybe she *was* the village witch and Karim was a superstitious old fool who consulted spiritualists and occult advisers. He wouldn't have been the first hard-headed businessman to do so.

One quick look told me the suitcases had been searched. I seldom locked them; a determined thief could easily break the flimsy catches and there was nothing I cared about in the bags anyhow. What had they expected to find? Drugs? A gun? A bomb?

The world in which Mr. Franklin D. Karim lived justified such suspicions. I had known who he was, and now he must know that I had not just blundered by accident into his private preserve. He had searched my purse too. Everything was there—passport, wallet, the folded clipping that proved I had been less than candid—but they were not in the compartments where I had originally placed them.

I ought to have had sense enough to realize that it was foolhardy to take chances with a man like Karim. I didn't know people like him, but I had read about them; if I had been caught trespassing by an ordinary angry householder the worst I had to fear was a dog, and I wasn't afraid of dogs.

I was afraid of Mr. Franklin Karim.

If he checked up on me he would find that I was the person I claimed to be. But I had lied about one thing, and now he knew I had lied. He had not returned the keys to my car.

My hands were a trifle unsteady as I took clean clothes from my violated suitcases and began to dress. There was only one way out of the mess I had gotten myself into. I'd have to tell him the whole story—and hope he would believe me.

TWO

Why is a garden's wildered maze
Like a young widow, fresh and fair?
Because it wants some hand to raze
The weeds which have no business there.

THOMAS MOORE

"My parents are dead."

I had practiced saying the words over and over and over, until I was sure I could repeat them with a steady voice and no tears. I thought I had succeeded, but Mr. Karim was not deceived. He said gently, "Both of them?"

Doreen had shown me to the dining room and offered the support of her arm. She didn't say much, and I made no attempt to start a conversation; I was anticipating the questions I expected to be asked, and trying to compose convincing answers.

Instead of an inquisitor I found a smiling, genial host who spared no effort to make me feel at ease. The food was excellent and we had served ourselves—no servants, no ostentation. Jennet and Karim did most of the talking; occasionally one of them would turn to me with a polite translation of some reference that had been obscure. I discovered that she owned quite a lot of property in town, including the hotel, the leading restaurant, and a shop. So, I thought, she isn't a witch—or else she's a very good one.

It was all very casual and friendly, except for the inimical presence of the fourth person. Jordan ate in silence until, over coffee, his father began the interrogation.

His tone was one of friendly interest, his questions casual—at first. "Is this your first trip to England? On holiday, are you? How long have you been here, what have you seen . . . ?" And then the smiling comment, "If I had a daughter your age I'd worry about her travelling alone. I hope you've sent lots of postcards to mother and dad."

"My parents are dead. . . ."

It was the beginning of the story I had known I must tell in order to convince Karim I was as harmless as I claimed, but I stuck after that statement, answering his next question with a wordless nod.

"I'm so sorry. A recent loss, was it?" His voice was as soft as velvet, but his eyes bored into me.

"What business is that of yours?" I hadn't spoken. The objection came from Jordan.

"I was just making conversation," Karim protested.

"No, you weren't," I said, meeting Karim's eyes with a hard stare of my own. I didn't need anyone to defend me. "Let's stop fencing, Mr. Karim. I'm not awfully good at it, and I'd like to get this over with. Have you finished checking up on me, or are you still waiting for a reply to your—faxes? Phone calls?"

Karim's round, brown face split into a toothy grin. "Both. You're a direct young woman, aren't you? I like that."

"Never mind the compliments. You haven't answered my question."

I kept my eyes fixed on him, as I would have stared down a dog whose temper was uncertain, but I felt much more comfortable now that he had stopped playing games. If he *had* stopped.

He spread his hands wide, in a gesture as practiced as it was unconvincing—the little old rug merchant in the bazaar. "You can hardly blame me for taking precautions. You played the role of a helpless female, sprained ankle and all, but you're a husky young woman." His eyes moved over my arms and shoulders. "What was I to think, especially when you came up with that preposterous name?"

It wasn't exactly an apology, but it came closer than I had expected. Slightly mollified—but only slightly, because this too might be part of his strategy—I said, "It is my name."

Karim nodded. "So I discovered. To answer

your question—yes, I have heard from my New York office. They were able to reach the chief of police in your hometown. He told them the whole story. It answered most of the doubts that had arisen in my mind—the expensive labels on the clothes in your suitcases, the receipts from four-star hotels. The insurance came to a considerable amount, didn't it?"

Jordan's movement was slight, but his father caught it. "Shut up, Jordan. I'm not accusing the girl of murder. It was an accident—a car crash. Wasn't it, Miss Tradescant?"

"Yes." I bit my lip. How much did he know? Too much, probably. Rigley was a smallish town, and the sheriff was—had been—a friend of my father's. He'd have been too awed by Karim's name to keep anything back, even if he had not been one of the world's most enthusiastic gossips.

It was as if I had spoken aloud. Karim's smile broadened. "Sheriff MacMillen is a nice fellow. We had a long chat. You are twenty-five years of age, an only child. You have a bachelor's degree in education from a small college within commuting distance of Rigley. Until last fall you lived at home and taught American history and English literature in the local high school. You also coached the soccer team, which won the state championship the year before." He looked me over. I had seen the same expression on the faces of farmers checking out a prize heifer, and I tried not to hunch my shoulders to make them seem narrower. He added, "Quite a diversification of talent."

"It's a small high school."

"And a small town. Fifteen thousand, right? Your father owned the hardware store and your mother gave garden parties and played bridge. You have been goin' steady with a feller name of DeWitt Sparks, up an' coming young accountant DeWitt is, reg'lar churchgoer, nice and steady—we all figured they'd get married one of these days but he—"

"Stop it!" His imitation of MacMillen's accent and speech patterns had been cruelly accurate. Everything he had said was true, but the woman he had described—a spinster school teacher too timid to strike out on her own, carrying on an insipid affair with an unenthusiastic swain—that wasn't me! DeWitt was just as boring as Karim had made him sound, but he had wanted to marry me, and he hadn't been the only one. Especially after word got out about the insurance policy.

I folded my arms across my chest. "You know a lot of things you have no business knowing, Mr. Karim, but you don't know the most important thing. My father and I had planned this trip for years. He was keen on gardening, probably because of his name; he believed we were descended from John Tradescant, the famous seventeenth-century English gardener—"

"Florists," Karim interrupted. "That was what they called themselves. It wasn't until centuries later that the word took on its present meaning."

"Of course. I expect you know as much about him as I do. There was a newspaper story about your purchase of this place and your intention of restoring the gardens—did you find the clipping in my purse, along with my passport and driver's license and other informative documents? My father clipped everything he could find that had to do with old gardens, and this project was of particular interest to him. According to legend this garden was the first project of John Tradescant the Elder. He went on to design gardens for the Earl of Salisbury, the Duke of Buckingham and, finally, King Charles I. His son, John the Younger, also worked here."

"You've done your homework."

"I told you. My father and I . . . I took some landscaping courses."

That didn't surprise him either. He probably knew how much I weighed at birth and when I had lost my virginity.

"Are you descended from John Tradescant?" he asked.

"I doubt it. We never found a direct connection."

"The name is unusual, though. I can understand why a—keen gardener, you said?—would be intrigued by the possibility."

"And why I might go to such lengths, even trespassing, to see this place? I came here yesterday, all polite and proper, to ask for permission, but they wouldn't let me in."

"You should have called for an appointment."

"How? You're not in the phone book."

Karim chuckled. "True. So, having been rudely rebuffed, you decided to break in? No, don't deny it. If I had been in your shoes I might have reacted the same way. So now you've seen the place. What do you think of it? What would you do if you owned it and wanted to restore the gardens?"

It was like wrestling with somebody who didn't know the rules; just when I thought I had his strategy figured out he came at me with a new move. I said warily, "I can't see that there's anything left of them."

"That's the opinion of an ignoramus—excuse me, a person who is ignorant of the subject. You claim to have studied it. You went to considerable effort to see this place. Why were you so interested?"

So I was still on trial. "All right," I said. "This place is unique for several reasons. It didn't belong to one of the great noble families, like the Cecils and the Stewarts. Roger Fallon, the original owner, was a simple untitled country gentleman who had a keen interest in gardening and enough money to experiment. More importantly, the garden was never extensively altered. The rich and famous families followed the fads—and there were fads in gardening, changes in fashion and in taste. The de Caus brothers and their water features, Andre Mollet's elaborate *parterres de broderie*, the Dutch influence, which used potted plants as a kind of mobile decoration—culminating in the landscape movement of the mid-eighteenth century, which replaced the stiff formal gardens of earlier times with romantic vistas, artificial parks and groves and pools. For some reason, possibly because the family fortunes declined, the Fallons never employed any later landscaping designers, not even the omnipresent Capability Brown. Fallon's garden represents the pure, unaltered design of the greatest of early seventeenth-century gardeners. Or rather," I ended, "it would, if there were anything left of it. Now are you satisfied that I do know something about old gardens or do you want me to lecture for another ten minutes?"

"You have done your homework," Karim admitted. "But you ought to know better than to say nothing is left. The plantings of Fallon's time are long gone, of course, but what might one hope to find out there?"

"Well . . . possibly the remains of structures like walls and terraces and garden buildings. Formal beds, like parterres and knot gardens might have left impressions in the soil. Fountains, statue bases . . ." I stopped with a gulp. Not only statue bases—at least one actual statue. I had no intention of mentioning it, or the leafy tunnel that, according to Jordan, didn't exist. I waited for him to mention it. He didn't say anything, he just watched me.

"Well done." Karim patted his plump hands softly together.

"Thanks." My coffee was cold. I drank it anyhow.

"Fair is fair," said my inquisitor. "Is there anything you want to ask me?"

Another flank attack, a feint designed to disarm me. I had no defense against moves like that. All I could do was tell the truth.

"I know who you are, of course. It was all in the newspaper story—how your great-grandfather started a small import and trading business, and your grandfather expanded it into a multinational corporation. What I don't understand is why you're living in a place like this. You're a very rich man. You could build yourself a mansion."

"I already have," Karim said. "I am a man of simple tastes, Miss Tradescant; I prefer to live quietly, without servants and sycophants around me."

Jordan didn't speak or move, but his father gave him a quick glance before continuing, in the same sanctimonious voice. "My hobbies are history and gardening. What more appropriate combination could there be than the restoration of an old garden? They aren't that easy to come by, you know. Most of them are in the hands of the National Trust, or private owners who take a dim view of American parvenus. When this place came on the market I snapped it up."

"So this is your new toy?"

"What's wrong with that? I've worked hard all my life and I am not a young man. I haven't looked forward to anything so much in years." He took his elbows off the table and leaned back in his chair. "I've only owned the place a few months and most of the time was spent in making the house habitable. It was in ruinous condition. I don't care about the house anyhow, it's the gardens that interest me. I'm still considering options; it isn't the sort of project one can rush into. How would you like to participate in it?"

"I—I beg your pardon?" I knew I must have misunderstood. The words couldn't mean what they seemed to mean.

"After the—er—accident, you quit your job and put the house up for sale. You've been wandering—some might say aimlessly—ever since. You inherited quite a lot of money, by your standards, but it won't last forever." His voice dropped to a murmur and he was no longer smiling. "I know what it is like to lose the only person you love in the world. I understand what you are going through. You are very young, and you are now alone. I am offering you—"

Jordan shoved his chair back and stood up, tossing his napkin onto the table. "For God's sake, Dad!"

"Keep out of this," his father said, without looking at him.

"Damned if I will. This woman is a total stranger, and she is obviously in a state of—to put it in the kindest possible terms—a state of extreme emotional confusion. As for you, Miss Tradescant—if that is your name and if you are who you say you are—what you need is a nice quiet rest home. My father is a lunatic, and you'll end up even crazier than you already are if you spend any time with him. Go away."

"Don't be so theatrical," Karim said coolly. "I'm just a sentimental old man who is trying to live up to the precepts of—"

Jordan interrupted him with a single four-letter word and stamped out of the room.

"I apologize for my son's language," Karim said. "It's entirely up to you, Miss Tradescant, of course, but I hope you will consider the idea. I'm not proposing to put you in charge of the job, you haven't the necessary skills. All I'm offering you is hard physical labor and the chance to participate in a project of the sort that is obviously dear to your heart. Good Lord, girl, most people would be speechless with gratitude at an offer like that!"

I was speechless, but not with gratitude. I might have stormed out of the room myself if Jordan hadn't beaten me to it. It was probably pure contrariness that moved me to pursue the insane idea. "What do you get out of it?" I demanded.

Karim rolled his eyes and pursed his lips. "Why, my dear, only the satisfaction of knowing I have helped a fellow human being."

Jennet spoke for the first time. "Don't overdo it, Frank."

Karim grinned. "I'll leave her to you then. Listen to Jennet, Miss Tradescant. She knows."

After he had gone, I said, "You *are* the village witch."

"Why, yes." Her smile looked as if she had practiced it—close-lipped, curving, mysterious. "You haven't visited my shop. Come round one of these days. You'll find it interesting."

"Another inducement to stay? Let's not fence. Why is he falling all over me? Is it my name?"

"In part. I suppose you would call him super-stitious."

"I certainly would, if he thinks my being here is anything other than pure coincidence."

"The separate chains of events that brought you and Frank here, at this time and in this place, involve quite a number of . . . coinci-dences. It would be more accurate to say that he feels you were meant to be here."

"Predestination? I don't believe in it."

She gestured impatiently. "That's irrelevant. Frank does believe in something of the sort, and that is his reason for wanting you to stay. His only reason. I hope you don't suspect him of having romantic designs on you."

"He's probably got a long queue of nubile females aching to become Mrs. Karim, or any reasonable facsimile thereof."

"You've got that right. And in case you were wondering, the same is true of Jordan."

"I wasn't wondering."

"So what's your problem?" She leaned forward,

her elbows on the table, her eyes holding mine. "A certain degree of caution is understandable, even commendable, but you're behaving like a little old lady who sees burglars under the bed and Martians in the shrubbery. Where's your sense of adventure? Seems to me you have a great deal to gain by accepting his invitation and nothing to lose except a little time."

I couldn't deny it, so I remained silent. Jennet rose. "It's up to you, of course. But I wonder what your father would say if he knew you had been offered a chance like this?"

ii

My ankle had stiffened while I sat at the table. I waited for a few minutes and then limped out of the dining room.

Where was I? Totally confused, that's where I was—spatially and in every other way. If Jennet wasn't the village witch, she was a good amateur psychologist. Her arguments had been irrefutable, and the last question had been a particularly shrewd hit. My father would have sold himself into slavery to Franklin Karim if his duties had included working on the garden, and he'd have been sorely tempted to include me in the deal.

I opened a door on my left and was pleased to find that my sense of direction at least was still intact. This couldn't be the main hallway of the house, it was too small, but there were the stairs I had descended with Doreen. I was about to start up when I saw something that brought me to a stop.

The portrait was full length and almost life sized, occupying the entire height of the wall on the upper landing. From this aspect it was impossible to miss. I hadn't noticed it coming down—probably because it had not been illuminated as it was now, with carefully directed lights above and on either side.

"Paying tribute to your ancestor?" said Mr. Karim, behind me.

The sneaky old devil must have switched on the lights over the portrait when he left the dining room. He had laid in wait for me and crept up like a cat.

"Not a good location," he went on. "I'll hang it in the library, I expect, after I finish remodelling. You recognized him, of course."

Now I knew why Sean had looked familiar. There was really no resemblance except for the beard, but it was quite a beard—neatly trimmed but fuller and longer than modern fashions in such matters decreed, with an equally luxuriant mustache.

I turned from the painted eyes that seemed to look directly into mine, and met the equally imperious gaze of Mr. Karim. He was smiling, but that didn't make him look any less imperious.

"John Tradescant the Younger," I said. "I've seen a portrait of him. Not that one."

"He's unmistakable, though, isn't he—that piratical beard and swashbuckling pose?"

"That's a shovel, not a sword, he's holding."

"Yes, I like that touch, don't you? He was a gardener like his father, and proud of it. They were explorers as well as 'florists,' though, travelling from the steppes of Russia to the wilderness of North America in search of rare plants. In the seventeenth century that took courage. Have you seen their tomb in that little garden in Lambeth, with the wonderful reliefs of pyramids and crocodiles and dragons?"

"Yes."

"A fitting start for your pilgrimage."

I didn't reply. After a moment Karim said, "I have some other mementoes that may interest you. Come into the library."

Favoring my ankle I went with him into an entrance hall and through a set of folding doors. The library was a large room with a fireplace on one wall and a triple Gothic window on the wall opposite the door. The furniture included a few fine antiques and a few pieces that could only be described as old—a cracking leather sofa and chairs, a worn oak desk. They must have come with the house, for nobody, much less a millionaire, would have bought them. Karim must have added the spanking new filing cabinets and the computer. Shelves lined two of the walls; books had been piled on them more or less at random, and a long table was covered with piles of papers, pamphlets, and folio volumes that were too big to fit on the shelves. The overall effect was appealing to a person who thinks any room is attractive if it contains a lot of books and a comfortable chair in which to sit while reading them, but it wouldn't have won any prizes for interior design. He hadn't been kidding when he said he wasn't interested in the house.

Karim settled me in a chair and went to the bookshelves. "Here is something that might interest you."

He offered it to me, using both hands; the book was an oversized folio and very heavy, as I discovered when my shoulder protested with a jab of pain. When I saw what it was, I caught my breath.

"You are familiar with it?" Karim asked, watching me.

"I've heard of it, but I never expected to see a copy." Reverently and carefully I began turning pages. "They're all in rare book rooms. You leave this lying out on the shelf?"

My voice rose to a squeak of outrage. Karim said, "I like to look at it. What is the sense of owning things if you cannot enjoy them? Examine it whenever you like. This is what I wanted to show you."

I hadn't observed the marker—an empty business envelope—until he inserted his finger and casually flipped over the intervening pages.

I knew that the engravings in the book had been based on seventeenth- and early eighteenth-century paintings. In those days before photography, when artists were regarded by the upper classes as merely a superior form of craftsman, wealthy landowners often commissioned paintings or drawings of their property. This one was what they call a bird's eye view; I wondered how the artist had managed it. They didn't have planes or helicopters in those days. It was almost as detailed as a map, showing not only the manor house but the parterres and orchards, terraces and ponds that had surrounded it.

I knew what it was even before Karim's finger indicated the legend under the picture. "Troytan House in the County of Lancashire, Seat of the Hon. Mr. Roger Fallon. 1609."

"But," I stuttered. "But—this is all you need. For the restoration. It's all here."

"Not quite all. You know better. What is missing?"

His tone was amused, paternal. I gave him a sheepish smile. "Oh, of course. I got so excited I didn't think. This shows the plan, but not the kinds of plants. You can make reasonable guesses about them, though. There are lists of the plants known to English gardeners— florists—in the seventeenth century. . . ."

My voice trailed off when I saw his smile broaden and his eyes narrow with amusement. "Don't tell me," I said. "Don't tell me, let me guess. You have John Tradescant's list. The one that was published in 1634."

"And that of John the Younger, published

twenty-two years later." He gestured casually at the bookshelf. "Look at them whenever you like. I have something better than that, however."

He had not handled this object so carelessly. A single sheet of paper, it had been sealed in inert plastic. I bent over it, frowning in concentration. The writing was big and bold, and not too badly faded, but the archaic spelling wasn't always easy to decipher. It wasn't until I had read several lines that the meaning of the greeting belatedly dawned.

"John," I repeated stupidly. "Not John Tradescant? This is a letter. From—"

"Roger Fallon, the owner of this property. Obviously a neat, well-organized fellow; he kept a copy for himself." Karim beamed at me; my awed disbelief obviously pleased him. "These are his preliminary instructions to John the Elder, including a list of some of the plants he wanted."

This piece of paper had survived the man who wrote it by over three hundred years. Even his bones were dust, but his handwriting—distinctive, individual, personalized—lay before me. It's impossible to explain the impact of something like that to a person who doesn't feel the pull of the past.

"Where on earth did you get this?"

Karim dismissed the question with a wave of his hand. "As soon as I purchased the place I put my people to work searching for source materials. I was fortunate to find this. The plans were almost certainly changed as work proceeded, but Fallon is quite definite about what he wanted, and he sounds like a man who would insist on having his own way."

"Yes, he does." I read the words aloud, savoring the archaic spellings and syntax. "'I did determine of a plott to be drawne, which I thinke will doe very well, & after may be chaunged or alltred at my pleasure.' No 'you,' not even a 'we,' in the whole letter. Plott," I repeated. "An actual plan? It would be too much to expect that you have . . ."

Karim stopped smiling. "Not yet. I have not given up hope of finding it, though. In the meantime, the engraving gives a good idea of what was there."

Remembering the comfortable but unpretentious dimension of my bedroom and the other rooms I had seen, I said, "Obviously this isn't the same house. What happened to the one in the picture?"

"There have been several houses on the site, in fact. Over three and a half centuries many disasters occurred—war, fire, simple abandonment for lack of funds."

He had not answered the question. I didn't notice at the time; he pulled out John Tradescant's plant list and I was gone.

Not until a patch of sunlight inched across the table and touched my hand did I realize how much time had passed. The triple windows were golden with sunlight. I had been sitting at the table for over two hours, while Karim trotted back and forth, fetching books from the shelves and papers from his files, while we talked and looked and argued, like equals and fellow fanatics.

"Time for tea," Karim said happily. "I am very fond of that particularly English tradition. I hope you are too."

"I can take it or leave it alone. Are you suggesting that it's getting late and that I may as well wait till tomorrow before I leave?"

He leaned back, folding his hands over his stomach. "I am suggesting that your foot and your shoulder—or was it a sore elbow that caused you to wince when you reached for the book?—are bothering you. A sensible person would not attempt to drive strange roads after dark with such disabilities when there is no need to do so. However, the decision is yours, of course."

He took out a set of keys—my keys—from his pocket and put it on the table.

It was probably suggestion, but when I leaned across to pick up the keys my shoulder gave another twinge. "All right," I said ungraciously. "I'll stay for a couple of days. Till my ankle heals. It's very kind of you."

His black eyes glittered with amusement. "Hasn't everyone told you that I have a selfish motive for everything I do? In this case my motive is relatively pure and simple. I am a lonely old man, Miss Tradescant. No one else is interested in my new toy; there is no one I can talk to. It has been a great pleasure to share the insights of a young, enthusiastic mind."

"Don't overdo it," I said.

Karim's jowls quivered with laughter. "That's another thing I like about you. You are so—"

"Refreshingly honest? I can afford to be, I've got nothing to lose. Why don't you try it? Don't give me that stuff about how you're tired of people fawning on you because you're rich and powerful, and that you're a lonely old man. If you want to talk gardens, you could hire all the experts you want."

"But they would fawn on me," Karim said, grinning.

I couldn't help grinning back. He was playing me like a violin, but he did have a certain charm—when he chose to display it. "Isn't your son interested in your gardening projects?"

"He is interested in nothing but dead gods."

Recognizing this as another example of Karim's purple prose, I raised my eyebrows and said, "Is that what he's studying—ancient history?"

"Something of the sort. It is very boring. Or perhaps it is Jordan who makes the subject boring. No doubt you would like to freshen up before tea. Do you need me to help you up the stairs?"

I took the hint but declined his assistance. The ankle felt better; it was my shoulder that was bothering me now. I used my left hand when I brushed my hair, and decided that was going to be the full extent of the freshening. If Mr. Karim expected me to turn up in a flowery frock and little white sandals he was due to be disappointed, and if he was applying for the job of father surrogate he was out of luck.

One of Karim's statements at lunch had hit me hard. "I know what it is like to lose the person you love best in the world."

He might have been referring to his wife. She had been dead for a good many years and he had never remarried. I had a feeling, however, that the loss had been more recent. If his lost love had been a daughter . . . She could have been about my age. Jordan appeared to be in his late twenties.

I was theorizing on little or no evidence, but the theory might help to explain Karim's interest in me. Maybe he was softer and more sentimental than he appeared.

He certainly wasn't sentimental about his son. It had been rather a horrible thing to say in Jordan's presence—thoughtless at best, deliberately cruel at worst. I doubted that Karim ever acted or spoke without thought.

Any fool, which Karim was not, would have known that I too had lost the most important person in my life, and that that person was not my mother. It made a nice, neat, sentimental equation—one lost daughter, one lost father.

But no two men could have been more different—the one gentle, straightforward and direct, the other as twisty as a corkscrew and as tough as a crowbar. I didn't trust him an inch, but I was beginning to like him. Whatever else he might be, he wasn't dull.

I had an ulterior motive too. His arguments and Jennet's had made perfect sense; I'd have to be crazy to pass up the chance of participating in the sort of project that had fascinated me for years. The interval would give me a respite, time to consider my future plans and come to terms with my loss. But my real reason for agreeing to stay was quite different.

I went to the window. Blue shadows turned the tangle of brush into a shapeless mass, vague as a storm cloud. I didn't like the look of it and I certainly didn't want to enter it again. But I had to, in order to prove to myself that I wasn't losing what was left of my mind. Jordan's certainty scared me even more than the panic attack. Could I have imagined the whole insane episode? If I had, a psychiatric hospital might be the best place for me. If I hadn't—if Jordan was lying or just mistaken— it was essential that I confront the panic and overcome it.

Tea was to be served on the terrace behind the house. I had refused an escort, saying I remembered the way. The door through which Sean had carried me led directly onto the terrace, but I decided to do a little exploring first.

So far all I had seen were the back parts of the house, and not all of those.

The dining room and kitchen were on the right of the staircase hall. On the left was a larger entrance hall, with the library behind it and a gloomy drawing room or parlor opening directly off it. Straight ahead was the front door.

Instead of a porch or terrace the front door led to a porte cochere that would have sheltered the elegant ladies and gents emerging from their carriages and motors. The driveway circled around and then curved, disappearing into a group of trees. Beyond them, I assumed, was the modern gate from which I had been turned away only the day before.

I had to go some distance from the house before I could get an overall view. It was the kind of house my mother would have had built if she had had enough money and had lived in the late nineteenth century. It combined the maximum of pretentiousness with the mini-mum of authenticity. Despite the pointed roof-lines and Gothic windows, it was pure Victorian, not Tudor or medieval. It even had useless bat-tlemented towers and parapets. To this hodge-podge the designer had callously added the porte cochere and the verandas along one side. The arched window over the porte cochere must belong to the bedroom across the hall from my own. Presumably there were other bed-rooms over the drawing room and dining room wings, which stuck out from the narrow central portion of the house. I had seen the window of one of them from my own window.

I turned my back on the monster and looked out over the front yard. If there was any remaining evidence of Fallon's plan it eluded my eye. Mine was not a trained eye, however; an expert might detect traces I had missed, in the very contours of the land: raised or sunken beds, the line of the original drive. I had read about such things.

And now I had a chance to see how they were done. The chance of a lifetime.

Following the driveway I discovered a narrower side road that appeared to lead toward a building whose slate roof was visible among the trees. I didn't hear the car; all of a sudden it was there, coming straight at me. It wasn't coming fast, probably because the surface of the drive was rutted and uneven. I jumped aside—an unnecessary move, since the vehicle had come to a stop.

No wonder I hadn't heard the sound of the engine. The car was big and silver and obviously expensive—a Bentley, a Rolls? What did I know? Toyotas were more in my line. The pirate who had carried me to my room that morning was at the wheel. He put his head out the window.

"Want a lift?"

"Where to?"

"The garage."

"No, thanks. I'm just taking a little stroll."

"Suit yourself." He turned into the side road. After a moment I followed. It wasn't far. By the time I arrived he had put the car away and was standing outside the building smoking a cigarette and waiting for me.

He was no more a chauffeur than I was a master gardener. It was partly the way he stood, balanced on the balls of his feet, like a spring ready to uncoil. It was partly the tilt of his head, as if he were listening for sounds no one else would hear. I wondered where he kept his gun. He wasn't wearing a jacket and his thin shirt and tight-fitting jeans displayed only the contours with which Nature had provided him— and very nice ones they were, too.

He tossed the cigarette away and gave me a real, honest to goodness smile that showed his teeth and narrowed his eyes. They were dark brown and a trifle protuberant. "Hello there," he said. "The ankle is better?"

"I just twisted it." I looked into the garage. It was a handsomer structure than the house, its mellow red brick walls covered with Virginia creeper. Possibly it had once been the stables. There were two other vehicles beside the—Rolls? One was a shiny new but very efficient-looking pickup, the other a Chevy. Jordan, being ostentatiously humble? Adjoining the main building was a smaller, rather charming cottage, also of red brick with a slate roof.

Seeing me crane my neck, Sean obligingly moved out of my way. "My humble quarters, formerly one of the servants' cottages. Office and kitchen on the first floor, bedroom and bath upstairs. Would you like to inspect them?"

"What, now?"

"Drop in any time." His voice had the caressing note that loaded the words with double meanings, but I sensed it was just a habit of his. His eyes were cool and speculative. "I hear from the old man that you'll be around for a while."

"Oh, really?" I started to go past him. He moved to block my way.

"How did you get in here?"

I wasn't particularly anxious to hear someone else tell me I was imagining things, so I avoided a direct answer. "Mr. Karim accepted my explanation and he has invited me to be his guest. I can't see that you have any right to question me."

"Oh, deary me, excuse me, ma'am. Are you going to report me for insubordination?"

"Not if you get out of my way. I'm late for tea."

"This way, ma'am." He sketched an insolent bow, and followed at a respectful distance.

The path led past several sheds and a walled enclosure that seemed to be a kitchen garden and then turned, paralleling a bank of rhododendron, before it ended at the base of a modern terrace. I knew where I was now. Beyond the terrace lay a wide stretch of grass and the great tree; under the tree was the table at which I had eaten Mr. Karim's breakfast. It seemed a century ago instead of only that morning.

I was beginning to feel like Alice in Wonderland. Less than twelve hours ago I had awoken in a strange hotel room, alone and friendless, and here I was about to have afternoon tea with a rich man who had accepted me, a stranger and a trespasser, into his intimate family circle.

Sean's question had brought home to me how odd it was that Karim hadn't pursued the little matter of how I had managed to get over or around that big high fence. He had quizzed me in detail about my family and my background and my knowledge of gardening, but he didn't seem to be at all worried about the violation of his privacy.

Maybe this was one of those stories in which the heroine (You a heroine? jeered a voice in my mind) had forgotten who she really was, and had invented an imaginary life for herself. Maybe I was Karim's long-lost daughter and crazier than a loon. Maybe I was just crazy, period.

I was quite close to the table before I realized that the man seated there with my genial host was not Jordan. Seeing me, he rose punctiliously to his feet. He was about Jordan's height, but fair instead of dark.

He looked tired. I don't know why that was my first impression; nothing in his physical appearance supported it. He was a little on the thin side but with good shoulders and an erect, easy carriage. His smile was friendly, his blue eyes unshadowed. I guessed he was in his mid-thirties.

Karim waved me toward a chair. "This is my neighbor and the former owner of Troytan. Giles Betancourt, meet Heather Tradescant. She's going to help me restore the gardens."

A bell rang somewhere off in the distance. Sean headed back toward the garage and Giles Betancourt, his eyes bright with interest, exclaimed, "It's a pleasure to meet you, Miss Tradescant. I believe our ancestors were well acquainted."

"I doubt it." I took the hand he extended and amended the brusque statement. "I mean, I doubt he was my ancestor. How do you do, Mr. Betancourt."

"Even if he wasn't, the coincidence is enough to justify the use of first names, don't you think?"

"I certainly do," said Karim complacently. "Heather is only a beginner, but she's very knowledgeable."

"Thanks, Frank," I said.

Karim chuckled. Giles Betancourt smiled, but not for the same reason Karim had chuckled. He was just being agreeable. "I can't imagine how he talked you into this. It will be an enormous project and he's too bull-headed to take advice or—"

He broke off with a stifled exclamation as two children came running across the lawn toward us.

The boy wore the same clothes he had worn the day before. The girl, who was several years his junior, was dressed in a female version of what must be a school uniform, with a pleated skirt instead of slacks, and a sweater of the same glaring, unbecoming blue. She was yelling, demanding that her brother wait for her and "give it back," whatever it may have been. Suddenly he stopped and turned, and the little girl went sprawling, flat on her stomach.

I understood then why Giles Betancourt looked tired. "Excuse me," he said, and started toward the children. Between the shrieks of the girl I heard her brother say, "Poor Laura! Did you trip?" She had. Over his foot.

I was beginning to wonder what had happened to mum when I saw her come around the corner of the house, accompanied by Sean. Checking on visitors was probably part of his job, but they were walking close together and she was smiling up at him, tossing her golden hair back with one hand. I had only seen her face when it was distorted by anger; when she smiled she was stunningly pretty. Long slim legs were displayed by a skirt that stopped several inches above her knees, and one could hardly doubt that her weight was in the lower limits of the proper category. I reached for a sandwich. It was probably an involuntary reflex.

Ignoring the children, she sauntered toward us and extended both hands to Frank, who took them in his. "Hello, Lindsay, how nice to see you. Heather, this is Mrs. Betancourt, Giles's wife and the mother of those charming children. Heather Tradescant, Lindsay."

She nodded indifferently at me and then did a classic double take. "Aren't you—"

"Yep," I said. "I am. How do you do, Mrs. Betancourt."

"Ah," said Frank. "You've met."

"Yep," I said. "Sort of."

Giles had picked his daughter up and brushed her off. I didn't hear what he said, but anybody within a square acre could have heard the boy's response.

"You're always blaming me! It wasn't my fault. I didn't do anything!"

Giles's reply was inaudible. The boy came running to his mother. "Mummy, he's picking on me again. He blames me for everything."

"That's all right, darling boy," Lindsay said vaguely. The boy edged closer to her as his father came up, holding the little girl's hand.

"As you have probably deduced, Heather, these are my children," he said. "Bob and Laura, say hello to Miss Tradescant and Mr. Karim."

Bob gave me a knowing grin. "Hello, Miss Tradescant." His tone was a deliberate caricature of his father's. "Hello, Mr. Karim. May I have one of those delicious little cakes, please, sir?"

"We can't stay," Giles said. "I was about to leave when you turned up, Lindsay."

"I was on my way home with the kiddies and decided I'd give you a lift."

"I told you I'd walk."

"You'll stay for tea, of course," Frank said. "You know you're always welcome. Sean, bring another chair."

Sean had remained standing. "There are enough chairs. I'm not staying. If any of you prefer beer to tea and crumpets I'll be serving shortly."

"Barbarian," Frank called after him.

"Mummy, can I have a biscuit?" Bob asked.

"Here." She gave him a handful. "Now run away and play, both of you."

"There's nothing to play with," Bob pointed out, with some justice.

"Find something." She gave him a little shove. Pouting like a baby he moved away, trailed by Laura. I thought that if Laura was hoping for a share of the cookies she was due to be disappointed.

Once the "kiddies" were disposed of, Lindsay turned to me. She was smiling, but her eyes were cold and curious. "I'm glad to see you again, Miss Tradescant, so that I can apologize for my behavior yesterday. I'm afraid we mothers revert to the primitive when our kiddies are in danger. You understand, I'm sure."

Her smiling lips were as full and pink and perfect as those of a romance heroine on the cover of a paperback novel.

"What's all this about?" Frank asked curiously.

Lindsay explained, her smooth white hands moving in graceful gestures. Did plastic surgeons do hands? I wondered cattily.

"It certainly wasn't Miss Tradescant's fault," she finished. Somehow it came out sounding as if it was my fault, though. "I didn't realize she was a friend of yours, Frank."

"That would have made it okay for me to run over your son?" I inquired.

Lindsay looked blank. Blanker, I should say. Visibly amused—more amused than the tasteless remark deserved—Frank said smoothly, "I hope we are friends, but I only met Heather this morning."

"Oh. Then it was Jordan who invited you."

I said, "Nobody invited me. I just dropped in."

Nobody believed this except Frank, who chortled. I suppose Giles interpreted it as a genteel attempt to fend off Lindsay's impertinent questions. He was flushed with embarrassment.

"One of his fellow students?" Lindsay persisted.

"No, I'm not a student."

"Heather is helping with the garden restoration," Giles said. "Speaking of gardens—"

"Really." She didn't believe that either. "All the same, it's rude of Jordan to ignore a guest. Where is he?"

Karim's face couldn't have been more bland. "Late as always. He'll be along, I expect."

Giles finally managed to get a polite conversation going. He asked the usual questions— was this my first visit to the area, had I had the opportunity to do any sight-seeing, did I enjoy hiking?

I wasn't surprised he should ask the last question. I look like the sort of woman who enjoys hiking. "There are a number of interesting walks hereabouts," Giles said. "But if I may offer a word of caution, you would be well advised to acquire a map or walking guide before you go any distance."

"The terrain isn't that rugged," I said. "Are there mine shafts or quicksand or something?"

"Parts of the moorland are rather boggy. Not that you'd be sucked under or pursued by a spectral hound," he amended, with a smile. "But there are rough stretches and it's easy to wander off the marked path in mist or fog. I have a walking guide if you'd care to—"

Lindsay jumped up. "There he is. Jordan!"

Jordan had come out via the kitchen door. She went to meet him, holding out her hands. Someone must have told her it was a graceful gesture, and it was almost impossible for the person she greeted to ignore it.

Jordan ignored it. Recovering smoothly, she twined those pretty white hands around his arm and drew him toward the table. "Poor boy, you look absolutely exhausted. Come and have your tea."

Jordan detached her as efficiently and unemotionally as a man pushing away an overly affectionate dog. "Hello, Lindsay. Giles, it's good to see you. I didn't know you were here."

"We mustn't stay." Giles glanced at the children, who were squatting on the ground some distance away. They were suspiciously quiet, and I wondered what they had found to hold their interest. "I just dropped in to tell Frank I'm hoping to get to those papers this weekend."

"Papers?" I echoed. "Relating to the garden?"

"Nothing so significant, I'm afraid," Giles said. "When we cleared the house out we found masses of rubbish in the attics, including some boxes of miscellaneous documents. I've been going through them a bit at a time—"

"At his leisure," said Frank. "I'll raise my first offer, Giles. Five hundred pounds for the lot."

"Frank, I can't imagine how you got the idea that there could be anything of interest to you in those papers," Giles replied. "It would be taking unfair advantage to sell them. I prefer to go through them myself. Who knows what ancient family scandals may require to be decently buried?"

"They weren't your direct ancestors," Frank said. "Why should you care? I'll make it guineas instead of pounds."

Giles laughed. "You're a frightful snob, Frank. In the unlikely event that I come across anything to do with the Tradescants and/or Roger Fallon, I'll give you first refusal. Allow me to—"

The sound that stopped him was the auditory equivalent of sticking your finger in a light socket—screams and squalls rising to a pitch that shocked the senses. Everybody froze, except Giles. He got out of his chair so fast it fell over, and sprinted off across the lawn.

I was the next to move. After several years of teaching you learn to recognize noises like those and respond fast.

Laura was still screaming, but the sounds were slightly muffled by the hands she had pressed to her face. Blood trickled down over her fingers. Giles's efforts to pull her hands away were hampered by her frantic squirming, so I squatted beside them and grabbed hold of her flailing legs.

"Stop that!" I ordered. "You're not hurt. Let your daddy look."

It worked. A firm, forcible order usually does, especially when it comes from a stranger. The child relaxed and Giles pried her sticky little fingers loose. It was difficult to assess the degree of her injuries since she had smeared blood all over her face. I couldn't find my handkerchief, so I pulled out my shirt tail and used it to wipe her forehead.

"No damage to her eyes," I said, relieved. "Just a few scratches."

"What happened?" Lindsay demanded. "Laura, I told you not to go near the hedge."

"I didn't!" Laura wept. "The kitty scratched me. Bobby was holding it and I was patting it and . . . Owooooo!"

I got to my feet and looked around. No kitty, no Bobby. Then I saw him, his hands in his pockets, looking up into the tree. He took something from his pocket, hauled his arm back, and threw. Leaves fluttered down, and something leaped from the branch. It hit the ground running and streaked for the hedge. It was a good-sized animal but I couldn't make out details; I saw only a blur of brown and fawn and black before it vanished into the brush.

I reached Bobby in time to catch his arm before he could throw another stone. There was something about the kid that brought out all my worst instincts and I was angry anyhow, but I had myself under control. I know I didn't hurt him. He shrieked, as I had expected, and then he lashed out with his foot, which I ought to have expected but didn't. It was a hard, calcu-lated kick, and it smashed into my sore ankle.

Flat on the ground I blinked away tears of pain and saw Jordan grab Bob by the collar. Bob didn't fight back this time. Looking limp and frail and helpless in Jordan's grip, he appealed to the others. "I say, I am sorry. I didn't mean to, my foot slipped when she shook me."

"I'd have done more than shake you, you little monster," Jordan said. He pushed the boy away and bent over me. "Are you all right, Heather?"

"Sure," I said bravely. But my ankle gave way when I stood up, and I lurched against Jordan, who put his arm around me. It was as imper-sonal as a back brace, but Lindsay gave me a long, measuring look before turning to her son.

"Apologize, Robert."

"I did. It was an accident, Mummy. She star-tled me, shaking me like that, and I slipped, and—"

"Dropped the stone," I said. My ankle throbbed and I was in no mood to be polite. "It's none of my business, Mrs. Betancourt, but perhaps your son could do with a lesson in kindness to animals."

"It's a wild cat," Bobby protested. "Dangerous. It hurt Laura."

"Oh, for God's sake," Jordan said, lip curling. "It wouldn't have scratched your sister if you hadn't teased or tormented it. Come and sit down, Heather, and I'll get some ice for that ankle."

So maybe I leaned on him a little more than was necessary. The look on Lindsay's face as she watched us gave me a contemptible satisfaction. I don't often get the chance to make beautiful women jealous.

THREE

Labyrinthus, hic habitat Minotaurus

GRAFFITO FROM A WALL AT POMPEII

Somehow I was not surprised to discover that Jordan's kindly concern had been prompted by annoyance at Bobby, not interest in my lovely self. After Laura had been attended to and stuffed with cookies, and I had been settled in a chair with my foot in a bucket of ice, Giles reiterated his intention of leaving. This time no one objected, not even Lindsay. The role of devoted mum appeared to be wearing thin. She left Giles to carry the little girl, and pushed Bob away, frowning, when he tried to take her hand.

As soon as they were out of sight Jordan started for the house.

"Where are you going?" his father demanded. "Come back and have your tea."

"No, thanks."

"Come here. I want to talk to you."

Jordan stopped, his back to us. His shoulders moved slightly; he might have been shrugging, or bracing himself. Returning, he gave me a look I had no difficulty in interpreting.

"Excuse me," I said. "I'll just leave you two alone."

"No, no, you must keep your foot in the ice a little longer," Frank said. "How does it feel?"

"Frozen stiff."

"Perhaps some Epsom salts."

"I don't need Epsom salts or ice. It's fine. He just caught me off-balance."

"He's a dreadful child," Frank said. "Badly spoiled, of course, by his mother, but don't you think there is some deeper psychological problem?"

"It's none of my business."

"How discreet. Aren't you curious? People," said Frank, pouring tea, "interest me. Their actions, their motives, their relationships. Giles is a nice fellow, don't you think?"

"Very nice." I drank my tea.

"He obviously enjoyed your company."

I smiled and sipped my tea. Frank tried again. "His wife is quite lovely, isn't she?"

If you like the Barbie doll type. I didn't say it, or any of the other things that came to mind. I knew what the old rascal was up to. "Quite lovely."

"But rather like a wax doll, isn't she?" I gave him a startled look. He grinned at me. "Some men prefer a woman with more character. Not Jordan, though."

Jordan wasn't ready for it. "For God's sake, Dad!"

"*Pas devant les domestiques?*" I quoted sweetly.

He came back with a quick, "*Pas devant les étrangères,* if you prefer."

"Why, Jordan, Heather isn't a stranger, she's practically one of the family," Frank said. "Anyhow, she could hardly help noticing how . . . fond . . . Lindsay is of you."

Jordan didn't respond. He had the look of a man who is walking down a dark street in a bad neighborhood, anticipating attack but not knowing from which direction it will come.

"It isn't her fault," Frank went on, with a hypocritical sigh. "The poor woman has a serious problem. She can't control herself. Jordan isn't the only man hereabouts she has—er—favored with her attentions, but of course he's the wealthiest. At least she assumes he will be."

I was speechless with horrified admiration. My mother had been good at putting people down, but she was a rank amateur compared to Frank. In a single speech he had implied that Lindsay was a promiscuous woman whose weakness his son had callously exploited, and that even a nymphomaniac would favor Jordan only because he was the heir of a wealthy man. If he was the heir.

Jordan might have fought back if he and his father had been alone; the presence of a stranger kept him from replying, but repressed fury darkened his face and tightened his mouth. I was angry too—not on Jordan's behalf, on my own. I resent being used as a stick to beat people with.

"So how do you come to be so well informed about Lindsay's little problem, Frank? You're the one who's wealthy; didn't she make a pass at you first?"

Frank's cheeks turned a rich purple color. I thought for a minute he was going to explode. He did—with laughter. He laughed so hard he had to lower his head onto the table. I felt a little ashamed of myself, but not much. Frank brought out the worst in me, and nobody could say he hadn't asked for it.

I waited until he had got himself under control—more or less, he went on sputtering and muttering for quite some time—before I sought a safer subject.

"Those papers you and Mr. Betancourt mentioned—family papers, he said. I take it that he's the collector from whom you obtained Roger Fallon's letter to Tradescant."

"No." Frank's eyes flickered from me to the face of his son and then back to me. Maybe my rude, unforgivable comment had had the desired effect after all; he wasn't willing to risk another one. "Giles is no collector. He's not directly descended from the Fallons; the connection is through the maternal line, I believe. The property has changed hands several times."

"Then why are you so interested in the papers? Five hundred pounds is a lot of money."

"It's Jordan who is interested in the papers. No sum of money is too great if it will make him happy, and assist a significant piece of research."

"You're a prince, Frank," I said. "But I saw the gleam in your eyes. You want those papers yourself, and you wouldn't want them unless you expect to find material dating from the time the gardens were laid out. How did they come into Giles's hands if he didn't inherit them?"

"You are a clever girl." Frank beamed approvingly at me, and Jordan let out his breath. "Most of the Fallon papers were dispersed two hundred years ago, when the direct line died out. Some ended up in collections like the one from which I purchased the letter. The majority have simply disappeared. But a few . . .

"Giles's great-grandfather, who built the present house, fancied himself as an antiquarian, and he claimed to be descended from one of Fallon's daughters. Like many of his contemporaries he had no taste and no training; he acquired old manuscripts the way a magpie collects sparkling objects. He bought up a lot of things from local families. When I purchased the house the attics were stuffed with the old gentleman's acquisitions, and with the accumulated junk of succeeding generations. There is a chance that the collection includes some seventeenth-century documents."

I shook my head. "Seems to me you're risking a lot of money on a remote possibility. He said he'd offer you any pertinent material he found. Don't you trust him?"

"He is too slow. I don't like waiting for what I want."

I believed that.

"If Jordan would show a little initiative I wouldn't have to wait," Frank went on. "I feel certain Lindsay would be happy to let him go through the papers. Some evening when Giles is out of town."

He was at it again. This time Jordan was saved by Doreen, who came storming out of the house. She stopped in front of Frank and glared at him, her hands on her hips.

"What's all this about my cat? I won't have nothing done to it, hear? That sodding little Bobby must have been tormenting it."

"It scratched the little girl quite badly," Frank said, shaking his head and pursing his lips.

"It's a gentle animal, reely. It wouldn't hurt nobody unless it was provoked."

"That's all right, Doreen," Jordan said. "Nothing is going to happen to the cat."

"Lindsay told Sean it had to be tested for rabies. The only way they can do that is to . . . It's had its shots, you can't let them hurt it!"

"Nobody is going to hurt the cat," Jordan repeated. He glowered at his father. "Tell her, Dad."

"Of course not." Frank looked at him in

shocked surprise. "How could you let her think that?" Glancing at me, he explained, "It isn't really hers, you know. It came with the house. I didn't realize you had become so attached to it, Doreen. Take it home with you if you like."

"I can't do that."

"Why not?" Jordan asked curiously.

"Oh— Well . . . you know how it is with cats. This is where it lives. It wouldn't be right to take it away. We all look after it," she added defensively. "It's a good mouser."

"That's quite all right," Frank said.

"Oh. Well. Sorry, sir. I fear I forgot myself."

Frank looked at her severely. "You did indeed. Such language, in front of a lady like Miss Tradescant."

Doreen glanced shyly at me. "Sorry, miss. Um—Sean said as how you'd stopped the little—the little chap when he was throwing stones at the cat."

"Knocked him flat," Frank said with a chuckle.

"I didn't mean to." Catching Doreen's eye, I laughed and admitted, "Okay, so maybe I did mean to. I don't approve of corporal punishment, but that young man needs a firm hand."

"So does his mother," Frank said. "A man's hand. Eh, Jordan?"

Dinner, I had been told, was at eight o'clock. That's late for Missouri and other unsophisti-

cated places, but I didn't mind. I had eaten quite
a few sandwiches and when I went back to my
room after tea and torture, I found that little
elves had been at work. My clothes had been
unpacked and hung in the wardrobe. The bed
and the window seat were piled with cushions,
there was a hassock in front of the easy chair
and a low table next to it. On that table was a
basket of fruit and a tin of fancy biscuits; on the
bedside table was a small clock and a cut-glass
carafe with a matching glass upended over it. I
sampled the contents. Water. What, I thought,
no champagne?

The elves had tactfully refrained from un-
packing my more personal possessions; my
toothbrush and the miscellaneous cosmetics
and first-aid supplies were jumbled up in the
suitcase as I had left them. The bags of chocolates were there too. I put the chocolates in the
drawer of the bedside table and the cosmetics in
the bathroom. Then I opened the drawer and
ate a few chocolates and lay down on the bed. I
had been up since before dawn, and encounters
with Karim—Frank, I reminded myself—were
tiring.

I slept, heavily and without dreaming, until
almost eight. Having been brought up to believe
that it is rude to be late for meals I paused only
long enough to smooth my dishevelled hair
before hurrying downstairs. I needn't have hurried. The dining room was deserted, though the
table had been laid as if for a party—flowers,

candles, damask cloth and napkins. There were four place settings. I stood around for a while, idly wondering who the fourth person would be, and then headed for the kitchen to see what, if anything, was going on.

Nobody was there but Sean. His feet on a chair, he was reading a newspaper. "Hi," he said. "Want a beer?"

"No thanks." I looked around the room. It showed the same peculiar blend of old and new that marked the rest of the house, as if the necessary modern conveniences had been added without regard for design or appearance. The end result was surprisingly pleasant, even if the cabinets weren't knotty pine and the appliances had not been color coordinated. There were pots of geraniums on the windowsills, and the wooden surface of the table at which Sean was sitting had the patina produced by age and innumerable scrubbings. The room was neat as the proverbial pin and there wasn't so much as a carrot stick in sight, not to mention a cook.

"Where is everybody?" I asked.

"If you mean Mrs. Greenspan and Doreen, they've gone."

"Aren't there any live-in servants?"

"Just me."

He was trying to provoke me; the insolent tone and lounging pose weren't those of a conventional servant. He hadn't even taken his feet off the chair, much less stood up. Had I treated him like a social inferior? I hadn't meant to; in my world those distinctions didn't exist, and his position in that household was certainly more complicated than that of a paid employee.

"Can I do something to help?" I asked.

From the dining room came the ringing of a bell—not a genteel tinkle, a loud, peremptory chime. Sean put the newspaper down and stood up. "The old man is ready. Since you were kind enough to ask, the answer is yes—you can help me serve the food. Mrs. Greenspan prepared it before she went home. I have many talents, but cooking isn't one of them."

He opened the refrigerator and began removing covered plates and dishes.

The food was all cold, but it was quite a spread—cold salmon with a delicately flavored green sauce, salads and homemade bread and sweet butter. At the head of the table, his brass bell at hand, Frank smiled benevolently at us as we served the food. His sole contribution was to open a bottle of wine. Sean filled the glasses and then sat down. So there wasn't another guest.

"Where is Jordan?" I asked, eyeing the food hungrily.

"Don't wait for him." Frank attacked his salmon. "He may or may not turn up."

"Oh."

"We live simply," Frank explained. "This is freedom hall, my dear Heather; come and go as you like, do as you like."

Catching my eye, Sean showed me a flash of white teeth. Frank did as he liked, but only because he had everybody else at his beck and call.

"How many people work here?" I asked.

Frank had taken a huge bite of bread, so Sean took it upon himself to answer. "The cook, Doreen, two teenagers from the village who come in three times a week to clean. Oh, and the guy who calls himself the gardener. He shows up when he feels like it. And me."

"What do you do?"

"A little bit of everything. Chauffeur, gate-man, waiter, personal trainer—when Frank can be talked into exercising, which isn't often—errand boy."

As the dusk deepened the candle flames took on new brilliance, forming pools of soft light across the damask cloth. Darkness pressed against the open windows.

"So there's nobody else here at night," I said.

"There's only me and Jordan in the house," Frank said. "Sean has his own quarters next to the garage. He likes his independence. You aren't worried about being here with us, are you, Heather? I assure you you couldn't be safer in your own home. It's not likely that Jordan would show enough normal human instincts to make improper advances to you, but if he should—"

"I'm not worried," I said stoutly. "Not about that. I was thinking about you, actually. The place is isolated and your security measures aren't exactly stringent. Not that Sean isn't worth an army—" I gave Sean a gracious nod, to which he responded with a grin and tug at his forelock, "but he's only one man."

"You think I should surround myself with armed guards?" Frank inquired. "There's no way of making oneself entirely secure, Heather. If someone is determined to kill you he'll find a way around or through any security system you could design."

He was right. If assassins could get at prime ministers and presidents, they could get at anybody. I wondered if Frank's calm acceptance of the possibility was due to his belief in predestination. Why fight it if it's going to happen anyhow?

Since I was not a fatalist I wasn't entirely happy about the situation. Not that I felt I needed a chaperone, but the house was old, the rooms were large and the ceilings were high; the floorboards probably creaked and I wouldn't have been at all surprised to hear things go bump in the night. There wouldn't be anybody in the house but Frank and Jordan.

Of course there was John Tradescant the Younger, looking down from the landing. Maybe he was the ghost. There had to be one. No servants living in, the cold meal, prepared by a cook who wasn't willing to hang around after nightfall—yes, it sounded like a conventional Victorian ghost story.

At least John the Younger would make a more interesting specter than the usual White

Ladies and hooded monks. Stepping out of the frame, drifting through the shadowy house with his piratical beard bristling and his shovel in his hand, looking for a place where he could plant . . . what?

No, I told myself. Young John wouldn't walk here. That little garden in Lambeth, maybe. He would feel at home there, it had been laid out with the plants and designs of his time. Did he and his father wander the paths in the dim starlight, checking for aphids on the roses and intrusive weeds in the neat pattern of the knot garden?

Frank saw me staring at the window and misinterpreted my expression. "I do take reasonable precautions, Heather," he said reassuringly. "Especially at night. Show her, Sean. It's time you turned on the outside lights anyhow."

"I was going to clear away first." Sean rose obediently.

"Leave the dishes. I always do," Frank said comfortably.

Of course he did. There was always somebody around to do what he didn't care to do. Tonight that somebody seemed to be me. The housekeeping arts are not my forte, but few women, I suppose, could have abandoned uneaten food to the tender mercies of insects and . . .

"The cat would have a great time with the salmon," I remarked, rising in my turn. "I'll cover it and put it in the fridge."

"The cat doesn't come in the house," Frank said. "But go ahead. Sean will help you."

Sean picked up a few plates and preceded me. He went to the back door and touched a switch. Nothing happened. "Damn," he said. "I'll have to go to the main board. Back in a minute."

He went out the door, closing it behind him.

I meant to look for plastic wrap or foil with which to cover the salmon, but instead I went to the window. There was enough moonlight for me to make out the shape of the big tree and the dark mass at the far end of the cleared space.

Somewhere in that dark tangle was the tunnel I had traversed. I knew it was there and I would prove it. But not tonight. I pictured how it would seem with only a flashlight to guide me—the green walls shiny with dew in the limited light, the scuttle and scratch of nocturnal animals through the roots. Their burrows and tunnels were there, narrow and low to the ground, unnoticed by taller, two-footed passersby. The cat must have gone through one such hole.

A blaze of light blinded me. The whole scene lit up like a stage—the terrace, to the right of the window; the tree; the lawn. The cold white illumination drained all color from grass and leaves like a black and white etching.

The back door opened and Sean came in. "Feel better?" he asked. "The lights are controlled from the master panel in my office, but there's another switch here. The cook keeps turning them off—by mistake, she claims."

"Show me," I said, joining him at the door.

"Why?"

"So I won't push the wrong buttons by mistake, like Mrs. Greenspan."

"There's no reason for you to push any buttons."

"One never knows. What's the big deal?"

"Oh, all right. These are the switches for the outside lights. They're all around the house and at the gate. This controls the alarm system, but you don't have to worry your little head about it; you can't turn it on or off without a key. I usually set the alarm when I leave the house at night, and it stays on until seven-thirty in the morning. So don't open any of the ground-floor doors or windows unless you want to announce your intentions to half the county."

"You mean I can't get out of the house between dark and dawn?"

"You can get out all right, you just can't do it without attracting my attention."

He looked so pleased with himself I felt the urge to snap back with some childish challenge: "Oh, yeah?" or "Wanna bet?" He saw my lower lip go out and continued, in an even more condescending voice, "If you have a heavy date or you think there's a burglar under the bed, call me. The extension is number four."

"Thank you."

"Any time."

By the time we had cleared the table and I had rinsed the dishes and put them in the dishwasher it was after ten, and Frank announced it was time for bed. When he went to bed, everybody went; Sean said good night and Frank escorted me to my room. After asking if there was anything I needed or wanted, he bade me a fatherly good night.

It wasn't until I had closed my door and switched on the lights that I remembered I didn't have anything to read. I considered going down to the library. Not seriously, however. There were lights in the hall, but not a lot of them, and I wasn't crazy about the idea of descending the stairs with John the Younger looking over my shoulder. I sat down in the easy chair and reached for an apple, thinking, ungratefully, that a host considerate enough to provide cookies and fruit would also supply bedside reading.

He had. There was a book on the table—the book about the Lancashire witches.

I bit into the apple and stared at the book. I hadn't noticed it earlier, but it might have been there, hidden by the fruit basket.

There were no other books; it was this or nothing. I took it and the apple to bed.

Old Demdike admitted everything. The Devil had first appeared to her in the shape of a boy, but he sometimes took the form of an animal.

As every educated person knew, all proper witches had such animal "familiars," which they suckled at the breast or at one of the extra teats which were the final, damning evidence of witchcraft.

The speediest way to take away a man's life, Demdike explained, was to "Make a picture of clay, like unto the shape of the person whom they mean to kille and when they would have them to be ill in any one place more than an other; then take a Thorne or Pinne, and pricke it in that part of the Picture you would so have to be ill; And when they would have the whole body to consume away, then take the remnant of the sayd Picture and burne it."

Torture was forbidden by English law, but the conditions under which the accused were confined and questioned amounted to torture, prolonged and painful. It is no wonder the old woman confessed—if she did. A common method of interrogation was to read out the charges and demand that the accused confirm them. A nod or a groan would be taken for agreement. The inquisitors already knew how to phrase the questions. The methods of witchcraft had been described by numerous authorities, the greatest of whom was the king himself. Had not a group of Scottish witches attempted to raise a storm that would sink his ship when he sailed to Norway to fetch his bride? Torture was permitted by Scottish law; James had personally supervised the "questioning" of some of the accused, and forced the reluctant jury to convict them.

Old Demdike was luckier than her children, both of whom were condemned and hanged. Her God showed her the mercy King James and the law would not; by the middle of May she was dead, whether from torture or disease the record does not state.

The dungeons of Lancaster Castle are still to be seen. . . .

The stone walls were slimy with lichen and wet with condensation. The only light came from a barred window, high on one wall. I lay on my side, my cheek resting on a stone covered with a film of filth. I could feel the fleas crawling over me, the dull pain of the sores that covered most of my body; I could smell decayed straw and urine and rotting human flesh. A rat walked unconcernedly across the floor a few inches from my face.

Torture is forbidden by English law.

I hadn't spoken aloud, but when I looked up someone was bending over me. Her face looked like crumpled linen. Her eyes were blank white circles, her bleeding gums completely devoid of teeth.

"This will pass," she mumbled. "You are one of us. You will be with her and with us in a fairer place than their Heaven."

I screamed at her. "I'm not one of you! You

aren't even real! I'm dreaming, and I hate this, and I'm going to wake up. . . . Now!"

I squeezed my eyes shut and held my breath and clenched my fists, mental muscles straining. Something gave way, as if I had broken through a wall. I smelled clean air and fresh linen, I felt the softness of the mattress under me. Gasping with relief, I opened my eyes.

She was still bending over me. Old Demdike, in her tattered black dress, her white hair matted with filth. Her eyes weren't blind, they were open and they saw me. Her hand reached for my face.

I rolled away, across the bed and off it, and when my feet touched the floor I did wake up.

I had closed the drapes the night before but I hadn't closed them all the way. There was enough light for me to see where I was going. I pushed the curtains aside and curled up on the window seat.

It was almost a relief to have an ordinary nightmare, without Freudian undercurrents. Not that I needed a psychiatrist to interpret those other nightmares; I knew what caused them, I just didn't know how to put an end to them.

Dawn was not far away. Beyond the glare of the artificial lights the sky had paled. The air was cool. I pulled my feet up under my nightgown and wrapped my arms around my bent knees.

I had seen a psychiatrist. At the end of the

third fifty-minute hour he had told me I needed four or five years of intensive psychotherapy. When I asked how much it would cost he informed me that mental health could not be measured in monetary terms.

The only other expert I consulted was my father's best friend, a woman of eighty-odd who lived on the next block. Her advice was simpler and just as hard to accept. "Stop feeling sorry for yourself. Get a life. You've never had one."

I had resented her comments even more than the shrink's glib diagnosis. Both of them had been wrong. All I needed was a little time to adjust, and some diversion. There's nothing like the troubles of other people to distract you from your own—hadn't she said something of the sort? She'd been right about that, at any rate. Between the Betancourts and the Karims, not to mention Jennet the village witch, there was plenty of distraction here.

The air was sweet with blended flower fragrances, and a genuine early bird let out a long, musical trill. A lark? I supposed it couldn't be a nightingale. I had always wanted to hear one.

If it hadn't been for that damned alarm, I could have gone for a walk. Exercise and fresh air were what I wanted and the fact that I couldn't get them made me want them all the more. I was half tempted to call Sean—he was probably still asleep—and demand he turn off the alarm. Waking him up would be less satisfying, though, than proving that I didn't need his permission.

I leaned out the window and looked down. The drop was sheer, straight down onto the concrete surface of the terrace. It was a graceless, relatively modern addition, that terrace—another discordant note, like the Victorian veranda.

The veranda. Jumping up, I went to the other window. It opened onto the south side of the house—and the roof of the veranda.

The light had strengthened; I could see the surface, shingled and slightly sloping. The roof had been repaired in a slapdash fashion—patched here and there, where shingles had blown off or rotted away—but it didn't look awfully solid. However, it was only six feet below the windowsill. I wouldn't have to jump, I could lower myself, testing the surface before I rested my weight on it. My ankle felt fine. No problem. There were no screens in the windows. No problem there either. Here was my chance to look for the tunnel through the hedge, to prove to Jordan—and myself—that I had not imagined it.

I dressed quickly and climbed carefully out the window. Preoccupied with this procedure I didn't notice the rectangle of light on the wall next to me until I had turned around.

Instinctively I dropped to hands and knees. Frank's suite, bedroom, and study and bath, was on the north side of the house. The window must be that of Jordan's room. What the hell was he doing up so early? Had he heard me?

I waited for a few minutes. No silhouette showed against the lighted window, so I concluded he hadn't heard me—yet. I'd have beat a hasty retreat if I had been certain I could pull myself back into my window without making a loud noise. The way my luck was going I would probably lose my grip and fall onto, possibly through, the roof. But if I went on I would have to pass close by that lighted window. Jordan's room occupied a square tower that stuck out from the house and was connected with it by only one wall. The veranda ran around two sides of the tower and if I remembered the lay of the land the only place from which I could safely descend was beyond his window, where grass and shrubs would soften a possible fall. Below the roof on my left, away from his room, was an extension of the terrace.

I had to risk it, there was no other way, unless I squatted there and waited for him to go downstairs. He might not do that for hours. I began to crawl, watching that lighted window and wincing when splinters pricked my hands. Avoiding the light spilling out onto the roof brought me uncomfortably close to the edge of the veranda. It had once been rimmed with an ornamental railing of typical Victorian gingerbread, of which only a few jagged bits remained. I looked down. It was a long way down, but at least there was grass under me now. Hoping for a drainpipe or a trellis, I crawled on. No drainpipe, no trellis. I'd have to settle for a post, and hope it was sturdier than it looked. At least the roof supports weren't smooth pillars or fluted columns; they bulged with carvings and were flanked at the top by openwork brackets.

My descent was far from graceful. It wasn't exactly silent either. One of the brackets gave way when my foot pressed it, and I slid down in a breathless flurry, arms and legs wrapped around the post, and toppled over into an azalea.

Lying on my back, half concealed by leaves, I looked up. Another smaller tower jutted out from the larger structure in which Jordan's room was located. Its window was lighted too. A bathroom, maybe. A rush of water nearby—the drainpipe I hadn't found—confirmed this assumption and I relaxed. If he had been in the bathroom, with water running, he couldn't have heard anything.

I crept out of the azalea and stood up, dusting off the seat of my pants. Childish triumph filled me, and for a moment I considered going to Sean's room and waking him up.

It was only a fleeting thought. Walking in on a man like Sean was likely to get a girl shot, or at least thrown hard across the room. Anyhow, I had other things to do. I pulled on my gloves and began walking along the hedge, looking for that damned elusive opening. There might not be a visible break on this side of the jungle. I had been running full tilt, my hands covering my face, when I came out; the panicky impetus of rapid motion might have carried me through several feet of brambles. But surely there would be some evidence of my passage, broken branches or scattered leaves.

I was moving slowly, inspecting the green barrier for such signs, when someone spoke. The words "Good morning" were innocuous, but the very sound of a human voice was enough to scare me half to death. I shrieked and spun around.

Jordan must have dressed in a hurry. His hair was rumpled and his sweater appeared to be on backward. He hadn't shaved, either. His smile could only be described as lacking humor.

I got my breath back. "That was a mean trick!"

"Turn about is fair play. Now you have a faint idea of my sensations yesterday morning. What the devil are you up to now? You must want something rather badly to risk that dramatic exit. The roof is in poor condition. You might have fallen off, or through."

"And you might have warned me."

"What, and interrupt the performance? I watched the entire thing. It was very exciting. Now, now, don't lose your temper; the fact is, I didn't see you until you were midway along, and I was afraid to call out for fear of startling you. A sudden, abrupt movement might indeed have proved dangerous."

It was, for Jordan, a fairly conciliatory speech, but I was in no mood for making up. "You talk like a professor," I said rudely. "Is that what you do? Or do you do anything?"

"I plan to do it one day. Profess, is that the word?" My rudeness didn't bother him one bit. Compared to his father's conversational habits, mine were absolutely innocuous. "I'm working on my dissertation at the moment, or trying to. These distractions are not conducive to concentration."

"At the moment, you are distracting me," I said. "Excuse me while I—uh—go on with what I was doing."

"You still haven't told me what that is." He moved to intercept me as I started forward. He didn't touch me; his hands were in his pockets. He was just there, in my way, and I couldn't prevent him from following me if he chose. I could tell him the truth or I could abandon the project, and I'd gone to too much effort to do the latter.

"You didn't believe me when I told you there was a way through that jungle. I'm going to look for it."

I brushed past him and began walking along the line of the hedge.

He followed. "You claim, I believe, that there is another opening outside the grounds?"

"Yes."

"Then let's go look for that one."

I stopped and turned to face him. "Why?"

"Do you mean, why am I offering to assist you, or why should we search for that entrance rather than the one that is—you claim—on this side? The answer to the first part of the question should be obvious. I hope to catch you in a flat-out flagrant lie, of course. As for the second point; this opening, assuming it exists, is obviously concealed. The other, according to you, is not."

"Damn it, it isn't. Concealed, I mean. It's there. Was there."

"Come on then."

He headed for the garage.

I could run to catch up with him or trail meekly along behind, like a servant—or a Victorian woman. Neither alternative appealed to me, but the second required less effort. Besides, if anybody was going to roust Sean out of bed I would rather it wasn't me.

He was already up and dressed, and when he saw me he gave me a long, thoughtful look. He must have concluded that Jordan had turned off the alarm, because he didn't mention it.

"Where are you going at this hour?" he asked.

Jordan didn't appreciate being interrogated. "We won't be long," he said curtly. Sean said no more.

Jordan backed the pickup out and gestured at me to get in, which I did. He didn't speak as we followed the drive to the front of the house and turned into the avenue leading to the gate. The trees lining it were oaks, and they were in terrible condition. People usually plant trees too close together; they want immediate gratification. But it doesn't take long for the growing trees to crowd one another out, fighting for sunlight and nutrients. Many of the old oaks were dying, all had dead branches, and the ground under them was littered with fallen wood. Some of them might be saved, with proper pruning and thinning, but it might be simpler to take them all out and start again. . . .

Jordan didn't ask directions. He must have known where my car had been found. We had gone a quarter of a mile along the track before he condescended to address me.

"How much farther?"

I glanced back. I could still see the line of the road. "I don't remember exactly. Farther than this." I glanced down at his neatly shod feet and added, not without malice, "We'd better get out and walk. The opening wasn't very big."

The mud through which I had squelched had hardened, but there were puddles. Jordan managed to avoid most of them. There was one particularly satisfying splash, though, and a couple of slithers. His shoes were no longer neat and his pants were spattered to the knee by the time we had gone another half a mile. I must admit I rather enjoyed it, even though he didn't complain or comment. How could he? It had been his idea.

We had gone quite a long way, past the curve I had mentioned, and there had been no sign of a break in the hedge, not even a hole big enough for a cat to pass through. Had I walked as far as this? Lost in my own thoughts I hadn't been paying close attention. Nothing looked familiar.

It was there, though. I was directly opposite the opening before I saw it. It was narrower and lower than I had remembered, but it was there. My exclamation brought Jordan hurrying to me.

"I'll be damned," he said.

"I told you so."

Not a very witty or mature comment, that one, but I couldn't restrain myself. Jordan gave me a critical look. He didn't reply.

We stood side by side staring at the opening. How the hell, I wondered, had I had the nerve to enter that constricted passage, walled with thorns, filled with shadows, floored with decaying leaves? It didn't look evocative and mysterious now, it looked like the entrance into a green hell. It was the sort of place an imaginative maker of horror films would construct, adding a skeleton or two tangled in the vines and a couple of boa constrictors and a grinning mummy. A breath of chilly dankness, heavy with the stench of rotting vegetation, came out of it.

The promise of the morning sun had not been fulfilled. Clouds were moving in out of the west. The sky was darkening, and it looked like rain.

Jordan's hands were in his pockets. I saw him shiver. He was wearing only a thin shirt, and the wind was cool. "Some animal must have made it," he said.

"A moose or a rhinoceros?"

"There aren't any moose in . . . Oh. Very witty."

"Only an animal with a hide like that of a rhino would force its way into that tangle. I tell

you, the growth was cut by a sharp-edged tool."
I studied the ragged, overgrown opening. "The
damned stuff has grown several inches since I
was here, but . . ."

Jordan took a step forward.

"Don't," I said sharply.

He stopped, hunching his shoulders. "Why not?"

"You're too tall. There were places where the
brambles scraped the top of my head, and I'm
shorter than you."

"Don't you want to have a look?"

"No."

"You were dead set on finding it."

"I had to find it. To prove to myself I wasn't
losing my mind."

My voice wasn't entirely steady. Until that
moment I hadn't realized how frightened I had
been.

After a long moment Jordan said, "I thought
you were lying. I didn't intend to question your
sanity."

"You wouldn't be the first person to question
it. Oh, hell, I didn't mean to say that. Forget it. I
know I wasn't imagining things and you know I
wasn't lying, and I see no point in ruining my
clothes and my hide again. It's not a—a nice
place. I don't remember which way I went or
how I got out. It's like a . . ."

"Like a maze? Wake up, you're not listening."
He took me by the elbow and gave it a little
shake.

"Ow!"

"What's the matter with you now?"

"I have a sore shoulder."

"First your ankle, now your shoulder. Stop whining and answer my question."

"What question? Oh. Well, the garden variety maze is a complicated series of paths bounded by hedges. The paths twist and turn, the hedges are too high to see over and too thick to break through. The more complicated type, the multicursal maze, is designed to confuse people and get them lost. But there's always a plan—a pattern. This path—tunnel—had no pattern."

"Maybe you simply failed to find it. People panic even in ordinary garden mazes and have to be 'rescued' by a custodian."

"Maybe. Let's go back now. It's going to rain."

Jordan ignored this. "Do you know the derivation of the name Troytan?" The question had been rhetorical; he went on without waiting for the answer I wouldn't have been able to provide anyhow. "It's a corruption of Troy Town. Some of the oldest mazes in England, patterns laid out in the turf without enclosing hedges, were called The Game of Troy or Troy Town. They may be Saxon in date."

"I suppose you're going to tell me why," I said resignedly. He had the car keys. Unless I wanted to walk I had to wait until he was ready to leave.

"There are references, in the *Aeneid* and other classical writers, to The Game of Troy. It appears to have been a religious ceremony that invoked the blessing of the god by following, on foot or on horseback, the windings of a sacred maze."

The wind blew a spatter of raindrops against my face, but I was beginning to get interested. "That is curious. How did the name get from ancient Rome to fifth—sixth, seventh?—century England?"

"Not just the name, the concept. There are a number of theories about the origins and function of the turf mazes, but they weren't just games. They had a mystical or symbolic purpose. As for the maze or labyrinth, it's much older than ancient Rome. In Minoan Crete—"

"Yes, yes, I know. Don't tell me about it. At least not now." It had begun to rain in earnest. Apparently oblivious to the water trickling down his face, Jordan stood staring at the hedge until I took his arm and dragged him away.

After Jordan had pulled into the garage he got out and trotted toward the house, leaving me to follow.

"You might at least apologize," I yelled after him.

No reply. He crossed the terrace and vanished inside.

There were two doors on the terrace, one opening directly into the kitchen, the other into the staircase hall. Since I had been trained not to drip on kitchen floors I used the second door and squelched up the stairs. I was stripped down to my underwear when there was a knock at the door.

I yelled, "Who is it?"

"Me." Doreen took the question for an invitation to enter. "Now what've you been up to? You're sure hard on clothes."

She gathered up my wet shirt and pants and I said ungraciously, "You don't have to pick up after me. What do you want?"

"Not me. Him. He's waiting for you in the library."

There were several men in the house, but I didn't have to ask who "him" was. "I trust he won't mind if I put on some clothes first? I had even thought of taking a hot shower and eating breakfast, but I wouldn't want to try his patience."

"He's short on patience, all right. But take your time. I'll tell him you'll be a while." She didn't leave, though. Her eyes were bright with what I took to be curiosity, and I expected a sly question about what I had been doing out in the rain. Jordan had gone through the kitchen; his equally saturated state must have been noted by Doreen or the cook.

Instead she said, "Thanks again. For keeping that rotten brat from hurting the cat."

"You don't have to thank me. It was pure reflex."

"Watch out for him," Doreen said.

"For Bobby?" I stared at her in surprise.

"I don't blame you for smacking him. But that was the second time you laid hands on him. It could be . . . well . . . dangerous."

"I teach school, Doreen. Spoiled kids are the rule, not the exception. I'm used to them."

"He's not just any spoiled kid. His—"

"I'd better hurry, if he's waiting for me." I turned my back on her and headed for the bathroom. She probably meant well, but I wasn't interested in her diagnosis of the boy's problems. She would probably recommend discipline, and firm hands, and maybe a good hard thrashing.

I decided to skip breakfast—not because he was waiting, just because. He was restlessly pacing the library when I got there, but his only comment was a smiling, "How nice you look this morning. Had a good long sleep, did you?"

Apparently he didn't know about my morning's adventures. I hadn't supposed Jordan would tell him, but I was surprised Sean hadn't reported at once, like a loyal employee. He didn't wait for an answer; he was itching to talk gardens.

I got carried away myself. We went through the list of plants Roger Fallon had ordered, and speculated about where they might have been placed. The old names sounded like poems: Love in a Mist, Love Lies Bleeding, Christ's Thorn. Some of the ones Fallon demanded were new and exotic in those days; several had been brought to Europe by Tradescant himself. They still bear his name: the white Michaelmas daisy, aster tradescantii, and the spiderwort, Tradescantia virginia. The list went on and on: pot marigold and winter cherry, salvia and summer jasmine and Virginia creeper—another of Tradescant's imports from the wilds of North America—and roses, autumn damask, rosa damascena, the White Rose of York . . .

My father and I had made lists too, every year. Limited lists; there had never been enough space or enough money. He had loved the old roses, but we only had two—Charles de Mills and the most glorious of white roses, Madame Hardy. The graceful heavy-laden boughs didn't make neat conventional bouquets like modern tea roses. She only liked flowers when they were in vases, in the house.

"Is something wrong?" Frank's voice broke into my reverie. "You didn't answer my question."

"Sorry, I was thinking about something else. What did you say?"

"Is it your foot that pains you? You weren't limping when you came in, I thought it was better."

"It is." My personal feelings were none of his business. "Uh—my shoulder is still pretty sore."

"It's almost lunchtime. What do you say we lunch in the village and consult Jennet about your sore shoulder?"

"Why her?"

"She knows a great deal about herbs and mental healing," Frank said seriously. "But if you would rather see a doctor—"

"No, there's no need. Okay. So long as she doesn't pray over me."

A trip to town would give me a chance to get some books. I had already checked the library shelves; Frank's idea of light reading appeared to be the *Wall Street Journal*. All the other books were about gardening. Jordan must keep his reference books in his room, but I doubted he would have any novels. Not the kind of novels I favored, anyhow.

Some of the things he had told me were interesting, though. The idea that a name could survive so long, even though its meaning had been lost and its syllables distorted, gave me a thrill. Raw American that I was, I had been impressed by a letter that was only three and a half centuries old; Jordan's lecture took me back at least two thousand years, maybe longer. The ritual described by Roman writers must have been ancient even in their time—perhaps as ancient as Minoan Crete. I had stopped Jordan from telling me all about the Cretan Labyrinth because I was getting wet, and because I knew it anyhow. Every schoolchild knows the legend of the labyrinth of Knossos, built to imprison the monstrous half-man half-bull known as the Minotaur, who fed on young men and maidens offered as tribute by the Greek cities that had been conquered by Crete. It had been Theseus, the heroic prince of—yes, of Troy—who killed the monster and made his escape through the winding pathways of the maze, thanks to the ball of string given him by the princess of Crete who had fallen in love with him. Poor dumb Ariadne; she had betrayed her father and her country for a handsome face and a set of bulging muscles, and then Theseus had sailed off and abandoned her on an island along his homeward route. Served her right for being such a fool.

I can't imagine why I was thinking about Ariadne during the drive to the village; it couldn't have been because Sean was driving. He dropped us at The Witches' Cauldron, which was, as I had suspected, a restaurant. The interior was dark and overpoweringly picturesque, but I was relieved to see that the theme hadn't been carried to excess. The waitresses wore mob caps instead of pointy hats, and only a few of the entrees had cutesy names. I decided not to indulge in Demdike's Delight, which was described as a "deadly" rich chocolate cake.

The Cauldron appeared to be the restaurant of choice for the town's elite as well as a popular tourist spot. Several people stopped by the table to say hello; Frank introduced me to a doctor, two solicitors and the vicar.

"You're a popular man," I said, after the vicar—who looked more like a big blond football player than my novel-derived notion of a Church of England clergyman—had slapped Frank on the back and gone back to his table.

"They think they will get money from me," Frank said coolly.

"Will they?"

"I have already contributed to the fund for repairing the church tower; it was about to collapse. The church itself needs extensive work. I haven't yet decided whether to underwrite the restoration. Most of it is eighteenth century, but the nave and the foundations—"

"So the vicar explained. At considerable length."

"He is, as one might expect, enthusiastic about the church. But he was also curious about you. People are like that in small towns."

"I know."

"Yes, you do, don't you? This is my first experience of the sort. I like it. The friendliness, the intimacy—"

"It's too damned intimate. People knowing every move you make, putting the worst possible interpretation on everything you do or say. . . ."

"Why should you care what people think?"

"That's easy for you to say."

"It's the only sensible way to live," Frank declared dogmatically. "Please yourself and tell other people to go to the devil. Do you want coffee?"

"No, thanks."

"I do." Frank gestured at the waitress. She responded with such alacrity that I deduced he must tip extravagantly.

"Now," Frank said, "we were talking earlier about the knot garden."

"Wouldn't it be better to postpone work on the gardens until you've finished remodelling

the house? You don't want workmen and construction machinery trampling down the beds."

"I'm not going to do anything to the house."

"It's going to look ridiculous," I insisted. "A
Victorian pseudo-Gothic hodgepodge in the
middle of a classic seventeenth-century garden?
At the very least you ought to tear off those
porches. They're ugly, they're dangerous, and
they may cover part of the gardens."

"No, they don't. The original house was considerably larger than the present one, and it was
differently oriented." Frank looked pathetic.
"I'm not a young man, Heather. I want to see
those gardens restored before I die."

"How old are you?"

His drooping mouth lifted into a grin. "None
of your business. What a cold, unsentimental
young woman you are."

"All right, then, if you're in such an all-fired
hurry why don't you get started instead of sitting around talking to an ignoramus like me?
Hire an expert like Sir Edwin Whitbread or one
of the other big shots. You can afford it."

"Hmm," said Frank enigmatically. "Have you
finished? Then let's visit Jennet."

Instead of going out onto the street he indicated a door on one wall of the restaurant. It
opened directly into the building next door.

There couldn't have been a greater contrast.
From the dim low-ceilinged shop, we entered a
space that was one big room, brightly lit and
entirely modern. Jennet must have gutted the

interior of the old house, and although my antiquarian instincts were appalled at such vandalism, I had to admit the result was far more likely to attract customers. That's what it was—a shop—though the merchandise was arranged with such restraint that at first glance it more resembled a museum. Glass cases and counters held a variety of objects. A lot of them sparkled. Articles of clothing hung on racks and were artistically displayed on the wall. The entire back section appeared to be a bookstore. Frank headed in that direction. I followed, glancing at the sparkly things. They were mostly jewelry and small ornaments—things that just sit there, to quote my dad. He was talking about Mom's collection of china ornaments—big-eyed cats and big-eyed kids and puppies with floppy ears. The ornaments in the cases here bore no resemblance to my mother's treasures. Many appeared to be carved of semi-precious stones, and they were all lovely.

Jennet was sitting behind a desk in the book section. Today her black hair had been twisted into an ornate coronet, bristling with fancy combs and pins. She wore a loose garment printed in gorgeous shades of topaz and brown and turquoise that flowed into one another with an odd suggestion of shapes that never quite solidified; the longer you focused on a particular pattern the more it shifted. She returned Frank's cheerful greeting with an abstracted gesture. Her cool gray eyes were fixed on me.

"So. You decided to stay on."

"For a while."

"I hear you've met Giles Betancourt."

"And his family," I said. That unblinking stare bothered me.

"How did you know that?" Frank asked.

"My crystal ball, of course." She looked amused. "Really, Frank, you are too much. Giles usually breakfasts at the restaurant and I often join him for a coffee. He spoke very highly of you, Heather."

"I can't imagine why. All I've done is slug his son. Twice."

"Yes, I heard about that too."

Tiring of the subject, I said, "You have a beautiful place."

"I'm rather proud of it," Jennet admitted. "It took forever to find the right craftsmen to carry out my theme, and even longer to develop a clientele. People come to me now from all over the world. Let me show you around. Oh, Frank, before I forget—here's that book Jordan asked for. Two hundred quid, please."

"Two hundred pounds?" Frank bellowed.

"It's rare and hard to find," Jennet said calmly. "I happened to have a copy because I've been on the lookout for garden books for you."

"Garden?" Frank took the book from her and read the title aloud. "*Mazes and Labyrinths.* Hmph. What does Jordan want with a book on mazes? He doesn't give a damn about gardening."

"You do love pretending to be an uncouth semi-literate lout, don't you? Jordan gives a damn about classical mythology and folklore. That's what his dissertation is about, remember?"

"I pay no attention to his academic nonsense. That's an outrageous price, Jennet. How about a discount for an old friend?"

They went on arguing about the price, more or less amicably, but I knew both of them were dead serious. My eye wandered to the bookshelf behind the desk. *The History of Witchcraft. The Werewolf. Phantasms of the Living. Mediums of the Nineteenth Century.*

I moved to the next section. All the books there had the word *fairy* in the title. They weren't books for children.

"Angels are hot too," Jennet said, behind me. "Come, let me show you the shop."

Frank trailed after us making disparaging remarks, which Jennet blandly ignored. Everything in the store carried out the theme whose nature I had already deduced from the books.

"So that's your clientele," I said. "People who believe in—uh . . ."

"The Old Religion. New Age, Wicca, the occult—it's a much broader clientele than you might suppose," Jennet said coolly. "Including people who come to look and end up buying something because it is beautiful. Then there's the natural food craze and the belief in herbal remedies. Americans are suckers for herbs." She stopped in front of a shelf and selected a small packet from one of the baskets. "Comfrey is especially good for bruises. Steep it in boiling water for five minutes and apply a compress soaked in the liquid."

Frank had not, in my hearing, mentioned my bruised shoulder. Did they really suppose I was gullible enough to be deceived by a simple parlor trick like that one? He must have telephoned her before we left the house.

"Comfrey," I repeated. "Isn't that the stuff that damages the liver?"

She recognized the challenge and accepted it. Her eyes sparkled. "You are up to date, aren't you? My dear girl, I wouldn't risk my reputation or my livelihood by offering you anything harmful. Certain of the recent studies strongly suggest one should be cautious about ingesting comfrey, especially over a long period of time, and I wouldn't prescribe it for asthma or respiratory congestion. As a compress it is perfectly safe and, I assure you, effective."

Touché, and touché again, I thought. I smiled at her. "Thanks. How much do I owe you?"

"Accept it as a gesture of friendship," Jennet said with an answering smile. "Is there anything else you fancy?"

The herbs had been wrapped in squares of printed fabric tied with colorful ribbon bows. I sorted through them. "Sorcerer's violet?"

"I like the old names. That's—"

"Periwinkle." I must have sounded rather smug. "And hokeypokey is nettle, right?"

"Also known as naughty man's plaything."

"I never heard that. Why . . . ? Never mind, I don't think I want to know."

"It's also known as devil's leaf. A number of poisonous or harmful plants have similar names."

Frank was examining the labels. "I see I must devote more study to plant names. What is scabby hands?"

"Hemlock, isn't it?" I said, still showing off. "Do you have any other deadly poisons around?"

"My dear girl, a good number of plants are poisonous to some degree, and even the medicinal varieties can make a person sick if they are misused."

Touché again. The foxglove, which looks so attractive at the back of a perennial border, produces digitalis, used to relieve various kinds of heart trouble and remove unpopular neighbors. The trumpet-shaped white blossoms of the datura look beautiful and are exquisitely scented, particularly at twilight. A handful of the pretty green leaves can kill you deader than a doornail. Even daffodil bulbs are deadly. That's why they flourish and spread; moles and mice won't touch them.

"You're quite right to be cautious about herbs, though," Jennet went on. "People assume that because they are 'natural' they are harmless, but some have unpleasant side effects if they are used to excess or in combination."

"Caveat emptor," I murmured, examining the pretty packaging. It would attract plenty of buyers.

"'Do no harm' is the motto of this establishment, not 'let the buyer beware,'" Jennet said sharply. "Each packet includes a descriptive folder identifying the plant and cautioning the buyer about its use."

"I didn't mean to imply you were unethical."

"Oh, quite," Jennet said. "I'd rather not risk a lawsuit either."

She was something of an enigma. One minute she talked like a mystic, the next like a sharp, calculating merchant. The two categories needn't be mutually exclusive. What did she really believe?

"You haven't seen my chief attraction yet. A number of my customers come for this purpose."

We had made a circuit of the store. On the wall opposite the door by which we had entered was a large hanging, ten feet high and six feet wide. I had assumed it was one of the pieces of merchandise. It was quite beautiful—a tapestry, in blended shades of green and brown. Before I could examine it closely Jennet pulled a cord, and the hanging lifted, to display an opening beyond.

And there she was, just as she had appeared in my dream—blind eyeballs glaring, dusty black gown trailing—Old Demdike herself.

FOUR

It was like the fabled Labyrinth constructed in
    mountainous Crete—
A maze of unbroken walls, with thousands of
    blind Alleys
To keep the venturer guessing and trick him, so
    that the right path
Into the heart of the maze was a puzzle to find
    or retrace.

VIRGIL, AENEID V, 588–91

Jennet emitted a ladylike yell. I had taken an involuntary step back—onto her foot.

"Sorry," I mumbled.

"I suppose I can't complain, since I designed
it to startle the kiddies and nervous little old
ladies," Jennet said, with what I had to admit
was pardonable sarcasm. "But it's not that fright-
ening, you know."

A second glance supported her statement. I
had seen grislier exhibits in Halloween haunted

houses. Life sized, the face carefully modelled, it was just an old woman in an old-fashioned dress. Her blind face was more pathetic than menacing and her clawlike hands were extended, palms up, as if in appeal. A length of chain connected the iron cuffs on her bony wrists.

"You don't have to go in," Jennet said.

It sounded like a challenge. Without replying I went on. My arm brushed the standing figure and the chain gave off a faint musical jingle.

Some of the exhibits were harmless and mildly interesting, showing how people lived in the sixteenth century, what they wore, what they ate; but the last room, the one to which no one under eighteen was admitted, made me sick to my stomach. Naturally it was the most crowded.

When I commented on this Jennet said, "It's not as bad as the Tower of London, or the jolly torture chambers in some of the European tourist spots. There's one in Italy where they use dummies to display how the thumbscrews and the rack and other devices were used. The dummies are very realistic."

"Yech," I said.

"That's one viewpoint. Another is that people should be made aware of the unspeakable cruelties human beings have perpetrated on one another."

"In the hope that they'll stop perpetrating them? I wish I could believe that, but I don't think it works that way. The same argument is used by the producers of horror films and video games, and it's not true. Exposure to explicit violence doesn't sensitize people, it hardens them. Look at that guy. He's revelling in every grisly detail." I indicated a man who was staring fixedly at a reproduction of a stone-walled cell. A rat nibbled at the hair of one of the emaciated figures sprawled on the floor. The other details were even grislier—and familiar. I turned my back on the exhibit and the ghoul.

Jennet said, "I'm inclined to agree with your general premise, but you are being a little judgmental, aren't you? Many of those who come here are pilgrims, visiting a shrine to the martyrs of their faith."

What faith? The unhappy victims of the witchcraft mania had been martyred by human ignorance and savagery; to compare them with Cranmer and Sir Thomas More, and others who had given up their lives rather than embrace what they considered a false religion was surely inappropriate. I didn't want a lecture, so I said repressively, "I'm sure your motives are above reproach."

"How kind of you to say so. In fact," Jennet went on, amusement coloring her voice, "I wouldn't deny that one of my motives is purely crass and commercial. The museum is a big draw, it brings a lot of business to the shop. The subject interests me, though. Are you familiar with the history of witchcraft, so-called?"

"I've been reading your book."

"My humble little pamphlet?" Her amusement was undisguised now. "There are better books on the subject if you want to read more about it. The Lancashire witchcraft trials are famous; there were two of them, you know, thirty years apart. The brutal sentences given the original Pendle witches didn't deter others from following in their footsteps. The appeal of—something—must have been very strong for them to risk death and torture."

"Something?" I repeated. "The worship of Satan, you mean? Some of the so-called witches may have practiced healing and primitive midwifery, but I doubt any of them flew on their broomsticks to adore the Devil in the form of a black goat." I had had enough of the exhibits and the conversation. I started back toward the entrance.

"You're right about that," Jennet murmured. "But the subject is rather more complicated than you make it sound." She paused by a glass case. "This is a rare manuscript—the original copy of a trial transcript from Scotland. See the last line? The verdict and the sentence: *Convicta et combusta.*"

Convicted and burned. At least she hadn't condescended to me by translating. She was deliberately baiting me, though, for reasons I didn't understand. I tried to match her cool, amused tone. "I'm surprised you don't have a tableau of someone being burned at the stake, complete with plastic flames."

"They didn't burn witches in England, they hanged them. It's an idea though—a gibbet complete with corpses. Quite a draw that would be."

She politely held the curtain aside for me. I had to walk sideways to avoid touching Old Demdike.

It was like coming out of a nightmare into bright day. The glittering, glowing objects in the display cases and on the walls carried no dark taint, whatever they were meant to suggest. I stopped to examine a caftan or robe—a long loose garment of silk that shone like a ruby and glittered with gold embroidery around the neck and sleeves.

Jennet was the professional merchant now, smiling and gently persuasive. "That's nice, isn't it? Scarlet isn't your color, Heather. This blue would look smashing on you, it would bring out the auburn in your hair."

My hair is mouse-brown. The color of the garment was marvelous, though—a blend of green and blue that shifted like running water as Jennet spread the skirt between her hands. "You could cinch it in with a belt like this one." The stones in the wide band matched the hues in the dress; if they weren't real gems they were darned good imitations of sapphires and emeralds, peridots and tourmalines.

"I couldn't afford—" I began, and then stopped, remembering that I could.

Frank said, "She will give you a discount."

"Frank, I keep telling you this isn't a suk. It's

in his blood, Heather. He always tries to talk me down on the price."

In some circles this might have been viewed as a racist remark, but Frank laughed as heartily as she did. "I always fail. She's as sharp a bargainer as any merchant in the bazaars."

Next to the door was a basket filled with a beautiful jumble of woven fabrics, the colors blends of earth tones—brown and beige and umber, black and white and pale turquoise. To judge from the examples that hung from a rack above, they were stoles and shawls. The fabric started to move, and a form emerged. The creature's soft fur had blended so well with the fabric it took several seconds for me to identify it as a cat.

Jennet snatched it up. "So that's where you'd got to! Wretched beast, how dare you nest in my hand-woven fabrics?"

She cradled it in her arms. It was quite large, its coat an unusual blend of brown and black and red, not in distinct patches like that of a calico, but shading gradually from one color to the next. Its face and feet were pure white.

"But that's Doreen's cat," I exclaimed.

"No, it's mine. A lot of the local cats have this coloring. The locals call them Demdike cats."

"I thought witches' cats were black."

"That's the traditional view. Pure superstition, like the belief that cats were familiars sent by the Devil."

The cat yawned. Its teeth were very long and sharp. "Is it a he or a she?"

"She—but only in the technical sense. I had to have her declawed, too; ordinarily I wouldn't approve of that, but she doesn't go outside, and my most expensive garments were her favorite sharpening post." The cat started to squirm, and she put it down on the floor. "Back to work, Fancie. She's supposed to pose elegantly on my desk or on a bookshelf. Another of my gimmicks, as you Americans call them."

"You do seem to have a lot of cat-shaped objects," I said, examining the contents of a glass case.

"Cat fanciers are big spenders. And cats are beautiful creatures."

"They're more shapely than dragons or bats, I admit. Can I have a look at that ring?"

"If you are going to talk about cats and jewelry I will return to the book section," Frank said.

The ring was silver, the recumbent, ruby-eyed cat shape curving around the shank. The carving was delicate and detailed. I slipped it onto my finger. It stuck at the knuckle.

"Too small," I said, returning it.

"I can have it resized."

"It's pretty, but I'm not a cat fancier."

"No? What are you then?"

I looked up. "What do you mean?"

After a long moment she said, "Never mind. Try this one, why don't you?"

She took my left hand firmly in hers and put the ring on my finger. The single rounded stone that formed the bezel was golden brown, and as she turned my hand a band of light shifted through its center.

"It fits," I admitted. "But—"

"It's a little loose. You're right handed, aren't you? Then it will be a trifle larger than the left." After she had transferred the ring she ran her fingers lightly over my palm. "The nettle rash is better, I see."

"Yes. Thanks." I tugged at the ring. It had gone on easily enough, but I couldn't seem to get it off.

"Keep it," Jennet said.

"No, really, I—"

"As a gift." Smiling, she took my hand in hers. "I gave you rather a hard time in the museum."

Frank had become bored with the books. "What are you doing?" he inquired, joining us at the counter.

"Not what you think, you evil-minded old man," Jennet said.

"I wasn't thinking anything of the kind. I know quite well where your interests lie."

"Frank, you're impossible. I'm not trying to get rid of you, but isn't that your car out in front?"

"Confound it!" Frank peered out the window. "It's Jordan. What's he doing here? I told Sean I'd call when we were ready to leave. Take your time, Heather, look around some more if you want."

"Jordan appears to be a trifle beleaguered," Jennet murmured.

"He can take care of himself," Frank declared. There was a note of amused malice in his voice that made me wonder what trouble Jordan had got himself into now.

"I'm ready to go," I said. "As soon as I pay for this."

Again her long slim fingers closed over my hand. "I will be offended if you don't accept it as a gift."

She sounded as if she meant it. I smiled and thanked her and went out the door Frank had opened for me.

Jordan stood by the car. In fact he was standing against the car, and Lindsay Betancourt was so close to him you couldn't have slid a sheet of paper between them without wrinkling it.

Lindsay pivoted neatly without putting any distance between herself and Jordan. "Frank! When I saw the Bentley I just had to run over and say hello."

"Ready to go, Dad?" Jordan asked. He did sound a little desperate.

"No. Why didn't you wait until I called?"

They would have gone on bickering if Lindsay hadn't intervened. "I was going to ring you, Frank, to tell you not to worry about Laura. The doctor said there probably wouldn't be a scar."

"Glad to hear it." I was learning to recognize that gleam in Frank's eyes, but I couldn't think

why he looked so cynically amused and Jennet
so sour until the latter said, "If anybody owes
Laura compensation, it's Bobby."

Speak of the devil, as they say. I hadn't seen
"the kiddies" until Jennet pounced, grabbing
the boy by his collar and pulling him away from
the door of the shop.

"Oh no you don't. I told you never to come in
my place again."

"I just wanted to look at the pretty things."
The boy's voice was sweet as sugar, but the look
he gave Jennet would have raised deep suspicions in any experienced teacher. His sister had
retreated behind a pillar box; her wide eyes
were fixed on Jennet and her thumb was in her
mouth. She looked like a frightened white rabbit.

"Take your hands off him," Lindsay exclaimed.
"If this is the way you treat customers—"

"Customers, hell. After his last visit I found
that three of the most expensive caftans had
been slashed."

"You haven't any proof it was Bobby."

"If I had been able to prove it I'd have called
the police."

Jordan opened the car door and gestured
peremptorily at me and his father. Frank
ignored the gesture; hands behind his back,
smiling benevolently, he was enjoying the argument too much to leave. Not until Jennet
turned on her heel and went back inside did he
allow me to take his arm and tow him toward

the car. I wanted to get the hell out of there. The scene had been unpleasant, and I had a feeling it wasn't over.

How right I was. Lindsay turned to her son. "Get in the Jag, Bobby. Mummy will be right with you."

"But, Mummy—"

"Do as I tell you."

"Yes, Mummy."

Laura trotted after him like an obedient puppy. Lindsay hadn't so much as looked at the little girl; she took firm hold of the Bentley's window ledge and leaned forward to address Jordan.

"Those papers you wanted, Jordan—why don't you come round this evening and have a look at them?"

Jordan tried not to look at his father. "Did Giles suggest it?"

"He'll be working late—as usual. The kiddies are spending the night with their gran, so you can take all the time you like."

I gave Frank a hard shove, and he finally consented to climb into the back seat. I scrambled in after him and slammed the door. Unfortunately I wasn't able to muffle his snort of laughter. Jordan heard it; his hands tightened on the wheel, and when he replied his voice was cold with fury.

"No, thank you. I'm busy this evening."

Frank's wide eyes moved back to Lindsay. The exchange did have a horrible kind of fascination, like those talk shows where people bare their most intimate private affairs to an audience of millions.

"Darling, how stuffy you sound! If your engagement is with your boring old books you can postpone it."

"It isn't with my boring old books."

"Then who—"

Only her firm grip on the window frame saved her from falling when the Bentley jerked sharply forward. The jolt, accompanied by the nasty crunch of crumpling metal, threw Jordan forward against the wheel. Lindsay staggered but managed to remain on her feet.

I should have realized the low-slung, spanking new vehicle immediately behind us was Lindsay's; it had been parked illegally but conveniently, and in her hurry to reach her prey she must have left the keys in the ignition.

Bobby might have miscalculated, but knowing him I assumed he had intended to ram the Bentley. This impression was confirmed when he reversed and slammed into the vehicle behind him.

"God damn that kid!" Jordan gasped. "So help me God, I'm going to kill him!"

Lindsay, her face distorted, ran toward her car. She wrenched open the door and yanked Bobby out so forcibly he fell to the sidewalk. I saw no more; Jordan pulled away with a suddenness that threw me into Frank's lap.

"What are you doing?" Frank demanded, not

of me, but of his son. "Someone might have been hurt."

"Nobody was hurt. Buckle up."

"But I want to find out—"

"What she'll do to Bobby? Something with boiling oil in it, I hope." He went on, in a pleased voice. "The kid may have overreached himself this time. She doesn't give a damn what he does to other people, but that car is her baby."

ii

As Jordan pulled into the garage Sean came out of his front door. Seeing the damage to the rear end, he let out a yell. "What the hell happened?"

He sounded as anguished as if the car were his property, and the glare he directed at Jordan made it clear he held him accountable. Frank hopped nimbly out, smiling in anticipation; I could see he wasn't about to get Jordan off the hook, so I said, "It was that little brat, Bobby Betancourt. I think he rammed us on purpose."

"Wouldn't surprise me if he had. The kid's a menace. Don't tell me it was Lindsay's Jag he was driving?"

"Trying to drive. How bad is it?" Frank asked, without much concern.

"Could be worse," Sean admitted. "Lindsay's car is probably in worse shape."

"Damn it," Jordan said suddenly. "I forgot my book."

"It's here." I picked the book up from the seat where Frank had tossed it. Jordan didn't move until I had emerged from the garage, and when I saw the way he held himself I remembered the crunch with which he had hit the steering wheel.

"Were you hurt?" I asked.

"No." He took the book and started for the house.

"Bruised ribs, I expect," Frank said. He did not sound concerned. "I've got to put in a few hours' work this afternoon. Can you amuse yourself?"

"Sure. Don't worry about me."

Sean was stroking the dent like a solicitous father. "I need to take the car in. If Heather could follow me to Birmingham and drive me back—"

"It can wait," Frank said. "I may have to run up to London shortly."

"If you say so."

"I do." He walked away.

Sean straightened. "You okay?" he asked.

"How kind of you to inquire."

He gave me a grin. "Not a mark on you."

"I was in the back."

"I figured. Can I offer you a cup of coffee?"

"Where?"

He gestured toward the door of the cottage. "All the comforts of home."

"I'm sure. No, thanks."

As I walked away I heard him say quietly, "You'll have to talk to me sometime, you know."

iii

The English climate demonstrated its famed inconsistency that day. The sun had come out; it was a fine, warm afternoon, too nice to spend indoors. Seeing a group of buildings and a brick wall behind the garage, I went that way. There was a gate in the wall. The space it enclosed was a kitchen garden; most of the green sprouts were too small to be identified from a distance, but I recognized the feathery tops of carrots and other things. A man was working there, scraping delicately at the ground with a hoe.

I know gardeners. I didn't want to walk into his domain without permission, so I gave him a hail. He straightened and turned, pressing his hand to the small of his back. I wondered if he had done it in order to prove how hard he had been working, because he wasn't that old. It's hard to tell with gardeners. They tend to be lean and wiry, and long exposure to weather doesn't do a lot for their skin.

"You shouldn't shout that way," he said reproachfully. "Look what you made me do to my sprouts."

I couldn't see that the brussels sprouts had

suffered damage, but I apologized anyhow. "I'm Heather Tradescant. Are you the gardener here, Mr.—?"

"Will. Just Will." He took the hand I had extended. "Monday, Wednesday and Friday are my days."

Another part-time employee. Could it have been he who cut that strange meandering path through the jungle? I didn't want to ask point-blank, so I tried subtlety. "Have you been helping with the restoration project?"

"Nay, not me." He gave me a sly, sidelong look, and waited a long time before adding, "I keep the beds weeded and mulched and the like, but I don't take much truck in flowers. Vegetables, now, they're useful."

I said politely, "Your garden looks terrific."

"Come in and have a look round."

I had a feeling he was going to introduce me to every individual carrot, but I didn't have the heart to turn him down. I piled on the praise, and managed not to sound too stupid about his beloved vegetables. We hadn't grown many, only a few tomato plants and an occasional zucchini. Dad had always wanted to try melons and asparagus, but . . .

"I'd better leave you to work in peace," I said.

He nodded. "The garden shed's along there if you want to do a bit of digging. Keeping those flower beds weeded is cruel hard on me back. Just be sure you put the tools back in their proper places."

"Of course. Thank you." What he was offering me amounted to an unpaid, part-time job—weeding is cruel hard on anybody's back—but my thanks were sincere. He knew, as I did, that gardening can be a cure and a catharsis. I offered him my hand.

Light shimmered in the stone on my finger. "Cat's-eye," he said.

"Is that what it's called?"

"Looks like one, dunnit?"

"Yes, I guess it does—the long slitted pupil."

"Same color eyes as the Demdike cats."

"Right again. Jennet gave it to me."

"Ah, did she then."

"Well—thanks again."

"You're welcome. Down there"—he pointed—"are my herbs. Guess I don't need to show you them."

"Some other time, maybe."

"Take what you want. Garden shed's that way."

He stumped slowly back to the place where he had left his hoe. I had been dismissed, but with courtesy. It had been kind of him to make me free of the garden.

I found the shed. Will was a pro—every tool in its place, not a speck of rust or a grass blade on them. Among the tools were several chain saws.

They were the only implements that might make a dent in the jungle, supposing anyone were inclined to tackle it. Secateurs and clippers would be about as much use as a pair of scissors. I was not about to tackle it, not then or ever. I closed the door.

The table under the oak tree was where I had ended up, sprawled ungracefully at Jordan's feet. I started toward it, trying to remember my exact position. I had fallen forward. Assuming I had proceeded in something like a straight line, I must have emerged from the hedge just about . . .

There was something on the table. It could have been a pool of dappled sunlight and shadow, but it wasn't.

I approached the cat with the caution of inexperience. It had raised its head and was watching me. Its eyes were greenish yellow. "Hello," I said tentatively.

Its mouth opened, and for an absurd instant I thought it was going to answer. Instead it yawned, displaying long sharp teeth. The tip of one ear was missing, giving it a mildly rakish appearance and there were burdocks and leaves stuck in its fur, but otherwise it looked healthy and well groomed. The pattern of mottled fawn and brownish red covered its entire body except for its face and a pair of white paws.

"He's waiting for his tea."

I had been so intent on the cat I hadn't heard her coming. My sudden movement startled the animal. It rose in a single fluid motion and jumped down off the table. I backed off.

"You needn't be afraid of him," Doreen went on. "Here, give him his milk."

She shifted the tray she was carrying to one arm and indicated a pitcher. I poured a little of the milk into a saucer and put it down on the grass. Purring, the cat tucked in.

"There, you see?" Doreen gave the table a casual brush-off and shook out a white cloth. I moved to help her. She had the cloth spread before I could do so, but she nodded her acknowledgment as she put the tray down and began unloading it with quick professional movements.

"I waited tables at The Witches' Cauldron before I came here," she explained. "Sit down, why don't you? The others will be along."

She knelt down beside the cat and picked a burr off its hindquarters. It growled at her but did not raise its head from the saucer.

"He's just an old softy, really," Doreen said fondly.

He didn't look like an old softy. He was even bigger than Jennet's cat and he had definitely not been altered, but the coloring was almost identical. It was not surprising that superstitious people would find something uncanny in the resemblance. Of course it was nothing more than the result of inbreeding and a particular genetic makeup, and I doubted that anybody knew what color Demdike's cat had been, if she had had a cat. As I had told Jennet, black was the preferred shade.

"Does he come to tea every day?" I asked.

"Unless there's company. He doesn't like strangers."

The cat had finished the milk. He pulled away from Doreen's hands and rubbed against my leg.

"Does he want more milk?" I asked apprehensively.

Doreen laughed. "He wants a pat. Go ahead, he won't bite you."

"I thought you said he didn't like strangers." The cat purred, preening under my tentative touch. He had come to me only because I had fed him and because he was tired of having Doreen pull his fur, but I couldn't help feeling flattered.

"I guess he thinks you aren't a stranger. His name's Tibb."

It sounded like a formal introduction, and the cat's response was amusingly appropriate. It jumped onto my lap. I said, "Oops," and stiffened.

"Don't you like cats?" She sounded puzzled.

"I like animals, I'm just not used to them. We— I never had a pet."

"You lived in a flat, did you?"

"No." Stroking the cat, I explained, "My mother said animals were messy."

"Nasty nice housekeeper, was she? How about your dad?"

"Oh, he loves—loved—animals, especially dogs. He always wanted one, but she wouldn't let—"

I broke off. Doreen seemed willing to overlook my abrupt dismissal of her the previous day, and I wanted to be on good terms with her, but not such intimate terms as that.

"It's the same with Mr. Giles," Doreen said. "Lindsay's not the kind to care about anything or anybody but herself and that rotten kid."

Obviously she didn't share my inhibitions about discussing people's private affairs. I had wondered why Karim, who brooked no defiance of his authority from other people, allowed Doreen such freedom of speech. I should have known. She kept him up to date on the neighborhood news.

A well-bred woman would have indicated, gently but firmly, that she didn't care for malicious gossip. A woman as uninterested in other people as I had been, only a few days ago, would have changed the subject. I said, "How long have they been married?"

Her conspiratorial smile warned me that I had inadvertently tapped a rich vein of gossip. "Twelve years. Bob will be thirteen in August."

I couldn't think what to say. It was irrelevant and immaterial and possibly not true, and certainly none of my business. Doreen went on. "He did the gentlemanly thing, did Mr. Giles, even if it wasn't his."

"Honestly, Doreen, I don't want to hear—"

"No, listen." She leaned forward, her eyes wide and solemn. "You have to hear this, it's for your own good. The boy's not like him at all, there's never been a streak of that in the Betancourts. It's not safe to interfere with him."

"Doreen—"

"You wonder why Mr. Giles won't keep a pet?

It's not because of her. They had a puppy when Bob was four. They've never dared to have another one."

I supposed she had selected her words with care in an effort to spare my sensitive feelings, but the simple statement was almost as bad as a detailed description of what the child had done. It left so much to the imagination.

"My God. How did he manage to get hold of Tibb?" The cat, lazily kneading my knees, looked up when I spoke its name.

"Fed him salmon sandwiches, I expect. He won't be so stupid next time. Cats have long memories, not like dogs."

I looked at the claws plucking gently at my trousers. I didn't need Doreen to tell me he was just playing, the claws only partly extended. I wouldn't have wanted to feel their full effect.

Doreen got to her feet. "There's the boss. I'll bring the tea. Guard the sandwiches, especially the fish paste."

They met midway and paused to exchange a few words, or a joke; I heard Doreen laugh. She obviously got on well with him, but he was "the boss" or "the old chap." I had heard her use first names when referring to Jordan and Sean and even Lindsay. But Giles still rated a "mister" in front of his name.

"So you have made the acquaintance of the cat," Frank said, eyeing the large bundle on my lap dubiously.

"Don't you like cats?"

"I revere all life," Frank said.

"I suppose that's in the Koran?"

"Probably." He grinned at me. "But nothing in the Koran or elsewhere says I must be intimate with them."

Sean sauntered up in time to hear the exchange. "I've been telling him he ought to get a guard dog, but he won't hear of it."

"They are too dangerous," Frank declared. "I have heard of them turning on their owners."

"Not if they're properly trained. If it would make you feel better, I could keep him chained up during the day and only let him loose at night."

"One day you would forget, and then he would attack me."

It was obviously an old argument which Sean continued only because he enjoyed teasing his boss. He gave me a sidelong smile, inviting me to share the joke. "We could get a little dog. A Pekingese or Chihuahua."

Frank was not amused. "What would be the point of that? Guard dogs should be large and fierce. No, I won't have one. They make droppings on the yard and dig up the flowers."

"I can't deny that. At least we have an attack cat." Sean reached out and scratched the cat under its chin. He went on scratching, the heel of his hand resting casually on my thigh, until Doreen came with the tea.

I couldn't think of a good reason for refusing to pour, as Frank requested, though I felt sure he expected I'd make a mess of it. I knew the routine—I had had it pounded into me—and I got through it without spilling anything. The cat refused tea, but accepted the scraps of sandwich Sean tossed him; after a time he walked off and found a patch of sunlight where he stretched out and started licking his paws.

"How did he know that was the last of the salmon?" Frank asked.

"He's a Demdike cat," Sean said seriously. "A witch's cat."

"Perhaps he would like more. Go and tell Doreen—"

Sean chuckled, and I said, "Don't be silly. He'd had enough, that's all."

"They are uncanny creatures, though," Frank muttered. "They know things."

Like the way through the hedge? Such knowledge wouldn't require supernatural powers, only the instincts of a semi-wild creature. I kept an unobtrusive eye on the animal, but he stayed where he was, curling up for a nap after he had finished washing himself.

Jordan didn't join us, but when Doreen came to bring more hot water she had a message from him. "He said to tell you Mr. Giles will be here for dinner."

"Oh?" Frank's scowl was not meant for her, though it was directed at her. "Who invited him?"

"He rang up to ask if he could drop in this evening," Doreen said calmly. "Lindsay and the kids have gone to her mum's, so Jordan asked him to come for drinks at six, and stay for supper. I've told Mrs. Greenspan. It's not as if you dine formally; there's always plenty of food."

"Have you made any other arrangements you'd care to share with me?" Frank inquired.

"No, sir, that's all," Doreen said, straight-faced. "I'll just take the tray, shall I?"

She collected the remainder of the sandwiches and cookies—biscuits—and went off without waiting for a reply.

"Well, well," Frank murmured. "I wonder what's up."

"Why should he be up to anything?" Sean asked. "He drops in all the time."

"Now, Sean, you know that isn't true. Giles is so confounded well-bred he never invites himself. Perhaps he has found a new attraction here."

He beamed at me.

iv

I decided to shower and change. Not because "we" were having a guest, just because. When I went into my room I found that something new had been added. Another day, another little amenity. This one was an electric kettle. It sat on an elegant silver tray with a sugar bowl and a folded napkin and a teaspoon and a cute little basket containing packets of tea, cocoa and instant coffee. I cannot resist food in any form, so I sorted through them and found that my every whim had been anticipated; there were several varieties of coffee and three kinds of herbal tea bags in addition to the standard Earl Grey and Lapsang Souchong. I wondered what Frank and/or Doreen would think of next. A fridge, maybe?

By the time I was ready the others were already on the terrace. I heard them from my window, Frank's emphatic voice rising over Giles's genteel murmurs and an occasional comment from Sean. If Jordan was there he wasn't talking.

Jordan was there. He just wasn't talking. They all rose when I came out the kitchen door, and I smiled to myself as I thought how pleased some women would be to receive the concentrated attention of four desirable men. Three of the four were young and good-looking. Frank was neither, but in one way he could be considered the most desirable of the lot.

Giles pulled out a chair for me. Jordan nodded vaguely in my direction and resumed the conversation my arrival had interrupted.

"You brought the papers with you?"

"Yes." Always the gent, Giles explained to me, "They're the ones we were talking about yesterday afternoon. Frank has convinced me I may as well dispose of them now as later, especially since you are willing to examine them."

I said brilliantly, "Huh?"

Frank said innocently, "Giles has decided he can trust us with his family scandals."

The old boy really was a pro at stirring up trouble. I couldn't imagine what lies he had told Giles about me—that I was a librarian, or a research specialist, or a trained secretary?—but I knew why he had done so; it was another jab at Jordan, who had assumed he would get the papers and who was certainly better qualified than I to examine them. I hoped he had sense enough to comprehend that and not blame me, but I couldn't tell from his face, which was as sullen and inexpressive as usual. He didn't look at me.

The innuendo directed at Giles had been even crueler. Giles flinched, but he didn't avoid the issue.

"It would be foolish of me to concern myself about ancient scandal when my current family problems are known to everyone in the area. I had planned to work this evening, but after I learned of Bob's latest exploit I decided I had better go home and deal with it. That was my principal reason for asking to see you, Frank. Naturally I'll be responsible for the damage to your car. I've notified my insurance company to that effect."

"I'll send you the bill," Frank said. "I trust you're planning to take it out of the boy's allowance, or possibly his hide."

Giles's tight lips relaxed. "There's something peculiarly comforting about your sledgehammer tactics, Frank. No doubt you'll be relieved to hear that I've almost persuaded Lindsay to send Bob off to school."

"You'll have to drag him, kicking and screaming," Frank said. "I trust it isn't an ordinary boarding school you have in mind. He needs a special school. Someplace where they have bars on the windows."

The speech was so outrageous that Jordan decided to intervene. "Let's finish our business, shall we? I presume the papers are in your car, Giles; we may as well take them in before dark."

"Now, now, what's your hurry?" Frank demanded. "Let the poor man relax for a while. Heaven knows he's entitled to it."

"I wasn't asking for help, Dad. I can handle them myself."

Really, Jordan was too easy. He kept setting himself up. Giles cut in before Frank could respond, tossing a set of car keys to Jordan. "Here you go, then. They're in the boot."

I could almost see the little wheels turning in Frank's mind as he tried to decide what course of action would be most irritating to the most people. It wasn't that difficult. He jumped up. "I'll give you a hand, Jordan. Only too happy to help out. No, Giles, you stay here—keep Heather entertained, eh? I'll write you a check. Five hundred, wasn't it?"

"Guineas." Giles sounded amused but firm.

"Yes, I expect you can use the extra money. Special schools are expensive."

He trotted after Jordan. Sean let out his

breath. "Jesus. The old boy's in top form tonight. I'll get us something to drink and see what Mrs. Greenspan has left in the way of food. He's generally better tempered after he's been fed."

Mrs. Greenspan had provided a particularly elaborate variety of canapés. Browsing, I said with a sigh, "That woman is too darned good a cook. I'm gaining weight hand over hips."

Giles laughed and made the proper polite demurral. Sean was more candid. "You could probably use some exercise. Why don't you come and work out with me?"

I couldn't decide which appealed less—having Sean see me in a leotard and/or spandex, or being at his mercy in a room full of weights and machines. "Thanks, but no thanks. I don't like exercise that consists of sitting or standing in the same spot repeating the same action over and over. It's boring." I popped another little yummy into my mouth.

"Do you run?" Sean inquired, watching me chew.

I swallowed. "Only when someone is chasing me. Maybe I should start jogging, though. How far is it from the house to the gate?"

"The drive is full of potholes and ruts," Sean said. "You'd be better off sticking to this area. It's about a quarter of a mile around the perimeter."

"What about hiking?" Giles suggested. "I brought that book for you, Heather—the one about local walks I mentioned. Remind me to give it to you before I leave."

Everybody seemed to be taking an inordinate interest in my state of health. I didn't know whether to be flattered or insulted.

When Frank came back Jennet was with him. "Look who's here!" he announced happily.

"Heather forgot her comfrey," Jennet said. "I thought she might want it. For her sore shoulder. Hello, Sean—Giles."

I had forgotten about my sore shoulder until then.

Frank insisted that Jennet stay for a drink. "Jordan has gone off with his dirty old papers. What were you talking about before we interrupted you? You appeared to be enjoying yourselves."

"We were talking about me exercising," I said. "There seems to be a general consensus that I need to."

"That depends on the kind of exercise," Jennet said. "Haven't you been running a lot lately?"

She didn't stay long. I wasn't sorry to see her go. The woman was beginning to get on my nerves. It was probably all part of her act—White Witch or Wise Woman (both capitalized, of course), or whatever she chose to call herself—but that seemingly innocent question about running hadn't been as innocent as the others believed. They hadn't heard the unspoken word—running "away." I had heard it, as she meant me to, and I resented both the criticism and the implication that she was Wise enough to see what I had tried to hide even from myself.

I could think of one reason why Jennet might have taken a dislike to little me. Giles Betancourt. Just before she left he had returned to the subject of hiking—or walking, as they called it around here.

"Would you care to go with me one day? I try to get out whenever I can find the time, and I could show you some of the more scenic walks."

"I'd like that very much," I said truthfully.

"What about Saturday, then, if it's fine?" I don't know whether he caught the vibes I was getting, or whether he was just being polite; he turned to Jennet. "You're a keen walker, Jen, or you were. Care to join us?"

"You know I can't get away. Saturday is my busiest day."

"Another day, then," Giles said obliviously.

She left right after that.

Dinner was a much more pleasant affair than it had been the night before. Giles made all the difference; he managed to keep the conversation light and casual, deflecting Frank's jibes and avoiding painful subjects.

Jordan didn't contribute much either. His eyes fixed on vacancy, he shovelled the food into his mouth as if eating were only an annoying distraction that had to be completed before he could get on with what he really wanted to do.

He started paying attention, though, when Frank asked Giles to tell me how much he remembered about the gardens.

"Not much," was the reply. "I was only six or seven when we moved away, you see."

"That long ago?" I blurted. Frank laughed, and I felt myself blushing. "Sorry, I didn't mean—"

"Of course not. Frank," said his guest amiably, "has a gift for finding double entendres where there are none. It was thirty years ago, to be precise. We had to move; the house was falling down around our ears, and maintenance was too expensive. My father did his best, poor old chap, but there was no money to hire help, and after he died everything except the house and approximately twenty acres went to pay the death duties. My mother would have sold it too, but no one was fool enough to make her an offer. Even the National Trust turned us down."

"He lights candles in thanks to me whenever he goes to his church," said Frank complacently.

Giles laughed. "That's not how it works, Frank. But if you like I'll mention you in my prayers."

"Then it looked much as it does now?" Jordan asked. He glanced at me, and glanced away. "Including the hedge?"

"Oh, it was a great deal worse. Keeping that damned jungle under control was one of the things that finally broke my father's back. One of my most vivid memories is of watching him trim it—not once or twice a year but over and over, week after week all summer long. There was something unnatural about the way it grew; I used to stand and watch it, fancying I could see the tendrils lengthening and reaching out for me." His voice was soft, his face remote; then he caught my eye and smiled self-consciously. "I had been warned to stay away from the place, because of the thorns and nettles, so I suppose it was inevitable I should come to think of it as nightmarish, like a great green dragon."

"And your dad was St. George," I said.

"Chain mail would certainly have been useful. He always ended up with a few scratches, though he wore heavy clothing."

"So you have no regret about leaving?"

"Not the slightest. I hated the bloody place."

After dinner Frank insisted we retire to the library "to help Jordan with those papers." I had expected Jordan would drag his prizes up to his own room so he could croon over them and play with them in private; either Frank had bullied him into sharing or there wasn't enough space in Jordan's room. The latter might have been the case; there were a dozen big boxes, all crammed with stuff.

After one look at the dusty, cobwebby, crumbling papers I declined to participate. Giles refused the treat too. "I've spent enough time on them already. Don't complain to me, Frank, if you find nothing earlier than World War One. I gave you fair warning."

Eventually Frank got bored with the papers and with heckling Jordan and announced that he was going to bed.

"It's time I was off, too," Giles said. "I didn't realize it was so late. This has been very pleasant. Suppose I ring you tomorrow, Heather, and we'll settle the arrangements for Saturday."

Jordan was still mumbling and muttering over his papers when I left the room. He didn't say good night.

FIVE

*In designing a garden everything trivial or
whimsical ought to be avoided. Is a labyrinth
therefore to be justified? It is a mere conceit,
like that of composing verses in the shape of
an axe or an egg.*

LORD KAMES, *ELEMENTS OF CRITICISM*, 1796

*For the next day or two I hardly left the house. The
weather was raw and dreary, but that wouldn't
have kept me from going out if I had wanted
to. I couldn't think of any reason to go anywhere.* My room was beginning to feel very
cozy, with tea and cookies laid on, and—the
newest addition—an excellent reading lamp by
the bed.

Everybody left me alone, even Frank. He had
apologized for his neglect, as he called it,
explaining that he was trying to clear away a
pile of business matters so he could concentrate on the restoration. One room of his suite

was fitted up as an office, with every telecommunication device you could imagine, and he spent most of his time there. Which was fine with me. Frank was interesting but tiring to be around.

Jordan's absence made things easier too. I was mildly surprised not to find him in the library the following afternoon, and even more surprised to discover that the papers had been returned to the cartons. He'd made such a fuss about them I hadn't expected he would lose interest in them so quickly. Mostly, though, I was pleased to have the place to myself, curled up in Frank's big leather chair reading, or looking through the rare old books on gardening. It wasn't until I wandered into the kitchen later that day that Doreen told me Jordan had gone away—to Oxford or Cambridge or someplace like that.

She and the cook were sitting at the table, their heads together over cups of tea when I came in. They looked up with the guilty expressions of interrupted gossips, so I started to back out, apologizing for disturbing them.

"No, that's all right," Doreen said. "I was just going to go looking for you to ask when you wanted your tea. Mr. H. is having his in his office. Do you want I should bring yours to the library?"

"There's no need to go to all that trouble. I'll just have a cup with you and Mrs. Greenspan, if I won't be in the way."

Apparently it was the right thing to say. Doreen pulled out a chair and fetched another cup. The cook gave me a shy smile and pushed a plate of pastry toward me. She was a huge, slow-moving woman who reminded me of those lumpy prehistoric female statues. I had never spoken with her before, just exchanged nods and murmured greetings.

Doreen did most of the talking. That seemed to suit her and Mrs. Greenspan just fine; the cook listened and nodded and smiled. It suited me fine too. Rain dripped at the foggy windows, the kitchen was a warm oasis of light, the tea was hot and sweet, the pastries were delicious. I ate three of them, with Mrs. Greenspan's silent, smiling approval. Women, sitting with their heads together and their elbows on the table, talking comfortably about nothing in particular, no men around. . . . It was probably a ritual as old as the human race, going back to a time when women wrapped in skins squatted around a rock eating berries and grunting at one another. Mrs. Greenspan would have fit right in.

When she started to pour me a third cup of tea I felt obliged to make a token protest. "Are you sure I'm not keeping you from your work?" Realizing that that might be interpreted as criticism, I added quickly, "It's nice of you to let me join you. I was getting bored with nobody to talk to."

That was when Doreen told me Jordan had gone off, as she put it. "I don't know what he does in those places. You'd think there was enough books here, wouldn't you?"

"Maybe they aren't the kind of books he needs," I suggested. "The ones in the library are all about gardening."

"His room is full of books," Doreen said, shaking her head. "Terrible dust collectors, books are."

"I wonder if he has any novels," I said hopefully. "I'm in the mood for something light and frothy and romantic."

"It's not likely Jordan would have anything like that," Doreen said with a grin. She fished in the bag hanging over the back of her chair. "You're welcome to this if it's not too trashy for you. I've finished it."

To judge by the cover, the book was what is known in the trade as a Regency. So standardized are the plot lines that I could have predicted that the girl in the diaphanous empire gown pouting at the gentleman attired in tight breeches and frock coat would end up in his arms after two hundred pages of saucy dialogue and mad escapades. I practically snatched it out of her hands.

Mrs. Greenspan rose and moved toward the stove. It was like watching a boulder walk. "We'd best be getting on, Doreen. Fog's thickening."

"Righto." In a few economical movements Doreen cleared the table and wiped it off. "Being it's such raw weather Mrs. Greenspan made a nice hot chicken pie for tonight, Heather. It's in the oven. On our way out I'll just remind Sean to turn it off in an hour."

"I can do that."

"No need to trouble yourself, he's used to doing it."

"I haven't seen him today. Did he have his tea?"

"Sean's not one for tea. Likely he's been sitting there all afternoon drinking his beer and watching sports on telly." She wrapped Mrs. Greenspan in her coat and reached for her own mac.

On a sudden impulse I said, "Doreen, do you ever stay here at night?"

She stood motionless for a moment, her back to me. When she turned her face was almost too innocent, as if she had wiped off another expression. "Here in the house, you mean? Where would I stay, then? There's no extra rooms, except for those nasty little cubbyholes in the attic, and they're not fit to be lived in."

"Of course. I just wondered."

"You're not afraid, are you?"

"Who, me? What's to be afraid of?"

She didn't reply immediately. Finally she said slowly, "Sean's there, you know. He'll come if you want him. He's good that way, Sean is."

I decided not to ask her what way that was.

ii

I was driven out of my room next morning by the "teenagers," as Sean had called them. They had high shrill voices like birds, and they giggled a lot. I was drinking tea and finishing *Lady*

Gertrude's Secret when I heard them coming, accompanied by a series of thumps which I took to be the vacuum cleaner being dragged up the stairs. They stood outside my door squawking and giggling for a minute, and then retreated, presumably into one of the other bedrooms.

They had been considerate enough not to disturb me, and I was in an excellent mood; so I decided I would get out of their way and let them get on with their work. I found them in Jordan's room dusting and emptying wastepaper baskets.

They looked, to my elderly eyes, about twelve years old, but that was probably because they followed the worst excesses of youthful style—exaggerated makeup, mops of frizzy hair and emaciated little bodies. So maybe I was prejudiced. Definitely skinny, though.

The starts and squeaks with which they responded to my greeting made me feel even older. One of them—the redhead—actually bobbed a curtsey. I said, with the graciousness of the Queen herself, that I hoped I hadn't disrupted their schedule, and they assured me I hadn't.

"Doreen said we wasn't to go near Mr. Karim's rooms," one of them—the blonde—volunteered. "So we've not got much to do today. You just go back and rest, miss, if that's what you was doing."

"My name's Heather," I said. "I wasn't asleep. I just wanted to finish my book."

As it happened Mitzie (the redhead) had also read *Lady Gertrude* and had liked it a lot, though not as much as the author's earlier work, *Lord Ronald's Escape*. They were more at ease with me by the time we finished our literary discussion, and I took advantage of the opportunity to inspect Jordan's quarters.

It was the first time I had entered that sacred chamber. It was almost twice the size of mine and obviously occupied the entire area of the square tower on the north side of the house. There were windows on two walls and another door opposite the one through which we had entered. Remembering the exterior, I cleverly deduced that the second door led into the smaller tower, probably a bathroom or dressing room.

It was a nice arrangement—cross ventilation, plenty of light, ample space—and he had made himself comfortable, in his own eccentric fashion. Except for a single bed, which was crammed into a corner, the room had been fitted up as a study, with a big table, a computer center, and bookcases on every available wall surface. The heavy blue drapes were a concession to those glaring outside lights, not a decorative feature; the rug looked like something he had picked up at a yard sale. There were two straight chairs, one at the desk and one at the table. The only comfortable articles of furniture in the room—I couldn't be certain about the bed, but it didn't look comfortable—were a big leather chair and matching hassock.

It wasn't the room itself that interested me. It was the books. I can no more resist a bookshelf than I can a candy counter. When Mitzie plugged in the vacuum and its noise put an end to conversation, I sauntered casually along the shelves.

The collection didn't look promising for someone who had just finished *Lady Gertrude*. Most of the volumes had titles like *Fertility Cults in Preclassical Greece*, and *Essays on Primitive Religion*. Some of them were in German.

Then my eye fell upon a thin book that was lying on its side atop one row. The gilt letters of the title were badly rubbed but they were still legible. *The Monster of the Maze*. That sounded hopeful. I was getting bored with witches, but I wouldn't object to an old-fashioned thriller. I opened it to the first page.

"He was barely seventeen when he saw her for the first time, crossing the stream near the mill. A mass of tangled black curls framed her rounded face, and her bright, tattered skirt had been lifted to display slender brown limbs. . . ."

The sound of the vacuum stopped and Mitzie said briskly, "That's it, then. Okay if we do your room next, Miss Heather?"

"Yeah, sure. Let me get my jacket and then it's all yours."

I took *The Monster of the Maze* with me. Surely Jordan wouldn't object to my borrowing it; he had probably bought it by mistake, because it had the word "maze" in the title. Anyhow, it was a short book. I could get it back before he noticed it was gone.

I don't believe I have mentioned why I was in an excellent mood. Giles had telephoned to ask if I was still interested in walking on Saturday. He had been brief and businesslike, perhaps because he suspected that Doreen, who had taken the call, was listening on the kitchen extension. Since I shared that suspicion I expressed my interest with relative restraint, and he said he'd pick me up at nine.

The weather was, as he had said, on the mend. The sun had made a watery but determined appearance, and I decided it would behoove me to limber up a bit before I set out on a four-hour hike. It had been a long time since I did anything that strenuous, and I did not want to fall by the wayside. Leaving the teenagers in possession I went downstairs and out the side door.

I had gone around the perimeter of the yard, sometimes running, sometimes—well—sometimes not running—three times when I saw Sean. He stood on the terrace watching me until I came around for the fourth time.

"You're a little out of condition, aren't you?" he remarked. "Sit down and take a breather."

I dropped onto the low stone wall and wiped

my face with my sleeve. "I'm not out of condition. I never was in it. Whew. It's getting hot."

"Muggy," Sean corrected. He sat down, not too close, and looked me over with the critical eye of a trainer or a coach. "What brought this on? I thought I heard you say you never ran unless someone was chasing you."

"I'm going hiking tomorrow. And don't pretend you don't know. Everybody around here knows everything about everybody as soon as it happens."

The combination of big black beard and large white teeth made a startling picture. I took it that the teeth indicated amusement, because he laughed. "Doreen's a great little talker. There are a few things she doesn't know, though. How did you get out of the house yesterday morning?"

The teeth were still visible, but I had a feeling they no longer indicated amusement. I considered telling him it was none of his business. However, that would not have been true. Security was his business.

"I went across the roof of the veranda and shinnied down a post."

"I was afraid it was something like that. Damn it, Heather, you're lucky you didn't break your fool neck. Why couldn't you have waited an hour or two?"

"I don't like being shut in."

"Oh."

Neither of us spoke for a moment. I was staring at my feet, wondering what had prompted me to make such an imbecile remark, when he put his hand over mine. "Okay. I think I understand. But if you're hellbent on climbing out windows I'll lend you a rope."

The kitchen door opened. "Anyone interested in a cup of tea?" Doreen asked.

I did not have a cup of tea. I did another mile, trotting lightly, head up and arms swinging—and then crept into the house via the side door and dragged myself up the stairs. The teenagers were still in my room. I overheard a few words that suggested they were making plans for their weekend entertainment before my appearance ended the conversation, and they took themselves and the vacuum cleaner away.

I ate too much for lunch and too much for dinner, and in between, there was tea. I hadn't planned to have more than a cuppa but Mrs. Greenspan had baked that morning, and it was cozy in the kitchen and Doreen was full of interesting gossip. Most of it concerned the Betancourts. After hearing of Bob's latest exploit I could understand why they provided the village with its chief entertainment.

"Burned to the ground, it did," Doreen said, shaking her head. "If Childers hadn't happened to come home just when it started he'd have lost all his chickens. Lost a dozen of the best layers as it was, he couldn't get 'em all out."

"I told him he shouldn't take old Towser to the pub with him," Mrs. Greenspan said enigmatically.

"That dog's not worth a thing as a guard anyhow," Doreen replied. "And he does like his little nip."

She went on to tell me about some of old Towser's exploits, including the time he had been run in by a local constable with a sense of humor for being drunk and disorderly (chasing a cat) on the public street. A beer-guzzling dog was new to me, and I was just as happy to talk about something besides those poor roasted chickens. Not until Mrs. Greenspan began shifting position, preparatory to rising, did I realize I'd been there for over an hour.

"I hope I didn't stay too long," I said.

"You're welcome any time," Doreen said graciously. "There's not much goes on here when the old boy is shut up in his office and Jordan's gone off. I expect you're bored."

"No." My spontaneous denial surprised me more than it did Doreen. "I suppose I should be bored but I'm not. I've been awfully lazy—sleeping late, and just lying around."

"You needed a good rest, I expect," Doreen said. "After all you'd been through." A gentle rumble from Mrs. Greenspan echoed this sentiment, and Doreen went on, "There's people hereabouts you'd enjoy meeting, I fancy. When you're ready."

It was the first time she had referred to my loss. No doubt she and Mrs. Greenspan had discussed the subject at length, shaking their heads and exchanging clichés. "Time heals all wounds.

What she needs is a good rest. Peace and quiet.
Something else to think about. A new interest in
life."

I had thought of this interval as a respite, and
so it had proved. I was sleeping better and
dreaming less. As for new interests, there were
plenty of them. I couldn't stay here forever, but I
had become so involved—so strangely and
strongly involved—it would be hard to leave
and never know what would become of them—
the Betancourts and their troubled marriage, the
dreadful, disturbed little boy, the restoration of
the three-hundred-year-old garden. I would
miss Doreen and Mrs. Greenspan (and the latter's cooking)—yes, and Frank. I would wonder
whether he and his son had ever come to terms
with one another. I would even miss Jordan's
caustic comments.

He would have plenty to say if he caught me
with his book. When I tucked myself in bed
that night with my tin of cookies I fully
intended to have another look at *The Monster* so
I could put it back next day. Instead I reached
for the guidebook Giles had lent me—a slim
green paperback, limp and worn with much
handling. There were some pretty colored photographs and a number of maps, all considerably more detailed than the ones I had acquired
from bookshops and tourist bureaus. After flipping through the book I turned back to the
table of contents.

I ought to have expected it. One of the suggested walks was labelled "the Pendle witch country."

iii

I had told Giles I would meet him outside the gate. I wanted to avoid any appearance of being called for by my young man, with Mrs. Greenspan offering him coffee and Doreen telling me not to get my feet wet and Frank making provocative remarks. Doreen and/or Sean must have passed the word on to Frank; at dinner he kept referring to my "date" and assuring me I was going to have a wonderful time. I couldn't understand why everybody seemed so pleased about it. You'd have thought I was a young lady in search of a husband and that Giles had come a'courting.

When I reached the gate he was waiting for me. He was wearing hiking boots and carrying a backpack, and in his shabby old windbreaker, with the wind ruffling his fair hair, he looked ten years younger.

"What's that?" he asked, indicating the brown paper bag I held.

"Mrs. Greenspan pressed it upon me as I was leaving. It's probably food; my appetite is becoming an open scandal."

"Good idea. I had planned to offer you lunch at a pub along the way, but it's a nice day; we

might picnic somewhere instead. Here, let me
take it." He opened his pack.

We walked single file along the road until we
reached the track I had followed on my first
visit.

"Here's where we start," Giles said. "The walk
is the one numbered twenty-seven in the guide;
it begins in Barley, but we can pick up the right
of way a little farther on."

"The witch walk?"

"I'm afraid we've made rather a feature of the
witches," Giles said with a smile. "It's our major
claim to fame, you see. If you're sick to death of
them I promise not to point out any of the traditional sites."

The air was cold and clean, and as I drew it
into my lungs in long breaths it seemed to penetrate and cleanse every square inch of my body.
Cloud shadows slid across the green slopes of
the hills. I pointed toward a single ridge that
dominated the horizon.

"Let's go up there."

"Pendle Hill?"

"I thought that might be it. The view must be
wonderful."

"Yes, but—"

"It doesn't look that steep. Do you think I'm
not up to it?"

I met his gaze with a challenging smile. After
a moment he laughed and slipped his arms
through the straps of the pack he was carrying.
"All right. Don't say I didn't warn you."

The first part wasn't hard walking, over stiles and across stretches of peaty moorland, and I was feeling fairly pleased with myself when the path turned into a narrow valley, and began to ascend. Giles set a steady pace. He didn't stop until we came upon a stream bubbling merrily across the way.

"Do you want to rest for a minute?" he asked. "There's a rather steep stretch ahead."

There was also no bridge across the stream. I squared my shoulders and said valiantly, "No, I'm fine. We—uh—we cross here, do we?"

I managed to get across without wetting my feet, hopping from stone to stone with Giles's hand steadying me. He hadn't been kidding about the next stretch. It was open hillside, rough with bracken and protruding stones, and I swear it went up at a forty-five degree angle. When the path finally levelled out I collapsed onto the ground and tried to catch my breath.

"Almost there," Giles said encouragingly.

"Almost?"

"The summit's only a few hundred yards farther on."

An involuntary groan escaped me as I turned to follow the direction of his pointing finger. The pillar that marked the summit looked about a mile away and a mile higher.

"We'll rest awhile before we go on," Giles said.

"No." I dragged myself to my feet, waving

away the hand he had offered. "If I sit here thirty seconds longer I'll never get up."

The path kept climbing, but not nearly as steeply as it had. It also crossed several more rocky streams. I would have fallen into one of them if Giles hadn't caught my arm and swung me neatly up and over and onto the bank. I found breath enough to gasp, "You Tarzan, me Jane. Thanks. . . ."

After that I let him hold my arm. I plodded doggedly forward, step by step, my eyes fixed on the path, until he transferred his grasp to my shoulder. "You can stop now. We've arrived. Sit down."

I didn't sit, I lay, full length. Giles sat down beside me. My breathing slowed from a series of whoops to ordinary pants and gasps, and I mustered enough strength to sit up.

"All right now?" he asked.

"You don't look so good yourself."

He mopped his perspiring face and brushed a lock of damp hair back from his forehead. "What were you trying to do, kill me? I'd have stopped for a rest half a mile back if I'd been alone."

"Serves you right," I gasped. "Male ego . . ."

"Serves *you* right. Feminist pride . . ."

"Don't make me laugh. Not enough breath."

We laughed anyway. He took a bottle of water from his pack and we both had a long drink. Then he said, "Now have a look and tell me if it was worth it."

"It was worth it," I said. I wasn't referring only to the view.

We found a rock to use as a table, and opened Mrs. Greenspan's package. She had done well by us—egg and cress and chicken sandwiches, squares of rich shortbread, pickles and celery. We passed the bottle of water back and forth, and Giles pointed out various sites of interest, the way men do. "See that house? No, not that house, the one to the right. Now see the grove of trees beyond it?"

I nodded and murmured at appropriate intervals. It was amazing how close together everything looked from up here—the village, Troytan House, Giles's house (I couldn't see it, but I pretended I could). I wasn't interested in the names of villages and rivers which meant nothing to me, but in the beauty of the panorama that stretched out all around. From that height it was as clear as an aerial photograph—green valleys and shadowed slopes, stretches of woodland and rolling foothills, little villages nestled in folds of the land.

"Sometimes one can see the Irish Sea and the hills of the Lake District," Giles said. "It's not quite clear enough today unfortunately."

"It's beautiful," I said dreamily. "Peaceful. Where is Malkin Tower?"

Giles gave me a startled look and then laughed. "I thought you didn't want to hear about the witches."

"I don't want to make a tour of the sites;

some people come here for that precise purpose, I suppose. But after reading that book of Jennet's I admit to a certain degree of curiosity."

"I find the whole business a bit morbid," Giles said. "And tasteless—profiting from a sad tragedy of that sort, even if it was over three hundred years ago. Not," he added quickly, "that I mean to criticize Jennet. The town owes her a great deal; in building her own business, which she did practically single-handedly, she has brought business to the whole village."

"Have you known her long?"

"Since infancy. She accuses me of stealing her toys and shoving her over when she was a toddler and I was a great brute of five. I can't remember doing so, but no doubt a psychologist would say I prefer not to."

"I can't imagine you being a bully."

"I can't imagine Jennet allowing herself to be bullied, even at two," Giles said with a laugh. "She's always been able to stand up for herself. Had to. Her family, like mine, were poor as the proverbial church mice."

"How did she manage to buy the hotel and the other property, then?"

"She came into a bit of money from an uncle. The hotel was badly run-down and the buildings were derelict, so investing in them was decidedly a gamble on her part. It's paid off, thanks to her business acumen and hard work.

"But you were asking about Malkin Tower, where Demdike and her family lived. I believe the precise location is still being debated by those who are concerned about such things, but there's a farm over in that direction"—he pointed—"of the same name. The house itself isn't old, but one bit of the field wall is popularly believed to be part of poor old Demdike's house, and until recently there was a stone-paved floor associated with it."

"The dancing floor?"

"I beg your pardon?"

"I don't know why I said that. It was the word *floor* that set me off. I overheard one of the girls who come to clean mention it. It's probably a pub or a restaurant. Your pubs have very peculiar names."

"So they do," Giles said amiably. "That's a new one on me, though. Well, are you ready to start back? It's downhill all the way from here."

"I'm not in a hurry."

"Nor am I."

"Except I'll probably want to eat again in a couple of hours."

"I can arrange that. Heather . . ."

"What?"

He wasn't looking at me or at the view. Head bent, he stared down at his clasped hands. "May I ask you something personal?"

I had to take a deep breath before I could answer. "Of course."

"It's about Bobby."

"Oh."

"I've no right to involve you in my difficulties,

but you're a teacher. You must have encountered similar problems."

"I'm no expert in emotional disorders. Perhaps you ought to talk to a psychiatrist or a . . . Oh, hell, Giles, I'm sorry. I didn't mean—"

"You needn't spare my feelings. I introduced the subject. I have consulted various specialists. Everyone agreed he needed help, but I didn't feel I could force him into treatment, especially when his mother . . . But recently he's become even more unmanageable. You've seen several of the incidents yourself, and I suppose you've heard about the latest—the fire at Childer's farm."

"How can they be sure it was Bobby?"

"He's done it before. Nothing as serious as this, but under similar circumstances. The one positive feature is that Lindsay has now agreed to send him away. I've had this school in mind for a long time. It offers the sort of treatment he needs, or so I've been told. The only thing is . . . Am I doing the right thing? When I told Bob, he was . . . He didn't take it at all well. He went so far as to threaten his mother. He'd never done that before."

"Threaten her?" I repeated. "Oh, Giles, don't take it so seriously. Kids do that when they're angry. 'I'm gonna kill you, you old witch!' They don't mean it."

Not quite true. I had meant it at the time. I'd been only five years old, but if I had had a blunt instrument and the strength to use it . . .

"He didn't mean it," Giles said quickly. "He adores her. She's taken the kids to visit their grandmother for a few days. She lives quite nearby, but they love staying with her. By the time they left, Bob was . . . better."

"Maybe he thinks he can talk her into changing her mind."

"No doubt he does. I don't believe he will succeed. Once she makes a decision she sticks to it."

Through hell and high water and headlong into a brick wall, I thought. It wasn't firmness of character but single-minded selfishness that directed Lindsay.

"I just want to be sure I'm doing the right thing," Giles repeated. "Not only for Bob but for Laura. She was almost as upset as he was. She's so attached to him—"

"Attached, hell. She's terrified of him."

"Do you really think so? She's never complained to me about him."

He looked so stricken I almost regretted my thoughtless statement. "Perhaps I put it a little too strongly. It's not unnatural for big brothers to tease and bully little sisters, but he does seem to pick on her. She might develop more self-confidence if they were apart for a while. You mustn't blame yourself, Giles. Sometimes it's easier for a stranger to see things like that. And I could be wrong. I am wrong now and then."

"You, wrong? I don't believe it. At any rate,

you've made me feel a thousand percent better. Thank you."

A romantic novelist would probably say I was looking so deeply into those wide blue eyes of his that I was unaware of anything else. I didn't notice that the sunlight was dimming until Giles let out an exclamation and started to his feet.

"Good Lord. Look at that!"

The valley floor had vanished under a blanket of fog. It moved quickly in even as we stared, enclosing the summit of Pendle Hill in a sea of gray.

Giles gathered up the remains of our picnic and stuffed them into his pack. "I really am sorry, Heather. I don't know where this confounded fog came from; it wasn't forecast. I'd never have brought you up here if I had known."

"I don't mind. It was lovely while it lasted."

He shrugged into the pack and handed me the jacket I had tossed onto the ground. "Let's go."

"Is something wrong? You do know the way?"

"Of course. Here now, I didn't mean to alarm you, there's nothing to worry about. The first part of the descent is a bit steep but it's a well-constructed path. Just stay close, okay?"

It was like climbing down into a bowl of milk. The farther down we went the more the mist thickened and curdled; I could see the ground under my feet, and Giles just ahead, and that was all. The path itself was clearly defined, though; there was no danger of wandering off it even if he had not held my hand. He didn't speak except to warn me of a drop or a turn. I could feel his tension in the tight clasp of his fingers, but I didn't understand why he was so concerned. Walking blind through nothingness was unnerving, even a little uncanny, but we couldn't go far astray; once we were down off the hill we would be among farms and houses.

Eventually a structure appeared dimly just ahead—something man-made, by the regularity of the outline. I was practically upon it before I recognized it as a metal gate. Giles stopped and let go of my hand.

"Don't neglect to tell me later how much you've enjoyed this," he said with a wry smile.

"I have enjoyed it. I'm even enjoying this; it's a new experience. For heaven's sake stop apologizing. You aren't responsible for the weather."

"It's unaccountable," Giles muttered. "I've seen fog come on quickly, but never as quickly as this, without the slightest warning."

"Witches," I said. "Weather control was one of their specialties, wasn't it? I shouldn't have been thinking rude thoughts about them."

"Unquestionably a grave error," Giles agreed. "All right, *excelsior!* The path's not so well defined from here on, and the landmarks won't be visible in this filthy muck, so for God's sake don't let go my hand."

A series of yellow-topped posts marked the next stretch, but I began to understand what Giles had meant when he said the usual landmarks wouldn't serve him now. The stile over a fence, which would have been easy to see in normal weather, took him several minutes of fumbling and swearing to locate. A wall guided him for another hundred feet, but when it ended I couldn't imagine how he knew where he was going. The ground underfoot was pasture, rough and hummocky, and it continued to descend.

I hadn't been exaggerating when I told Giles I was enjoying this new experience. Perhaps enjoying isn't the right word, but it had a certain eerie charm. I felt as if I were enclosed in an egg-shaped bubble that moved with me across unseen land; I was alone with him in that small universe, free of responsibility and selfishly content that it should be so. It was with a certain sense of regret that I realized the bubble had expanded, and that I could see the dark shape of a low wall—at least it looked like a wall—ahead.

I don't know how I lost hold of his hand. One second he was there, the next second he was gone. The wall—if it was a wall—had vanished too. I heard him call out, but his voice was weirdly distorted and I couldn't tell which direction it came from or how far away he was. I took two tentative steps and stopped with a scream as something rose up out of the ground right in front of me.

He caught hold of me as I turned, and spun me around into his arms. "Stand still! You're right on the edge of a ravine."

He was holding me so close I couldn't see anything except his face, slick with moisture and pale as the mist that had veiled it. When he let his breath out, it felt cold against my face.

"Move back a step—this way. You're all right now. Sorry about that."

"If you apologize once more I'll hit you," I gasped. "What happened? Did you fall? Are you all right?"

"Yes, certainly. What about you? You're trembling."

"I do that when I'm terrified."

"Sorry—" He let out a muffled sound that might have been a laugh. One of his hands moved to the back of my head and pressed it down against his shoulder.

After a while his hold loosened, and he said conversationally, "I think the fog's lifting. Can you hang on for another mile or so if I promise you tea at the end of it? There's a decent little cafe in Barley."

"Offer me food and I'll follow you to the ends of the earth." The fog was dissipating, and I saw that the shape I had taken for a wall was its opposite—a ravine or gully cutting across the field. It wasn't very deep, but if I had walked over the edge I could have broken a bone or two.

"Did you fall in?" I asked, as Giles led me down the slope.

"Not exactly. I had to throw myself flat to avoid going over, though. I called out to you, told you to stand still."

By the time we reached the village of Barley the fog was gone and the sun was shining. Giles made no objection when I suggested the pub instead of the cafe. Settling me at a table he went to the bar and came back with glasses and bottles.

"I've rung Sean and asked him to bring the car round," he said. "You look as if you've had enough for today."

"That bad, huh?"

"I don't look so hot myself," Giles said gravely. "Heather . . ."

"Watch it, Giles."

"All right, no apologies. And no thanks—you don't allow them either, do you? However, if I were to be allowed I would tell you you're absolutely wonderful."

I had a horrible suspicion that I was blushing, which I never do. With a mumbled "Excuse me," I fled to the lavatory. The comb I had tucked into my pocket was some help, but without makeup, which I had not brought along, there wasn't much I could do to my face except wash it. I had chewed off every speck of lipstick and my nose was pink and shiny.

When I went back to the table Sean was sitting in my chair drinking my beer.

"Get up, Goldilocks," I said, nudging him.

"I'll get you another," Sean said. "You look as

if you could use it. What did you do to this woman, Giles, drag her all the way downhill by her hair?"

Giles did not find this amusing. He said stiffly, "We had rather a nasty descent through the fog. Heather was a real trooper."

"Fog? What fog? It's been sunny and clear all day."

iv

"So," Frank said with a fatherly smile, "did you enjoy your walk?"

My mouth was full of Mrs. Greenspan's cottage pie, so I nodded. Sean said, "Wading through streams and crawling through weeds isn't my idea of a good time. What's there to see once you get up there?"

"I thought the view was lovely," I said.

"In the fog?"

"The fog didn't come in until later. I know, I know," I said, anticipating his reply. "There wasn't any fog here. It must have been what they call a local phenomenon. It was bad while it lasted, though. Even Giles had some trouble finding his way, and he's done it a dozen times."

"So that's why you were so long," Frank said. "We were beginning to worry."

"There was no reason for you to worry. We were never in any danger."

"Hmmm."

"What's that supposed to mean?" I demanded.

"Nothing. Nothing at all." He ate in silence for a while and then said, "I've almost finished my business chores. One more day should do it. I'm going to London tomorrow; as soon as I get back we can start working on the garden."

"Tomorrow's Sunday," I pointed out.

"Is it?"

One day was the same as any other to him, of course. When Franklin Karim called a meeting, the meeting took place, at his convenience. When he wanted to see someone they came— from a honeymoon or a deathbed, probably.

Then it hit me. I said slowly, "Sean is driving you, I suppose."

"Yes. But don't worry about being alone in the house. I've telephoned Jordan and told him to come home. He'll be here tomorrow."

"You shouldn't have done that," I protested. I didn't want to admit, even to myself, that the information came as a considerable relief. "What about his work?"

"Pooh." Frank waved Jordan's work away with an airy gesture. "He'll never finish that dissertation, it's just an excuse to avoid responsibility. Sunday, you said? I'm afraid you'll have to get your own breakfast, then."

"You mean Doreen and Mrs. Greenspan get one day a week off? You're all heart, Frank. Don't worry about me, I'm perfectly capable of making toast and coffee, I do it all the time. I'll get something for you if you like. What time are you leaving?"

"Don't trouble yourself, my dear. We'll stop somewhere along the way. Have a nice lie-in, as they say in these parts, and a restful day; you could lunch at The Cauldron and go shopping—Jennet is open on Sundays, it's a good day for the tourist trade—see the church, the tower is quite—"

"I don't need a tour guide, Frank. I can entertain myself quite nicely."

"I want you to be happy here."

The flip reply I had been about to make stuck in my throat. He sounded so sincere. The candle flames reflected in his wide eyes and made them look twinkly, like those of a jolly old St. Nick. I told him I was happy. And the funny thing is, it was almost true.

After Sean and I had cleared the table Frank ordered him to go to bed. I asked Frank if he needed any help with his packing. He gave me the same blank look he had given me when I reminded him the next day was Sunday, and Sean, lingering at the door, laughed.

"Honey, people like Frank don't pack. He's got a duplicate wardrobe and everything else he might need in his London flat. Among other places."

Frank scowled at him. "Go, go," he ordered, making shooing motions at Sean. "We are leaving at six, be ready. Don't forget to set the alarm."

"Yes, boss." Sean sketched a salute, winked at me and went out.

"I didn't mean you should go to bed," Frank said, as we left the dining room and started up the stairs. "It's still early and you can sleep as late as you like."

"I may as well. There's nothing else to do."

He stopped. "I didn't think. It is boring for a young person. Would you like . . . What would you like? A television, perhaps, and a VCR? I never watch the confounded things myself, but Sean has a TV; I'll call him to bring it over now and then on Monday we can find you something better."

The bearded face of John Tradescant the Younger, high on the landing, appeared to be smiling cynically. Maybe I was just imagining how Sean would look if I allowed Frank to rob him of his major source of entertainment.

"Don't do that." I caught hold of him; he appeared to be on the verge of plunging back down the stairs. "For heaven's sake, Frank, it would take a long time to haul the thing over here and set it up. I don't want it. Really."

"Monday, then. Is your room comfortable?"

"I have everything I could possibly want. Doreen keeps bringing me things."

"Good. That's good." His room was to the left of the landing, mine to the right, along the corridor. He stopped at the top of the stairs and held out his hand. "Good night, Heather. Now don't worry, I told Jordan he must be here by noon tomorrow."

"Good night, Frank."

I had taken only a few steps when he spoke my name. I turned. He had opened his door; the light from the room behind him left his face in shadow. "Don't go walking alone," he said. "It could be dangerous."

"What do you mean?"

His silhouetted shoulders lifted in a shrug. "Falling and hurting yourself, meeting a snake or a rabid dog—"

"How about a tarantula? This isn't the Arizona desert, Frank. But if it will make you feel better, I have no intention of exerting myself tomorrow. I'll probably be stiff as a board anyhow, after all that unaccustomed exercise. Jogging around the yard is about as far as I intend to go."

"Good," he repeated. "Very good."

"Good night, Frank," I repeated.

I turned down my bed and plumped up the pillows and arranged my water bottle and my tin of cookies on the bedside table, all ready and waiting. *The Monster of the Maze* was already on the table; I reminded myself I had better get it back before Jordan noticed it was missing. I ought to be able to manage that in the morning, after Frank had gone and before Jordan returned.

Instead of getting undressed, I went to the window and leaned out. The outside lights glared brightly, but I could see the window of Frank's office. It was dark. The office was in one of the little towers that protruded here and there from the main block of the house; it cut off my view of his bedroom windows, so I couldn't tell whether he had gone to bed.

I still hadn't made up my mind what to do. Perched on the window seat, I considered the object that lay on the floor under the window. When I had seen it for the first time, after returning from the pub, it had been in shadow, and for one eye-popping moment I had taken it for a living thing, crouched on the floor.

What it was, investigation proved, was a ladder—one of the emergency escape types that cautious people buy in case of fire. It had been fixed to the windowsill. All I had to do was toss it out.

SIX

It is an intricate and difficult Labour to find out the Centre, and (as the Vulgar commonly like it for) so intricate as to lose one's self therein, and to meet with as great a Number of Stops therein and Disappointments as possible.

STEPHEN SWITZER, *ICHNOGRAPHIA RUSTICA*, 1742

For all I knew, every upstairs room might have been provided with such a ladder. I hadn't seen one in Jordan's room, but I hadn't been looking for it. Frank's quarters I knew only from Doreen's casual references; he had never invited me in.

A farsighted home owner would have provided ladders like that one for all the bedrooms. The house was old, the wooden floors and frame dry as tinder, and there was only one staircase. In a pinch the veranda outside my window and Jordan's could serve as an emergency exit but the windows of Frank's suite opened onto a two-story drop.

I was pretty sure I knew who had provided the ladder, though. Sean had offered to lend me a rope—and there it was.

It was probably a lovely night. There were probably lots of stars. I couldn't see them because of the glare of the lights. There was no sign of life on the terrace, not even the cat, but I would have been willing to bet money Sean was somewhere around, watching my window and wondering whether I would accept the challenge.

If it had been Giles out there, waiting for me in the starlight . . . I closed my eyes and remembered, not only with my mind but with my entire body—the hard pressure of his arms, the movements of his hand stroking my hair, the rapid rise and fall of his chest. Within the white wall of fog we had been alone, free of responsibilities and obligations.

I opened my eyes. Memory could make anything it liked of that moment, but common sense told me to forget it. Not passion but passionate relief had prompted that brief embrace. He had told me I was wonderful; he might just as well have called me a swell kid or a plucky little thing.

Sean hadn't even told me I was wonderful. He had smirked and rolled his eyes and made a few ambiguous remarks, but I felt sure he behaved that way with all women and that he didn't always spend the night in his quarters—at least not always alone. The cottage was some distance from the house and he controlled the security system; he could come and go, and make it possible for others to come and go, unnoticed. So what did he want with me? He must have better fish to fry, younger, sexier and more willing.

I changed my skirt for pants and my sandals for sneakers before I lowered the ladder out of the window. The metal fittings clanked faintly when I climbed over the sill. It did occur to me, as my foot came to rest on the topmost rung, that this might be a handy way of disposing of an unwanted guest. Even a broken leg would require a hospital stay and I'd be lucky to get off with a single broken bone after landing splat on the stone terrace.

Since such things occur only in romantic suspense novels it didn't occur this time. I crossed the terrace, out of the glare of the lights and stood still waiting for my eyes to adjust. There were stars up there, all right. A moon, too—round and shiny as a silver dollar. Very romantic. At least it could have been romantic, if anyone of the male persuasion had been there. He wasn't.

Relieved (and somewhat deflated), I walked across the dew-damp grass, pulled a chair out and sat down, with my back to the lights.

There was Orion, with a row of three stars for a belt, and Cassiopeia. I had known them since I was a child. We would lie on the grass in the backyard on summer nights, when she was at a meeting of the garden club or the bridge club or one of the others; he would point out constellations and planets and stars, and tell me the legends about them, and I would "say" a poem. I had a capacious memory and a child's love of the rhythmical beat of the words; he was immensely proud of me and loved hearing me recite. "Twinkle twinkle little star" was the first one, when I was three or four; I went on to Shakespeare and Keats and the rest. But it was not those words that came back to me now.

"'Sunset and evening star, And one clear call for me—'"

"'Let there be no dah dah dah dah dah, When I put out to sea,'" said a voice behind me. "You're in a morbid mood tonight."

"Damn it, Sean, don't sneak up on people like that!" He dropped lightly to the grass, grinning, and I added, "I wouldn't have taken you for a lover of poetry."

"Had an old battle-axe of an English teacher who made us memorize some poems."

"You didn't memorize that one very well."

"If you'd rather, I could tell jokes or talk about my unhappy childhood."

"Was it?"

"No complaints. Want to talk about yours?"

"No. Why don't you get to the point? You must have had some reason for enticing me out."

"Enticing! Is that what I did? Well, for one

thing, I wanted to see if I was right about you. I figured you for the kind that couldn't resist a challenge. For another thing, I want to ask you a few questions. It's hard to get you alone during the day."

"You have a nasty, suspicious mind. What do you think I am, some kind of industrial spy, or an assassin hired by one of Frank's business rivals?"

Sean chuckled. "Worse. I thought you were a reporter."

"What?"

He settled himself more comfortably. "Your ideas about modern business practices must come from thrillers, honey. Oh, sure, there are plenty of people who don't like the boss and a few others who would love to know what he's going to do next. They have more effective methods of getting information than sending an amateur to break into the place. You'd have been out on your attractive ass five minutes after you arrived, sprained ankle and all, if it hadn't been for your name."

"It is my real—"

"Yes, I know. But taking advantage of that coincidence is the sort of thing that might occur to a bright, ambitious young journalist. A little research could discover the importance of the name, and the fact that restoring this garden is one of the old boy's vulnerable spots. He hasn't got many. Then you made him persuade you to stay. That would have been smart psychology. He always wants what he thinks he can't have."

He leaned back, supporting himself on his elbows, and continued to contemplate the heavens. It was a pose that displayed his lean body and long legs to best advantage. There was nothing wrong with his brains, either. He was handling me just right—a casual compliment here, a casual endearment there, and the appearance at least of candor. I was intrigued. That was one hypothesis I hadn't thought of.

"It would have been a smart plan, all right," I admitted. "A little too ingenious, though. Why would anybody go to so much trouble just to get an interview?"

"Ah," said Sean. "You don't read the gossip columns or the tabloids, do you? Or watch anything on TV except PBS?"

"No."

He sat up, crossing his legs. "Honey, you're so far out of the mainstream I'm not sure I can explain it to you. Frank has a nasty temper and a big mouth. He's extremely rich and extremely antagonistic to reporters, and he's pulled off some stunts that make the Trumps and the Milligans look like Elsie Dinsmore—and gotten away with them. He is also . . . eccentric, isn't that what you schoolteacher types say? Crazy is what I'd say. Didn't you read about his setting up a school for prostitutes in Rome, so they could learn typing and office skills? Or the Institute for the Study of Extra-Terrestrial

Intelligence he funded to the tune of five million bucks?"

"I can't believe he'd be that gullible!"

"Well, actually he isn't. Right now he's unfunding the Institute, and the former head of it will probably spend quite a long time in jail." Sean sighed. "I've managed to keep most of his wilder stunts out of the papers, but the sensationalist press would love to find out about this setup."

"I don't see why."

"Don't you? Here's a man whose lifestyle included a couple of private jets and a fleet of cars and a staff of hundreds. There were a couple of dozen people in security alone. Now he's buried himself in the country with only a cook and a couple of maids—and me. What is he doing here? What's he really up to?"

"It couldn't be anything so obvious as the truth, I suppose," I suggested sarcastically.

"I'm not denying the possibility, I'm telling you how a cynical journalist would react. Old Cutthroat Karim sentimental about flowers? Tell me another one."

"People change," I said. "He's not that old; maybe he's had a midlife crisis or something."

"There's no maybe about it."

I leaned forward, trying to see his face more clearly through the shadow that hid it.

"Let's stop playing games, Sean. You know I'm not a reporter, you've checked on me seven ways from Sunday, and you're not worried about the imaginative inventions of the tabloids. What are you worried about? What's going on here? Why has everybody accepted me as part of . . . whatever it is? You didn't even ask me how I penetrated your famous security system."

"No security system is perfect. There are a couple of possibilities. As it happens, however, I know how you did it."

"Jordan told you?"

"Jordan and I don't talk much," Sean said flatly.

"And that's another thing. Why don't you talk much? Why is Frank so hard on him? Why are they—"

I shied back as Sean sat up in a sudden movement that brought his face into alarming proximity to mine. "You'll have to ask Frank about that. As for your so-called tunnel—"

"It's there. Jordan saw it."

"I know. What I don't understand is how you found it."

"I was looking for a back gate or a place where I could climb the fence," I admitted. "I told you why I wanted to see the grounds. That was the truth."

"The truth, the whole truth and nothing but the truth?"

"Yes!"

His stiff, aggressive pose relaxed and he stood up. "All right. It's getting late. Time for all good little girls to be in bed."

"You haven't answered any of my questions."

"Maybe I don't know the answers. Come on, will you? I've got to be up at dawn and I'm not going to leave you alone. If you fell off the ladder Frank would crucify me."

"I am perfectly capable of climbing that ladder without help."

"I said, come on!" His hands closed over my wrists and pulled me to my feet.

The sound cut through the quiet night like a siren, rising from silence to a falsetto scream before it ended. Already off-balance, I fell heavily against Sean.

"What in God's name was that?" I gasped.

"Some kind of bird or animal, I suppose." His arms had gone around me when I stumbled. He went on coolly, "Some of them make weird noises, especially when they're mating. Relax, Heather. Look at me."

I had never kissed a man with a beard before. DeWitt had a mustache, stiff and prickly as a dry toothbrush. The hair on Sean's face was as soft as a cat's fur; the brush of it against my cheeks and chin set up a thousand little tingles, an interesting contrast to the hard assurance of his mouth.

I won't claim I didn't enjoy it, but under the layers of pleasure and need was the bitter knowledge that this was a substitute for what I had wanted that afternoon, when Giles held me in his arms. Another reason for my enthusiastic cooperation was even more ignoble; I wanted to prove that the soft, cuddly little women aren't always the sexiest. I was pretty sure I had convinced him when he finally raised his head and gave me a blank, bemused stare.

"Hey," he whispered, getting a firmer grip.

I turned my face away. "It's late. You need your sleep."

"Honey, that's not what I need."

"Be sensible, Sean. You didn't think you were going to get me onto my back so easily, did you? Especially in this wet grass."

He took my chin in his hand and turned my face to his. I would have resisted—I think I would have resisted—if I hadn't seen that he was laughing. "You're really something. And you're right. Wet grass is only one of the problems. Up you go, then. I'll hold the ladder for you."

He waited below until I had hauled the ladder up, and blew me a kiss before he walked away.

I should have been tired. My muscles were aching, as predicted, but I was wide awake and I knew I wouldn't be able to sleep for a while. It had been quite a day for a spinster schoolteacher.

Sean had taken my rejection more gracefully than I would have expected. I wondered if Frank was one of the "problems" he had mentioned. In his own eccentric way Frank was an old-fashioned gentleman. He had never used a swear word, not even a little "damn" in my presence, and he had never come to my room except for that first time, when he had brought Jennet with him as chaperone. He had never invited me to his room. No, I thought, Frank wouldn't be well pleased to find Sean "taking liberties" with me, and he'd be even less pleased to find me encouraging them. Not that it mattered; for a number of other reasons I wasn't inclined to add myself to the list of Sean's conquests. Even if he did look like John the Younger.

I got into bed with my book and my tin of cookies and pried open the lid of the latter. Doreen had emptied out the remains—mostly crumbs, I admit—of the first offering and replaced them with another variety, chocolate over a wafery center. They ought to compensate for the dullness of my book.

The Monster of the Maze turned out to be another version of the Pendle witch story. At least, parts of it were the same; Old Demdike was one of the characters, along with her children and a couple of other people whose names I recognized from Jennet's book. However, the author of *The Monster* had tried to spice up the story by making Demdike's daughter Alizon, who had been described as ill favored and homely, into a bewitching village maiden—the one with the sable curls and long slim legs. He had also added a couple of characters, the most prominent being a local landowner who was the villain of the tale. Having tried in vain to seduce the pure maiden Alizon, he had been the most damaging witness against her and her family, claiming she had bewitched him with love potions and killed his cows and called up a storm that ruined his hay crop. His name was Roger Fallon—of Troytan.

If that now-familiar name hadn't caught my attention I might not have finished the book. However, it got better as it went on. The eponymous maze was the one Fallon had had built, and it was there that he had attempted to force his vile attentions on the innocent Alizon, pursuing her along the twisting paths whose secret was known to him alone, and cornering her at last in the center.

Mindful of the sensitivities of his Victorian readers, the author hadn't gone into detail, but there were enough references to bare white shoulders and writhing limbs and sobs and vain pleas for mercy to make it clear that Fallon had in fact succeeded in his "vile attentions."

So why harass the girl and her family after that? I wondered, munching cookies. Poor and humble (though virtuous) they couldn't take legal action against a man of property, and rape, especially of the poor and humble, wasn't considered a crime.

The author of the book had obviously wondered about this too. He had to come up with a motive for Fallon's vindictiveness against the girl he had wronged, and his explanation was fairly ingenious. Fallon, a man of his time, sincerely believed in witchcraft. He was also a pompous, pious hypocrite. He had accused Alizon and her family of casting a spell over him—using black magic to make him lust after her. It sounded perfectly reasonable to the court, and Fallon's accusations were the final straw that condemned the Pendle witches.

However, Old Demdike had had her revenge. She had cursed Fallon from the very scaffold, in words that curdled the blood of the spectators and tacitly admitted her guilt. Why shouldn't she admit it? She was already condemned, the rope actually around her neck, the hangman waiting.

"Never believe, vile betrayer, that you will get away scot-free. You have escaped the vengeance of the law but you will not escape the vengeance of Another. It waits for you in the heart of the maze!"

The description of the old lady on the scaffold made it clear that a good part of the story was pure fiction. As I knew from Jennet's book, Demdike didn't live long enough to be hanged. She died in prison. I flipped to the end, skipping pages of pious moralizing, to find out whether the monster got Fallon and what it was like.

"He was found next morning in the heart of the maze, at the foot of one of the classical statues he had brought from abroad to ornament his gardens, a look of indescribable horror on his dead face. There was not a mark on the body, but beside it, on the dust of the path, were the prints of bare feet—the slim, dainty feet of a young and beautiful woman."

I closed the book. The author had exhibited more restraint than I would have expected—no torn flesh, no clawed prints—but the description had an eerie suggestiveness. I wondered whether the statue had been that of a hooved and horned god.

ii

I treated myself to coffee in bed next morning. I felt very pampered and upper class lounging against the pillows, even if I did have to get out of bed and make the coffee first. The sun was well up and the outside lights were off, so it was probably safe to assume that Sean and Frank had gone; but the possibility that they might have been late getting away was another reason for remaining in my room.

It felt good to know I was alone in the house, with nobody around to fuss at me or make ambiguous remarks or expect me to talk to them. Stretching lazily, I decided I wouldn't bother getting dressed until after I had made myself a large breakfast. I might as well make the most of my quiet time before Jordan showed up. He'd be even grumpier than usual after being dragged away from his precious research to play nursemaid to me. I doubted he would be there by noon. I wouldn't have been, I'd have showed my resentment in some relatively safe and harmless way, like being three or four hours late. However, I figured I had better return his book before I forgot about it. In robe and slippers, uncombed and unwashed, I padded down the hall. I was reaching for the door when it opened.

After I had swallowed my heart I said weakly, "I owe you one for that."

Very slowly Jordan's eyes moved from my face down to the book on the floor where I had dropped it, and then back to my face. He looked as if he hadn't shaved in two days, his eyes were puffy, and his pajamas were a mass of wrinkles. He looked, to sum it up, like a man in the grip of a massive hangover.

Silently he returned his gaze to the book. I picked it up and offered it to him.

"I didn't know you were here," I explained.

"Obviously."

"When did you—?"

"About three hours ago."

"Oh. I'm sorry I woke you up. Excuse me. Go back to bed." I started to edge away.

"Stop right where you are." He wasn't hungover, he was tired—and mad. His voice rose. "What the hell were you doing in my room? Who told you you could make free with my property?"

"I was going to put it back before you got home."

"Oh, well, that's all right then."

"I just wanted something to read. The teenagers were here cleaning, and—"

"The who?"

"The girls from the village. That's what Sean calls them, the teenagers. They were in your room, and your door was open, and I was—"

"Going to put it back before I got home."

"Uh-huh. I apologize. I didn't look at anything except the books, honest."

Jordan weighed the book in his hand. "Go away," he said.

"I was going to. I really am—"

The door closed.

I needed nourishment more than ever after that encounter, so I proceeded to the kitchen and began rummaging in the fridge. My discomfort was partly shame and partly resentment. Mostly shame, though. He had been in the right. It was his rudeness I resented, not his point of view.

I assumed he'd gone back to bed, so he got another squeak of surprise from me when he entered the dining room. There were still visible shadows under his eyes, but he was clean-shaven and fully if informally dressed. Neat as a pin, though—not a wrinkle in shirt or slacks. The comparison was not to my advantage and if I had been a suspicious-minded woman I'd have thought he had done it on purpose. He appeared to be in a more amiable mood, however; contemplating the platter of scrambled eggs and bacon on the table he said, "You didn't have to fix breakfast for me."

I also contemplated the platter of scrambled eggs and bacon on the table. "I didn't. I mean, uh, I thought you . . . Help yourself. I'll make more toast."

He calmly proceeded to eat most of my breakfast, though by that time—if not before—he must have suspected I had intended it for myself. I didn't feel I was in any position to object.

"So," he said, elbows on the table, "what did you think of *The Monster of the Maze*?"

"Fairly typical of third-rate Victorian literature," I said with a shrug. "There were just as many bad books being written then as there are today. Mercifully, most of them have been forgotten."

"I had a hell of a time finding that one," Jordan said. "But I didn't acquire it for its literary qualities."

"I can't imagine why you did buy it."

"Can't you?" He reached for the coffeepot.

"The connection with Troytan and Roger Fallon? Surely that part was pure fiction. Jennet's book never mentioned him. A number of other elements were obviously imaginary, like the curse and the innocent beauty of Alizon."

"And the cat."

"What cat? Oh, the one our imaginative author claims belonged to Old Demdike. That's right, the trial records described the old lady's diabolical familiar as a dog named . . . uh . . ."

"Tibb," Jordan said.

"Yeah. Tibb. Interesting, how some names survive. The author obviously made that part up."

He filled my cup and then his own. "The same is true of other novels written about the Pendle witches. Have you read Ainsworth and *Mist over Pendle*?"

"No, and if they're as bad as this one I don't intend to. I'm not interested in finding out any more about the local case. I only read *The Monster* because I'm a compulsive reader and there wasn't anything else around."

He was silent for a moment. Then he said, "You taught English and history, I believe."

"Junior high level. If you're looking for a research assistant, you're out of luck."

"Hmph," said Jordan.

"Do you want this piece of toast?"

"No, thanks." He watched me eat the toast. "What are your plans for today?"

"I told you, I am not qualified—"

"Yes, you told me. I was going to suggest a visit to the village. We might have lunch and stroll gently along the high street. See the local sights."

"Hmph," I said.

"You could get something to read. I agree that only desperation could have driven you to— er—borrow *The Monster of the Maze*."

The idea tempted me, but I saw one serious objection. "The shops are closed."

"Jennet's place will be open. She has quite a

good selection of books, including sensational fiction."

"Well . . . Okay." I added grudgingly, "Thanks."

"You're welcome. Suppose we leave around noon. I'm going to work for a couple of hours."

I hadn't expected he would offer to help with the dishes.

I am a messy cook. By the time I had restored the kitchen to the pristine condition in which I had found it, and restored myself to a civilized appearance, it was almost noon. When Jordan knocked at my door—rather pointedly, I thought—I was ready.

"I suppose you want to eat first," he remarked, as we drove toward the village.

"I can always eat. The Witches' Cauldron, is it?"

"There's a McDonald's in Roughlee, if you prefer that. Or the local pub."

"The Dancing Floor?"

He came to a sudden stop at an intersection. The seat belt cut painfully into my stomach and I said irritably, "Didn't you see the sign?"

"I saw it. What did you just say?"

"I don't know. Oh—the pub. That's not its name? No, I guess it can't be; Giles would have recognized it."

"Where did you hear it?"

"Mitzie." He looked blank, so I elaborated. "She's one of the girls who comes to clean. Don't you even know their names?"

"I avoid them like the plague. They giggle. What did she say?"

"I can't remember exactly. Something about meeting at The Dancing Floor on Saturday. I assumed it was some local hot spot. I would prefer the pub, as a matter of fact. All right?"

"Okay," Jordan said.

We had a glass of beer and a nice lowbrow lunch, loaded with fat and calories, at The Green Man. Jordan seemed abstracted, but he condescended to lecture me on pub names. "The derivation of *The Green Man* is interesting. Did you notice the sign—the human figure with vegetation sprouting from his face and body? It's obviously derived from some primitive agricultural ceremony—"

"Ah, yes," I said. "The god reborn and resurrected. The growth of the crops from the body of the sacrifice. Osiris and Adonis and that crowd."

Jordan put down his fork and stared at me. "Have you been reading *The Golden Bough*?"

"No, I got it from a novel. A romance novel," I added.

He didn't believe me. "If you're familiar with the history of fertility cults—"

"Can I have some of that cake?"

He continued to stare. I said defensively, "Well, this is my main meal of the day. I'd offer to cook dinner but I don't know what's there, and anyhow I can't cook anything but eggs and macaroni and cheese."

Jordan's lips tightened, but he went to the counter. By the time he returned—with the cake—I had repented of my teasing. He was trying to be nice. It wasn't his fault if he didn't know how.

"I'd help you with your work if I could," I said. "But honestly, I don't know anything about the subject except what I've picked up here and there. Why don't you hire an assistant?"

"I don't need . . . Never mind. Have you finished?"

We strolled—gently—along the high street. Prodded by me, Jordan provided a grudging commentary. "There's not much of historic or artistic interest. The building Jennet converted into her shop is sixteenth century, and so is the restaurant. Do you want to go in?"

I wouldn't have minded another look at Jennet's merchandise, but not with him along. Shopping with a man is no fun. They keep glancing at their watches and looking patient.

"Not particularly. That newsstand is open. Maybe they have some paperbacks."

Jordan kept glancing at his watch and looking patient while I selected some reading material. He let me carry the parcel.

"Where now?" I asked.

"May as well have a look at the church."

"Frank said it had been largely rebuilt. What's to see?"

"There are some points of interest. A little exercise won't hurt you."

"I got plenty of exercise yesterday." I proceeded to tell him about it, in indignant detail, as he led me on. He didn't comment.

St. Mary Magdalen under Pendle was, for all its imposing name, a small parish church of simple design and moderate size, built of the local gray stone. The tower was square and squat with a single pointed window and machiolated roof. In a small side chapel was the monument Jordan had brought me to see. It was set against the wall in an arched alcove: the kneeling life-sized figure of a man wearing a scarlet gown and short cloak. His eyes were closed and his joined hands were raised in prayer. The inscription under it was in Latin, but the name was immediately identifiable.

"Roger Fallon! Our Roger?"

"None other."

I studied the plump cheeks and pious smirk critically. "He doesn't look at all the way I imagined him. But maybe it's not a good likeness. How old was he when he died? No, don't tell me; I studied Latin in high school, let me see how much I can translate. '*Hic jacet . . .* Here lies Roger Fallon of Troytan, born February 19, 1576, departed this life October 31, 1612. With fire . . . *tandem in gratium redit.*' Okay, I give up. What does that mean?"

"With fire he will at last be restored to grace."

"Odd epitaph. Sounds as if he expected to go to hell."

Jordan responded to this uncouth comment with the silence it deserved, and I continued blithely, "Thirteen plus—uh—twenty-four. He was only thirty-seven."

"Brilliant," said Jordan. "You didn't even have to count on your fingers. Anything else strike you?"

"No."

"Sixteen twelve is the same year the Pendle witches were hanged."

"So? Oh! Maybe the coincidence is what gave the author of *The Monster of the Maze* the idea of using Roger as his villain. Is that what you mean?"

Jordan gave me the same look he might have given a dog that had suddenly broken into English. "Very good."

"Don't be so damned condescending." I started down the aisle toward the door. "Incidentally, why was the author of that book so modest? All it says is 'A Gentleman of Lancashire.'"

"That's one of the things I'm trying to find out."

"Ah. That's why you wanted Giles's papers."

I got another "what a clever dog" look. "Right. His great-grandfather fancied himself a litterateur and antiquarian. Just the sort of man to have written a book like that—and to have considered it too trivial to bear his dignified name."

"So you're looking for . . . what? Notes? A manuscript?"

"Whatever. If he did perpetrate that book he ought to have left some reference to it."

"Seems reasonable."

"You don't sound as if you're convinced."

"I'm just wondering why you give a damn. It's a very minor point and can't have anything to do with your dissertation."

The doggie wasn't as clever as it had first appeared. Jordan shrugged, scowled, and did not reply.

We walked through the churchyard on our way back to the street. Most of the markers were small and simple. According to Jordan, some of them were Fallons. I took his word for it, since the alternative would have been kneeling in the dirt and scraping away the lichen that blurred the worn inscriptions.

"Roger was the only one who rated a fancy monument in the church," I remarked.

"He was the only one who could afford it," Jordan answered. "The family fell on hard times. After the manor house burned—"

"Was that what happened to it?"

"Do you make a habit of interrupting people? Yes, that's what happened to it, and to a lot of other dwellings. Open fires, candles and torches for light—it's a wonder any houses of that period survived, especially when you consider the drinking habits of the gentry and anybody else who could afford wine and beer."

"Ale and wine were safer than polluted water, which a lot of it was."

"I doubt that's why they were preferred," Jordan said dryly. "The germ theory of disease was centuries away. The scientific ignorance of the period is one of the reasons why the witchcraft mania flourished. Curses are a convenient explanation for unknown disasters, including illness."

"Maybe that's why Roger was so hostile to the Demdike family. Things started going badly for him."

"Things did go badly. I don't know exactly what—I haven't found any records—but the next generation had been reduced to poverty. They must have lived in the ramshackle shell of the house, because it wasn't rebuilt until the end of the sixteenth century."

"What does this have to do with your dissertation? The Fallon–witch connection is pure fiction."

Jordan grunted uninformatively.

We had to walk the length of the High Street to reach the car, which Jordan had left in front of the pub. I was ambling along looking in shop windows when Jordan stopped short and said something under his breath.

Lindsay and Giles stood by the Bentley. They appeared to be arguing in the typical Betancourt style: Giles's voice barely audible, Lindsay's high-pitched and angry. "No, I will not! He can't be much longer, where is there to go in this wretched hole?"

Turning to look along the street, she saw him and ran toward him. "Jordan! Where've you been?"

"Showing Heather the sights," Jordan said. "We didn't have an appointment, did we?"

His tone and his words were rude enough to make her flush. She raised the handkerchief she was clutching to her eyes. "I recognized the Bentley. They said in The Green Man you had left an hour ago, so I waited. You've got to help me, Jordan. Help me find him."

Jordan shoved both hands in his pockets and looked at Giles. "Bobby?"

Giles nodded. "Hello, Heather. Jordan, I'm sorry about this, but . . . Yes, it's Bobby. He's run away."

"Again?"

"I'm afraid it is 'again,'" Giles said, addressing me. "He's done it before. We thought when we saw the car that Frank was in town and Lindsay wanted to . . . She thought perhaps . . ."

He stuck at that point, since he couldn't come up with a sensible excuse for Lindsay's behavior. She unveiled her eyes—which were, I couldn't help noticing, undimmed by tears—and looked imploringly at Jordan.

"I thought perhaps you might have seen him. I've looked everywhere. I don't know what to do!"

"You've notified the police?" I asked. I didn't doubt the little devil had absented himself out of spite, to scare his parents; he was probably holed up somewhere pigging out on sweets and reading comic books. But if he wasn't, if he had tried to hitch a ride or catch a bus . . . The idea of a child, even a juvenile monster like Bobby, falling into the wrong hands, was terrifying. I couldn't help feeling some sympathy for Lindsay; her mascara was unsmudged, but she did seem upset.

"Yes, of course," Giles said wearily. "They promised to make inquiries, but one could see that they weren't taking the matter very seriously. As I said, he's done this several times."

"Where did he go the other times?" I asked.

"His grandmother's. But he can't have gone there this time. It was from her house that he left. He's not come home either."

Jordan no longer bothered to conceal his lack of interest. "He'll come back when he gets hungry."

"No, he will not!" Lindsay directed a blazing look at her husband. "That's why he ran away, the poor darling—because you threatened to send him to that awful school."

She had agreed with the decision. However, Bobby wouldn't blame her, nor would she take any of the responsibility. Giles didn't bother pointing this out. He was used to being the ogre.

"We won't find him standing here, Lindsay. We'll go home and—"

She twisted away from the hand he had placed on her arm. "You can take me to Mother's. I'll be living there from now on, until I can get a divorce. You have the number, Jordan?"

It was obvious from Giles's face that this was the first he had heard of her intention. She couldn't have humiliated him more completely if she had hired the town crier. Impulsively I offered him my hand.

"We'll let you know at once if we hear anything," I said. "I'm sure he'll be all right."

"Thank you." Not just for the reassurance,
his eyes told me, but for trying to leave him a
few rags of dignity. "I hope you suffered no last-
ing effects from yesterday's excursion."

"Not a twinge. I had a terrific time, Giles."

"So did I. I'll ring as soon as we hear anything, Heather."

Lindsay had already started down the street.
He went after her.

"Get in, quick," Jordan muttered. He opened
the door of the car and shoved me in.

"I hope the boy is all right."

"He's probably back at his grandmother's by
now," Jordan said with a twist of his lips. "The
last time he ran off she kept him hidden for two
days while Giles was scouring the county looking for him. Lindsay knew where he was, of
course."

"God," I muttered. "Poor Giles."

"He may be on a roll. She might go through
with the divorce this time."

The sunlight lay golden across the grass when
we returned.

"Ready for tea?" I asked.

"You had lunch an hour ago!"

"Three hours ago."

"I have work to do." He unlocked the kitchen
door.

"It's too nice a day to be indoors. Hey—look!"

Jordan jumped. "Don't yell like that! I don't see anything."

"I never noticed it before. Maybe the sun wasn't right. See that line of shadow ten feet from here? And the one, farther along? They're the old terraces, I'd bet my life on it."

"Oh," Jordan said.

I was too thrilled at my cleverness to hear the flatness of his tone. "And that sunken area south of the tree—it's not much of a depression, just a largish dimple—there was a small artificial lake on the plan. It must have been filled in or was silted up. When the shadows lie this way you can see the whole plan! We need to do some digging. Frank ought to get a horticultural archaeologist out here."

He didn't respond. I turned on him, scowling. "You think it's just my imagination?"

"No. He said the same thing."

"Who? Frank?"

"The guy who was here in February. Name was Burton, I think; Dad got hold of him through English Heritage, he was some kind of archaeologist." Hands in his pockets, he stood staring out across the sun-dappled grass as if he were seeing something I couldn't see. "He dropped in his tracks, right out there, under the tree. Heart attack."

*   *   *

iii

"Why didn't you tell me?" I demanded.

"I'd forgotten about it," Sean said.

"You'd forgotten about a man dropping dead in the backyard?"

Jordan had found a message from Frank on the answering machine, saying they were leaving London earlier than he had expected and would be back around midnight. When they finally arrived, at twelve-twenty, I was perched on the window seat, hidden by the curtain. Thanks to the bright lights I could see every line in their faces and every crease in their clothes. Frank looked rumpled, grumpy and sleepy; after Sean had opened the door Frank dismissed him with a brusque gesture and went inside.

I put my head out the window, stuck two fingers in my mouth, and whistled.

Sean looked up. Grimacing furiously, he put his finger to his lips.

I mimed my intentions. He shook his head. I repeated the gestures—heaving something out the window, pointing down.

Entering into the spirit of the thing, Sean jabbed his finger emphatically at the window of Frank's bathroom, laid his cheek on his hands, held up ten fingers and ten again.

Ten minutes later Frank's light went out. I waited another ten minutes.

Sean was at the foot of the ladder when I descended, his hand ready to steady me. I shook it off. "I don't need that."

"Nimble as a mountain goat," Sean agreed. "Let's get out of the light."

We crossed the grass into the shadow of the tree. It seemed to loom larger that night, as monumental as any church or temple. Many man-made structures are older, but none of them were alive. Of all living things only trees have a life-span that can be measured in multiple centuries. Compared with the giant sequoias, this tree was a mere infant, but it had seen ten generations of humans live and die, and the man who had supervised its planting had been dusty bones for three hundred years.

I shivered. Sean turned one of the chairs and straddled it, arms resting on the back. He had changed from his business suit to a dark sweatshirt and pants. "What's on your mind that couldn't wait till morning? I'm tired."

I told him what was on my mind and he said, "I'd forgotten about it."

"You'd forgotten about a man dropping dead in the backyard?"

"Who told you that? He's not dead. He had a stroke. That sort of thing happens to people. He was an old guy, overweight, out of condition—"

"How old?"

"How the hell should I know?" He caught himself, swallowed audibly, and went on in a lower voice. "Damn, you can be irritating! Are you implying that it wasn't a stroke? He was alone, nobody near him, not a mark on him."

"What are you so defensive about? I wasn't accusing you."

"It sure sounded like it." The moon slid behind a cloud; shadows concealed his face. I sensed rather than saw him shift position slightly. "So okay, I still feel bad about it. Not guilty, just . . . bad. He'd been lying there in the cold for over an hour before I found him. It was a near thing. If I hadn't gotten him to the hospital when I did, he might not have made it. I should have kept an eye on him."

For a man who carried a gun and was presumably prepared to use it, he had a surprisingly sensitive conscience. "That's silly," I said.

"Silly? Me?" He let out his breath in a sound that might have been a muffled laugh or a grumble of exasperation. "You sure have a way with words, lady. Have you finished the interrogation?"

"No. Why is his father so brutal to Jordan?"

"Are you still harping on that?"

"Yes."

Sean sighed. "I don't know why I bother being discreet. You'll wring it out of somebody sooner or later. In the simplest possible terms, Frank resents Jordan because he's alive and his brother is dead."

"I didn't know he had a brother."

"You're unreal," Sean said in exasperation. "Don't you ever read the papers or watch the news?"

"Not that kind of news. So that's who Frank

meant when he said he'd lost the person he loved best in the world."

"Mitch," Sean said. "He was six or seven years older than Jordan, and as unlike him as the son of a different mother—which he wasn't. I don't know how Jordan turned into such a nerd. Mitch was a carbon copy of the old man—looks, personality, temperament. You might not believe it, but Frank was a handsome guy when he was young, and something of a daredevil."

"I'd believe it. You knew Mitch?"

"Hell, yes. That's how I came to work for Frank." Sean shifted position slightly. "Went to school with Mitch. We hit it off. Did—things—together."

"All sorts of—things?"

"Mmm-hmmm." It was only a murmur, amused and reminiscent. "Neither of us was exactly interested in academic subjects, but Mitch was a lot smarter than I was; he managed to keep his grades up. I didn't. Flunked out, senior year."

"You don't suppose daddy's money had anything to do with Mitch's getting passing grades?"

"Maybe. That's the way the world goes. Anyhow, I didn't have any particular career prospects, so Mitch arranged for me to come to work for him. Bodyguard, companion, gofer—whatever you want to call it. I was a fair athlete and I can look respectable and talk good grammar when it's necessary. It worked out."

"And what did Mitch do?"

"Oh, he was a vice president or something.

We travelled a lot—Europe, South America."
Something in the tone of my voice or the qual-
ity of my silence must have gotten through to
him, because he added defensively, "He needed
me. I got him out of a number of situations that
could have been embarrassing if the newspapers
had found out about them. Frank appreciated it.
That's why he kept me on after the accident."

I thought I understood the things he hadn't
said. Mitch must have had the old man's charm
and all the money in the world; as his companion, Sean had enjoyed first-class travel, luxurious hotels—and other luxurious things.

"I'm surprised Frank doesn't blame you," I
said bluntly. "What was it, a car crash? Why
weren't you with him?"

"Plane, not car. I should have been with him,
at the controls. He had his pilot's license too but
he . . . On that occasion I was baby-sitting
Jordan. He'd gotten into some mess with a
woman and the old man wanted him kept
incommunicado. Mitch thought it was pretty
funny, his stuffy kid brother going off the rails.
He ordered me to stay with Jordan. Promised
me he wouldn't do anything stupid. He wasn't
supposed to fly that plane, they had lifted his
license the month before—"

He broke off, turning his head away.

So much for my sentimental fantasies about
dear dead daughter. The person Frank mourned
sounded to me like a typical playboy, selfish and
spoiled and dangerously attractive. Everybody—

including, I didn't doubt, Jordan himself—
blamed Jordan for his brother's death. Frank
resented him because he wasn't like Mitch, Sean
despised him because he wasn't like Mitch, and
Jordan was trying his damnedest to be as unlike
Mitch as he possibly could. I did not think I
would have liked Mitch very much.

"If you've finished the inquisition I'd like to
go to bed," Sean said.

I gathered I was not going to get a good-night
kiss. "Okay," I said.

The kitchen door opened. "I thought I'd save
you the climb," Jordan said. "But I can wait, if
you haven't finished what you were doing."

Sean said emphatically, "Oh, shit!" and
stalked off.

Jordan politely held the door for me. Then he
slammed it. "Where did you get that contraption? Sean?"

A good offense is the best defense. I scowled
at him. "How did you find out about it? Were
you in my room?"

"I ran out of coffee and came down to the
kitchen to get more." He rubbed his forehead. I
remembered he had only had a couple of hours
sleep the night before. No wonder he needed
caffeine to keep awake. I was beginning to
understand why he drove himself so hard, and
to feel a little sorry for him, when he said coldly,
"How many men do you want?"

"Huh?"

"You don't suppose I missed those tender

glances Giles was giving you? Now you've got Sean jumping through hoops, and the old man is making a fool of himself, and . . . What's the matter with you? Are you laughing? It isn't funny!"

"Oh, yes it is." I grabbed a paper towel and wiped my eyes. "You'll never know how funny. Look at me, Jordan. Can you seriously believe that Frank would want me when he could have his pick of swimsuit models and cheerleaders?"

"I'd rather believe that than . . ."

"Than what? I can't think of anything less attractive from your point of view, unless . . . That he wants me for you?"

He hadn't thought of that one. I am not a vain woman, but his look of incredulous disbelief roused my worst instincts.

"Well, why not? I'm young and healthy—good teeth"—I bared them—"wide hips, suitable for childbearing—humble background—sensible, practical, unsentimental—"

"Go to bed," Jordan snapped. "And don't forget to haul that ladder in."

"Sturdy," I went on, "muscular. Good with children."

He stamped out of the room. "Knows a lot about old gardens," I said.

It was funny. The funniest thing I had heard in a long time.

SEVEN

The quaint mazes in the wanton green
For lack of tread are indistinguishable.

SHAKESPEARE, *A MIDSUMMER NIGHT'S DREAM*

In case I haven't mentioned it, breakfast was country-house style, with chafing dishes set out on the sideboard. When I came down next morning empty place settings and a rack of leathery toast suggested that the others had already eaten and departed. Wondering absently what idiot had ever invented toast racks, I got myself some scrambled eggs and croissants. There were three kinds of marmalade. I had thought it only came in orange.

Three kinds of marmalade, two servants who didn't even live in—and Sean. I'd been thinking about what he had said the night before and I could see why he found the situation puzzling. Secretaries weren't absolutely necessary in these days of instant electronic communication; the gadgets in Frank's office enabled him to be in direct touch with his employees all over the world. Electronic gadgets could also reduce the need for bodyguards, but protecting this place was a heavy burden for a single man.

If a person truly, wholeheartedly believed that his destiny had been forecast from the day of his birth and that nothing he did could alter it, he might reasonably consider bodyguards an unnecessary expense. It was hard to imagine Frank being so resigned to the workings of Fate, though. He was a fighter if I had ever met one, and a dirty fighter at that.

The kitchen door opened and Doreen poked her head in. "'Morning. How'd you make out yesterday?"

"The cooking wasn't as good," I said, returning to the sideboard. "Otherwise no problem. I suppose you've heard about Bobby Betancourt. Has he been found yet?"

"Oh, he goes off like this all the time. He'll turn up when he's good and ready. Can I get you anything?"

"More coffee would be nice, if it's not too much trouble."

"Decaf or regular?"

"Whatever you've got. I'm not fussy."

"No, you're not." She watched me pile butter and marmalade on the tail end of my croissant. "I thought Americans worried about cholesterol and calories."

Jordan entered by the other door in time to

hear her comment and my reply. It was brief and to the point. "Not me." I put the croissant in my mouth.

"I'll get the coffee," Doreen said, and vanished.

"Good morning," Jordan said. I nodded at him; my mouth was full. He went to the sideboard and helped himself.

Doreen came back with a fresh pot of coffee. "I'll clear this lot away if you're through with it," she said, indicating the chafing dishes.

"I may as well finish the bacon," I said. "There are only a couple of pieces left and it would be a shame to waste them."

"Do you always eat like that?" Jordan asked, eyeing the remains of egg, mushrooms and bacon on my plate.

"I consider the modern obsession with calories a meaningless affectation."

"Obviously."

I ignored the comment. Jordan retired behind the book he had brought and I finished my bacon. When I got up to go Jordan said softly, "I'd like to talk to you."

"I don't want to talk to you. After all those nasty things you said last night—"

"For God's sake, lower your voice!" He indicated the kitchen door.

"I'll do better than that, I'll leave. Go back to your damned dissertation."

Frank was at his desk in the library. Sean was there too, perched on one corner of the desk.

He mumbled a greeting. Frank jumped up from his chair and hurried to meet me. "Good morning, good morning! I was just about to go looking for you. How did you get on yesterday? Did Jordan behave himself?"

I could have killed Jordan for putting ideas into my head. Now I'd be hearing sly hints in everything Frank said. Sean's sidelong glance wasn't any easier to interpret.

"He was very nice," I said primly, avoiding Sean's eyes. "He took me to lunch and to see the church."

"You slept well?" Frank asked. His eyes were wide and innocent. "Nothing disturbed you or worried you?"

Had Sean come clean and thrown himself on his boss's mercy? I didn't think so, but if the old boy was hoping to induce confidences and confessions from me he wasn't going to get them.

"I wasn't nervous, if that's what you mean. I wasn't alone for a second. I don't know what you told Jordan, but he drove half the night to get here before you left. That wasn't necessary."

"It was the least he could do. Well, good. I hope you have made no plans for today. Mr. Barnsley will arrive this afternoon, and you'll want to watch him begin the survey."

"Mr. Barnsley?" I repeated. "Survey?"

"Didn't I tell you?" He knew he hadn't. "I followed your advice, you see. You said, 'Hire an expert,' and you said, 'You must find out what is there before you decide what to do.' So

I have hired one. Barnsley has worked at a number of historic gardens, including Hatfield House, and his qualifications are excellent. I made the final arrangements with him yesterday."

I looked at Sean. His expression was about as animated as that of Roger Fallon's effigy in the church.

"That's nice," I said. "How old is this Mr. Barnsley?"

Sean choked and started to cough.

"That is a strange question, Heather. Aren't there enough young men around for you?"

"Oh, yeah," I said. "If he's coming, I suppose you'll want my room. I was thinking I ought to—"

"You can't leave now, just when the work is getting underway. He will stay at the hotel. Which reminds me, what is this I hear about the Betancourt boy?"

"You probably know more about it than I do, if you've talked to Doreen."

"Doreen is an entire intelligence staff in herself," Frank agreed, chuckling. "That's why I hired her. I think we will have a party this evening. To welcome Mr. Barnsley."

"And celebrate Bobby's departure?" I said. "Frank, you're not thinking of inviting the Betancourts, are you? Not even you would have the gall to ask them to come to a party when they're worried sick about a missing child."

"Who says they're worried sick? If I were Giles I would be celebrating."

"You're disgusting," I said.

Frank grinned. "Yes, I am. I speak the truth, and truth often is unpalatable. There's no cause for alarm about the wretched child, he's always running away."

"They won't come."

"Well, we'll see, won't we? Excuse me now, I must talk to Mrs. Greenspan about the food. Perhaps I can induce Doreen to stay late if Sean drives her home. You wouldn't mind doing that, would you, Sean?"

He left the room, smiling and rubbing his hands together.

"Now what's he up to?" I demanded.

"Being a pain in the ass," Sean said.

"You didn't tell me Frank had hired another archaeologist."

"You didn't give me a chance. Do you think this guy is going to be struck down by some deadly curse—or by me?"

"Don't be silly. Does Frank know about the ladder?"

"Sssh!" He put his hand over my mouth. "Between Doreen and the old man the walls around here definitely have ears. Come for a drive."

"Where?" I inquired indistinctly.

"There's something I want to check out; you may as well come along."

I had a hunch I knew what Sean had in mind, and I knew I was right when he turned off the road onto the track paralleling the wall. The same idea had occurred to me.

If there was ever a hiding place that would appeal to a child, that jungly tunnel was it. Its height and width, its very randomness, suggested a child's hand at work. I wouldn't have put it past Bobby to steal a chain saw and try to cut his way into a place where he wasn't wanted, and wasn't supposed to be. I didn't see how he could have managed it by himself, but he might have had help—friends his own age and older, co-members of a gang or a secret club.

The wild grasses in the pasture had grown several inches, and weeds spread green stems across the track. "Who owns this?" I asked, indicating the pasture.

"Frank. His property line runs along that row of trees."

"It doesn't look as if it's ever been cultivated."

Sean didn't answer. I went on talking, more or less to myself. "It must have been, though. Or at least used for grazing. Something has controlled the spread of the brambles. Goats? They'll eat almost anything."

Sean came to a stop. "We walk from here."

"I know." I scrambled out of the pickup. "You did investigate my wild story, didn't you?"

"I would have been derelict in my duty if I had failed to do so."

"You needn't show off, I suspected you could talk proper English when you chose. Did your sense of duty impel you to tell Frank about the rope ladder?"

Hands in his pockets, eyes on the ground, Sean said morosely, "I didn't tell him, but I'd be willing to bet he knows. He knows everything."

"I don't care if you don't," I said.

"I guess I don't. He knows I . . . I mean, the only way I could get in trouble is if you complained."

"About what? You supplied the ladder, but it was my decision to use it. If Frank gets on your case I'll tend to him."

"I'll bet you would at that," Sean said. He sounded more cheerful.

"Damn right." I stopped. "There it is."

The gap was visibly narrower than it had been, and it looked more like a natural break. I couldn't believe how much the vines had grown even since Jordan and I were there. One long tendril, armed with vicious thorns, festooned the upper part of the opening.

Sean started across the grassy strip that separated the track from the hedge. I yelled, "Stop!" He did, but by that time it was too late; his booted feet had crushed a wide swath.

"What's the matter?" he demanded.

"You thought Bobby might have come here, didn't you? You've just stamped on the evidence."

"Hell. I forgot." Sean scratched his chin.

"Oh, well. It's not likely the grass would retain traces of footprints, it's too green and springy. Don't touch anything—that's a nettle you were about to swat. Don't you have gloves?"

"Not with me." He raised his foot and swore as a bramble hidden under the weeds wrapped around his ankle. "It's as tough as barbed wire," he muttered, pulling his foot away. "I can't see how anyone could get through this without being torn to pieces."

"It was wider before. At least it seemed wider."

"Shall we have a look inside?"

The last word seemed to echo in some empty space—my mind, no doubt. I remembered what Doreen had said. "You were inside? Right in?"

I said, rather more emphatically than I had intended, "Not me. And not you either, if you have an ounce of common sense. You aren't even wearing a hat."

"Chicken," Sean said. He ducked under the hanging vine and went in.

He wasn't in long. A loud "Damn it!" preceded his sudden reappearance.

"What?" I ran to him. "What happened?"

He straightened and raised one hand to the crown of his head. When he held it out the palm was sticky with blood.

"I just about got scalped."

"I told you so."

"You're not great on womanly sympathy, are you?"

He started back along the path. When we reached the Jeep I asked, "Can you drive?"

Sean scowled at me. "I may faint from loss of blood, but I'll give it my best shot."

He settled himself behind the wheel. I stood, so that I could see the top of his head. "It's stopped bleeding."

Even that slight indication of interest soothed his temper. "I'll be damned if I can figure out how you got through that place without being torn to pieces."

"I'm shorter than you are. And I did get scratched pretty bad."

"That tunnel sure as hell wasn't designed for normal human beings."

"What?"

He laughed. "What do you think I mean—the pixies? Funny you should say that, though . . ." I hadn't said it, he had; he went on, "Some people believe they weren't just fairy tales for kids. They were the prehistoric inhabitants of Britain, small, dark people who built their houses underground for warmth and safety and ease of construction. Archaeologists have actually found some of those houses. When the Angles, or the Saxons, or whoever, invaded, they had iron weapons. The stone arrowheads and bronze spears of the little people didn't stand a chance; they were driven back into the hills and under the hills, where they lived for centuries, coming out only at night and giving rise to the legends about brownies and elves and so on. That's why the fairy folks hate iron; they remember the terrible weapons of the men who hunted them like animals."

"Where did you hear that?" I asked, wondering what had prompted this uncharacteristic speech.

"I'm part Irish." Sean grinned. "I got that from Jordan, if you must know. He's into folklore and fairy tales and all that jazz."

"Right. So then who did make that tunnel, if it wasn't pixies or normal human beings?"

"Kids. You had the same idea—that he might be hiding in there."

"It had occurred to me."

"I thought so. I was afraid you might decide to investigate on your own; that's why I wanted to show you how unlikely a theory it is. The kids may have cut the thing, but Bob wouldn't stick around there very long. It's too uncomfortable for a spoiled brat like him."

"He couldn't go to a hotel," I argued. "A child, alone—"

"There are places," Sean said. "Empty houses, barns, abandoned buildings. During the day he'd hang out in shopping centers and amusement parks."

"You sound as if you know about places like that."

"I ran away a few times." The gates swung ponderously open and then closed behind us. "That's why I'm damned sure he's not hanging around here. If he were, he'd want food, among other things. He'd be spotted immediately if he went into a shop. Stop worrying about him. He's not your responsibility."

Thoughtfully I followed him toward the house.

At least he had been sufficiently concerned about the child to investigate the tunnel. Except for his parents, nobody else seemed to care what happened to the boy.

Mrs. Greenspan was washing vegetables at the sink. Sean put his arm as far around her as it would go and announced, "This woman is the real love of my life. How about a cup of coffee, Matilda darling? And I wouldn't say no to a slice of your homemade bread."

Mrs. Greenspan giggled—an astonishing sound, from a woman of her size and dignity—and pushed him away.

"Crushed again," Sean said, seating himself at the table. "But I think she'll take pity on me to the extent of a bite and a sup. Heather?"

The cook, who had taken a cup from the shelf, looked inquiringly at me. "Thanks, but I have some errands to do. I'm going to the village."

ii

It was already beginning to seem familiar and friendly. People smiled and said good morning; the vicar greeted me by name and asked what I had thought of the church. As I left the parking lot I recognized the highway robber whose car had rammed mine; he touched his cap, grinned, and said it was nice to see me. Small towns are like that, and I didn't doubt that all Frank's activities were a subject of consuming interest; even so, this wholehearted acceptance was extraordinary. It was as if I were a long-lost daughter who had returned home after a prolonged stay abroad.

When I reached Jennet's shop she was behind one of the counters, showing jewelry to a pair of older women who were obviously American tourists. They were talking in high-pitched voices and debating the respective merits of a ring with a cat on it and a necklace with cats dangling from it. I gathered that the matching earrings also had cats on them.

With a wave and a smile at Jennet I went toward the book section. She certainly had a wide selection, including some fiction. I ended up with an armful of books. One of the clerks offered to relieve me of them; seeing that Jennet was occupied with another customer I let the girl take the books and went on browsing. I was in no hurry. And, I reminded myself, I was rich. I could buy anything I wanted.

Jennet hadn't overlooked a single aspect of her theme. Cats, of course—patchwork cat pillows, silver and gold cat jewelry, stained-glass cats and porcelain cats. Angels, wizards, fairies; crystals, incense, music for meditation, framed mottoes that advised the reader to seek serenity and start on a journey to self-discovery. If the object didn't have an obvious mystical significance, the label supplied it;

"The Goddess Top" was a flowing garment with butterfly sleeves, "one size fits all." The beautiful knit stoles were "like the shawls worn by Wise Women and White Witches in times gone by."

I collected a few bags of herbs and a ring set with reddish stones that struck my fancy; to judge by the price, the gems weren't rubies but they sure as hell weren't glass, either. I was inspecting the silky caftans when Jennet joined me.

"Do you want to try the blue one on?" she inquired.

"I like the red one better," I said perversely.

"Try both. But you'll see I'm right." She lifted the dresses down and led the way toward a curtained booth.

She *was* right. The red looked like a costume. The blue actually made my hair look as if it had auburn highlights.

"I'll take the blue," I said. "Though I'm damned if I know when and where I'll ever wear it."

"Try the belt. Stay where you are, I'll get it."

She brought a selection of jewelry too—a heavy gold necklace and a couple of pairs of dangling earrings. After seeing the necklace on me she shook her head. I was surprised; I had seen the price tag. When she offered a pair of the earrings I shook my head.

"I don't have pierced ears."

"They can be converted. Just hold them up."

The ones she approved were dangles of iridescent peacock blue stones. Red and gold sparks danced in them. When I looked at the discreet little tag I let out a gasp. "Holy God!"

"Fire opals," Jennet said. "By one of my best young designers. Her stuff is going to be worth money someday."

"This isn't money?" I indicated the tag.

"I'll convert them for free. Or I'll pierce your ears for you, gratis."

I could see her with a long needle in her hand. "No, thanks. I'll take the earrings, though."

"Anything else?"

I looked at my watch. "I think I'll break for lunch. Will you join me?"

"I suppose I'd better," Jennet said coolly. "Since that was your real purpose in coming."

The restaurant was crowded, but the owner of an establishment never has any difficulty getting a table. After we had ordered Jennet waved the hovering waitresses away. "You didn't have to go to all that trouble and expense for the privilege of a private conversation with me," she said dryly. "What's on your mind?"

There were a lot of things on my mind. I started with the least provocative. "You've heard about Bobby, I suppose."

"Of course." She raised both eyebrows and smiled faintly. "I don't need a crystal ball, you know. News spreads quickly in small villages."

"Has there been any trace of him?"

"Just the usual rumors. One of our less reputable citizens claimed he saw him get into a lorry sometime after midnight, and another claimed her nephew's bike was stolen last night." She stared at her untouched glass of wine. "It's not Giles's fault, you know."

"I wasn't blaming him. It's none of my business. I hardly know them."

"You're a teacher. I thought modern educational theory holds the parents accountable for everything that goes wrong with a child."

"Mum is usually the one who's blamed."

"Not around here. The man is the head of the family and it's up to him to control the kiddies—with a stick, if necessary. Giles is too soft. A good walloping would set that kid on the right track."

"Surely you don't believe that."

"There are times when I do. Giles is a damned fool. He's too soft in some ways and as unyielding as granite in others." She looked up at me. "He told me how kind and sympathetic you've been."

"I haven't done anything. I mean . . . Look, I don't want to talk about that."

"What do you want to talk about, then?"

It was hard to find the right words. Finally I said, "Two days ago I didn't know any of you people existed. Now you're talking about Giles as if he were a—a close friend of mine, and Frank treats me like a member of the family, and Doreen has told me things a stranger shouldn't know. I feel like an actor who's been pushed onto the stage without a script. The rest of you know your lines, and you behave as if I'm supposed to know mine, but I don't. I don't know what I'm doing here!"

"Perhaps this is where you were meant to be all along. Your place was prepared and waiting for you. Accept it."

When people make speeches like that one, they usually intone the words and look solemn. Jennet sounded almost angry.

"I think you really believe that," I said.

She shrugged. "'There is a fatality that shapes our ends, Rough hew them though we may.'"

"And 'all the world's a stage,'" I said. "'And all the men and women merely players.' I can quote Shakespeare too. It's an elegant metaphor, but that's all it is."

"Then why don't you pack your bags and leave?" She leaned toward me, her eyes intent. "I don't think you can. You're caught in it now—part of the pattern."

If she wasn't dead serious she was putting on a superb performance. Uncomfortable, trying not to show it or admit it, I inquired sarcastically, "Lost in the maze?"

"Another metaphor," Jennet said musingly. "It's interesting that you should choose that particular one."

"Was Bobby the one who cut that tunnel through the wilderness?"

She hadn't expected that. She stared at me

without speaking and I said impatiently, "That's no metaphor. Don't pretend you don't know about the tunnel. You saw the condition I was in the other morning—the scratches, the nettle rash. You didn't ask how I'd gotten them or how I had gotten past the gate. You knew. What is it about that place?"

"I didn't suppose you'd be interested in local superstitions."

"You're stalling. Doreen knows something too. She said . . ."

But I didn't repeat the words. A couple of prosaic prepositions hold no suggestion of the uncanny. "In—inside." It had been her tone of voice and the way she looked.

"Are you sure you aren't letting your imagination run away with you?" Jennet asked.

"The strange noise I heard night before last wasn't imagination. It was like a scream, and it came from the direction of the wilderness. I thought perhaps Bobby had gone there."

"Ah, I see." Jennet's taut pose relaxed. "As I said, there are some foolish local superstitions connected with the place. At least you would call them foolish, since you don't believe in such things. I can assure you, however, that Bobby Betancourt doesn't know about your tunnel, nor would he have any reason to go near the place. You must have heard an animal or a night bird. Foxes make strange noises."

"Yeah, right. Then who—"

She tossed her napkin onto the table. "I've

been away long enough. Take your time. Have a coffee."

"No, thanks. I think I'll browse the shop some more. Who knows, I may find something else I want."

We exchanged tight smiles. I followed her into the shop. She went straight to her desk and picked up the phone—as direct a dismissal as I had ever seen. I browsed.

It might have been embarrassment that made her unwilling to enlarge on "local superstitions." People seem to think it reflects on them if their friends and neighbors harbor such beliefs. Jennet was a shrewd businesswoman who had capitalized very successfully on a basic human need, and her implied role as Village Wise Woman didn't do her business any harm; but I felt sure she was more than that. She was a believer too. In something.

So far as I was concerned she could believe in angels, garden fairies (faeries seemed to be the preferred spelling) and Old Demdike. She was entitled to her opinions, so long as she didn't try to foist them on me.

She didn't approach me again until I went to the cash register with my purchases.

"I thought you'd like to know. Giles called just now; they think Bob is heading for Birmingham. He told one of his school chums that's where he would go the next time he ran away from home."

"Without money or transportation, in the middle of the night?"

"He had money. Nicked over a hundred quid from his mother's handbag. She didn't realize it was missing until an hour ago. It's only six miles to the nearest train station. If he waited till after sun-up before buying a ticket no one would think twice about it."

She waited for me to comment. I couldn't think of anything to say; she had covered all the obvious objections.

When I got back to the house I found Jordan and the cat having tea on the terrace. The cat's nose was in a saucer of milk and Jordan's nose was in a book. Neither looked up until I dropped one of the boxes I was trying to balance.

Neither of them offered to give me a hand, either. Doreen emerged from the kitchen so promptly I wondered whether she had been watching for me.

"Back so soon?" Jordan inquired, closing his book.

"Sit down and have your tea," Doreen said, relieving me of my bundles. "I'll take these up for you."

"No, that's all right." I tried to hold onto the last of my purchases, which was hanging over my arm. It had been tenderly encased in a plastic clothes bag. Not just any old plastic bag; it was silvery white, tied to the hanger with pastel ribbons.

Doreen recognized it. Before I could stop her she had snatched it from me and whisked up the plastic covering. Silk shimmered in the sunlight like running water. "Whoo!" she exclaimed. "That's gorgeous."

I didn't mind her seeing the dress; what I minded was letting Jordan see it. From his expression you'd have thought I had brought back a spangled G-string or one of Frederick of Hollywood's more uninhibited creations.

After one disgusted look he opened his book again.

"Just leave them on this chair," I said, without much hope that she would do as I asked.

"That bloody cat will be all over the dress if I do. You know how they are."

She went off, holding the garment bag high. I felt certain Mrs. Greenspan was waiting to have a look-see too. Well, why shouldn't she? A place had been set for me. I sat down.

Jordan went on reading. It was Matthews on mazes; I could see the title, since he was holding the book up in front of his face.

"They think Bobby has gone to Birmingham," I said.

"Lucky Birmingham."

"Are the Betancourts coming?"

"What do you think?"

The cat bumped its head against my ankle. Jordan said, still from behind the book, "He's already eaten all the ham sandwiches. There's nothing left but cress."

"You heard him," I said to the cat. "Want more milk?"

It didn't, but I had to peel back the bread and show it the cress before it believed there was no more ham. With a sniff it stalked away. I ate the sandwich.

Doreen hadn't offered to carry my other parcels upstairs. Since nobody seemed to want to talk to me I examined my purchases. I decided I would wear my new ring on my right hand, but when I tugged at the cat's eye Jennet had given me it still wouldn't come off. Maybe I had been eating a little too much.

Sucking my finger, I looked up to find that Jordan was watching me. "I'm wetting it so I can get the ring off," I explained.

"Oh. You bought a few books, I see."

I gave up on the ring. "Uh-huh. Have a look if you like. I've decided to go in for witches. It was that or angels."

"Hmmm." His eyebrows lifted. "Murray's *God of the Witches*? That's pretty heavy stuff."

"I am not entirely devoid of intellectual capacity."

"Her theories are generally considered unsound."

"So I understand."

"I suppose you read that in one of your romance novels."

"That's right." His skeptical expression moved me to elaborate. "Murray proposed the idea that witchcraft was nothing more than a survival of a prehistoric nature religion—the worship of the mother goddess in one of her many forms, maiden, mother and crone. Her consort and/or son was a horned god. It was easy for Christian theologians to turn him into the devil."

"The superimposition of the inquisitorial scheme on a preexistent stratum of generic superstition."

"Huh?"

"Don't go out of your way to sound stupider than you are," Jordan snapped. "The idea of witchcraft as a compact with the devil was developed by theologians and inquisitors and imposed on the public through sermons, books and the witchcraft trials. Eventually many of the accused came to believe it themselves."

"Oh. Right. That's what the woman who wrote the novel said. I've never read Murray's book, so I figured I'd give it a try."

"It's not worth your time. If you really want to read up on the subject I have some books I can lend you."

I took the last sandwich. "What are you trying to do, get me educated enough so you'll have somebody to talk to?"

Jordan's forehead furrowed. "Maybe you're right," he muttered. "Maybe I need to talk to someone. I've been getting some of the craziest ideas. . . ."

"Like what?"

He glanced at the door of the kitchen. "Never mind."

The kitchen door opened. I wondered how long Frank had been lurking there, and whether

Jordan had been aware of his presence. Our voices hadn't been loud, but Frank had ears like a cat's. Not that it mattered if he had overheard. We hadn't said anything personal.

"Ah," he said, smiling. "Having a nice time together, are you? I hope I'm not interrupting."

"No, I've finished the sandwiches," I said, collecting my purchases.

"Then you had better hurry and get dressed, my dear. The party is all arranged. Jennet is bringing Mr. Barnsley and the Betancourts will be here at six."

"You really are the limit," Jordan said in disgust. "Inviting a pair of worried parents to a party—"

"We're not having balloons and dancing girls," Frank said. "Just a quiet gathering for drinks and dinner. It will do them good. Who knows, I may be able to bring about a reconciliation. Marriage is a sacred institution, not to be lightly dissolved. No doubt Lindsay was upset and worried or she wouldn't have—"

"Oh, for God's sake." Jordan fled into the house.

Frank sighed. "The boy always puts the worst possible interpretation on everything I do and say. Now, Heather, run along and make yourself beautiful. Even more beautiful, I should say."

I was glad to get away from him. What he had in mind I didn't know, but the situation he had arranged had all sorts of potentials for serious embarrassment if not actual physical combat. Giles and Lindsay on the brink of divorce, Lindsay in hot pursuit of Jordan, Jennet in more dignified pursuit of Giles, Sean—well, I wouldn't have been surprised to learn that Sean had been or was involved with Lindsay and Doreen, and Lord only knew how many other women. And then there was me.

From my window I had a good view of the preparations and I sat watching, like a spectator at a play, as Sean carried an extra table and chairs across the lawn to the area under the big tree. Doreen followed with tablecloths and trays; Frank ran back and forth spouting orders. As the shadows lengthened the buried features I had observed earlier seemed even more prominent. I wondered what Barnsley would make of them. I was beginning to relax, safe in obscurity, when Frank stopped on his way back to the house and looked up at my window.

"Hurry, Heather. They will be here in fifteen minutes."

He made sure I would obey by sending Doreen up to help hurry me. I was getting used to her popping in; when I heard her knock, followed immediately by the opening of the door, I finished hooking my bra and said resignedly, "Now what does he want?"

"That you should hurry up, what else?" She went to the wardrobe and removed the blue silk gown.

"I'm not going to wear that."

"Saving it for Buckingham Palace, are you?

The boss said you should put it on." She advanced on me and dropped the garment over my head. I swore. Doreen giggled.

"How did he know about this damned dress?" I demanded, as she arranged the flowing skirt. "Did you tell him?"

"He has his little ways. Now come on, why fight it? Lindsay will be dressed to the teeth, it will do her good to have some competition."

"I can't believe she's coming. There hasn't been any news about the boy, has there?"

"Not that I've heard." Doreen opened the bureau drawer and took out the earrings I had bought. "Want some help with your hair?"

"No. And don't offer to pierce my ears, either. I've already refused to let Jennet do it."

"She knows how to do those things," Doreen said seriously.

I decided to let that one pass. Since I couldn't wear the earrings, I slung them back in the drawer, passed a brush over my hair, and started for the door.

Then I went back. It took ten more minutes to do what I had decided to do. I avoided the mirror. If the overall effect was that of an ugly duckling trying to imitate a swan I didn't want to know. Hoisting my skirts with all the grace of a charwoman I descended the stairs and went out the side door.

Jennet and Barnsley had arrived. Frank trotted to meet me. He took my arm and escorted me toward the table. I tripped over my skirts.

Barnsley was a tubby little man with a mustache; although he appeared to be in his mid-forties, he was already losing his hair. When Frank introduced me as "my dear friend and guest, Miss Tradescant," he actually blushed with excitement. "Not really! How absolutely thrilling! What is the relationship, Miss Tradescant?"

"There isn't any," I said. "And it's Ms. Tradescant." The poor little man flushed, and I regretted my bad manners. He had done nothing to deserve them. "But please call me Heather," I added, with a smile. "Pleased to meet you. Hello, Jennet."

She looked me up and down and smiled as sweetly as if we hadn't been exchanging innuendoes a few hours earlier. "That outfit is definitely you, dear. You should have left the earrings to be converted. Or have you decided to let me pierce your ears?"

Jordan was the next to appear. He hadn't bothered to put on a coat or tie, and he could have used a shave. He was being deliberately naughty, and his air of defiance would have been funny if it hadn't been rather sad.

The Betancourts came separately. Giles looked absolutely exhausted, but his face brightened when he saw me. He drew me aside.

"No news yet," he said, before I could ask. "I've left this number in case something should turn up. It was kind of Frank to arrange this, wasn't it? Very thoughtful."

He meant it. If I had said yes, it was thoughtful, my nose would have shot out like Pinocchio's, so I just smiled.

Lindsay was the last to arrive. Just like her, I thought, but I regretted my evil-mindedness when I saw that her eyes were shadowed and her smile strained. She selected a chair next to mine and accepted a glass of wine.

"How nice to see you, Heather. That's a delicious frock; I was tempted to buy it myself, but it's not really my color."

"Jennet made me do it," I said. "You look—you look very nice."

In fact she looked even more attractive with that wistful droop to her mouth and a minimum of makeup.

"A trio of lovely ladies," said nice Mr. Barnsley, with a gallant bow in Jennet's direction. "Forgive me, Miss Tradescant, but I am fascinated to meet a bearer of that distinguished name. You are an American, aren't you? I didn't realize . . ."

He was a nice little man. We discussed the Tradescants and speculated on how the name could have gotten to America. Nobody mentioned the missing child.

There were salmon sandwiches. I had just about decided the cat wasn't going to show up when I saw it emerge from the hedge, flat on its belly like a furry snake. I stared. Was that the tunnel entrance? Not necessarily. Cats can squeeze themselves through holes you wouldn't believe; it has something to do with their shoulder blades.

When I failed to respond to a question of Mr. Barnsley's, he turned to see what had distracted me. "What a handsome cat," he exclaimed. "Here, puss, puss."

He held out his hand and made peculiar noises. The cat stopped and fixed him with a cold stare. Barnsley chuckled. "A definite snub. Cats can make one feel completely inferior, can't they?"

"Try the salmon sandwiches," I suggested.

"May I? I am very fond of cats. Bewitching creatures. I have three of my own. Here you are then, my friend." He started toward the cat, holding the sandwich out at arm's length.

It advanced a few feet and then stopped, pawing at its mouth and shaking its head.

"It has a mouse or something," Lindsay said in disgust. "Don't let the creature come any closer."

"It's not a mouse," Jennet said.

"Here, puss, puss," caroled Mr. Barnsley. "It appears to have something caught in its teeth. Shall I fetch it? Will it bite?"

The cat stopped again in a patch of sunlight a few feet away. Jennet got to her feet. The animal didn't resist when she scooped it up and carefully removed something from its mouth.

Not a mouse, not a mole, not a piece of string. A long strand of bright blue yarn, twisted and crimped, as if it had been unravelled from a larger piece of knitted fabric. I had seen that particular, distinctive shade of blue before. It was the identical color of the sweater Bobby Betancourt had worn.

EIGHT

What is this mighty labyrinth—the earth,
But a wild maze the moment of our birth?

ANONYMOUS, "REFLECTIONS ON WALKING IN THE
MAZE AT HAMPTON COURT," BRITISH MAGAZINE, 1747

The sunlight turned solid, like a skin of gold over
leaves and grass and the cat lying in the curve
of Jennet's sun-gilded arm. Not even a breath
broke the stillness until Lindsay fell out of
her chair, all in one piece like a block of
wood.

Jennet lowered the cat to the ground and gave
the piece of yarn to Jordan. She went to Lindsay
and knelt beside her.

The faces of the others were almost as pallid
as that of the fallen woman—except for Mr.
Barnsley, who was trying not to stare. He didn't
have a clue as to why everyone was behaving so
strangely. It was typical of Giles, I thought, that
his first words were directed at Barnsley.

"You must please excuse us. This must seem
rather—"

"Oh, stop being so damned polite," I said.

"You're sure it's from the kid's sweater?" Sean asked. He sounded a little shaken.

"His mother is," Frank said. "How is she?"

Jennet hauled Lindsay to her feet and deposited her in a chair. "Fainted," she said brusquely. "Head on the table, Lindsay." Lindsay just sat there staring at nothing; her arms and legs stuck out at odd angles. If it had been up to me I wouldn't have got her up so soon, but I wasn't the village Wise Woman. Jennet arranged her as she would have arranged a rag doll, arms on the table, head on her arms. "Brandy, Frank?"

"I'll get it." Sean headed for the house.

Holding the stained yarn at arm's length, Jordan muttered, "The evidence is inconclusive. This doesn't necessarily mean—"

"Oh, for God's sake!" I exclaimed. "Why are you standing here talking? It may not mean . . . anything, but we've got to look, haven't we? If he's in there . . ."

The others turned to stare at the wall of living green from which the cat had come.

Giles hadn't spoken a word or moved to help his wife. Now he started walking toward the hedge. Frank caught his arm.

"Wait a minute. Heather is right, but we need to plan before we act. Take your wife home, Giles."

"No."

"No," Lindsay echoed. "I just need to rest— lie down for a minute. . . ."

"Right," Frank said. "Give her a little of that brandy and then help her upstairs, Doreen."

Doreen had returned with Sean and the brandy. He must have told her what had happened; avid curiosity marked her face, and before she followed Frank's orders I saw her eyes move quickly and comprehensively across the lawn. I looked too. The cat was gone.

Briskly and efficiently Frank took charge. Barnsley was dismissed, with apologies and the briefest of explanations; Lindsay, white-faced and silent, was led away by Doreen. Everybody had brandy except Jordan and me—not that I didn't need it, but I hate the stuff.

"Now, then," Frank said, setting the bottle of cognac on the table with a decisive thump. "Where's that tunnel of yours, Heather?"

"How did you know about it?"

"I know everything that goes on here," Frank said flatly. "If I choose not to pursue some matters, it is for reasons of my own. Never mind that now. It will be dark in a couple of hours. What's the best way of getting into the place?"

I had already considered that question, and tried to emulate his cool, practical tone. "From the outside, I think. We'll need a chain saw. And gloves, boots, protective clothing. I'll go up and change."

"Hold on," Jennet said. "I'm not surprised that Frank has gone off the rails, this is the sort of wild escapade he enjoys, but what in heaven's name is wrong with the rest of you? You can't demolish that jungle with a chain saw, and there is no reason whatever to suppose the boy is there. All the children who attend the school wear the same sweaters; the cat could have picked up that scrap anywhere."

"This is blood," Frank said, fingering the stiffened end of the yarn with what struck me as unpleasant relish.

"You don't know that. And even if it is—any child, Bob or one of his mates, who explored the wilderness, might have been scratched, his clothing torn."

Sean stroked his beard thoughtfully and Jordan said, "She's right. We could report this to the police—"

His father cut him off. "As you were the first to point out, the evidence is inconclusive. If you're afraid of scratching your manicured hands, stay here. Jennet may be right, but I'm going to have a look. Those of you who want to go with me had better hurry and change. Five minutes."

He trotted toward the house.

"Damn the man!" Jennet exclaimed. "Jordan, can't you talk sense into him?"

"I'm the last person he'd listen to," Jordan said. "I'll have to go with him. The rest of you suit yourselves."

He ran toward the house. I followed him; Jennet followed me. She was muttering under her breath—curses, directed at Frank, I assumed. As we mounted the stairs she said,

"Have you a jacket or long-sleeved shirt I might borrow?"

"Oh, you've changed your mind?"

"No, I have not changed my bloody mind. But if the rest of you are going to do this I have to go with you."

"I can lend you a shirt and jacket, but my shoes would never fit you, and those sandals—"

"I'll manage."

"That's stupid. There are enough of us without you." When I opened my door I saw Lindsay sitting on the edge of the bed. I had forgotten about her. "Stay with Lindsay."

"She doesn't need me," Jennet said. "You do."

"What? Lie down, Lindsay, or you'll pass out again. Where's Doreen, I thought she was with you?"

"I want to go home," Lindsay mumbled. "Home to Mother."

"Oh, for God's sake! Doreen, where the hell are you?"

Jennet went to the wardrobe and opened the door. Torn between two women who appeared to have lost their wits, I was on the verge of slapping one or both of them when Doreen sidled into the room.

"You were supposed to stay with her," I exclaimed.

"She wanted some aspirin." Doreen displayed the bottle.

"I want to go home," Lindsay repeated. "I'm sorry if I caused trouble. I didn't mean to faint.

It was the shock . . . But the cat—the cat couldn't . . ."

Unwilling sympathy tempered my dislike of the woman. I suppose the same horrible image had flashed into all our minds. A small, still body, claws and sharp teeth digging into the blue yarn. . . .

"No," Jennet said sharply. "Don't even think it."

"What about me?" Doreen asked. "I want to go home too."

Jennet stripped off her tunic and stepped out of her pants. "There's no need for you to stay; we won't be partying tonight. Take her home to mum."

"Me?" Doreen's eyes popped. "But what if she—"

"I won't, I won't do anything." Lindsay caught Doreen's hand and held on, despite the latter's effort to pull it away. "I promise. I just want to get away from here."

Jennet turned. "It will be all right, Doreen. Do as I say."

"Well . . ."

"It will be all right," Jennet repeated.

Doreen looked from her reddened hand, which still bore the imprints of Lindsay's fingers, to Jennet. Stripped to bra and panties, her hair dishevelled and her face taut with new lines of strain, the older woman was not a particularly impressive figure. The flowing tunics she favored had softened a body that was not so much boyish as sexless—virginal, you might say, if that word could be applied these days to any woman of Jennet's age.

Doreen's mouth relaxed. "Okay. If you say so."

"What a fuss about nothing," I said angrily, after Doreen had led Lindsay out. "Hey, that jacket is the one I was planning to wear. You'll have to make do with the blue one, if you're still determined to come along."

As we passed his door I heard Frank's voice raised in a wordless bellow. Jennet stopped. "He's misplaced his shoes or his pants or something. I'd better help him find them before he has a stroke. Go on, and don't let them leave until we get there."

"What do you want to help him for? We don't need him, he'll just be a nuisance. You keep him occupied and I'll go with—"

"No!" She turned, her hand on the doorknob. "No one is to enter that place without me. Do you understand?"

I didn't understand, but she didn't wait for me to say so. She went into Frank's room and closed the door.

The men were waiting. Jordan had added a shabby windbreaker to his attire; Sean had changed into work boots and jeans with a matching denim jacket—designer, I couldn't help noticing. Giles hadn't done anything except remove his tie and button his blazer. Sean was yelling at him.

"You can't go like that. You haven't seen the damned place."

"I know what it's like," Giles said. He smiled at me. "A suit of armor would be more suitable, but I'll settle for gloves, if you have an extra pair."

Control like that may be admirable, but it is also unhealthy. I wished he would yell and swear. I could see the quiver of muscles and nerves under every exposed inch of skin.

Jordan suffered from no well-bred inhibitions. He accepted the gloves Sean handed him and wrinkled his nose. "Disgusting objects. The gardener's, I presume. You'd think he could wash them every year or so. Where's the old man? Why are we waiting for him? He'll only be in the way."

"Jennet asked us to wait for her," I said.

Jordan tossed the filthy gloves onto the table. "I've changed my mind. This is insane. Sean, you're supposed to protect the old fool. Why don't you stop him?"

"Because he can fire me," Sean snarled. "Why don't you stop him? I wish somebody would. I'm not crazy about doing this either."

"There's no reason for any of you to do it," Giles said quietly. "If I may have the chain saw—"

Frank's appearance put an end to what would certainly have developed into another argument. Giles meant precisely what he said, but neither of the other men could let him go alone without losing face. So we all piled into the pickup, Frank and Sean in the cab, the rest of us sitting or standing in the back, and started off. The sun was far down the sky and the shadows were lengthening. Jennet had been quite right, this was a futile gesture, probably pointless, possibly dangerous. I wished I hadn't suggested it.

Sean must have noted certain landmarks when we were there before. He couldn't have seen the opening; it was now almost hidden by new growth. There was something uncanny about the rapidity with which those vines had lengthened and intertwined, as if they had been directed by a guiding intelligence. Giles looked dubiously at the wall of greenery. "I don't see—"

"It's there," I said.

"Fascinating," Frank murmured.

Jennet stood to one side, her hands twisted tightly together. Her lips were moving. I heard a low mutter of what might have been profanity, but I couldn't make out the words.

Sean obviously didn't like what he was doing, but he went about it with the same efficiency he had demonstrated in other ways. The chain saw was gasoline-powered. When Giles reached for it Sean silently shouldered him away and gave the starter a hard yank. The engine caught with a sound like the angry roaring of a large invisible animal.

The rankest of the new growth was on the outside, where it had ample light and room to expand. Once he had penetrated into the tunnel

Sean began hacking at the vines that roofed it. His progress was slow, and even over the racket the saw made I could hear him swearing.

The rest of us had gathered around the opening. Frank had started to follow Sean, and had been yanked back by Jordan. When he started to protest Giles said, "I'm next in line, Frank. As soon as he's made more room."

His tone brooked no argument. It shut even Frank up.

When the engine suddenly cut off, the silence was deafening. "Get the hell away from the opening," Sean shouted. "You're blocking the light. It's dark enough in here."

"I've got the flashlight," Giles said. "Shall I—?"

"Yeah, come on. Give me plenty of elbow room."

The bright, narrow beam shifted and settled, focusing on the roof and Sean's raised arms. The sleeves of his jacket had slipped back and the strained muscles of his forearms were outlined in dark shadow. In the glow I saw that Giles was hunched over, his head bent. He was a couple of inches taller than Sean and the latter hadn't left any extra headroom.

When they had gone a few more feet Frank made another attempt to follow. I had anticipated it, and apparently Jennet had too; we moved in on him with the practiced precision of a pair of cornerbacks on a receiver.

"You try that one more time and I'll break your leg," I said between my teeth. Frank laughed.

Jordan had gone back to the truck for another flashlight. He didn't look at his father. When he shone the light into the tunnel I saw that both men were out of sight. The tunnel had started to curve.

"It's almost dark," I said uneasily. "I didn't realize they were going to make such a project of this. I should have gone in alone, I got through before."

"Damn fool," said Jordan distinctly.

"They have to stop," I insisted. "There are twists and turns and dead ends and—and things. . . . It's too dangerous in the dark."

"I agree," Frank said. "Jordan, go after them and tell them to quit for the night."

I don't know whether Jordan would have done it or not. I didn't wait to see. He was even taller than Giles, and he'd left the nasty dirty gloves behind. I pushed past him and went in.

It wasn't as bad as I had expected. An occasional thorn plucked at my sleeve and the cut twigs made a slippery surface underfoot, but the light accompanied me and once I caught a glimpse of shadowed sky through a gap in the roof. When the tunnel curved, cutting off the flashlight beam, I could see another light ahead and before long I made out Giles's silhouette. He hadn't heard me because the saw made so much noise. When I touched him he started, but he kept the light steady.

"Jennet?"

"No, it's me. Heather. Frank says to stop."

He didn't move or reply. "You have to, Giles," I said. "Please. Maybe there's been a message from the police—maybe they've located him— seen him—"

"And if they haven't?" He had to yell; we were both shouting to be heard over the noise of the saw. "You go—all of you. Leave me the chain saw. I've tried to persuade Sean to let me take over—"

"Do you suppose any of us would leave you here alone?" I caught hold of his sleeve. "We'll come back as soon as it's light, with better tools. Please!"

The arm under my hands was as hard as a stone. I could only begin to imagine the frustration he must feel, the pain of waiting inactive and helpless. This was something to do, at any rate. It might be futile but it was better than doing nothing.

Sean's arms were shaking with strain; I don't think he knew I was there. He moved forward another step, and then, without warning, the steady roar of the saw changed to a high, screaming whine. The blade rebounded, throwing Sean off-balance. His foot slipped and his back struck the brambly wall and the white, skull-sized object that had fallen from the underbrush ahead bounced off his shoulder and hit the ground.

It rolled and came to a rest. The empty eye sockets stared blindly at me, and the shadows moved across the twisted mouth so that it seemed to smile.

Jennet was the only one who refused Frank's invitation to dinner. She said she was too tired, and her appearance bore it out. Giles had said she was a few years younger than he, but that night she looked sixty, her face lined and pale, her shoulders bowed.

After a quick wash and brush and a change of clothing I went to the kitchen. I was ravenously hungry. It must have been stress; I hadn't done anything except stand around and cause trouble. I knew that if I wanted something to eat I'd have to get it myself. Giles had gone to telephone, Sean was in his quarters changing his clothes and Jordan had disappeared. Frank had taken his place at the head of the dining room table with an air of patient expectation.

Mrs. Greenspan had started to prepare an elaborate meal. She had obviously departed in haste; the oven had been turned off and a bowl of plain, unadorned lettuce had been put in the refrigerator. I turned the oven on, took a tray of canapés from the fridge, and carried it into the dining room.

"When is dinner?" Frank inquired, studying the little dainties without enthusiasm.

"Damned if I know." I crammed a tiny biscuit loaded with shrimp into my mouth. "Unless you like your roast beef rare on the ends and bloody in the middle, you'll have to wait. Have a cheese biscuit."

"I don't want one. Where is Mrs. Greenspan? Where is Doreen?"

"Gone home."

"I didn't tell them they could go home!"

"You didn't expect them to hang around and serve a fancy dinner, did you? I'll get something on the table when I'm good and ready. I'm not ready."

"I would like something to drink."

He looked like a chubby, irritated, brown baby. "Get it yourself," I said.

I never knew how Frank was going to react. Instead of pouting or yelling, he gave me a bland smile and rose from his chair. "Would you care for something?"

"Yes, I would. I don't care what, so long as it's strong. Where is Jordan?"

Busying himself with the glasses at the sideboard, Frank said, "I've no idea. He wandered off with that statue head cradled in his arms. Just like him. Ah, here is Giles. Make yourself a drink, old chap."

I didn't have to ask; relief and renewed hope made Giles look ten years younger. "Good news," I said.

"Encouraging, at any rate." He took the hand I had extended and squeezed it. "Someone reported seeing a boy of Bob's description in Birmingham. The police are following it up."

"I'm so glad."

"And how is your wife?" Frank inquired, handing Giles a glass.

It was a characteristic query, but if he had hoped to embarrass Giles—and me—he failed. Giles gave my hand another squeeze before releasing it and accepting the drink. "Better," he said. "She was resting, but I spoke with her mother and passed on the good news."

Sean was the next to appear, and between the three of us—obviously I do not include Frank— we managed to get a scratch meal together. Nobody seemed to want his beef rare, so we hacked up the roast and fried the ragged slices. It had been a beautiful roast. Mrs. Greenspan would probably faint when she saw what we had done to it.

Jordan had to be summoned to dinner; he had gone to roost in the library, and when he joined us he was carrying the marble head. Removing a bunch of roses from the vase in the center of the table, he replaced the flower arrangement with the head, settling it carefully into place. The neck fit neatly into the wide mouth of the vase.

"Lovely," I said.

Jordan began shovelling food into his mouth. I don't think he was aware of what he was eating—just as well, the beef was definitely over-cooked—or maybe burned would be more accurate. He couldn't seem to take his eyes off the stained marble. The blade of the saw must have struck it on the neck, because the features had not been damaged. It was even uglier than I had thought—the nose lumpy, the twisted lips thick, the brow low and receding. The streaks that had run down its cheeks looked like dried green blood.

"This is the one you saw?" Jordan asked.

"I think so. Yes."

"You might have mentioned it was there," Sean said. I noticed he had shifted his knife to his left hand. His face was speckled with red spots, like measles.

"I did mention it."

Giles dropped his fork. "What the hell are you talking about? Heather, did you go into that damned . . . Excuse me. None of my affair, is it?"

I'd be lying if I claimed his outburst didn't please me. I had never seen him come so close to losing his temper—and on my account. I explained; I apologized. He apologized again. I told him there was no need for him to apologize. Frank sat there grinning like a spectator watching the Marx brothers until Jordan said impatiently, "Enough already. Did you know the statue was there, Giles?"

"No. I was never allowed to go near the wilderness." He was still looking at me, with a mixture of reproach and admiration. "I never tried to get into it."

"So the tunnel wasn't there in your day?" Jordan persisted.

"If it was, I wasn't aware of it. There was certainly no opening on this side, I'd have seen it."

He took hold of the vase and turned it so that the thing was grinning straight at him. I was sorry to see antiquarian interest replacing his tender concern for me. "Fascinating to think this has been there for hundreds of years."

"You believe it's part of the original garden layout?" Jordan asked.

"Must be. No major changes or additions were made after the middle of the seventeenth century."

"Were garden designers importing classical statuary that early?" I asked.

It was a casual question, prompted by nothing in particular, but Jordan's head snapped around as if I had uttered an obscenity.

"Were they?"

"I don't know. That's why I asked."

"Statuary and urns were common by the end of the seventeenth century," Frank said.

I wasn't above showing off either. "There's mention, in a list of l679, of a marble statue—spelled statua. I can't recall anything earlier, but I'm no expert."

"Then why did you raise the point?" Jordan demanded.

"Damned if I know. I'm sorry I did. What difference does it make? Some later lord of the manor might have picked up this little atrocity; they were goofy about the Gothic around the turn of the nineteenth century and mad about miscellaneous antiquities for the next hundred years."

"Cute," said Jordan, his lip curling. "This isn't Gothic. It's almost certainly Roman. Probably a copy of a Greek original."

"How do you know?"

"It's my field. The material is marble, the workmanship excellent. Look at the carving of the curls." His finger flicked one of the horns. "This is Pan or Silvanus."

"It could be an anonymous faun or satyr," I said perversely. "They had horns too. Or the Devil."

Somehow or other it had turned into a personal duel, and I was secretly relieved when Sean broke in.

"Who gives a damn? It's ugly as sin, and I hope nobody expects me to go back there tomorrow looking for the rest of it—or explain to that old grouch of a gardener how the chain saw got smashed up. He acts as if he owns those tools. Incidentally, it's the only one that was gas powered."

Jordan gave him a horrified look. "Chain saw? You can't use anything like that. We'll have to proceed carefully. Clippers—is that what you call them?—and, uh—"

"Toenail scissors?" I suggested.

I think, for a few seconds, he took me seriously.

Sean flatly and profanely refused to have anything to do with the project, and Frank didn't insist. Giles indicated his intention of participating. He didn't have to explain why. The news about his son had been encouraging but inconclusive; until the boy was found there was always a possibility that he had been—"had been," not "was," I couldn't bring myself to believe that—inside the maze. It was assumed by everybody but me that I would make up one of the group.

The party broke up shortly after that. Giles helped clear the table before he left. It was obvious from the way Sean moved that his shoulder was bothering him, but when I asked about it he bit my head off so I didn't offer to give him a back rub. He herded Giles out.

I had refused Jordan's invitation to join him in the library. It wasn't my company he wanted, it was a sounding board for his theories.

Frank must have gone to the library too. Nobody had turned on the hall or stair lights and I had to fumble for the switches. Avoiding the interested eyes of John Tradescant the Younger, I trudged wearily up the stairs.

The bedspread was wrinkled and the indented pillow had a few golden hairs. I gathered them up and examined them. The root ends were considerably darker than the rest.

"Bitch," I thought, detaching the clinging strands and putting them in the wastebasket. I was referring to myself. Whatever her failings, the poor damned woman was worried sick about the kid. So was his father. When I thought of Giles going into his empty house I found it hard to feel sorry for Lindsay. Shared worry ought to bring people closer.

Sean had turned on the outside lights. I closed the drapes to shut out the glare and started to undress. I had no intention of descending the ladder that night. Even if I had been in the mood, which I wasn't, I doubted Sean would be waiting for me. He claimed he hadn't been hurt, but he had favored his right shoulder all evening, and a couple of times I had seen him wince when he moved his arm. He probably blamed me for instigating the insane expedition.

In a way it was my fault. If I hadn't put the idea into their heads . . . But cool reason, in the shape of Jennet, might have prevailed if Frank hadn't taken up the crazy scheme. His jeer at Jordan had prompted a matching macho response from the other men, none of them could back out without losing status. It was pure dumb luck that someone hadn't been seriously injured. The decapitated head might have struck Sean square in the face, the blade of the saw might have ricocheted onto him or Giles, close behind him. . . .

The only one whose actions were understandable and excusable was Giles. He was at a pitch of anxiety where he'd grasp at any straw. I pictured him alone in that empty house, waiting for the telephone to ring and hearing only silence—not even a voice or a presence to share the worry, to offer and receive comfort.

I got into bed and reached for a book—any book, anything to distract me. The one on top

of the pile was *The God of the Witches*. I threw it
onto the floor and took up the next. It was one
of the romances I had bought in town. On the
cover a raven-haired lovely lay back against a
pile of cushions, long slim legs exposed by a slit
skirt, white shoulders bared. The hero was nuz-
zling her neck. He had flowing fair hair and
more muscles than he needed for the job at
hand. The possibility of distraction looked
good. I opened the drawer of the bedside table
and fumbled for the bag of candy.

It was empty. Outraged as only a chocolate
freak can be, I got out of bed and searched the
drawer, hoping for an overlooked nugget. Had I
eaten the whole damned bag? Apparently I had,
unless Doreen had been nibbling at my supply.

Maybe she was trying to reform my food
habits. She had refilled the biscuit tin, not with
cookies but with crisp crackers coated with
some kind of seeds, and very salty. Far better for
me than chocolate, I was forced to agree. They
weren't bad.

I was well into the first seduction scene
before I realized that it wasn't just the salty biscuits that made my mouth dry; I was picturing
myself in the position of the heroine, and the
man whose hands and mouth were doing all
those interesting things had the features of Giles
Betancourt.

I threw that book aside too, and disarranged
the neat stack of books trying to find something
that wasn't scary or sensual. The only candidate

seemed to be the book on historic gardens, most of which I had already read. So, I thought, I'll read it again. After gulping down a glass of water I propped the book against my raised knees and forced myself to concentrate on . . . mazes.

By a strange coincidence, if it was a coincidence, that word was the first to catch my eye when I opened the book at random.

Topiary toys, someone has called them, sources of innocent merriment; and so they are today. I had visited the one at Hampton Court, the oldest surviving hedge maze in England. Not because I had ever been particularly interested in mazes—they weren't the sort of feature you can reasonably add to a suburban garden—but because it was there. It's a multicursal maze; there are junctions and alternative routes instead of the single winding path of the unicursal variety, and wrong choices can lead the visitor into one dead end after another. According to the custodian who admitted me, the average time for unravelling the maze is fifteen minutes. I had done it in ten, perhaps because I wasn't having fun or feeling merry.

Older mazes weren't walled by hedges, they were just patterns laid out with colored pebbles or cut into the grass; the center of the maze symbolized the goal of a seeker for truth. Paradise, in Christian times, but before then . . . what? Death and rebirth, according to some theories; retracing the path from the center took the initiate back into the world. Success, the blessing of the gods, for the youths who ran the passages of the Troy Town mazes. . . .

I was still pondering that arcane question when my door was thrown open. I was too startled to cry out. Clutching the book to my chest I stared open-mouthed at Jordan, who stared open-mouthed back at me.

"You're here!" he said.

"Where the hell did you think I was?"

"Sssh!" He edged into the room and closed the door. "Dad's gone to bed, but you'll wake him up if you yell like that."

I lowered the book. My nightgown was chastely high necked and even a woman more confident of her charms than I could not have suspected Jordan's intentions. His shirt was rumpled—and buttoned—his hair stood on end, and the dark stubble shadowing his jaw looked like sandpaper.

"I thought it was you," he went on, somewhat incoherently. "But it's not. Who is it?"

"What are you raving about?"

"There's somebody out there. I saw a light."

"Where?"

"Where do you think? Naturally I assumed you were on the prowl again." He parted the drapes and peered out. "Damned lights! Too much glare. Come on."

I scrambled out of bed and got between him and the door. "You're crazy. You can't go back into that jungle—"

"I've no intention of doing so."

"Where the hell are you going then?"

"Will you please stop shrieking? I'm going downstairs to turn off the lights, what do you suppose? Come with me or go back to bed."

I was sorely tempted to select the second alternative. It must have been later than I had realized because I was so tired my legs felt like lead. Curiosity, and the fear that he might do something stupid, moved me out of the room and along the hall. I stumbled on the stairs, catching the bannister just in time. Jordan, several steps ahead of me, didn't stop or turn around. By the time I reached the kitchen he had switched off the lights and gone out onto the terrace. He had left the door open. I stopped and leaned against it.

"I don't see anything."

"It was a moving spot of light."

I said, "Mmmf."

"Might have been a flashlight beam—diffused by the leaves, carried by someone walking through the tunnel," Jordan went on. "No trace of it now. If I hadn't wasted time debating with you . . ."

"You imagined it." That was what I meant to say. All that came out was a gurgle. I closed my eyes.

His hands closed over my shoulders in a grip hard enough to rouse me a little. I tried to push him away but my arms wouldn't move, they hung like lead weights, and when he pulled me into the kitchen my feet dragged. A light shone through my closed eyelids. I could hear voices somewhere off in the distance, but I couldn't make out what they were saying. The light brightened. I tried to close my eyes again but something was holding them—one of them?—open. Eyes and mouth. I couldn't breathe, I was choking and vomiting and making ineffectual attempts to free myself from the hands that held my arms and my head and my shoulders. Surely that added up to more than two hands?

It was my last coherent thought for some time. After a long, unpleasant interval I found myself sitting in a chair wrapped in a blanket. There was a very nasty taste in my mouth and liquid was running down my chin.

"I think she swallowed some of it," said a voice.

"Get her up and walking again," said another voice.

Two voices. "Ha," I croaked triumphantly. "Two people. Four hands. Ha."

"First sensible remark I've heard out of you," said the first voice.

"You call that sensible?" was the reply. "Open up, Heather. Drink this."

"Will it make me shrink?" I inquired.

"One never knows." The voice was Jordan's, though it was deeper and not as steady as his normal tones. "Give it a try, why don't you?"

The liquid was coffee, hot, bitter and black. I had to drink it or choke; Jordan's fingers pinched my nose shut and Sean had the cup jammed against my mouth.

"What are you doing here?" I asked, when I was able to speak.

"Came over to find out why the lights were out," Sean said. "Feeling better?"

"I feel awful."

"Get up."

"I can't. I want to lie down."

"Up," Sean repeated, and made it so. Supported by his arm I stumbled up and down, back and forth, for an endless number of hours. Then I had more coffee. Then I walked some more. And finally my head began to clear.

I pushed the fiftieth or sixtieth cup of coffee away. "I won't drink any more goddamn coffee. I'm hungry. I want a doughnut or a sandwich."

Sean put the half-empty cup down on the table, rose from his coffee-stained knees, and dropped into a chair. "Jesus," he muttered.

"A ham sandwich," I suggested. "Or some of that roast beef."

"Christ," Sean continued.

Moving slowly and carefully, as if his joints had gone stiff, Jordan got out of his chair. "Mustard or mayonnaise?"

"What was it?" Sean asked. "Crack, coke, sleeping pills?"

"What are you talking about?" I took another bite of the sandwich.

The two men exchanged glances. Sean shrugged, Jordan shook his head.

"Wait a minute," I said indistinctly. "Are you implying . . . Was that what . . . I don't take drugs! Search my room if you want. Hell, you've already searched my suitcases and my purse, you must know—"

"Calm down," Jordan said. "Or at least swallow before you choke. I don't want to have to resuscitate you a second time."

I swallowed. "God damn it!"

"Her outrage appears to be genuine," Jordan remarked. "You were the one who went through her belongings, Sean. How thorough were you?"

"I'm always thorough," Sean said. "She could have acquired it later. . . . Okay, Heather, okay. So maybe I was wrong. But it was a drug of some kind, I know the signs. If you didn't take it yourself, how did you get it?"

"I don't know."

"You haven't been nibbling on exotic plants?" Jordan asked. I glared at him.

"It wasn't in the food at dinner," Sean said. "The rest of us ate and drank the same things. Have you eaten anything since?"

"Probably," Jordan murmured.

I gave him another glare. "Only a few of those little crackers."

"What little crackers?" Sean asked.

"They're in the tin on my bedside table."

"Did you buy them?"

"No, I did not. There's always been food in

my room—fruit, cookies and crackers, fancy bottled water. I assumed it was part of the amenities," I explained.

The corners of Jordan's mouth twitched. "Did you? I have heard of such a custom, but the rest of us don't get such attention from the old man."

I drained the glass of milk that had accompanied the sandwich and picked up an overlooked piece of lettuce. They appeared to have accepted my word, but I was still indignant. "If you believed I had taken an overdose of some poisonous substance, why didn't you call a doctor? I could have died!"

"He was concerned about your reputation," Jordan said.

Sean scowled at him. "You weren't in any danger of dying. I told you, I know the symptoms—"

"Of cocaine? I won't ask how you know," I said politely. "Maybe it wasn't, though."

Sean looked a little shaken. "Maybe not. I think we'd better have a look at those mysterious crackers."

"Can I go to bed now?" I inquired.

"Are you sure you wouldn't like another sandwich?" Jordan asked.

"Well—"

His beard twitching, Sean scooped me up—or started to. The arm that had lifted my legs gave way and he returned me to the chair with a painful thump.

"I may be a little overweight," I began indignantly, "but that wasn't a very nice— Oh. You did damage that shoulder, didn't you?"

Sean unclamped his teeth. "It's just bruised. I forgot about it. You'd better carry her, Jordan."

Jordan folded his arms. "Up all those stairs? Not me."

So I walked. Jordan condescended to take my arm; his grip was as efficient and wooden as a crutch. Sean trailed after us.

"Perhaps I should look in on the old man," Jordan said casually. "It's not like him to sleep so soundly."

Sean gave him a startled glance and ran to Frank's door.

"You don't think—" I began.

"No." Jordan pushed me at the bed and picked up the tin of crackers. "Is this it?"

"Then why did you . . . Yes, that's it."

"Snoring like a buzz saw," Sean announced, returning. He took the tin from Jordan, who was prying ineffectually at the lid, and popped it open. "Hmmm. Store-bought, similar to other varieties I've seen. Are those sesame seeds?"

"More likely poppy seeds," I said.

"Opium comes from poppies," Jordan muttered.

"Don't be absurd," I sneered. "You have to stew the liquid or something to get opium. People use poppy seeds all the time on muffins and buns and rolls and things."

"You should know."

"Cut it out," Sean snapped. "I'll take these

along and have them tested, though I'll be damned if I can see how they could have been tampered with."

"You could smear them with butter or oil and then sprinkle on the seeds," Jordan said. "A lot of seeds are poisonous."

"What about the fruit?" Sean picked up a withered, brown banana peel.

"I ate that this morning," I said. "And an apple—yes, that's the core."

"And an orange?" Jordan inquired, exhibiting part of the peel. His voice sounded peculiar.

"I like fruit. Fruit is good for people."

"She'd have felt the effects earlier if it was in the fruit," Sean said.

"How could someone poison a piece of fruit?" Jordan demanded. "Dip an apple in the brew, like the witch in Snow White?"

"Hypodermic?"

"Don't be an idiot."

They appeared to be enjoying their investigation so much that they had forgotten about the victim. I wanted to go to bed. I ached all over, as if somebody had been pummelling me. Come to think of it, somebody probably had. I picked up the empty water bottle and headed for the bathroom.

The sound of running water apparently reminded them of my presence. "What are you doing?" Jordan asked, coming to the door.

"Getting some water. I'd like to take a shower, or at least change my nightgown if you'll go away and allow me a little privacy."

I shut the door in his face. When I came out, they had gone. The tin of crackers and the fruit bowl had gone too. I went to bed.

And dreamed, of course. Not about the witches; it was the old familiar dream of danger, but the characters as well as the plot had changed. He was smiling at me, his eyes shining and his hair gilded by the sunlight, unaware of the thing that was coming up behind him. White marble, stained and streaked, hooved feet thudding, broken arms reaching for . . . Not my father.

I fought to free myself from the invisible bonds that held me, and then I was awake, struggling in the dark against arms that bruised my ribs. Warm, real human arms.

"Giles," I gurgled.

"Sorry, but no." He lowered me onto the pillow and pulled the blanket up over me. "You were dreaming. Go back to sleep."

"I need a tissue."

"Definitely. Here." He put it in my hand. I wiped my wet cheeks and blew my nose. He'd been sitting on the bed. It lifted when he stood up, and I started to babble. I didn't want him to go away and leave me alone.

"I'm sorry. Did I wake everybody up? Did I make a lot of noise?"

"No." He hesitated for a moment. "I was already here."

"That was nice of you."

"I relieved Sean about half an hour ago,"

Jordan said coolly. "We agreed it was advisable for someone to keep an eye on you tonight."

"Oh. Thank you."

"Go back to sleep."

"I can't." I didn't want to. A slit of light caught my eye. "Is it morning?"

"Seven o'clock." A hint of amusement softened his voice. "I suppose you want breakfast."

"I wouldn't want you to go to any trouble on my account. I can wait. Believe it or not."

"How about a cup of coffee, then?"

"Well . . ."

He moved to the window and opened the drapes. I blinked in the light. The sky was blue; it was a lovely day.

Jordan filled a cup and brought it to me. I pushed the pillows into a pile and sat up.

"Now that you are relatively compos mentis," he said, settling into a chair, "I'd like to ask a favor. Don't tell my father about this."

"Why not?" The coffee was black and unsweetened, but I drank it anyway. My head still felt fuzzy.

"He enjoys dramatizing things. If you didn't take some unorthodox substance yourself—"

"Give me a break. I'll bet you boys had another look around last night while I was dead to the world. You didn't find any drugs, did you?"

"Yes, we did, and no, we didn't. Kindly allow me to finish my syllogism. If you didn't take it, there are only three possibilities: some unknown enemy is after you, or you accidentally partook of something mildly poisonous, or you were just plain sick. Could have been a virus, or an allergic reaction, or even food poisoning."

I thought about it, sipping my coffee. "Obviously you don't believe I have an unknown enemy."

"Do you?"

"No name comes to mind," I admitted.

Jordan stretched out a long arm and took the cup. "We'll have to take turns, I only have one. What about your fiancé? Is he the jealous type?"

"Who? Oh—uh—DeWitt?" I laughed. The idea of DeWitt consumed by mad passion, pursuing me halfway across the world, was too hilarious. "He's not my fiancé, I never said I'd marry him. Anyhow, who would he be jealous of?"

"I am simply eliminating possibilities, however far out," Jordan said. His voice absolutely dripped icicles. "How much money did you inherit? Who would get it if you died?"

"You're a real chip off the old block, you know that?" I said, feeling my cheeks redden. "Frank couldn't have put it more bluntly. Since you ask, the money came from an insurance policy. One million bucks. She made him take it out. The premiums cost the earth. There was nothing left for anything he wanted—travel, clothes, tuition for me at a good college. She expected to outlive him. She probably would have if she hadn't insisted he drive her to the

mall that day when the roads were icy and he
wasn't feeling well, and . . . It was wonderfully
ironic, when you think about it."

"Stop it." If he'd sounded sympathetic I
would have broken down. The curt command
and cold voice had the same effect as a slap. He
filled the cup again and handed it to me. "So
that's it. I wondered."

"That's what?"

"That's why you've been so irrationally ob-
sessed with your father's death. It's not grief and
loss, it's anger and hatred. You blame her—"

"Shut up!" If he had been closer I would have
hit him—or tried to. Since he was out of reach I
clenched my fists and shook them. "How dare
you sit there looking smug and spouting cheap
psychoanalysis at me? You're a fine one to talk
about irrational obsessions, and blame, and
anger—over a man whose death resulted from
his own arrogant stupidity—"

"That's enough." His voice was low but not
soft; it had an edge like a piece of broken glass.
He was as white as a man of his complexion
could get, and his breathing was quick and
uneven. We stared at one another in silence,
while he fought to control his temper and I
tried to decide whether it was fury or shame
that made me feel so awful.

"Let's call it a draw," Jordan said finally. The
color had returned to his face. "Now, as I was
saying. Who would inherit if you died?"

"You're absolutely inhuman," I informed him.

"And you're way off the track besides. I made a will. My lawyer insisted on it. I left everything to an animal shelter."

"Scratch that motive, then," Jordan said, not visibly moved by my insults.

"Scratch all of them. You may enjoy these little intellectual exercises, but I don't, and they aren't necessary. I see your point. Eliminate all other possibilities and the one remaining, however improbable, must be the truth. It was an accident."

Jordan glanced at the window. "There's somebody at the back door. Must be Mrs. Greenspan, smack on time and undoubtedly rabid with curiosity."

"Oh, Lord," I said in alarm, remembering certain of the nastier effects of my—accident. "Did either of you clean the kitchen?"

"Not to say clean." Jordan stood up, stretching. "But I did scrub the sink. Breakfast will be ready shortly, you'd better hurry and get dressed if you want to be first at the trough."

"You have such a graceful way of putting things." I got out of bed. There didn't seem to be any point in being modest with a man who had held my head while I threw up. My slippers weren't in sight. I knelt and rummaged under the bed.

My exclamation stopped Jordan on his way to the door. "Now what?" he demanded.

Mutely I held out the object I had found on the floor, concealed by the ruffled bedskirt. It was not a slipper. It was a crude clay figure about four inches long, roughly modelled and featureless, but unquestionably intended to represent a human form. I knew who it was meant to represent, and what it was.

And so did Jordan. The look on his face was a dead giveaway.

NINE

*Like every other defunct mode, the topiary
labyrinth is liable to temporary revivals by
lovers of the antique, but there is little reason to
hope or to fear that it will ever again secure a
position of any dominance in the affections of
the gardener.*

MATTHEWS, MAZES AND LABYRINTHS, 1922

My first impulse was to throw on whatever garments came to hand and rush into town. A telephone call wasn't good enough, I wanted to confront her face to face.

Then I remembered that Giles meant to have another go at the jungle that morning. If he had changed his mind after hearing that a boy of Bobby's description had been traced to Birmingham, he had not mentioned it to me, and I wasn't about to let him tackle the job alone.

He was in the dining room with the others when I arrived, and his face lit up when he saw me, ready for action in work clothes and heavy shoes. "I might have known you'd be game," he said approvingly. "But the expedition is cancelled, Heather. There's no need to look there now."

He held a chair for me, so I had to sit down. Jordan, loading his plate at the sideboard, gave me a knowing look. "Do let me get you a little something to go on with," he said. "A few pounds of bacon and a half dozen croissants, perhaps."

I turned my back pointedly and returned Giles's smile. "You've found him?"

"Not yet, but we've heard from him. His grandmother found the note this morning. It had been slid under the front door."

"He's somewhere in the neighborhood, then?"

A plate of croissants appeared in front of me. "Marmalade?" Jordan inquired politely, offering the jar.

Frank spoke for the first time. "Jordan, if you can't stop behaving like a six year old leave the room. Get yourself something to eat, Giles, and tell Heather—and me, of course—all about it."

Giles hadn't seen the note, but he could practically recite it by heart. "He said he'd been hiding in a secret place. Yesterday he found someone—he didn't mention names—who agreed to take him to Birmingham. He told his mother not to worry, he'd call or write in a few days."

"Thoughtful of him to reassure her," Jordan murmured.

"He'll telephone when he runs out of money," Frank said. "This whole stunt is blackmail pure and simple, Giles. I hope you aren't going to give in."

"For heaven's sake, Frank, that's hardly the issue now," I snapped. "At least he was safe until yesterday, and surely the police can locate the person who took him to Birmingham. The secret place must be the wilderness. He ripped his sweater crawling through, and the cat found the piece of yarn. Damn that woman, she lied to me!"

"What woman?" Giles asked curiously.

"Oh, well, maybe she didn't know."

"Then the boy who was seen in Birmingham wasn't Bob?" Jordan frowned. "He couldn't have left the note until late last night after everyone had gone to bed, so he was still in the area yesterday."

"That was only one of several false leads," Giles said. He jumped up and held my chair again. "I'd better be off. I didn't mean to intrude, but I thought you'd want to know at once."

"Of course," I said. "Don't rush off, Giles, you haven't eaten anything."

"That's kind." He smiled at me. "But I had a bite before I left home, and I want to question some of his chums again. They all denied knowing anything, but now I have a bit more to go on."

He went out through the kitchen, and I heard Doreen's voice raised in interested inquiry before the kitchen door closed in its turn.

"Damn," I said. "I could have bummed a ride into town with him."

"Finish your breakfast," Frank said. "You can go in with Sean; he's supposed to pick Mr. Barnsley up at nine. What do you want in the village?"

"Toothpaste." It was the first thing that came to my mind.

"Sean can get it for you."

"He can't get the other things I want," I said. "You're going ahead with the landscaping, then?"

Frank abandoned the interrogation. He probably thought I was referring to embarrassing female needs.

"Barnsley's time is limited, he has other engagements. Now that we are reassured about the child there is no reason why we shouldn't proceed, is there?"

I couldn't think of one. In fact, there were several reasons why I was looking forward to hearing Mr. Barnsley's views on old gardens.

Jordan was watching me with an expression that could only be called enigmatic. He had known what the image signified, but he had refused to discuss it, saying only, "Someone's playing silly games. One of the cleaning teenagers, probably."

It wouldn't have surprised me to learn that a number of local women played around with magic, and not because they were superstitious rural types; shops like Jennet's did a thriving business in cities like New York and London. But if the girls had put the clay image under my bed, they must have been following someone else's orders. They had no reason to dislike me, and the image was intended to do harm to the person it represented.

Frank appeared a trifle preoccupied; even his insults hadn't been up to the usual standard. I felt certain he would have referred to my bout of sickness if he had known about it. Apparently Sean and Jordan had succeeded in cleaning the kitchen.

Not well enough to deceive Doreen and Mrs. Greenspan, though. When I went through the kitchen on my way out, the cook gave me a curious look but left it to Doreen to ask the questions.

"What were you all up to last night?" she demanded. "The place looked like you'd thrown a party."

"Sorry. I guess we did make a mess." Frank would have left it at that. In fact, he wouldn't have said that much. That's what servants were for, to clean up messes; he wouldn't have apologized or explained. I shuffled my feet and went on, "We—uh—some of us—decided to have a snack and some coffee and—uh—we got to talking." And then, because I am a damned fool and a moral coward, I added, "I went to bed first and left them—uh—talking. You know men, their idea of cleaning a room is somewhat primitive."

"Sean is usually pretty good about picking up after himself," Doreen said.

"Is he? Oh, well, I suppose he was tired. I'd better hurry if I want to catch him."

I beat a quick retreat before I dug myself in deeper. A woman with an ear for gossip, which Doreen had, could find all sorts of interesting ideas in my stumbles and stammers.

Sean had backed the car out. He was giving it a last loving polish when I reached the garage.

"You treat that car like a baby," I said.

"Good morning to you, too." He tossed the cloth aside and came to me, taking my hands in his. "How do you feel?"

"Fine. Thanks for last night."

"Looking for somebody?" He wasn't speaking to me.

"Excuse me," Doreen said. "Cook wanted to know if Miss Tradescant will be back for lunch. Excuse me. I didn't mean to interrupt."

I mumbled something in the nature of an affirmative reply and heard her footsteps retreat. I hadn't heard her coming.

Sean had found the exchange highly entertaining. He knew enough about women to interpret Doreen's cool voice and exaggerated apologies correctly. She must have heard me thank him "for last night."

"Coming with me?" he asked, squeezing my hands.

"I have an errand in the village." My tone was as frosty as Doreen's.

"Hop in then. I'll be with you in a minute."

As I fingered the rough clay in my jacket pocket it occurred to me that the teenagers weren't the only suspects. Doreen was an even more likely prospect; she had opportunity, means and motive. I had suspected she was interested in Sean, and if she considered me a rival for his affections—all-inclusive though they seemed to be—she might not think it was wrong to cripple me a little.

Sean had gone into the garage. I took the doll out and examined it.

It didn't look like me. At least I hoped not. It resembled the gingerbread men people bake for children, the arms and legs stiff, the face a flat oval, but it was definitely female. Two insultingly small blobs of clay indicated breasts. The body had been pierced in three places, not by nails or pins but by thorns, driven deeply into the clay. One at the shoulder, one at the foot, and the third straight into the center of the body.

I had read enough of the books I had bought from Jennet to have a vague idea of the underlying logic of magic, if you could call it logic. There were only a few basic types. Charms to protect and cure, charms to hold or win a lover—and this one, meant to harm or kill. The little dolls, or poppets, as they were sometimes called, could be constructed of various materials, including cloth or wood or straw. The Pendle witches had modelled them of clay. The important thing was that the image represented a particular person. If Doreen had pushed the thorns into the poppet she hoped to cripple me more than just a little, and she could have made sure the magic would work by adding something nasty to the water.

"What's that?" Sean was at my window.

I returned the image to my pocket. "Nothing. Aren't you going to be late?"

"It's only a ten-minute drive." He tossed a paper sack into the car and got in. "Did you say anything to the old man about last night?"

"I didn't say anything to anybody. Jordan thinks it was food poisoning or a simple digestive upset."

"He could be right. You're a hearty eater."

"A pig, you mean."

"Not at all. I don't like skinny women."

"Oh, stop it," I said irritably.

Sean laughed. "Back to business, then. It may be a waste of time, but I want someone to have a look at those crackers, especially the seeds. I figured I'd ask Frank's doctor. If he can't test them he'll know who can."

"What are you going to tell him?"

"Don't worry, I won't mention you. I'll invent some likely story."

I felt certain he could.

Cruising slowly along the high street in search of a parking place, he asked whether I had come along for the ride or whether he should drop me somewhere. I said I'd go back

with him if he didn't mind waiting for a few
minutes.

After he had gone into the hotel I went to the
shop and found, as I ought to have expected, that
it wasn't due to open until ten-thirty. I banged on
the door a few times, partly from frustration,
partly in the hope that Jennet was at her desk. If
she was, she didn't respond. I was passing the
restaurant on my way back to the hotel, when I
remembered something Jennet had said.

She was in the restaurant. Giles wasn't—but she
was expecting, or hoping, he would be. She lowered the newspaper she had been reading when I
reached her table and her welcoming smile froze
when she saw it was me. Her greeting was perfectly polite but less than enthusiastic.

"Good morning, Heather. What are you doing
out so early?"

I was in a hurry and I was mad all over again.
I took the doll out of my pocket and slammed it
down on the table.

For once I succeeded in making her lose control. Her eyes widened and her hands flew out,
covering and then cradling the little image.
"Don't handle it so roughly!"

"If I break it my arms and legs will fall off?"

"You know what it is?"

"I've been doing my homework. The books I
bought the other day were very helpful. I don't
know why you're doing this, Jennet, but you're
wasting your time. It only works if people
believe in it. I don't believe in it."

Shielding the thing with one hand, she bent closer to examine it more carefully. Her fingertip moved from the thorn that had pierced the shoulder to the one in the foot. "Where—" she began, and then stopped with an audible gulp, looking up over my shoulder and cupping protective hands over the doll.

"Good morning," Giles said, with a deprecating little laugh. "You must think I'm following you, Heather."

"Not at all," I said stupidly.

"You've told Jennet? About the note?"

I said, "Uh . . . no, I hadn't gotten around to that."

"I already knew." Jennet's polite social smile was back in place. Deftly as a conjurer she slid the image off the table onto her lap and concealed it under her napkin. "But it was good of you—both of you—to come round and tell me. A pity we didn't know this last night, before that insane expedition."

Giles looked grave. "Yes. I'm glad Sean wasn't hurt. Bob is still missing, but at least we know he was alive and well as recently as last night. Are you joining us for breakfast, Heather?"

Considering that he had just watched me stow away enough food for two grown men, I thought it was a very tactful question. "No, Sean is waiting for me. We came in to get Mr. Barnsley."

Jennet's expression dared me to say more. When I ignored the challenge she indicated the napkin-wrapped object in her lap. "I'll take charge of this for you, shall I?"

"I certainly don't want it back. Goodbye again, Giles."

"I may drop by later this afternoon," Jennet said. "I'll be interested to hear what Mr. Barnsley has to say about the gardens."

I couldn't express myself candidly, so I tried subtle sarcasm. "I'm sure Frank would be tickled to death if you came to tea. You too, of course, Giles."

Sean and Barnsley were waiting in front of the hotel. He brushed my apologies aside. "Not at all, not at all, I was late myself and it is a lovely warm morning; I was enjoying the fresh air and the charming ambience. Is this your first visit to Lancashire, Miss Tradescant . . . ah, if you insist—Heather. Most kind. Please call me Terry. Mr. Karim assured me I might take advantage of you today—in the way of assistance, I mean, of course. I hope that is all right with you? My usual assistant is ill, one of those spring viruses, so she was unable to accompany me, and I would be very grateful. . . ."

"I'll be happy to carry your briefcase and hand you your pencils," I said, when he paused for breath. "But don't expect anything in the way of professional assistance. I'm a rank amateur."

He brushed my modest, and honest, demurral aside. Frank wasn't the only one who seemed to believe anyone bearing the hallowed name of Tradescant must have inherited talent.

I learned more from that fussy little man in one day than I could have learned from a dozen books. Hands-on experience, as they say. He loved to talk, and once he had gotten it through his head that I was as ignorant as I had claimed, he lectured unceasingly. The experience didn't convince me that I wanted to make a career of garden restoration, but it made me realize I'd be a fool to pass up the chance of participating in this particular job. I even forgot, for a few hours, that there was any other reason for wanting to remain.

After I saw Terry's tool kit I wondered if it had been my muscles rather than my presumed expertise that made him ask for my assistance. He did have a briefcase and a lot of pencils. He also had stakes, bottles and jars and envelopes for samples, probes and trowels for digging. I forget what else, but there was a lot of it and it was heavy, especially after he had also acquired a few tools from the garden shed.

He had already studied the plans and preliminary surveys, the plant lists and drawings Frank had sent him, and he led us straight out into the garden, explaining that the morning light might show up features that would be difficult to see otherwise. I couldn't see any. Sometimes I couldn't see them even when he pointed them out. He knew exactly where to look. He must have memorized the plan, he hardly ever referred to it.

By the end of the morning there were colored

stakes all over the place, marking off areas to be excavated or cleared, and careful digging (by me) had brought to light a low, weathered stretch of stone that had faced a terrace wall. I held one end of the tape while Terry measured along a line invisible to my eyes and poked in another stake.

"The corner should be hereabouts," he announced. "We'll have a look after luncheon. If I may have the use of a lavatory? . . ."

Frank beamed approval. He liked a man who knew his own mind, and he was obviously impressed. He escorted Terry to his room and I made use of my own lavatory. I needed it more than Terry did; I had done most of the digging. When I went downstairs I found them already at the table. Frank was asking about aerial photographs.

"Not at this time of year" was the dogmatic reply.

"But I've seen photographs of buried gardens that show almost as much detail as an actual drawing," I said, reaching for the bread. "The shape of parterres and buried terraces and even paths."

"Parchmarks," said Terry. "Yes, but they are most visible in grassy areas after long periods of drought. Oblique lighting will serve our purpose just as well. I'll have another look late this afternoon, when the sun is low, and we might try shining automobile headlights across the lawn at night."

"Great idea," Frank said. "That method was used at Monticello, wasn't it?"

Terry nodded, being unable to speak with his mouth full.

"I don't know why you need lights," I said. "You've found so much already."

Terry patted his lips with a napkin. "My dear, we've barely begun. The plotting I've done is only an educated guess; it will require excavation to confirm the layout. The East Garden, the orchard and the maze are yet to be investigated."

Jordan wandered in, looking even vaguer than usual. "Hello, Mr. Barnsley. Sorry I'm late."

"We didn't wait for you," his father said.

"I noticed. Pass the ham, will you, Heather?"

I passed the ham. Also the mayonnaise and mustard.

"How's it going?" Jordan asked.

"Quite well, no thanks to you." Frank was back in form. "You might have offered to give us a hand instead of letting poor Heather do all the work. Her back must be killing her."

Terry looked stricken. "Oh, I say," he began.

"Knock it off, Frank," I said. "My back feels fine and I've enjoyed every minute of it. I'd have fought for the privilege."

"You won't have to fight with Jordan," said Frank.

"Damn right," Jordan agreed. "I'll emulate my esteemed father and watch while Heather does all the work."

"Oh, are you joining us?" I inquired.

"I might. Later."

"And how is your work going?"

"Nice of you to ask. Quite well, actually. I've found some new material."

Frank's ears pricked visibly. "In those papers of Giles's?"

"No," Jordan said.

Frank announced that it was time we went back to work and Terry rose obediently. I went with them before Jordan could make some crack about how little I had eaten.

As we went through the kitchen Frank said, "You'd better plan on staying for supper, Terry. We can try the car lights tonight."

He nodded at Mrs. Greenspan to make sure she had heard and I said self-consciously, "Oh, gosh, I almost forgot. I hope you don't mind, Frank. I asked Jennet and Giles to come to tea."

"Not at all," Frank said. "I'm glad you feel enough at home here to issue invitations."

"Jennet invited herself, actually. And Giles was there, so I thought it would be rude if I didn't ask him too."

"Quite right. Poor Giles needs our support and sympathy just now."

By the time we had finished plotting the lines of the terrace my back was beginning to ache. Jordan had joined us. He didn't offer to help, he just stood looking on, his hands in his pockets. Finally he broke a long silence—his own, Terry had been lecturing steadily—to ask, "Are you going to have a look at the wilderness?"

"There was no . . . Oh." Terry glanced in the direction he had indicated. "You are giving the word its common usage. In gardening terminology a 'wilderness' was not wild at all; it was carefully designed, with rows of trees and, later, informal plantings of various kinds. There is no wilderness shown on the plans of this garden."

"Then what's that?" Jordan asked.

Terry looked pleased. Here was a fresh audience, even more ignorant than the people he had lectured all morning. "It is certainly wild. If I am not mistaken it occupies the site of the former maze. We can have a look if you like; I had planned to do so."

We strolled across the lawn, pausing to admire the ancient oak tree. "It is a holm oak," Terry explained to Jordan, who had not asked. "As I told Mr. Karim and Heather this morning, it is one of the most extraordinary features of the garden—as large or larger than the one at Westbury Court, which I had believed to be the oldest in England. Three hundred years, my dear fellow, at least!"

"Fascinating," Jordan said in a bored voice.

"As for this—er—jungle," Terry continued. "The only thing I find puzzling about it is why it exists at all. The rest of the grounds have been kept fairly clear. No doubt as the family fortunes declined the formal gardens were abandoned as unproductive and difficult to maintain, and the area was used for vegetables and other practical purposes. If it had not been constantly cultivated, the whole area would resemble this." He indicated the thorny hedge.

"It would?"

"Dear me, yes." Jordan's question had reinforced his impression that he was in more need of education than I and Frank. He decided to start with the basic. "A plant requires three things—sunshine, water and nutrients. I simplify, of course—"

"Please do," said Jordan.

"Well, then, in the simplest possible terms, any plant, if uncontrolled and undamaged, will grow to fill the space available to it. The fitter survive by crowding out the weaker, cutting them off from the light necessary for photosynthesis, and monopolizing the supply of food. I well remember my first sight of the garden of Pitheath—one of my earliest and most challenging jobs. A solid mass of blackberries, fallen trees and saplings, higher than my head and a good two acres in extent!"

"Goodness!" I said, since he obviously expected admiration and awe and he obviously wasn't going to get it from Jordan.

"It was a daunting sight, my dear. However, a wilderness—I use the word in the common sense—like that is easier to deal with than an area in which some valuable plantings have survived."

"You mean you just whack it all down," I said.

"Well, er—yes, in a nutshell. There is obviously nothing here worth preserving."

"How do you know?" Jordan demanded.

"What could there be?" The little man sounded huffy; he had recognized the remark for what it was, not a request for information but a challenge. "This was unquestionably the site of the maze. Mr. Fallon's plant lists suggest that the material used for bordering the paths was yew. The plants would have died out centuries ago."

"What about the maze at Hampton Court?" Jordan asked. "It's as old as this one."

"That is a different case entirely. The Hampton Court maze has been constantly maintained, and even with such care there is very little left of the original hornbeam of the hedges. They have been patched and replanted with boxwood, privet, yew, and other shrubs. Historically the place is of great interest, but aesthetically . . ." He shook his head disapprovingly.

"So there would be no possibility of tracing the original pattern of the paths?" Jordan persisted. "Differences in elevation, even slight ones—traces of gravel or paving stones?"

"Hmmm." Terry looked thoughtfully. "It is an intriguing idea. The chance would be slight, I believe, but to the best of my knowledge such a project has never been attempted. I wonder . . ."

Frank broke in. "I don't know why this sudden interest in a subject that has never concerned you, Jordan, but if you want information go to the library and do some basic reading. I am not employing Mr. Barnsley to instruct the ignorant."

Nice little Terry tried to smooth things over. "Your son has raised an interesting point, Mr. Karim. I had intended to have a closer look at this area anyhow. If you have a chain saw we might see what's there."

"I told Sean to buy a new one," Frank said. "Where the devil is he? He ought to be helping. Heather, go get him, I'll look in the garden shed. Jordan—"

"I'm going to do my basic reading."

We scattered in three different directions and Terry strode briskly toward the hedge, drawing on a pair of heavy gloves. I heard him cry out and spun around. He was sprawled facedown on the grass.

My feet felt as if they were rooted to the ground. I was the first to move, though, and even before I reached him Terry had rolled over and raised himself on his elbow. Breathless with relief and haste, I had almost reached him when he put out a peremptory hand.

"Watch where you step, Heather, there's something under the grass. I tripped over it."

He had done more than trip. His pant leg was ripped and blood trickled from a cut across his shin.

"How bad is it?" Frank asked.

"Not bad, not bad at all. Just a cut. I've had

worse. Clumsy of me; I ought to have looked where I was going."

I had been fumbling in my pockets in a vain search for a piece of cloth clean enough to be used as a temporary bandage. Jordan handed me his handkerchief and bent over to pluck something from the ground.

"Scissors."

"Secateurs," I corrected automatically. "Someone must have forgotten them."

"They haven't been there long," Jordan said. "No rust." He ran his finger lightly along the opened blades.

"Watch it," I said, a little too late. "Will keeps his tools well sharpened."

Jordan wiped the streak of blood off on his pants. "He wouldn't leave them lying around, then, would he? Are you the culprit?"

Before I could voice an indignant denial Frank said, "Will may be the world's neatest gardener but everybody has memory lapses from time to time. Stop wasting time on academic discussions, Jordan, and help Terry to the house. Sean can take him to a doctor."

"No, no, there's no need." Terry got unassisted to his feet. "Soap and water and a bit of Elastoplast and I'll be good as new."

With an irritated glance at his son, who showed no signs of moving, Frank said, "I'll show you. Heather, get the chain saw."

I took the secateurs from Jordan, who was squinting at them as if he had never seen such a tool. Maybe he hadn't. "I'll put them back in the shed."

"I suppose they all look alike," Jordan said. He sounded as if he were talking to himself, so I didn't reply. It was a stupid question anyhow.

Or maybe the question wasn't stupid. It was pure coincidence that two landscapers should suffer an accident—mercifully slight, in this case—near the hedge, and another coincidence that Terry's path had crossed the spot where the clippers had laid. But that spot was on the direct line I had followed on my morning run.

I touched the point of the blade with a gingerly finger. It was razor sharp, but how much damage could it have done, if I had tripped over it or even stepped on it? No one could count on my foot coming down on that precise spot; an inch or two in either direction would leave me unscathed.

Unbidden and unwelcome, the memory of something I had recently read came back to me: "To cause an enemy to cut himself. Smear the blade of the knife with his blood or other body fluid, and repeat the following words . . ." I couldn't remember the words. Something about darkness swallowing the sun, and blood calling to blood, and a litany of unfamiliar names— those of evil spirits, I presume.

Sean, or somebody, had bought another chain saw. It took me a while to get it in running order; when I returned to the hedge Frank and Terry were waiting. The latter seemed none the worse for wear, but when I offered to wield the saw he didn't object, except to warn me to be careful. I didn't need a warning. I hate to admit it, but I had wiped the blade with a cloth before I picked up the saw.

The roar of the motor brought Sean out from wherever he had been—washing the car, probably. I refused his offer to take over, and Terry was kind enough to approve my efforts.

"You're doing a splendid job, Heather. A certain delicacy of touch is required, odd as that may sound when applied to a tool of this sort. . . . Over here, if you will, please."

He called a halt to the proceedings before my arms tired. "Yes, it is as I had expected. There's no sign of anything except brambles and scrub trees. Quite a tangle, I must say! There's nothing for it, Mr. Karim, but to—er—hack it down."

"The whole thing?" Sean asked, raising his eyebrows.

"With the proper equipment and a trained crew it won't be such an undertaking as you may suppose," Terry said reassuringly. "I can recommend several firms who specialize in this sort of thing."

"I'll have to think it over," Frank said. "How long will it be before you can start on the terraces?"

"My dear chap, you haven't even seen my preliminary estimate." Terry laughed gaily. "I'll start working on it as soon as I get back to my office. If you approve it . . . well, I really can't give you a definite date until I've found out who is available and what their schedules are. Then there's the question of—"

"Don't tell me what you have to do, just do it. I'll pay whatever it takes to get the job done in a hurry."

Even I wouldn't have made an ingenuous offer like that to a person I planned to hire. On the other hand, Karim's reputation was such that only a fool would try to take advantage of him. What surprised me most was his urgency. He had sat on his hands for over six months without taking action, now he was hellbent to get on with the job. Maybe he had been waiting for an omen. Maybe I was it.

Devout people often begin a new, important enterprise with prayer. The old gods—the dead gods, as Frank had called them—demanded more than words in exchange for good luck. The word *sacrifice* came to mind.

Also the word *idiot*. I shouldn't have read those books about the history of magic. Obviously I was more susceptible to suggestion than I had realized.

And maybe I wasn't the only one.

At 4 P.M. precisely Terry asked if someone could drive him back to the hotel. "I believe you said you were expecting guests for tea, Mr. Hakim. I would like to freshen up and change clothing."

"Certainly. Sean will take you in and wait for you." He turned a fond but critical eye on me. "You could do with a change of clothing too, Heather. Make yourself beautiful."

Making myself beautiful was beyond my powers, but I needed freshening more than Terry did. Since I didn't want to trail dirt and grass through Mrs. Greenspan's nice clean kitchen I went in the side door.

There was no avoiding Doreen, though. She must have been watching from the kitchen window. I had stripped down to my underwear when I heard the knock on the door.

"It's me," she called.

"I figured. What do you want?"

Taking this for an invitation to enter, which it had not been, she opened the door. "I thought you might need fresh towels."

I reached for my robe. I'm not overly self-conscious, but my body isn't designed for public display. "Why do you always come when I'm undressing? Are you looking for witchmarks or something?"

She looked as if I had hit her. "I didn't think . . . I wasn't . . ."

"I was kidding. I've got all the towels I need. What do you really want?"

"I—um—I was just going to apologize about this morning."

"For what, interrupting a romantic tête-à-tête? Come on, Doreen, you know perfectly well Sean hasn't the slightest interest in me or I in him."

"Then what . . . None of my business, I guess."

"No." I softened the curt word with a smile. I had come around to considering Jennet my leading suspect but there was no harm in making it clear to Doreen that I was a friend, not a rival.

Visibly relieved, she smiled back at me. "Are you going to wear that gorgeous frock?"

"What for? Lindsay isn't coming. What I would like," I said pointedly, "is some privacy so I can shower and change into plain ordinary clean pants and shirt. We'll probably get in some more work this evening."

"Okay. I'll take these along to the laundry. You ought to buy more clothes, Heather, you've only got just the one pretty frock and the way you get things mucked up with that digging and all, you should have . . . Okay, okay, I'm going!"

Now why, I wondered, had I made that inane comment about witchmarks? I had witchcraft on the brain these days.

I stepped into the shower, and as the water washed off the sweat and stains I scrutinized my body with detached curiosity. I had several moles in various places, and a small reddish birthmark on my left wrist. Moles could be witchmarks. So could any other unusual, or even usual, excrescence, reddening or bruise, if the witchhunters so determined. The most damning physical mark was an extra nipple—obviously the place where the witch suckled her diabolic familiar.

Quite a few people, male and female, have supernumerary nipples. It's a recognized medical condition, called polythely. It wasn't recognized in the seventeenth century, though. God help the poor woman who was born with one of them; she must have lived all her life in a cold sweat of terror, praying she would never come under suspicion. Or, believing herself already damned by the mere possession of that sign, she might turn to the forbidden worship.

If the hunters failed to find a visible witch-mark they could locate an invisible one—a deadened spot impervious to pain. In her museum Jennet had one of the needles witch-hunters used for that purpose—steel probes really. One example had a retractable point, like a stage dagger. A "witch" touched by that device wouldn't feel anything, and if the man wielding the thing did it deftly enough, the witnesses wouldn't notice the trick. Experimentally I pinched a fold of skin between my fingers. It hurt.

After that morbid excursion into superstition I had to hurry to get dressed. Doreen was right about one thing, I could use a few more changes of clothing, but not from Jennet's overpriced, over-elaborate stock. I'd have to make a trip to a larger town. That was what I needed, city streets and boring familiar chain stores like the ones back home. The atmosphere of Malkin and environs was getting to me.

Doreen and I were friends again; she graciously allowed me to carry a tray, and we discussed shopping possibilities as we went to the table under the oak. Frank was already there. So was the cat, coolly occupying the second chair. The two of them were staring at one another, and it would have been hard to say which looked more suspicious.

"Give it its tea," Frank said out of the corner of his mouth.

"I don't know why you're so uptight about him," Doreen scolded. "Here, you give him the saucer of milk."

Frank shied back. "No, no."

I took the saucer from Doreen and put it down on the grass, several feet away. The cat went to it and Frank let out his breath.

"I don't wish it any harm," he said loudly. "It is welcome here."

Chuckling, Doreen went back to the house and I sat down. "I'm surprised at you, Frank. I thought you feared neither man nor beast."

"That is not an ordinary cat. It is—"

"Yeah, yeah, I know. Here's Terry. Is he limping?"

He was, but he denied anything except slight discomfort. "In our profession we are accustomed to bumps and bruises. You should speak to your gardener though, warn him to be more careful where he leaves his tools."

"I hardly ever see him," Frank grunted. "I don't know what the devil I'm paying him for, he shows up once in a blue moon and—ah, there is Jennet. Good evening, my dear."

"What are you complaining about now?" she asked, distributing a smile and a nod between me and Terry.

"The gardener, whatever his name is. You were the one who recommended him, Jennet, why didn't you warn me he is so lazy?"

"He needs the money," Jennet said coolly. "Not many people can afford gardeners these days. Don't be such a skinflint, Frank, you can well afford it." She turned, studying the rows of painted stakes. "You have been busy. Any exciting discoveries?"

Terry launched into a lecture. Doreen returned with trays of canapés and the teapot, which she placed in front of me.

"You pour," I said to Jennet. "I'll watch you."

She acknowledged my not-so-subtle jibe with a slight smile.

I wasn't watching for Giles, I just happened to be the first to see him. I could tell by his face he hadn't heard anything, so I didn't ask and for once, probably because he wasn't particularly interested, Frank didn't pose the question either. Terry picked up the lecture where he had been interrupted, but he didn't get far; seeing Jordan sauntering toward us, Frank had to make a rude remark.

"What an unexpected honor! I dare not assume it is on our account that you joined us; are you expecting someone else?"

Jordan wisely ignored this, and Giles got Frank off the track with a question about the garden. Terry was happily holding forth when Sean joined us. He had come from the kitchen and he was carrying a basket, which he put on the table. The basket contained crackers—round, crimped around the edges, sprinkled with small black seeds.

With a meaningful look at me Sean took a cracker and bit into it.

"What are those?" Frank asked.

"Crackers." Sean popped the rest of it into his mouth and chewed with apparent relish. "They're good. Try one."

Frank curled a fastidious lip. "Some common commercial brand, I presume. I prefer Mrs. Greenspan's excellent little sandwiches."

Sean passed the basket around. Giles and Terry were the only takers, probably because they were too polite to refuse.

"They look vile, Sean," Jennet said with a smile. "If you like mass-produced junk, you should stick to your favorite pretzels and chips."

"They have an interesting flavor." Sean took another cracker. "Maybe it's these little black things, whatever they are."

He thrust the basket at Jennet. She shook her head. "They look like poppy seeds. Wasn't there a list of ingredients on the packet?"

"Why the devil are we carrying on a conversation about crackers?" Frank demanded. "You said you wanted to have another look around at sunset, Terry."

Giles put his cup in the saucer. "It's time I was—"

"Don't be so damned sensitive," Frank snapped. "That wasn't a hint."

"He never hints," Jordan said. "If he wanted you to leave he'd say so. Anyhow, the sun won't set for another couple of hours."

"You don't have the faintest idea what we're talking about," Frank said.

Mild-mannered though he was, Terry was not to be bullied in his own field of expertise. He took another sandwich. "There's no hurry, Mr. Karim. The longer the shadows, the easier it is to discern slight differences in the terrain."

Jennet leaned back, hands folded in her lap, eyes lowered. I didn't doubt she had had some specific reason for coming, but I wasn't sure what it was. A private conversation with me, if that was her purpose, wouldn't be easy to arrange with so many people around.

I had underestimated her patience and her social skills. It was her questions, not Frank's nagging, that got Terry onto his feet offering to conduct a tour and explain what had been done. Everyone except Sean went with him. Jennet slipped her arm through mine and let the others draw ahead.

"I want to talk to you," she said.

"So talk."

"Not here. It's almost impossible to get you alone, you know. There's always some man or other in attendance on you."

I liked the sound of that, but honesty and my sense of humor compelled me to admit that my charm was not as overpowering as she had implied. "So pretend you want to be buddies, why don't you, and invite me to lunch or a shopping trip. Women do things like that all the time."

"When?"

"Any time." I added, pointedly, "I wouldn't mind a private conversation myself. I hadn't finished all I wanted to say to you this morning."

"The sooner the better then. You need to be set straight about—"

"Heather!" Frank was beckoning and bellowing.

"Ignore him," I said.

"It's impossible to ignore Frank." She had that right. Frank trotted toward us, demanding my attendance and attention.

"Tomorrow, then," Jennet said. "What time?"

"What about tomorrow?" Frank demanded. "Where do you want to go? Sean will drive you."

"You're the bossiest, nosiest man I've ever met," I said. "I don't want Sean. I need to buy some clothes. I didn't bring many, and all this gardening is rapidly destroying them. Jennet knows the right shops."

Jennet gave me a look of grudging admiration. She hadn't expected I would be so inventive on such short notice. "I'll pick you up at half past nine, if that suits."

"Now that you have settled that important matter, come and listen to Terry. You ought to be taking notes."

I let him lead me away.

Frank kept Terry and me hard at it for another hour. Jennet and Giles had gone by then, and Sean hadn't returned after opening the gate for them. Jordan had settled himself at the table with a book. He was still there when Terry informed Frank, politely but firmly, that he was finished for the day.

"There's not a great deal more I can do here. I'll want to organize my notes and go over the plans again at my leisure. If I might impose on you to . . ."

He led the way toward the house, talking incessantly. For once Frank had met his match. He couldn't get a word in.

I let them go ahead. Jordan put his book down when I approached him. He waited for me to speak first.

"I think I know why you've suddenly become interested in mazes."

He raised his eyebrows. "Oh you do, do you?"

"Yes. The fact that this place is named Troytan suggests that there may have been an older maze here, one of the turf mazes."

"There must have been at least the memory of one here in the sixteenth century, or Fallon wouldn't have given his estate that name. It can have had no other significance for him."

"Fair enough. But what makes you think the ancient maze and the one Fallon had built shared the same site and the same plan? That is what you're thinking, isn't it?"

"It's only a theory. There's no proof, for or against. I can't even find documentary evidence of an older maze."

"You won't find it in there." I gestured.

"Not documentary evidence, no," said Jordan.

"Don't be so damned pedantic. You know what I mean."

"Yes. And you are probably correct. But the pattern itself, if there is one remaining, may be significant. If it's a complex spiral, like the ones at Saffron Walden and Alkborough, that would strongly suggest an early date."

"So why haven't you gone in for a look?"

"Why should I go to all that trouble? There's an easier and more efficient way of finding out, if I can convince the old man to investigate the place before he hires a brigade of bulldozers to tear it down."

"That's why you were sweet-talking Mr. Barnsley."

"Certainly. He can reason with my father. I can't." He hesitated for a moment and then said, "It was I who found this place, you know."

"I thought Frank did."

"Oh, yes, he always claims the credit. I ran across it when I was in England a couple of years ago, starting my research. The Pendle witch case offered interesting possibilities. I met

Jennet while I was staying at the hotel. She was very helpful. She's an intelligent woman and well informed about the subject."

"She's also a witch."

"If she wants to call herself that, I've no objection. It's probably good for trade. The modern version of witchcraft, so-called, is a perfectly harmless—" He broke off, and his eyebrows went up again. Higher this time. "You don't suspect Jennet of putting that poppet in your bed, do you?"

"Poppet," I repeated. "Such a cute, harmless-sounding name. Yes, as a matter of fact, I do suspect her. Among others."

"I don't believe she'd do anything so childish. Or that Sean will find anything wrong with those crackers."

"No," I said. "I don't think he will either."

TEN

*Your maze may be in your garden, but it will
lead you into another world.*

GRAHAM BURGESS, HORTUS III, 2, 1989

*Jennet was smack on time next morning—half past
nine on the dot.* She was wearing a grubby old
mackintosh in which she looked as drab and
unimpressive as I had ever seen her. Trying to
be inconspicuous, in case we ran into someone
she knew? A raincoat was appropriate; the
weather had changed—again—with gray skies
and a chill, damp wind, but there was something about Jennet that made you expect she
would wear scarlet and gold when she scrubbed
her kitchen floor.

"Do you really want to go shopping?" she
asked.

"Why not? I do need clothes. Plain, ordinary
clothes—jeans, shirts, socks and underwear."

She gave me a sour smile. "We may as well
kill two birds with one stone, then. There's a

Marks and Spencer in Preston, if that isn't too common for you."

"I'm pretty common myself."

"Self-deprecation can be disarming, Heather, but it isn't always a good idea. Some people will take you at your word."

"How much do you charge for counselling?"

Her lips tightened, but she didn't take her eyes from the road. "If sarcasm will clear the air, go ahead. Get it out of your system. We shouldn't be at odds with one another."

Raindrops speckled the windshield, and she switched on the wipers.

"I don't go around picking fights with people," I said. "But I prefer not to beat around the bush. I suppose you're going to deny that you put that nasty thing in my room?"

"Of course."

"You'd say that anyhow."

"Why should I deny it if it were true? They haven't hanged a witch in England for two hundred years."

"There's got to be some law against . . . whatever it is."

"Ah, that's the point. What is 'it'? There's a Fraudulent Mediums Act, but it, and other legislation of the kind, refer to extorting money under false pretenses." She turned onto the highway and picked up speed. The rain was falling more heavily now; eyes narrowed, she went on, "As for malicious intent . . . Well, wishing someone to death would be the perfect crime, wouldn't it? In today's skeptical world such a killer could confess—even boast—of having committed murder and he wouldn't be believed, much less charged and convicted."

Rain poured down the windows. The wipers slapped back and forth, clearing a brief view before water hid it again. It was like being in a glass box under a waterfall. She was driving a lot faster than I would have done under those conditions and her voice had changed, from the delicately ironic to the deadly serious.

"Only one problem," I said. "You can't commit murder that way."

"It can be done. It has been done. I've got a fairly thick file of verified cases—not from medieval histories, but from twentieth-century newspapers."

I braced my feet against the floor. "I've heard of such cases too. But you've got it backwards, Jennet. People don't kill other people by wishing them to death. People kill themselves by believing they are going to die. It's not murder, it's suicide."

"You have such nice simple views of the universe," Jennet murmured. "It would make a good plot for a thriller, though, don't you think? Suppose you want to kill someone. Having selected your victim, you begin by arranging a series of misadventures—nothing life-threatening at first, just a succession of accidents and bad luck. Everyone has a buried streak of superstition; the people who deny it most vehemently are often the most susceptible. You play on this susceptibility—casually, innocently. I can think of a number of ways, can't you?"

Like persuading them to read books about witchcraft and providing them with amulets to protect them against evil. I had looked up cat's-eye in one of the books I had purchased. The gem was a chrysoberyl; only a certain percentage of the stones showed the reflected band of light that looked like a cat's slitted pupil. It wasn't one of the extravagantly costly gemstones, like emeralds and rubies, but it was valuable. It was also a defense against evil spirits.

The fact that I couldn't seem to get it off was a perfect example of the kind of suggestion Jennet was so good at. I couldn't get it off because, deep down in my subconscious, I didn't want to. *Not that I believe in such things, but . . . It can't do any harm.*

Jennet went on in the same musing voice, as if she were thinking aloud. "Yes, I think it might work quite nicely. Having got your victim in a proper frame of mind, you inform him that he is doomed. The beauty of it is that you've risked nothing. Whether it works or not—"

A truck roared past us in the outer lane and a flood of water covered the windshield. I let out an involuntary yelp. Jennet glanced at my stiff knees and feet.

"Does fast driving make you nervous?"

"In bad weather, yes." I wasn't going to admit that her fictional plot had gotten to me. It was a damningly accurate description of what had happened over the past few days.

"I'm sorry," Jennet said smoothly. "I had forgotten about your parents. Relax, we're almost there."

I had forgotten too—until she reminded me. It might not have been her fault that everything she said sounded insincere.

Preston was a largish town just off the main north–south highway. The wind drove the rain straight under Jennet's umbrella and soaked my coat, which had long since lost its weatherproof qualities. Jennet suggested I buy a new one. She was stalling, but that was okay with me. The busy aisles of a department store were no place for the kind of discussion I had in mind. I was determined I wouldn't let her get me off the track again.

Anyone overhearing our conversation would have taken us for two ordinary women enjoying a day out. I wasn't ashamed to ask her advice; many of the brands were unfamiliar, and I still had to stop and count on my mental fingers before I could translate pounds into dollars. I ended up buying several colored shirts—the ones she indicated—instead of plain white, and a green plastic raincoat I would once have considered tasteless and garish.

Once or twice I had to remind myself I wasn't having a good time.

The restaurant she chose for lunch was large and expensive and uncrowded. No doubt the first two features affected the last. A smiling waitress carried our wet coats away and Jennet ordered a half carafe of wine.

"None for me," I said.

"*In vino veritas*," Jennet said. "But you don't need wine to loosen your tongue, do you? Have some anyhow."

The pale golden liquid looked like watery sunlight. I knew why she wanted me to join her in a glass. You don't have to be a witch or a wisewoman to know that alcohol does loosen the tongue. Sharing food and drink with someone is a symbol of hospitality offered and accepted, bargains struck, differences settled.

I let her fill the glasses. She'd done most of the talking so far, and I expected she would go on. Instead she sat in silence, turning the wineglass in her hand.

"What have you done with the dolly?" I asked.

"It's safely hidden away where no one can get at it. I took out the thorns."

"Gee, thanks. No wonder I feel so much better."

"Mr. Barnsley cut himself rather badly yesterday."

It sounded like a non sequitur, but I caught on. Maybe I wouldn't have been so quick to follow her meaning if I hadn't had the same idea. "It might have been me, you mean? If that's the way your magic works I don't think much of it. Did you have to turn the curse on poor harmless Terry?"

Anger wrinkled her face, but the appearance of the waitress with our salads prevented her from voicing it. By the time the young woman had finished she had herself under control.

"You're on the wrong track, Heather. Obviously you've done some reading or you wouldn't have understood the purpose of the poppet, but you've stuffed your head with miscellaneous misinformation and old superstitions. Modern witchcraft isn't what you think."

"So you admit you are a believer?"

"Is that what you wanted to ascertain from me?" She gave me a faint, cynical smile. "I haven't admitted it. But if it will clear the air and make you more receptive to my suggestions . . . Yes, I am. What else do you want to know?"

I had expected she would go on equivocating. The flat-out statement, and the question, left me momentarily at a loss. Then I said, "I want to know who's in charge—head witch, chief of the coven, or whatever you call it. You?"

Her lips tightened. "I don't call it either. It's not that sort of organization. I am not in charge, that's not how we function. You could say I have a position of authority and respect."

"Who else is involved?"

I might have known it wouldn't be that easy. Jennet shook her head. "I can't tell you that. I will not betray the confidence of others."

"That's very high-minded and noble," I said angrily. "But if you're in charge— Oh, all right, damn it—if you do have authority over the others, then you must know who's trying to scare me. Do you condone that sort of thing?"

"Of course not." She poured herself another glass of wine, and I realized she wasn't as much at ease as I had believed. "It's hard to explain, but I'll try. And you might try to keep an open mind."

"I'll do my best."

"Most of us prefer not to talk about our beliefs; we despise the people who court publicity, via telly or sensational newspapers. Wicca is a religion, not a game or a means of acquiring power over others. It holds that the divine permeates all life and all nature; that individuals are solely responsible for their actions and their own salvation. It is matriarchal in structure; individual groups are headed by women, but men fill important positions too. Its most important precept is 'do no harm.'"

I didn't doubt she was telling the truth, as far as it went, but there were a lot of gaps in her account. "'Do no harm,'" I repeated. "What about the dolly?"

"It was meant to harm you, yes. What you must understand is that modern witchcraft isn't a single entity with a central organization. Like other religions it has its schisms and sects, and—like other religions—it attracts a certain number of mentally unstable individuals."

"And individuals who are attracted by those stories about dancing around in the buff."

"That's precisely the sort of ignorant misinterpretation that makes us reluctant to discuss our beliefs," Jennet said angrily. "Those who come to us expecting orgies and indiscriminate sex don't last long. They fail completely to understand the basic truths of the craft. We don't believe in Hell or the Devil. We don't parody Christian ceremonies; why should we? Our own rituals are older than Christianity."

"The Old Religion," I said. "The Mother Goddess."

"The goddess, yes. Why shouldn't the divine principle be female? She has a male counterpart, whom we also honor." Jennet dismissed the approaching waitress with a brusque, "No dessert, just coffee," and leaned forward, planting her elbows on the table. "I can't go into detail. I don't want to. I'm only telling you this much because I want you to understand that Wicca doesn't perform black masses or recite the Lord's Prayer backwards, or any of that nonsense. Or cast spells. The directing of power which some of our ceremonies attempt to achieve is channelled only for good, to help or to heal."

She could cast a spell of her own. The words were oddly compelling and the eyes fixed unblinkingly on mine had an almost hypnotic power. I had to make an effort to look away.

"Can I have dessert?" I asked.

I thought for a minute she was going to swear. Then her lips curved in a tight smile. "You do have a talent for the mundane, Heather.

I ought to get back to the shop, but I wouldn't want to deprive you. What do you want?"

What I really wanted was more of her time. She had managed to avoid direct questions by discoursing eloquently and vaguely on the principles of whatever it was. I needed answers, not theology. I ordered something that sounded fattening and full of cholesterol—if I was under a curse I might as well die happy—and got to the point.

"If you didn't put the dolly in my room, who did?"

"You are persistent, aren't you? Haven't you heard anything I said? I don't know who was responsible for the poppet, Heather. That's the truth."

"Any ideas?"

"If I did, I wouldn't tell you. It would be unfair. Suspicion isn't proof." She cut my protest short, firmly and authoritatively. "Listen to me, Heather. That little image can't hurt you. If you don't believe in its powers you're in no danger from it, right? Anyhow, it's harmless now. I've taken steps to neutralize it."

That statement sounded like a contradiction of the first, but I wasn't to be distracted again. "I'm not worried about the damned doll. What worries me is the intent behind it. I am familiar with the literature—only too familiar, thanks to you and Jordan—and I know that when suggestion failed, an impatient sorcerer often took more direct action. I was sick last night. And don't tell me that it was because I overate. I didn't."

She didn't reply because the waitress had arrived with my dessert. I didn't really want it, but I forced some of it down. Jennet watched me in frowning silence, and then called for the check. "What had you eaten?" she asked abruptly.

"When? Oh, last night? Just what everybody else ate. At dinner, I mean. Later, I had some of the crackers that were in my room."

She paid the check and we collected our coats from the rack. Buffeted by wind and rain, we made our way back to the car.

"So that's why Sean made such a point of those nauseating nuggets," Jennet said thoughtfully. "I shouldn't have refused them, should I? Obvious evidence of guilt."

"Or evidence of good taste," I admitted. "They weren't the originals. He took those off to be tested."

"I can't imagine a chemist will find anything. How could one tamper with them?"

"The seeds?"

"Another point against me? Come now. You know something about herbs and poisonous plants yourself. I defy you to name a poisonous seed of that color and size. And how could one scrape off the original poppy seeds and replace them without leaving visible traces?"

"I agree. But there was something wrong with me and it wasn't an upset stomach."

"Then what are you suggesting?"

"It was in the water, of course. The crackers were very salty. I drank practically the whole bottle."

The rain seemed to be letting up. Jennet drove without the panache she had displayed on the way over.

"Are you absolutely sure—"

"That I didn't overdose on sleeping pills or absentmindedly munch on a handful of foxglove leaves? I have better sense than to do either. And if you think I'm making it up, ask Jordan and Sean. If they hadn't made me throw up and poured coffee into me— Hey! Watch the road, damn it!"

I reached for the steering wheel. Visibly paler, Jennet returned her gaze to the road and the car to its lane.

Fortunately nobody had been trying to pass.

"Are you implying someone wants to kill you?"

"What the hell have we been talking about?" I demanded.

"I thought we were talking about a mild case of indigestion. Are you telling me you actually . . . I'd better talk to Sean."

"He can give you a vivid description. I think he was the one who stuck his finger down my throat. It might have been Jordan, though. I was semi-comatose by that time."

She said something under her breath. "Jordan too? What time of night was this? Don't mistake my motive for asking, Heather, I'm just trying to make sense of this business."

I had no idea what her motive might be, but at least she was taking me seriously. "Around midnight, I guess. He just happened to come to my room because—"

I stopped with a gulp. The coincidences were getting a little too thick to swallow. That Jordan should just happen to come to my room with a wild story about lights which he just happened to see, at a time when it just happened that I was beginning to show the effects of the drug I had been given. . . . The intent might not have been murder. A thorough scare might be enough to persuade me to leave, supposing that was the intent. A cautious man, which Jordan was, wouldn't risk a murder charge. But if Sean hadn't just happened to be awake, if he hadn't come over to find out why the lights were out. . . .

Jennet gave me a quick, curious glance. "Are you all right? You're making strange noises."

I swallowed. "I . . . guess I shouldn't have had dessert."

"If you're going to be sick let me know so I can stop."

"I'm not going to be sick." Not throwing up sick, anyhow.

"Go on with what you were saying."

"Huh? Oh."

I gave her a brief, probably badly garbled, account of what had happened. Neither of us spoke during the rest of the drive. She looked worried, and I was preoccupied with some unpleasant suspicions of my own.

The more I thought about it the more the evidence mounted up. Jordan had easy access to my room. He was thoroughly conversant with the tricks and methods of "the craft," as Jennet had called it. It had been Sean, not Jordan, who took my illness seriously enough to investigate the crackers. Jordan had tried to make me believe it had been an accident. He didn't want me there; he had made that clear from the first.

And it wasn't difficult to come up with a more substantial reason for his dislike than general antipathy. Threatening to cut ungrateful children out of the will is a favorite form of harassment for some elderly people; but more than one doddering old fogey had left the lot to a young stranger. Frank wasn't doddering, he was just mean as a pit bull, but that only made it worse. Jordan would have a hell of a hard time proving that I had exercised undue influence on a senile old man.

ii

Jennet dropped me off and went on her way. I splashed through the puddles on the terrace and went into the kitchen. Mrs. Greenspan and Doreen were seated at the table, heads together over their cups of tea. The cook started guiltily when she saw me; Doreen jumped up and divested me of my parcels.

"You're soaked to the skin. Don't go dripping through the house, get out of that wet coat and have a nice hot cup of tea."

The kitchen looked warm and inviting after the blustery gray outside and at that particular moment I preferred the company of Doreen and Mrs. G. to that of anyone else in the house. A distant roaring, which I identified as the sound of the vacuum cleaner, was an additional inducement to remain; the teenagers were obviously in possession.

So I let Doreen take my coat and accepted the mug Mrs. Greenspan handed me. The liquid was so dark it looked like coffee. I added milk and sugar—when in Rome, as they say—and smiled apologetically at the cook.

"I've tracked up your nice clean floor."

"It's a hopeless job on a day like this," Doreen said, bustling around with newspapers and cleaning cloths. "What's needed here is a covered porch or a mud room like. Get those wet shoes off and I'll see what I can do about drying them. Had a nice day shopping, did you?"

She turned a predatory eye on my parcels and I said, "Take a look if you like. I didn't get anything very interesting though, just pants and blouses and underwear."

Doreen's reaction to the sedate cotton panties and plain white socks made it clear that she had hoped for something livelier. With a sniff she returned them to the bags.

"Mr. Jordan was looking for you." Mrs. Greenspan had never addressed me directly before. It was like hearing a rock speak—a slow, deep monotone. Considering what I had been thinking about Jordan, I may have overreacted.

"What did he want?" I demanded.

Mrs. Greenspan looked even blanker. Doreen said, "Well, he wouldn't tell us, would he? He's not one to stand round chatting. His dad, now, he's always ready for a bit of gossip. He wants to see you too. Said to tell you to come to the library when you got back. But I wouldn't hurry myself if I was you, you'll catch your death if you go running around in wet clothes."

Mrs. Greenspan refilled my cup and removed the top of a tin. The cookies—biscuits, I reminded myself—were homemade. They smelled of butter and cinnamon. I reached for one and then pulled my hand back with a squeal of surprise as something snaked across the table toward the tin. It was covered with fur and it had claws.

The cat must have been sitting or lying on a chair, hidden by the tablecloth. Finding that the cookies were out of reach, it stood up, front paws on the table and tried again. With a guilty look at me Mrs. Greenspan broke off a piece and tossed it onto the floor. The cat followed it. I heard crunching noises.

"Frank said the cat never came in the house," I remarked.

"It comes when it pleases and goes when it likes," Mrs. Greenspan said seriously.

"What Mr. Karim don't know won't hurt him," Doreen added. "It doesn't bother you, does it?"

"Of course not," I said stoutly, managing not to jump when two paws and a head suddenly appeared on my right knee. I broke off a piece of cookie, which the cat accepted as his due. "I didn't know cats ate sweets."

"Some do, some don't. He's just being sociable," Doreen said fondly. "There now—he likes you, you see?"

The cat was now on my lap. "He likes my cookie," I said, meekly handing over the last bit. However, it appeared the cat had had enough. He shoved and nudged at me until I had arranged my legs to his satisfaction and then settled down and began to purr.

I decided it was safe to take another cookie. "These are delicious, Mrs. Greenspan. Is Mr. Barnsley still here?"

"He went off after he'd had his lunch," Doreen answered. "Back to London, he was going; Sean drove him to the train station."

Mrs. Greenspan glanced at the window and rumbled softly. Doreen interpreted. "Not much he could do outdoors in this pouring rain."

I nodded. "He finished most of the survey yesterday."

Doreen pulled her chair closer. "What was all that about the headlamps of the car?"

I explained as best I could. Mrs. Greenspan's expression didn't change. I wondered what it would take to get a visible reaction out of her. Doreen stopped me after a while.

"So he's really going ahead with it, then? When?"

"That depends on Mr. Barnsley. As soon as possible, if Mr. Karim has his way."

The cat appeared to have gone to sleep. I was trying to figure out how to move him without injury to myself when the back door opened and Sean came in. His black hair dripped and raindrops sparkled in his beard.

"Hello, girls. Is this a private party, or can you spare a cuppa for a tired, wet, hard-working man?"

Tibb vanished soundlessly under the table. Apparently he didn't care to compete with a larger male creature, who was getting all the attention. Doreen rushed at Sean with a towel and Mrs. Greenspan clumped to the cupboard to get him a cup.

"So you got Mr. Barnsley to his train all right?" Doreen asked.

Sean rubbed his hair and wrung rain out of his beard. "Yeah, no problem. Don't go just when I come in, Heather, or I'll take it personally."

"I've got to take these things upstairs and change my clothes." I wriggled a bare foot at him and began collecting my bags.

"Want some help?"

"They aren't heavy," I said, pretending I hadn't noticed the tilt of his head and the gleam in his eye. Doreen pretended not to notice too.

Hearing giggles and high-pitched voices from across the hall I deduced that the girls must be in the drawing room, dusting or doing whatever they did in that room. The library door was closed. My bare feet made no sound on the stairs, or along the carpeted upstairs corridor. I was congratulating myself on having avoided all the people I didn't particularly want to see when Jordan opened his door.

"There you are," he said.

He must have been listening for me. "Here I am," I agreed. One of the plastic bags slipped through my fingers and hit the floor, spilling white cotton panties across the corridor.

He stood watching, his arms folded, while I picked up my underwear and carried them and the other things into my room. When I went back to close my door he was standing in the open doorway.

"Come to my room for a minute. I want to talk to you."

The autocratic order, with not so much as a please to soften it, and the supercilious expression had an unexpected effect. He didn't look like a villain. He looked like a man who didn't give a damn whether I trusted him or even liked him. I said shortly, "I'm busy."

"Doing what?"

"Like, for instance, putting on socks and shoes. I'm not wearing either."

"I noticed that. Hoping the old man wouldn't hear you?"

"Hoping you wouldn't hear me. What do you want to talk to me about?"

He strode into the room. I backed up a couple of steps. Jordan picked up a pair of sneakers from the chair where someone, presumably the girls, had put them—it certainly hadn't been me, I always kick them under the bed—and thrust them at me. "Put 'em on, then. I'll wait."

He retreated to the doorway, however. I took out a pair of my nice new socks, unwrapped them, removed pins and labels. . . . In other words, I took my own sweet time. I didn't succeed in provoking him into profane comment, or in giving up. He waited until I was ready and then preceded me into his room. He left the door open.

"Do you want to sit down?" he asked.

"I don't know. How long is this going to take?"

"Please," said Jordan, emphasizing the word, "sit down."

I took the seat he indicated, the only comfortable one in the room. He pulled up one of the straight chairs and straddled it, facing me. "You may remember that I said earlier I was getting some crazy ideas. I want you to listen to them. You owe me."

"For burgling your room?" One thing you

had to say about Jordan, he didn't waste time with social amenities. "I don't know why you think listening to crazy ideas is appropriate recompense. I'll jeer at you if they're that far out."

"That is precisely what I want you to do—pick holes in my theory and tell me where I've got off track." His eyes shifted, avoiding my steady stare, and I realized that his hectoring manner had concealed a certain discomfort. "You see, you're the only one I can talk to. You do seem to have the rudiments of a logical mind."

"How can I resist a florid compliment like that?"

"I'm sorry," Jordan said stiffly. "I'm not in the habit of flattering people, or asking favors."

"That's part of your trouble. Okay, okay," I said quickly, as his brows drew together. "No more smart remarks. Go on. I'm listening."

Again he went straight to the point. "You said something the other day about a place called 'The Dancing Floor.' Are you sure those were the precise words?"

"Yes. Why?"

"It's not a pub or a restaurant or public amusement place. I've checked."

"So maybe it's a private club."

"I tell you there is no such place. Not around here. Not now." He was beginning to sound a little rattled, and when he closed his eyes and spoke in the sonorous accents of someone who is reciting poetry, or quoting from the classics, I seriously wondered whether he was losing his marbles. "'Upon it he worked a dancing floor, like the one Daedelos made in Knossos for curly-haired Ariadne. There young men and beautiful maidens danced, holding one another's wrists.'"

He opened his eyes. Seeing my alarmed expression he smiled faintly. "I said it was crazy. The structure Daedelos made in Knossos was the labyrinth. That passage, which is from *The Iliad*, calls it a place for dancing. Sacred dances or races were performed along the pathways of the Roman mazes. Dancing has had ritual significance in many religions; David, if you remember, capered before the Lord. They still 'tread the maze' in some villages on May Day, which was one of the holy days of the Old Religion. In other areas the young men and women run along the pathways to the center and back out again—and, as one of the participants reported, 'Something unseen ran with us.' These days they perform such rites in order to attract tourists, but not long ago—"

"Wait a minute," I said. "Wait just a minute. Are you suggesting that—"

"That something of the sort has survived here. There are a number of indications. That pathway through the wilderness, deliberately cut and regularly maintained—the statue of a horned god inside it—even the cat, which is obviously a genus loci—"

"A what?"

He gestured impatiently. "A guardian spirit, located in a particular spot. Doreen was horrified at the idea of taking it home with her. It belongs here, she said. She's one of them. She knows—"

"For heaven's sake, Jordan," I exclaimed. "You think Doreen and the teenagers are worshipping the Devil out there in that jungle?"

"Don't be absurd."

"Me, absurd?"

"It's just some harmless local group of occultists," Jordan said disgustedly. "Wicca, or whatever they call themselves these days. What's important is that the ritual this bunch follows derives from local tradition and legends. Talk about survivals! Now look, what I want you to do is talk to them—get them to talk to you. Ask them about the Dancing Floor. They won't tell me anything, I'm an outsider and a man—"

His voice trailed off and his face was as rapt as that of a man dreaming about his lover. To each his own, I thought, and wondered what the hell I was going to say to him. In view of what I had learned from Jennet that afternoon, his wild theory wasn't quite as crazy as it sounded. I hadn't promised Jennet I would keep silent, but for some reason I was reluctant to betray her confidences—especially to Jordan.

I was saved by Frank. Jordan had left the door open; I could hear Frank's heavy footsteps while he was still on the stairs. Jordan jumped up, made an abortive movement toward the door, realized the futility of closing it, and said a bad word.

I had left my door open too. One glance must have told Frank I wasn't there. He began yelling for me. I said a bad word, and called, "Here I am."

"Ah," said Frank, in the doorway.

He looked from me to Jordan and back to me. Then back to Jordan. He didn't have to say anything. He had his son so on the defensive that a blink would have started him babbling.

"I wanted to consult Heather about something," he said feebly.

"Ah," said Frank.

"What do you want, Frank?" I asked.

"You didn't tell me you had come back."

"No, I didn't."

"Did you enjoy yourself?"

"Yes, thank you."

"Good. I want you to enjoy yourself, Heather. I want you to be happy here."

Involuntarily I glanced at Jordan. Leaning against the table, hands in his pockets, shoulders braced, he was staring fixedly at the floor like a bad boy who is expecting a scolding.

No, he didn't look like a villain. He looked like a damned fool.

I sighed. "What the hell do you want, Frank?"

"Why, to tell you we are going out this evening. Come for drinks, she said—don't dress, nothing formal. I didn't feel I could refuse. What are friends for, but to rally around in time of trouble?"

I knew him well enough by now to read between the lines, but I couldn't believe what I was thinking.

"You don't mean . . . Lindsay?"

"And Giles." His eyes were as bright and merry as a bunny rabbit's. "They are together again. Isn't that nice?"

Frank knew a good exit line when he said one. He closed the door gently behind him.

"Tough luck," Jordan said. "I was going to break it to you more gently."

"You can be almost as vulgar as your old man when you try hard," I said, with as much dignity as I could command. The information had surprised me, as Frank had meant it to. "How can the woman be so tasteless? Throwing a party when her son is still missing—"

"If one were charitably inclined one might suppose she is not throwing a party but gathering her friends around her for comfort and encouragement."

"Yeah, sure. She can't possibly consider me a friend."

"If one were not charitably inclined, one might suspect she is reestablishing her claim. It's your own fault. She wouldn't want Giles back if you hadn't indicated that you want him."

"I was wrong. You can be even more vulgar than Frank." I wrenched the door open.

"So you're going to decline the invitation?" Jordan inquired gently.

I slammed the door.

iii

There was no question of declining. Among other reasons, and never mind what they were, I didn't want to stay alone in that house at night. The rain had ended but the wind seemed stronger; from my window I could see the tree tops bowing and hear the melancholy susurration of the branches. I put on one of my new shirts and a pair of my new jeans.

The Betancourts' house was exactly the sort of place I would have expected Lindsay to favor—fake Tudor with a square of manicured lawn and spindly new plantings. It took us almost twenty minutes to get there, but as Frank mentioned—in his most innocent voice—the house was less than a mile from Troytan as the crow flew or the hiker hiked.

Sean had driven us over, but he flatly refused to come in, though Frank tried to persuade him.

"Lindsay will be disappointed, Sean. You know the Betancourts consider you a dear, close friend."

"Damned if I'll sit on that snow white sofa of hers with my toes together, sipping wine," Sean said sourly. "I'm going to the pub. Back in an hour. I'll come to the door; that will give you an excuse to get away."

"That's very kind of you, my boy," Frank said.

Lindsay didn't ask about Sean. She wore casual clothes and her hair had been pulled back into a simple ponytail. The effect was to make her seem younger and more vulnerable, and she greeted me with a warmth that made my inconvenient conscience squirm. I didn't like her and I doubted I ever would; but some of my reasons for disliking her did me no credit. One of them especially. She probably had few women friends. Perhaps she felt the need of them now.

We went to the living room, as I would have called it—Lindsay referred to it as the lounge—and I lowered myself gingerly into a chair. It was ivory, like everything else in the room, including the wall to wall carpeting. The only color accents (I could hear the decorator calling them that) were a couple of purple cushions and a huge modern painting over the fireplace—three perpendicular bands of color, purple, red and turquoise. It made my eyes ache.

Giles served drinks and passed around bowls of nuts and crunchy bits. He didn't say much. Occasionally I would catch his eye and then he would smile at me, and my stomach—the part of the body that really hurts when you care about someone—would contract painfully. He'd been so hopeful that morning. Disappointment is all the more grievous after your hopes have been raised.

I asked about Laura, and Lindsay said she was still at her grandmother's.

"It's easier for her there," she said with a sigh. "Where she isn't constantly reminded of Bobby."

I would have thought it was better for the child to be with her parents—especially her father—but I didn't venture an opinion.

We had been there for almost half an hour, and I was counting off the minutes when the doorbell rang.

"That must be Jennet," Giles said, rising.

"It's typical of her to be late," said Lindsay. "Inconsiderate, under the circumstances."

"We didn't give our friends much notice," Giles said quietly. "It's good of them to come. Under the circumstances."

He left the room. Lindsay leaned forward, her eyes fixed on the doorway, her hands tightly clasped, her lips parted. Something strange and unpleasant had entered the room. The others were aware of it too. Frank had fallen silent and Jordan was watching Lindsay with narrowed eyes.

She jumped up when Jennet came in and ran to her. "Did you bring it?"

"No," Jennet said curtly. "I told you I prefer not to use that method."

"At least let Jennet have a drink first," Giles said wearily. He knew what Lindsay wanted. I thought I knew too. So that was why she had asked us to come. I ought to have realized it wasn't because she needed comfort from friends.

Turned out I was wrong. Part wrong, at any rate. Jennet refused a drink. "Let's get at it," she said. "I need something of Bobby's. Something he's handled or worn."

"Why won't you use the map?" Lindsay demanded.

"Because it's not one of my . . . talents. I told you that. I've had some success with the other, I'm willing to give it a try."

She avoided my eyes. Her discomfort was palpable; after lecturing me about the lofty ideals and ethics of her religion she was about to resort to parlor magic of the most obvious kind. I didn't think less of her, though. She had yielded, against her better judgment, to the pleas of a woman in distress. I didn't blame Lindsay either, any more than I would have blamed a man with terminal cancer for consulting faith healers. If you're desperate enough you'll try anything.

However, I was relieved to learn that we hadn't been summoned there to take part in a séance or watch Jennet pretend to go into a trance. Thanks to my recent research—and my novel reading—I understood what Jennet was talking about. Some police departments have actually used psychics in the hope of locating missing persons. One method is to hold a pendulum over a map. Theoretically the psychic's powers will direct the swaying pendulum and stop it at the right place. Jennet had rejected this technique in favor of clairvoyance, focusing

on an object that had been in intimate contact
with the missing person in the hope of making
contact with him.

"An article of clothing?" Giles asked. He was
even more uncomfortable than Jennet, though
he hid it more successfully.

Jennet shrugged. "What about the note he
left? He's touched that more recently than anything in the house. Or did you give it to the
police?"

"No, they didn't seem to want it. I'll get it."

He came back almost at once with a folded
paper.

Jennet opened it. I could see writing—printing, rather, today's computer-habituated children don't write unless they are forced to—but I
couldn't read the words. Jennet barely glanced
at them. Taking the paper between her hands
she leaned back in the chair and closed her
eyes.

It was so casual. I had expected a ritual of
some kind—a prayer, or at least a solemn
demand for silence. I didn't know what I was
supposed to do. We all stared at Jennet. Frank
was perched on the edge of his chair, eyes bright
with interest; Jordan's forehead was creased in a
slight frown. Giles was frowning too; he
appeared to me to be more anxious than critical.
Lindsay's expression could only be described as
avid. She hardly seemed to breathe.

Time stretched, the way it does when you're
in the dentist's chair or taking an exam you

haven't prepared for. I sneaked surreptitious glances at my wristwatch. The hands crawled. Jennet had been at it for less than five minutes when she started convulsively. Her head jerked forward and her hands clenched, crumpling the paper.

Giles must have expected something of the sort. He was at her side instantly, clasping her hands, speaking quietly and insistently.

"Enough, Jennet. It's all right, dear. Open your eyes. Look at me."

She drew a long, shaken breath and lay back in the chair. "Yes, it's all right," she murmured.

"What was it?" Lindsay demanded shrilly. "What did you see?"

Giles turned and said, in a voice I had never heard him use to her, "Be quiet. She was decent enough to do this for you, the least you can do is give her time to recover. Jennet, what can I get for you?"

"I'll take that glass of wine now," Jennet said, in her ordinary voice. "Sorry, Lindsay. I couldn't get anything."

"Nothing?" Her voice cracked. "Nothing at all?"

Jennet took the glass Giles handed her. "Only an impression of darkness. There was something in the way—a barrier. I couldn't get through it."

"Fascinating," Frank muttered.

"Fascinating," Jordan repeated, with quite a different intonation. "If you don't mind my asking,

Jennet, what caused that violent muscular spasm?"

Her lips curved in a faint, ironic smile. "You would probably say it was a deliberate theatrical effect. No, that's quite all right, Jordan, you needn't protest; you're an honest skeptic and I've no quarrel with that. In fact I wasn't aware of a muscular spasm, only of intense, frustrated mental effort. I'm sorry, Giles. I tried."

"You know how I feel about this sort of thing," Giles said. "I didn't want you to do it."

"Yes, darling, I know." She might have been speaking to a child. "Just let me sit quietly for a few minutes."

She leaned back and closed her eyes.

The courteous persons present—I do not include Frank and Lindsay—tried desperately to find some neutral subject to talk about. Giles refilled glasses and pressed peanuts on everybody, but it was Jordan who actually got a conversation going. On second thought, he probably wasn't being polite, he just wanted to find a subject that interested him.

"I haven't found anything in those papers," he said to Giles. "You're sure that was all there was?"

"I don't believe I overlooked anything. I am sorry—" He glanced at me. His strained face relaxed into something that was almost a smile, but, being Giles, he couldn't refrain from trying to help. "It's still the author of the monster book you're after? As I told you, my grandmother always claimed her grandfather had written it, but if she ever owned a copy she must have disposed of it. Wait a sec, though—I do seem to remember her saying her brother had one. Great-uncle Andrew, that would be. His son was a barrister in . . . York, I think. We've not kept in close touch with that branch of the family."

Jordan had stiffened like a hunting dog on a scent. "Could you find out where his son lives?"

"For pity's sake, Jordan, don't bother poor Giles with that nonsense," Frank said. "You already have a copy of the book. Set me back over fifty pounds."

"It's no trouble, I assure you," Giles said. Frank's bad manners always amused him. "I got a Christmas card from the old boy last year, as a matter of fact, together with one of those long tedious letters about children and grandchildren I'd never heard of and couldn't care twopence about. Let me see if I can't locate it."

Lindsay got up. "It's in the escritoire, isn't it, darling? I'll have a look."

"I think I filed it," Giles said, giving her an odd look. "Go ahead, though, if you like."

Lindsay was still rummaging in the little desk when he came back with an envelope in his hand. "York it was, Nottingham it is. It's possible that he had some family papers, but Lord knows where they would be now, he seems to be in some sort of nursing home. You can ring him if you like—"

"I'll go to see him," Jordan interrupted. "If

you wouldn't mind letting me have the address?"

"Take the card," Giles said. "Please do, I don't want the damned thing. Are you sure you want to go all that way on such a slim chance? Judging from his letter he's not senile, just hopelessly loquacious, but—"

The doorbell pealed, and I tried not to sag with relief. Good old Sean, right on time. It had seemed a lot longer than an hour.

Lindsay went to let him in, and Giles detached himself from Jordan and prepared to play host. Sean refused a drink; he wouldn't even sit down. "No, thanks, Giles, I've already had my quota. I'll just wait in the car if you people aren't ready to go."

"I'm ready," I said, with a pointed glare at Frank.

Jennet opened her eyes and sat up straight. "Me too. No, thanks, Giles, no more wine. I'm a little tired."

"You're exhausted," Giles said. "I'll drive you home. I insist."

I said quickly, "Let me. Sean can follow us and pick me up, that way Jennet won't be left without her car."

There was a brief argument. Frank didn't want to leave, Jordan remarked that he was more likely to get Jennet home in one piece than I, and Jennet insisted she didn't need to be chauffeured. Giles didn't argue, since my suggestion obviously made better sense than his.

Lindsay didn't offer her opinion. She sat in frowning silence until we were ready to leave, and then made a visible effort to behave like a proper hostess. Her thanks to Jennet were almost gracious. She really sounded as if she meant them.

Jennet waited until the others had gotten into the Bentley and closed the doors before she spoke.

"I'll drive."

"Are you sure?"

"It's not far. I'm perfectly fit, just a little tired."

Jennet had parked on the street, some distance from the nearest streetlamp. She waited until I had buckled up before she started the engine. I waited for her to speak. She didn't, so I decided to initiate conversation.

"So what was that all about?"

"You never take anything at face value, do you?"

"Depends. Never mind the—uh—business this evening. You wanted to tell me something in private. What?"

"Not tell, ask." The headlights of the big car following us glared in the rearview mirror. She adjusted it before she continued speaking. "I've got to go into the maze. Will you go with me?"

The breath literally went out of me. Her performance had been more effective than I had been willing to admit. All I could think of was

the violent shudder that had gripped her, and
what might have caused it.

"My God, Jennet! Are you telling me you
saw—"

"I didn't see anything." She laughed, a
breathless, ugly laugh. "Why bother asking?
You don't believe in that sort of thing, do you?
My reasons don't concern you. I want to have a
look, and I want a witness. You've already been
inside."

That word again. We were on the outskirts of
the village before I answered.

"Okay. When?"

"That simply?"

"My reasons don't concern you," I said.

"Oh, well done." She sounded as if she were
smiling. "You're a gutsy lady, Heather. I take off
my hat to you."

"Your pointy hat, I presume."

Jennet brought the car to a stop. We were in
front of the hotel.

"Is this where you live?" I asked.

"Didn't you know? I have an apartment on
the top floor." The Bentley had pulled up
behind us. Jennet glanced over her shoulder
and said quickly, "Can you meet me outside the
gate tomorrow at eight? Find some excuse. No
one must know what we're planning to do."

"Make it nine. I'll tell them you're taking me
shopping again." I opened the door.

"Good." She waited until I was out of the car
before she added, "Thank you."

I closed the door and put my head in the window. "I'm looking forward to it *so* much."

iv

Frank sulked all the way home. He had wanted to ask Jennet to come back with us to dinner and had failed to do so only because he was too lazy to get out of the car and go after her himself. Nobody else would.

"She wouldn't have accepted," I said, for the tenth time.

"How do you know if you didn't ask?"

Mrs. Greenspan's curried lamb en casserole improved his disposition a trifle, but he kept harping on his desire to discuss the evening's performance (Jordan's word) with the star performer. "What did she say to you?" he demanded of me. "Don't tell me you didn't discuss it. Haven't you any normal curiosity?"

"We did not discuss it," I said more or less truthfully. "She didn't tell me any more than she told you and the others. She saw nothing."

"I'm surprised that she consented to do it," Jordan said. "I thought better of her."

"Nobody cares for your opinion," his father retorted.

"You mean you don't. I'm well aware of that."

It was a ruder exchange than usual, and the

way they were glaring at each other portended worse to come. It was Sean who intervened.

"What did you think, Heather? I don't know Jennet all that well, but she doesn't strike me as the kind of woman who'd fake a performance like that one."

Jordan began, "I didn't say she—"

"If she did," I said loudly, drowning him out, "it was because Lindsay asked for her help. What else could she do?"

"Just say no," Jordan said.

"You said 'if,'" Sean persisted. "Do you think—"

"I don't know what I think! Except that I'm sick of the subject." I scooped a sizable lump of the casserole onto my plate. "Anybody else want seconds?"

I must have sounded pretty emphatic. With more tact than I would have expected, Frank started talking about the garden. I agreed to join him in the library after dinner so he could tell me about Mr. Barnsley's most recent ideas. I had missed, said Frank with a mildly reproachful look, their discussion that morning.

He wasn't the only guy who asked me for a date. While Sean and I were clearing the table he made a hopeful reference to ladders and windows.

"Don't wait up," I said.

"Chicken?" Sean inquired.

"It's damp and chilly and the grass is wet."

"Are you sure you aren't copping out because you're scared of Jordan?"

"Ha," I said.

Frank and I spent a couple of hours talking garden. He had made copies of Barnsley's notes and it was interesting to go over the old plans with Barnsley's comments and interpretations in mind. One feature that was designated for destruction was the vegetable garden. Barnsley believed it occupied one part of the former East Garden, which had contained some of Fallon's choicest plantings.

"It's a pity," I murmured. "Will is so proud of his brussels sprouts. That area has been plowed and dug over intensively; surely there can't be anything left of the East Garden."

"Even if there isn't, I don't want carrots and cabbages growing in the middle of my grounds," Frank said. "The gardener will still have a job if he wants it, helping with the restoration."

I remembered Will's opinion of that project. He might have been playing the curmudgeonly country gardener for my amusement, though. No sensible man would turn down employment so cavalierly.

I wasn't sorry to be distracted from thinking about what I had agreed to do next morning. There was no way I could have refused without looking like a coward or a wimp or a believer in the very superstitions I had derided. But I wasn't looking forward to doing it.

Frank finally dismissed me with a mixture of royal condescension and fatherly concern. When I went into my room there was a cat on the bed.

Tibb. Or another of the Demdike cats? Whoever, whichever, it was, I was damned if I could figure out how the creature had gotten in. The door had been closed.

I got hold of my common sense and gave it a little shake. Maybe the cat had crept in while the teenagers were cleaning. No, that wouldn't wash. The girls had done my room while Tibb and I were in the kitchen pigging out on cookies. The door had been closed when I went upstairs. Maybe he was Doreen's latest addition to the amenities. Coffeemaker, carafe, cookies, cat.

Keeping a wary eye on Tibb, who turned his head lazily to follow my movements, I sidled around the bed and inspected the cookie tin. It contained the same spice cookies I had eaten that afternoon. So, Doreen had entered my room later that day. The cat must have slunk in and hidden under the bed until she left, for she wouldn't have knowingly shut it in the room. Unfamiliar as I was with cats, I knew enough about their habits to know that would not be a smart idea.

The cat gave no indication of moving, and I wasn't about to move it. I went back to the door and opened it. The cat yawned. Leaving the door ajar I retreated into the bathroom and got ready for bed. When I emerged the cat was still there.

A silent confrontation followed. I lost. Turning out all the lights except the lamp on the bedside table I climbed into bed, plumped up my pillows, and settled down with a book—knees well up. The cat watched me with an expression of poorly concealed amusement, but it didn't move.

I did not open the tin again, though it cost me a pang to abandon those delectable morsels. It was unlikely to the point of extremely unlikely that there was anything wrong with them, but it would have been stupid to take chances. I had emptied out the water bottle and rinsed it thoroughly before filling it from the tap in the bathroom. I had also replenished my chocolate supply at the newsstand, while Jordan wasn't looking. Those chocolates couldn't have been tampered with. If you have ever tried to put the foil back on a chocolate kiss, with the little strip of paper sticking out just far enough, you know it can't be done.

Fortunately the cat did not ask for chocolate. I didn't know then that it's bad for them, and I would have handed it over, quick as a wink, if I had been asked. I read for longer than I would have done if I had been alone, hoping my uninvited visitor would depart, but after he had fallen asleep, sprawled across a disproportionately ample area of the bed, I gave up and turned out the light. It took me a while to get to sleep. Wherever I tried to put my feet I found cat. It was so damned annoying I didn't even remember I had expected to lie awake brooding about the maze and Jordan's goofy theories about Dancing Floors.

ELEVEN

The way into the labyrinth represents the path
to the underworld, whereby the return to
Mother Earth is combined with the
hope for rebirth.

KERN, ARTFORUM 19, MAY, 1981

I thought about it next morning, though, when my sleepy eyes saw a crack of sunlight between the drawn draperies. I had been hoping for heavy rain so I'd have an excuse to pull out of the expedition.

The second thing I thought about was the cat. I was lying on the extreme edge of the bed, with one foot hanging off, but the cat had gone.

It had left me a note. Such was my first foggy impression when I saw the envelope propped against the cookie tin. However, the note turned out to be from Jordan.

"I'll be away for a few days. Don't let the old man do anything to the wilderness." That was it, except for scribbled initials. Not even "best wishes" or "sincerely."

Since my door had been left open I couldn't really complain about his coming in to leave the note, though I was surprised he had taken the trouble to inform me of his intentions. It must have been a sudden decision. He hadn't mentioned it before, at least not to me.

In mounting exasperation I reread the terse message. Why bother to tell me he was going away and not tell me where? He had talked with Giles the night before about some elderly relative who lived in . . . Nottingham, if I remembered correctly. Maybe that was where he had gone, in hot pursuit of the monster book and its anonymous author. The real mystery was why he was so fixated on the subject.

It was a little after eight when I went downstairs. There was nobody in the dining room and nothing in the chafing dishes, so I followed the smell of bacon into the kitchen, where I found Mrs. Greenspan in action.

The sight was so astonishing I stopped and stared. She wasn't moving fast, she just rolled relentlessly and unceasingly from stove to counter to refrigerator, stirring, chopping and rinsing, using both hands to pick up and discard implements. If I had stopped to think about it I would have wondered how she managed to get those gargantuan breakfasts on the table by eight-fifteen if she didn't arrive until eight. Now I understood. Practiced and oddly graceful, her movements resembled those of a grave ritual dance.

Doreen was dealing with the coffeemaker. As I entered the contraption made the uncouth noise that signified it had finished. Doreen filled two mugs and handed one to me.

"'Morning. You're up bright and early."

"Can I help?" I asked.

"Good Lord, no. Don't get in her way."

Five minutes later Mrs. Greenspan turned off the last burner and Doreen leaped into action, turning eggs, bacon, mushrooms and God knows what all into heated serving dishes. The cook sat down and picked up the mug of tea Doreen had prepared for her.

I said sincerely, "That's the most impressive thing I've ever seen."

Mrs. Greenspan ducked her head. "There's porridge," she murmured. "Mr. Jordan likes his porridge."

I didn't have the heart to tell her Jordan had left, sans porridge and, one presumed, breakfast. So she wouldn't be hurt I ate some of the porridge myself. Oatmeal is not one of my favorite dishes, but with thick cream and brown sugar it isn't at all bad.

Frank wasn't aware of Jordan's defection until Sean told him. He complained bitterly—just for the fun of complaining, I assumed, since he usually didn't care whether his son was there or not. I did not mention the note. When I said I had a date with Jennet, Frank turned his annoyance on me.

"You're always going off somewhere. You went shopping yesterday. I want you to help me today."

"I'm sure Sean will play with you if you ask nicely," I said.

"Not if it has anything to do with the garden," Sean said.

"Of course it has to do with the garden." Frank gave me a sly look. "I thought we might dig out more of that stone wall."

"You mean you want me to dig. I don't think Mr. Barnsley would approve of an amateur messing around out there."

"He has nothing to say about it. It is my property."

"True." I was curious about that wall myself. Rough homely foundation stones—but they had been laid over three hundred years ago while Roger Fallon looked on, and consulted the plan drawn up by John Tradescant himself.

The maze had been laid out by Tradescant too. Suddenly sobered, I said, "We'll work on it this afternoon, Frank."

"You'll be back in time for lunch?"

"I hope so," I said.

I didn't suppose either of the men would notice I wasn't dressed for a shopping trip, but I stole out the side door in order to avoid questions from Doreen. I had to cool my heels for a few minutes before Jennet pulled up and beckoned me to get in. Like me, she was wearing denim pants and stout shoes, and she looked as if she hadn't slept. The sight of her haggard face sent my spirits plummeting—and they had not been high to begin with.

Buckling myself in, I said casually, "I left a note."

She might be tired, but she wasn't slow. Understanding produced not resentment or scorn but open amusement. "The thrillers you read must be very badly plotted. A sensible murderer has better sense than to dispose of the victim when they are known to have gone off together. You did tell Frank we were going shopping, didn't you?"

"Yes, but it never hurts to be on the safe side."

"I can't argue with that." Her smile faded. "What are you looking for, Jennet?"

"Clues, my dear, what else? No, don't ask any more questions. Not yet. I rather think you'll be full of them before we've finished."

She stopped the car and we started off along the now-familiar track. The sun shone bright and dimmed briefly as a brisk wind sent fat white clouds rolling across the sky. The long ridge of Pendle Mountain brooded over the horizon. As we walked Jennet shrugged into her jacket and adjusted her fanny pack. We exchanged only a few sentences.

"You have gloves, I hope."

"Yes. I would have brought secateurs, but that might have raised questions."

"I have them."

Even in two days the harsh gashes of Sean's chain saw had been softened by new growth. I touched a pale green tendril, so soft I could have pinched it off with a fingernail, and marvelled at the tenacity of plant life. In time that fragile strand would harden into a stem as tough as rawhide and twine around a branch tightly enough to strangle it.

Jennet didn't pause. She pulled on a pair of gloves, took the clippers from her pack and went in.

In daylight, with a companion who obviously knew what she was doing, the place wasn't as bad as I remembered. The thinning of the roof allowed considerable light to enter. It was easy going at first, along the path Sean had widened and raised, but I couldn't believe how short a distance he had covered. I had wandered for what seemed like hours before I came across the statue. In less than a minute I saw the end of Sean's cutting.

Instead of continuing along that path Jennet turned and thrust both hands into the green wall. My involuntary exclamation of warning was never uttered. She pulled the vines aside, and I saw they were thornless—honeysuckle and Convolvulus, woven into a tight, living curtain. Beyond was the dim open space of another passage.

It was darker there, and lower, and there were thorns. "It is a maze," I breathed. "The multicursal type. Easy to follow if you know the pattern;

just as easy to lose your way if you don't know it. I still don't understand why it took me so long to reach the statue, or why I panicked, or how I got out, or—"

"People often panic even in conventional, open garden mazes. And this one isn't . . . conventional." She pushed through another curtain of vines and turned to face me. "There is only one true path to the center. You followed a false path, which led you to . . . something . . . that had been designed to guard and protect."

"Guard and protect what?"

"You'll see. Wait."

She moved more slowly now, pausing after each step to subject the ground to a searching scrutiny before she went on, sometimes turning from the visible way into another side passage. At last she stopped and spoke.

"Please bear in mind that what I'm about to show you is held in reverence by me and certain others. I can't swear you to secrecy. I must throw myself on your good will."

Covering her face with her hands she plunged through a thicker, darker veil of vines and disappeared.

It was my own fault. Her voice had been so grave, her manner so intense, I thought she had covered her face as a gesture of respect—reverence, to use her own word. I knew what lay beyond that veil of vines. The heart of the maze, the center of their worship. I might respect that belief, but I did not share it.

So I didn't protect my face, and of course I ended up with a couple of nasty scratches. I didn't feel them though. I had thought I knew what occupied the heart of the maze, but I had been wrong. What I saw literally took my breath away.

A hemisphere of living green enclosed a space less than ten feet in diameter, which was carpeted with velvety emerald moss. She stood in the center, white arms curved. In that first breathtaking moment I didn't see the chips and nicks and stains, or the lines of repair across neck and arms and slim ankles, I saw only the grace of her body and the proud tilt of her head. The short tunic left her legs bare and exposed one rounded breast. Through the clustered curls on her brow protruded . . . not horns, but the tips of the crescent moon.

"Diana," I said in an awed whisper.

"Artemis, Isis, Herodias; Demeter, Cybele, Kore, Hecate. She has had many names. All are One."

Jennet's hand moved in a gesture I couldn't see precisely. When she spoke again it was in her old brisk, practical voice.

"We don't worship statues. This is a symbol of the life force in its feminine aspect."

"It's the most beautiful thing I've ever seen." Even the air was a soft luminous green, sunlight diffused—appropriately—by new growth, rebirth and renewal. At the apex of the dome the vines were so thin that there must have been an opening there very recently. At certain times of the year, moonlight would shine down into the hidden glade and the moon itself would be visible.

As the first, stunning impact of that vision faded, something less comfortable occurred to me. The virgin goddess, whose symbol was the moon, was only one aspect of the threefold "feminine principle." Maiden, Mother, and Crone—the Virgin, the Nurturer, and the Wise Woman whose embrace meant darkness and death. The Maiden wasn't always benevolent either; the hounds of Artemis hunted, to the death, those who had offended her. I looked at the lovely, arched marble feet and remembered the ending of *The Monster of the Maze*—the girl's footprints, next to Roger Fallon's dead body. Fiction, of course. Right. But here I was, in the heart of a thorny wilderness whose paths I did not know, with a woman who worshipped "the feminine principle" in all its manifestations.

I cleared my throat. "Uh— Do you come here often?" I inquired, and could have kicked myself for the inanity of the words.

Jennet was walking around the perimeter of the space, peering closely at the ground. Apparently she didn't find the question as pointless as I had. She frowned. "I've already disclosed more than I ought. The details are none of your affair."

"I don't give a damn about your religious activities, Jennet, but I'm tired of enigmatic remarks, and I have a feeling some of those details *are* my affair." Confronting her so bluntly might not have been wise, but I wasn't really afraid of her, or of the place itself. Not any longer. I demanded, "Why did you bring me here?"

She completed the circuit and came to stand next to me. "Two reasons. For one thing, I wanted a witness in case I found . . . But you can see for yourself. No one has been here."

Her outflung hand indicated the soft un-marked turf. Moss is delicate. Heavy shoes would have torn and crushed it, especially if the wearer of the shoes were of a destructive nature.

"Not Bobby, at any rate," I agreed. "He'd probably have ripped the arms off the statue. You thought he might have come here? But you told me, the other day, he didn't know about it."

"He should not have known. But it's possible he found out. Are you sure about that light Jordan saw?"

"I didn't see it. Why don't you ask him?"

"He may have imagined it. Or seen reflected moonlight."

"Or invented the whole thing." The slim white shape drew my eyes like a magnet. I could see the small disfigurements wrought by time more clearly now, but it was still beautiful. "Wait till he sees this," I said. "He's got some theory about the pagan origins of mazes—"

"That's not a new idea," Jennet said abstract-edly.

"—and that this maze has something to do with the Dancing Floor."

Jennet spun around. "Where did he hear that name?"

"From me, I guess. I heard the girls talking about it."

"Jordan is on the wrong track," Jennet said flatly. "This is not the Dancing Floor."

"Then there is such a place?"

Jennet's eyes narrowed. "You're as persistent as a wasp. Yes, there is such a place, and it's none of your business where it is or what goes on there. This isn't it. This is a sacred spot. It is only visited on special occasions."

Such as the four great festival days of the Old Religion? One, as Jordan had reminded me, was May first. That would explain why the path had been clear and open when I stumbled on it, and into it, a week later.

No wonder the followers of that belief considered this a holy spot. There she stood, as she had stood for centuries, the embodiment of the principle they worshipped. And so beautiful, in a setting so perfect, I was tempted to bend the knee to her myself.

"Wow," I said, under my breath. "Jordan is going to flip when he sees this."

"Heather, you don't owe me anything and there's no reason why you should do me a favor, but I'd rather you didn't tell Jordan about this. If Frank goes ahead with his landscaping schemes the entire area will be razed to the ground. There will be nothing left of it."

"But if they don't know she's here, they'll

bulldoze right over her. It would be a crime to destroy something so old and so beautiful."

"I agree. That won't happen if you'll give me time to make other arrangements."

"Oh. I see."

"Is it so unreasonable?" She was deadly earnest, her voice deep and unsteady. "To Jordan, even to Frank, it's an interesting survival. It means a great deal more to me. She has been here, in the heart of the maze, for over three hundred years. There were other . . . images. They are all gone now except for her. The horned god was the last, and his destruction means that what this place symbolized is gone forever. Her presence will consecrate some other place, if you'll let me do what I want to do."

"Well . . . I won't do or say anything without consulting you first."

"That's more than fair. Thank you."

"Can we go now?"

"Yes, certainly. Watch where you're going, you've already acquired a few scratches that will take some explaining."

I followed her example as we left the glade, protecting my face with gloved hands. "This is even more confusing than the maze at Hampton Court. Where's the other entrance, the one I came out?"

"There isn't another entrance." Jennet went on without looking back at me. "You found the one narrow spot where it is possible to get out, and plowed straight through twelve inches of brambles and vines. I don't know how you did it."

"Me neither. You said you had two reasons for bringing me along. What's the second one?"

"That was it. You're involved with this place now, whether you like it or not. Without protection you could never have found your way in and through."

"It was pure accident."

"There is no such thing. This way." She didn't speak again until we had emerged into the sunlight. Then she said, "Frank was right about you. You are part of the pattern, and you were meant to be here. Apparently the destruction of this place is also part of the pattern. I must accept that."

"So you don't blame me?" I inquired hopefully.

"How could I? You are only a tool. One does not blame the scissors that cut the web."

I was relieved to hear it.

ii

I had intended to sneak in the side door, but as luck would have it Frank and Sean were on that side of the house inspecting the veranda. I didn't see them until it was too late to retreat. Frank broke off in the middle of a sentence that had started, "It's dangerous and in the—" to demand what I had done to myself.

"I tripped getting out of Jennet's car and fell against the gatepost," I said glibly. "Some of those stones have sharp edges."

"You should be more careful," Frank scolded. "Go clean yourself up and then come to lunch."

"Is it that late?"

It was. How long had we stood in that green haze where the goddess lived?

Sean gave me a knowing smile. "I'd like to see the other guy."

"I never laid a glove on her," I riposted wittily.

"No packages?"

"I couldn't find anything that fit. What's going on with the veranda?"

"Frank's decided it has to come down, or off, as the case may be. I'm supposed to spend the afternoon finding someone to do the job."

"It's a wise decision. The darned thing is ugly and it's falling down anyhow."

"You should know. I thought you might object to having your means of egress removed."

"I have my handy-dandy ladder."

"I—uh—may not be around this evening."

I gave him a haughty stare. "I wasn't planning to use it this evening."

"Just thought I'd mention it."

"Kind of you." I marched off, my nose in the air.

At lunch Frank elaborated on his plans. "I've

been reconsidering my views concerning the house, Heather. You were right about the veranda, it's a useless appendage and it looks terrible. I don't want to rebuild, but a moderate amount of remodelling could make the place more comfortable and convenient. What do you think?"

"I think it's entirely up to you," I said.

He folded his hands and beamed benevolently at me. "Ah, but what I need is a woman's viewpoint. Imagine that you owned the place and planned to live here. What changes would you make?"

Surmises as wild as weeds burgeoned in my brain. Was Frank planning to take a wife? Was it me? The last idea—courtesy of Jordan, damn his eyes—was so lunatic I almost laughed out loud—at myself. Frank had found himself another new game. He had probably never remodelled or redecorated a room, much less a house, in his life.

Neither had I. She had always selected the furniture, the curtains, the ornaments. As a game, a purely theoretical exercise, it had a certain fascination. Supposing I had all the money in the world and could do exactly as I liked . . .

"Well . . ." I said.

After a while we retired to the library where Frank could take notes and I could sketch floor plans. "Once the veranda is gone the drawing room will have more light. It's no wonder you hardly ever use it now, it's so dark and out of the way. You could put another staircase in the main hall outside the drawing room—you really need two sets of stairs in a house this size."

"There is another staircase, the one the servants used." Frank sounded as if he were as interested as I. "It's been blocked up for years, but it might be feasible to repair and reopen it."

It was fun. I even found myself talking about color schemes and furniture. When I wound down, Frank carefully collected my scribbles and his lists and put them in a folder. I couldn't be sure how seriously he had taken my suggestions. Some of his ideas had been even more extravagant than mine, though.

"You can't just go around tearing down walls," I protested, after he had proposed throwing two of the upstairs bedrooms into a single suite. "They hold up the roof. Anyhow, you should ask Jordan before you start destroying his room."

"His opinions are inconsequential," said Frank, with a wave of his hand. "Compared with yours."

"Well, if you're going to make a mess of his quarters don't blame it on me. How long is he going to be gone?"

"Who knows? A day, a week. That reminds me, I had almost forgotten—Lindsay called earlier asking for you. I said you would call her back."

"Looking for me? Why?"

"She didn't say. Do you want to return her call now, before we start the digging?"

"I don't want to return her call at all, but I suppose I should."

"Yes, you should, it would only be polite," Frank said. "She left the number. She has gone back to her mother's."

I didn't say anything. After a moment Frank volunteered the information for which I had not asked. "They quarrelled again last night. Doreen didn't know what about, but I think perhaps Giles was angry with her for asking Jennet to use her talents. He has no sympathy with such things."

"I don't either. But I can't blame Lindsay; if I were in her place I'd try anything. There's still been no trace of the boy?"

"Not that I've heard. It distresses you, doesn't it?"

I turned away. "It's the uncertainty that's so horrible—and the fact that it could continue indefinitely. Thousands of children go missing and are never found. I can't imagine living with that for months, maybe years. Nothing could be worse."

"Nothing?"

I didn't know whether he was referring to my loss or to his own. His own, probably. Since I wasn't supposed to know about it—and would not have been inclined to discuss it anyhow—I said, "I may as well call and see what she wants."

Lindsay's mother answered the phone. Her voice was faded and overly genteel and my name did not inspire any warmth. "No, she's not

here. I'm sure I can't say when she'll be back. I'll
tell her you rang."

She hung up before I could repeat my name
or ask, as I had meant to do, about Laura. She
was there; I had heard her, whining in the
background. If it had been any of my business
I would have been worried about that child
too.

"Let's dig," I said, returning the phone to the
cradle with more force than was strictly necessary.

On my way to the shed to get a trowel I
glanced into the kitchen garden and saw a back-
side I recognized, upended over a row of
radishes. It was partly courtesy that moved me
to speak and partly the hope that I could enlist
a helper. I knew Frank wouldn't do anything
except look on and make impractical suggestions.

I hailed him, and he straightened slowly,
clutching his back in a practiced gesture.

"Why don't you kneel instead of stooping?" I
asked. "It wouldn't be so hard on your back."

"It's my knees, you see. Got the arthritis terrible bad. You can help with the weeding if you
like."

I was tempted to ask how old he was. He
probably wouldn't tell me; complaining about
aches and pains is a habit with gardeners. He
wasn't all that antiquated. The sandy hair sticking out from under his cap showed no gray, and
his hands, though callused and hard, weren't

deformed by swollen joints. I'd have guessed his age at around fifty, about the same as my father.

"That's very kind of you," I said. "Actually I was hoping to talk you into helping me dig. We found some foundation stones the other day and Mr. Karim wants to see how the line runs."

He shook his head and set his lips. "I have naught to do with that. I stick to my vegetables."

"Okay. He's waiting for me, so I'd better get back. I'm going to borrow a trowel, if that's all right."

"Just so you clean it off and put it back. Doesn't do to leave tools lying about."

I had turned away from the gate. I went back and leaned on it. "You'd never do that, would you?"

He narrowed his eyes at me and waved the insulting question away. "So it's true that the old man is going to have all that lot down?"

"I don't know exactly what he's planning. It depends on what the landscape architect suggests."

"Ah." His expression clearly indicated what he thought of landscape architects. He waited until I had turned to go before he spoke again. "Seen my herb garden, have you?"

"I'm afraid I don't have time—"

"Come when you like. Take what you like. They're all there."

This time it was he who turned away. Like royalty, he claimed the right to end a conversation. I called "Thank you," and got a grunt for an answer.

I selected a trowel and started back. Had that comment about leaving tools around been a general warning or a reference to poor Terry's accident? Will had probably heard of it; the grapevine worked efficiently in these parts. It could have been both. I was the only other person who used those tools.

As I had expected, Frank confined his assistance to looking on and indicating places where he wanted me to dig. We, to use the word loosely, uncovered another two-foot stretch of the wall before he conceded that "we" had done enough for the day.

"It is almost teatime. But it goes so slowly! You could use a shovel."

"No, I could not." I brushed the dirt from the knees of my pants. "Good heavens, Frank, those stones are practically sacred relics. A spade might dislodge or break them. You go in, I'm going to put the trowel back and clean up."

"We will have tea in the library today," Frank said. "It's too windy to eat outside."

"Good idea." I grabbed at my shirttails in time to prevent them from being blown up over my head. Tibb wouldn't get any salmon sandwiches this afternoon.

I wiped the trowel and put it back in its place. On my way back I looked over the gate into the kitchen garden. Will was gone. The man came and went like one of the little elves in the story, unheralded and unobserved, but he did manage to get through a lot of work in a short time. The rows of veggies were weed-free and healthy looking.

Twice now—on the only two occasions when I had seen him—he had made a point of that herb garden. It might be the crown jewel of his little domain, but I was beginning to think there was another reason for his harping on that theme. I unlatched the gate and went in.

If I hadn't known better I might have thought Will had abandoned his prejudice against flowers in this part of the garden. Walled off by a hedge of miniature hollies, the sheltered spot blossomed with patches of pink and bright blue, feathery white and yellow. The plants weren't arranged in parallel rows but in clumps, and I followed the narrow paths between and around them.

He hadn't labelled them. Why should he? He knew what they were. Some weren't what I would have called herbs—the trailing stems and deep blue blossoms of periwinkle and the soft crumpled rosettes of foxglove. I recognized yarrow and comfrey; others I could only guess at. A handsome plant with spotted leaves had to be a variety of pulmonaria, or lungwort—an ugly name for a very handsome plant. It was covered with dainty pink blossoms.

Many of the standard culinary herbs were there—rosemary and thyme, parsley, and the elliptical leaves of some variety of allium. One corner boasted a clump of velvety green catnip, bordered by a lower growing variety of Nepeta with grayish green foliage. Both were a bit mashed, probably by Tibb rolling in them. I couldn't identify the fernlike foliage of the tall plants set behind the catnip.

Some people would have found it touching that the gruff gardener grew herbs for a cat. Tibb wasn't just a cat, though. He was a genius loci. A benevolent guardian spirit appreciated offerings, and what more appropriate offering for this one than catnip?

Basil and marjoram and some of the other culinary herbs had another function. They were for protection against evil spirits and for un-crossing—cancelling a curse. Periwinkle was used in love charms, and yarrow was woven into wreaths to protect dwellings on Midsummer Eve, another of the old pagan festivals. Even parsley had occult connotations; the safest time to plant it is on Good Friday, when it is free of the devilish influences it possesses at other times.

And of course it is one of the ingredients in the brew that can turn a person into a werewolf.

Was Will one of them? It boggled my mind to think of the stony-faced gardener footing it lightly across the Dancing Floor with Doreen and the teenagers. But he knew something; he had spotted the cat's-eye stone and pressed me to take whatever herbs I liked.

I took nothing, not even a sprig of periwinkle.

When I entered the kitchen Doreen looked me over, lips pursed critically. I expected a comment on my scratched face and general dishevellment, but she said only, "You'd better hurry up. The old man is yelling for his tea and he won't have it until you're there."

"Go ahead and take it in. Tell him I'll be down in a few minutes." I lifted the tablecloth and peered underneath.

"What are you looking for?" Doreen asked.

"The cat."

"Haven't seen him."

"He spent the night with me. Part of it, anyhow. How did he get in my room?"

Mrs. Greenspan had been arranging tea sandwiches on a plate. Her plump hands stopped moving, and she and Doreen exchanged a long look.

"It wasn't me that put him there, if that's what you mean," Doreen said.

"I didn't suppose you had done it deliberately. I just wondered."

They looked so ordinary, but with only a slight stretch of the imagination I could see them in other roles. Mrs. Greenspan the quintessential earth mother, feeding the hungry and watching over the hearth; Doreen a younger, more sensual aspect of the goddess, vine leaves in her flaming hair, treading the maze hand in hand with . . .

"Excuse me," I muttered, and fled.

iii

I dreamed I was being pressed to death. That, in case I have neglected to mention it, was one of the many interesting ways in which they disposed of witches. It was a very realistic dream—the heavy weight on my diaphragm, the struggle for breath, the jeering howls of the torturers. Oddly enough, my arms seemed to be free. I grabbed wildly at my chest. Sharp nails stabbed into my hand.

I'm not sure precisely when I realized that I was awake, and that the lump on my chest was warm and covered with fur. Tibb figured it out before I did. He stood up, all four feet pressing painfully into various sensitive parts of my anatomy and let out another peremptory howl. I had never heard him make a noise like that.

The room was dark but the door stood open. The glow of the hall light seemed dimmer than usual, as if the bulb were about to go. My throat was dry, and I heard a sound like paper crumpling or . . .

"God!"

I got out of bed and bolted for the door. I could see the flames even from there; the fire was blazing brightly in the hall below. The floorboards were hot enough to singe my bare feet as I dashed for Frank's room. How much time did we have? Minutes, maybe seconds, before the dry, varnished wooden flooring burst into flame.

The smoke was thicker in his room, a gray fog that clogged my lungs and made me cough. He lay unmoving, a humped shape under the blankets. I grabbed an arm and pulled with a strength I hadn't known I possessed, dragging him bodily out of the bed and onto the floor. The jarring impact, and the fact that the air was clearer there, roused him a little; he stirred feebly and started to cough. Some part of my mind I wasn't using at that moment thanked God he was still capable of responding. I snatched the water bottle from the table and dumped the contents over his face and chest.

Alternately pulling and pushing, cajoling and cursing, I got him onto his feet and draped his arm over my shoulders. He was six inches taller than I and fifty or sixty pounds heavier and only half aware of what was going on, but I got him to the door and out in one long staggering rush. Only a few more yards, to the door of my room, and we had a fighting chance. If he couldn't get down that ladder I would get him down it—somehow. The stairs were gone. Glancing to one side as we stumbled down the passage I saw a bright fringe of flame stroke the frame of John the Younger's portrait. The bearded face was beginning to dissolve into blisters.

Closing my door gave me a false but comforting sense of temporary safety. I dropped Frank onto the floor and pulled back the drapes. The wind roared in. It blew away some of my panic and confusion, and I forced myself to take a few seconds to assess the situation.

Thank God for the wind. It was blowing from the north, against the flames. The fire must have started in the kitchen, which was blazing merrily, but thanks to that blessed wind the north wing of the house was still untouched. We would have to hurry, though, before the flames ate their way up through the floor.

I ran into the bathroom, dumped all the towels into the tub, and turned on both faucets. It wasn't until then that I remembered the cat, and I spared an entire vital minute—which seemed like twenty—calling it and looking for it under the bed and in the wardrobe. There was no sign of it, and no response to my calls. I could only pray it had found a way out.

Smoke was curling in under the door, so I jammed one of the wet towels into the crack before I turned my attention to Frank. I didn't need the wet towels. The fresh air must have restored him, he was on his feet—leaning for support against the wall, but upright and, I hoped, aware. I spared enough breath for a muttered "Thank God," as I heaved the rope ladder out the window. Then I grabbed him by the arm and tugged at him, trying to turn him toward me and toward the window. He was as heavy and unresponsive as a dead man.

"Frank? Can you hear me? The house is on

fire, we've got to get out. For God's sake, Frank, move it!"

Between the outside lights and the fire the night was as bright as day. I could see the drops of sweat on his cheek and the graying stubble along his jaw.

The face he had turned on me might have belonged to a genuine monster of the maze, gray and rigid as stone, blankly staring. I don't think he recognized me or even saw me, except as an obstacle in his way. His right arm struck me with an impersonal violence that flung me back across the bed. By the time I got up he had reached the door and vanished into the smoke outside.

The truth slammed into my brain so hard it felt like another blow. Pausing only long enough to grab the wet towel, I went after him. I couldn't see, the smoke was too thick. I didn't have to see. I knew where he had gone, and I knew why.

He had left Jordan's door open. I slammed it shut and headed for the window, the one opposite the door. The veranda roof under that window was our only chance now. I pulled the drapes back and drew the clean air deep into my lungs before I went to help Frank.

The smoke wasn't as bad here, but Jordan was obviously one of those people who is hard to wake up, especially after he has had only a couple of hours' sleep. Frank was trying to drag him out of bed. Through the roar of the fire I could hear Jordan swearing sleepily and Frank coughing.

I slapped Jordan across the face with the wet towel. "Get up, damn you! The house is on fire."

"Fire," Jordan repeated. "Fire?" He sat up. "Fire! Why the hell didn't you say so?"

Frank doubled up, clutching his chest. Jordan shot out of bed in time to catch him as he fell. "Get him out," I gasped. "Quick. The window."

By that time Jordan's breathing wasn't very good either. He didn't waste time trying to lift Frank, he dragged him across the room and draped him over the sill. Neither of us could speak even if we had been inclined toward conversation, we were too busy trying to breathe. I scrambled out onto the roof and managed to keep Frank from rolling off it when Jordan pushed him out the window. We slid and crawled in an ungainly tangle toward the edge.

"You first." Jordan reinforced the order with an emphatic push.

"How are you going to get him—"

He just looked at me. It had been a stupid question. Any place, any way, was better than this. Flames curled around the far end of the veranda; everything except this farthest corner must be blazing by now. It was a miracle the roof hadn't fallen in.

Without further debate I lowered myself off the roof and climbed down the post. Halfway down, I should say; I fell the rest of the way. My

knees were very wobbly and I felt sick at my
stomach, and the lurid hellish light I saw
through the windows of the drawing room
made me willing to risk broken bones rather
than hang around any longer than I absolutely
had to.

I crawled out of the azaleas and found myself
looking up at the soles of Frank's feet. Jordan
had lowered him by his wrists. "Out of the
way," he called, adding a string of epithets for
emphasis, and let go. Frank crashed down into
the bushes. A few seconds later so did Jordan.
Between us we hoisted Frank out of the bushes
and staggered off across the lawn. My heart was
banging around in my chest and my lungs felt
as if they were about to burst and my eyes were
blurry. I went on moving mechanically until
Jordan stopped, pulling Frank's feet free of my
grasp. I fell to my knees, and my body decided
to go the rest of the way. Facedown on the grass
I whooped and gagged until Jordan's foot came
in hard contact with my ribs. At least he wasn't
wearing shoes.

"Go for help. Where's that bastard Sean?"

"Sean!" I sat up and brushed my hair out of
my eyes. I was sticky all over with sweat, but all
of a sudden I felt cold, and not because of the
wind. "Yes, where can he be? You don't think
the cottage—"

Jordan was bending over his father, rhythmi-
cally pumping on his chest. "We may need the
manual override to open the gates. The key is—"

"You go, you know where things are. I'll take over." I waited for the right moment and substituted my hands for his. "God, he looks bad. All that smoke."

"Heart," Jordan said curtly. "I'll be back as soon as I can. Put this over him." He stripped off his pajama top and tossed it to me and went running off across the grass, his shadow black and distorted by the flames.

I managed to get the extra layer of cloth over Frank without breaking my rhythm. His own pajamas were clammy cold from the water I had poured over him and he didn't seem to be breathing. I was shivering too, though I could feel the heat on my back and see, out of the corner of my eye, that flames were spouting from the roof. Where the hell was Sean? Why hadn't someone called the fire department? The flames must be visible for some distance.

It wasn't until much later that I realized the whole business couldn't have lasted more than ten minutes, from start to finish. It wasn't until later that I was able to think at all. Right then every brain cell and every muscle had narrowed in on a single set of movements. I was only dimly aware of the roar when the roof fell in. I didn't hear the sirens. I went on pushing and counting as mechanically as a machine until someone lifted me to my feet.

"All right, Heather, you can stop now."

I rubbed the sweat, or maybe it was tears, out

of my eyes and looked around. People were running around all over the place. Two men were lifting Frank onto a stretcher. Sean was there too, staring down at the old man's still face. He looked different, but I was too confused to figure out how. Jordan was talking to another man dressed in some kind of uniform. Bare-chested, his face streaked with soot and his hair standing on end, he resembled a refugee from a prison camp. I looked down at the smoke-stained rags of my nightgown, and then up into the face of the man who held me by the shoulders. I should have been surprised to see him, but I wasn't. I was long past feeling anything as complicated as surprise.

"Hello, Giles," I croaked. "Nice of you to come. Can I throw up now?"

He made a funny choking noise and took me in his arms. I leaned against him. He felt so nice and warm. My teeth were chattering.

"Very pretty," said Jordan, behind me. "But she probably will, you know, she's swallowed quite a lot of smoke. Hold her head and then give her your jacket if you want to make a useful contribution."

I didn't throw up, but they did some nasty things to me at the hospital before they let me go and sit in the waiting room with the others. Frank was in intensive care, with a couple of doctors monitoring him. He was still alive, but it would be a while before they knew . . . Before they knew.

They had made some attempt to brighten the waiting room with plastic flowers and blue and white striped curtains, but it had the depressing atmosphere of all such places—places where worried people wait to hear whether loved ones will live or die. There was a rack of crumpled, out-of-date magazines on the wall.

Giles got up and led me to a chair. He had given Jordan his jacket. I was tastefully attired in my shredded nightie and a faded cotton hospital gown.

"You ought to be in bed," he said. "Wouldn't they admit you?"

"I don't want to stay here. Damned if I know where I am going to sleep, though."

"You're coming home with me, of course. Both of you." He glanced at Jordan.

"There's no need for you to stay," Jordan said. He added, "Either of you."

"Don't be an idiot," I said, rearranging the folds of fabric across my chest.

"Would you like some coffee?" Giles asked. "It's pretty vile, but it's hot."

"Try her on a couple of sandwiches and a few slabs of cake," Jordan said. "If she can't eat she should be in the hospital."

"Where's Sean?" I asked.

"Still in emergency. His hands were pretty badly burned."

His face hadn't gone unscathed either. That

was why he had looked so strange—his eye-brows were gone, and half his beard.

"What was he trying to do?" I asked.

"Get a ladder up to Dad's window. I had to knock him down before he'd listen to me."

"Poor Sean. He must have been beside him-self."

"He was drunk," Jordan said. He rubbed his scraped knuckles. "You don't suppose I could have landed a blow if he'd been sober, do you?"

"No," I admitted.

"Thanks."

Giles came back with a couple of paper cups and I sipped the coffee, which was indeed vile. If anything else were needed to complete the catastrophes of that night, Sean's defection would have been it. He hadn't seen the fire until it was too late; he had been drinking, and I felt sure he had not been drinking alone. It looked as if we were in for another round of heavy guilt.

When Sean joined us he was accompanied by an angry nurse. "You just get yourself back downstairs, young—sir. The doctor hasn't fin-ished with you."

"I'm finished with him," Sean said. "Get lost, honey."

The skin on his face was bright red and shiny and blistered. His beard was a ragged fringe. His hands would have turned a sensitive stomach, but they didn't bother me as much as the look in his eyes.

"Sit down," I said. "Coffee? I'll hold it for you."

"No, thanks."

The nurse stamped out, shaking her head. Sean subsided slowly into a chair. "You got him out," he said, addressing me.

"It was pure luck," I said, with some vague notion that the disclaimer would make him feel a little less guilty. "If the cat hadn't waked me—"

"What cat?" Jordan demanded. "You didn't tell me that."

"There hasn't been time to talk about . . . about much." I put my head in my hands. "The cat. You know—Tibb. I've heard of animals doing that, smelling the smoke and rousing the people in the house. I don't know what happened to him. I'm afraid he . . . Why am I getting so upset about the poor damned cat?"

My voice rose to a wail. Giles put his arm around my shoulders. "Heather, dear, you're about to fall apart. And high bloody time too. Let me take you home."

Home. What a beautiful word. I sat up and rubbed my eyes. "Not till we find out about Frank. I didn't know he had a bad heart. Why didn't somebody tell me he had a bad heart?"

"What could you have done about it?" Giles asked reasonably. "You did what had to be done, and it was a hell of a lot more than most people could have accomplished."

"I tried to get him to go down the ladder," I muttered. My nose was running. I wiped it on the back of my hand. "He pushed me out of the way. I didn't even know you were there, Jordan. He knew. Why doesn't somebody tell me to shut up?"

"Shut up," said somebody.

Jordan, of course. I blew my nose on the tissue somebody else had handed me. Giles, of course. Sean said again, like a recording, "You got him out." No one spoke again.

When the doctor finally came I knew by the look on his face what he was going to say. Doctors don't smile when they tell you somebody is dead. He told us to go home—home!—and come back next day.

"Thank God," Giles said sincerely. "Now let's tend to the rest of you."

I creaked to my feet. Every joint felt as if it needed lubricating.

"You can't walk far, especially in that ensemble," Giles said. "It's almost morning. I'll go and bring the car round to the emergency entrance. Jordan, will you . . . Jordan? Are you all right?"

Jordan hadn't spoken, not even in response to the doctor. He turned an expressionless countenance toward Giles and nodded.

"Come along with Heather in a few minutes, then," Giles said. "You too, Sean; there's plenty of room, if you don't mind sleeping in . . . in one of the children's rooms."

"I'm staying," Sean said.

There was no arguing with a statement that had been pronounced with the flat finality of a basic truth. "Right," Giles said. "Come later, if you like. Any time."

After he had left the room I touched Sean's shoulder. "Let them take care of your hands."

"Don't worry about me," Sean said. "Giles needs your TLC more than I do."

"I suppose that's true. The worst is over for us, and Lord knows it could have been a lot worse. He's still in limbo, not knowing whether his son is alive or dead."

"He's alive."

"What do you mean?"

"He never went to Birmingham. He's around here, not far away. Who do you think started that fire?"

TWELVE

Expatiate free o'er all this scene of man;
A mighty maze! But not without a plan.

POPE, *AN ESSAY ON MAN*, 1733–4, EPISTLE 1

It wasn't difficult to understand why Sean wanted to believe the fire had been deliberately set. He had been the last to leave the house and he was responsible for its security. If he had been in a hurry, thinking about his plans for that night, he might have failed to notice something wrong. He would feel responsible anyhow, but this theory made him less negligent, and when you're talking guilt, every little bit helps.

My thoughts ran into a dead end at about that point. I was out on my feet, barely capable of moving, completely incapable of thinking about anything except a bed. I shook my head helplessly at him, and staggered out.

Things got rather blurry after that. When I opened my eyes and saw Jennet seated beside

the bed it took me a while to remember how I
had gotten there.

The room looked like an illustration from a
home and garden magazine, all flowered chintz
and tastefully coordinated colors. It was obviously a guest room. There was a horrible taste
in my mouth, and my lips were gummy. I pried
them apart and sorted through the miscellaneous jumble in my head for an appropriate
word. "Coffee," I croaked.

"I thought you'd say that. Back in a minute."

By the time she returned with a tray I had
found another word. "Frank?" I asked, taking
the cup she offered me.

"Coming along nicely. They're planning to
move him out of intensive care tomorrow."

"Have you seen him?"

She shook her head. "No visitors allowed.
Except Jordan, of course."

"That must have been some meeting. I wonder what they said to each other."

"Nothing. They stared at one another for a
couple of minutes and then Jordan left." My
skeptical expression produced a faint smile.
"No, I wasn't there, and no, I didn't use clairvoyance. One of the nurses is a good customer
of mine."

"Where is he? Where is—"

"If you'll stop asking questions I'll bring you
up to date." She crossed her legs. "Jordan is at
the hotel. He's taken a room for you too—if you
want it. Giles said you were welcome to stay

here as long as you like. He's gone to the office. I persuaded Sean to let me work on his hands. Strange as it may seem, he has more confidence in my methods than in conventional medicine. He's gone back to the hospital. I brought you some clothes, and a toothbrush and comb and a few other odds and ends. More coffee?"

Mutely I held out my cup. She refilled it from the carafe, and I considered the information she had rattled off so glibly. I still had a lot of questions, but she had certainly covered the main points.

I was in Giles's house—and in his pajamas. They were miles too big, even for me; the sleeves kept unrolling and sliding down over my hand. Obviously I couldn't stay in them, or in his house. Jennet had provided me with the necessary means to leave and a place to go. An efficient woman, Jennet.

The garments she had placed on a chair by the bed weren't my style, but they were probably the best she could do on short notice. The full skirt had an elasticized waistband, one size fits all, and a design that featured stars, suns, and moons. There was a matching Goddess Top in pale blue, and even a pair of sandals—with cats on them.

It hadn't hit me till then. Those bizarre garments were my sole possessions. Thanks to its slate roof the garage hadn't burned, so I assumed my car was intact, but it was a rental car. Clothes, money, passport, credit cards; shoes, purse, luggage . . . everything I had owned was gone. Including my past—the letters and snapshots, the greeting cards with their loving messages, the gifts.

"Would you like something to eat?" Jennet asked.

As a rule that question gets my attention, but for once I was too dazed to respond. The sheer enormity of the change in my life was difficult to assimilate all at once. I shook my head. Then I threw the blanket back and stood up.

"I'm going to get dressed and go to the hotel, if you don't mind driving me."

"That's what I'm here for," Jennet said. She was looking at my feet, hidden by the overlapping folds of Giles's pajamas. It didn't require a talent for clairvoyance to know what she was thinking.

I hoisted up the pajamas and headed for the bathroom.

ii

Jennet dropped me at the hotel. We hadn't talked much; I had thanked her, awkwardly but sincerely, for providing me with the things only a woman would think of, including shampoo and soap scented with a strong clean herbal perfume. I had to wash my hair twice to get rid of the faint, sickening smell of smoke.

It took some nerve to walk into the lobby in

those clothes. The skirt billowed around my ankles and the top flapped and the sandals pinched my feet. They are quite large—my feet, I mean. However, I was received with flattering attention and outpourings of sympathy and good will; apparently the whole village was under the impression that I had been the hero of the occasion. Among the messages awaiting me was one from the editor of a local newspaper, asking when—when, not if—he could send a reporter to interview me.

I fled for the elevator, refusing the unnecessary assistance of a bellman. Since I had the key it didn't occur to me to knock before I unlocked the door and saw Jordan ensconced in a chair watching television.

There was no bed in the room, only chairs and a sofa and a couple of tables. "Oh," I said. "They must have given me the wrong key. You, of course, have a suite."

"*The* suite," Jordan corrected. "Sitting room and two bedrooms. That's yours. There's a bolt on the inside of the door."

He returned his attention to the TV. The program appeared to be a game show. It was the first time I had ever seen Jordan do anything so frivolous. But then he had lost everything too. His notes, his books, his script. Years of work gone up in smoke.

"Where did you get the clothes?" I asked. He was wearing tan slacks and a white shirt, neither of which fit very well.

"Giles." He looked me over, from sandals to damp hair, his lip curling. "New wardrobes are definitely in order for both of us. We'll deal with that problem tomorrow morning."

I sat down, more suddenly than I had intended, on the sofa. "I don't have any money. Or credit cards."

"The old man has all the credit you'll ever need."

"I can't take—"

"You'll have to, unless you plan to go around dressed like a raggle-taggle gypsy for the rest of the week." He pointed the remote at the television set. The screen went dark. "Don't be disingenuous," he said roughly. "The least he can do is replace what you lost. You saved his life. And mine, for what that's worth."

I thought of him standing by his father's bedside with that same closed-in look, too proud to display his feelings, and Frank glowering back at him, too stubborn to admit his, and of the waste of something as precious as it was forever at risk.

"It's worth a lot to him," I said, choking with rage. "Worth more than his own. I wasn't the one who saved your life. I didn't even know you'd come back. He was barely conscious when I dragged him into my room and tried to get him to go down that ladder, but he knocked me down—knocked me flat!—he was so frantic to get to you. If you could have seen his face . . ."

I didn't really expect he'd dissolve in tears or

thank me, in broken accents, for breaking down the barriers between him and his father. What I really expected was that he'd sneer at me for being a sentimental jerk, or yell at me for being an interfering, sentimental jerk. He didn't say anything. Not a muscle in his face moved.

"And you," I said. "You knew about his bad heart. That's why you were living there instead of locating in a city with a major library or university—to be near him in case he needed you. Not that you'd ever admit it. Men! Honestly, I wonder sometimes how you—"

The telephone rang. Jordan picked it up. His end of the ensuing conversation wasn't very illuminating. It consisted solely of monosyllables—yes, no, right, fine. Then he held the instrument out to me.

I shied back. "It's not that reporter, is it?"

Annoyance—the first emotion he had displayed for several minutes—darkened his face. "I'll deal with the reporters, just pass them on to me. No, it's Giles."

"Oh."

"You will no doubt ask him to join us for dinner," Jordan said. "Jennet suggested we have it sent up here. Seven, if you can wait that long."

He went into his room and closed the door.

I did ask Giles to join us, after I had thanked him for his hospitality and his pajamas and reassured him as to my state of health.

"Not tonight, I'm afraid."

It wasn't like him to be so brief, without

explanations or apologies. "What's wrong?" I asked.

"I can't pull the wool over your eyes, can I?" He hesitated for a moment. "I hadn't meant to tell you. You've got enough to worry about just now."

"Oh, my God. You don't mean—"

"I don't think it can be Bobby," Giles said quickly. "There are, tragically, only too many missing children. But they want me to have a look and of course I must. Brighton. I'll probably drive straight back."

"Call me as soon as you know. Any time."

"I will. Oh, and I'd appreciate it if you wouldn't mention this to anyone—except Jennet, of course. I don't want it to get back to Lindsay. It's probably a false alarm, and there's no sense in worrying her unnecessarily. She's been prostrate ever since she heard about the fire."

"Oh. You've seen her?"

"No. I went there hoping to see Laura, but I wasn't allowed in. Darling, I must go. I'll ring you later."

After I had replaced the receiver I stood looking vacantly around the room, wondering what to do next. One answer immediately suggested itself. I filled the electric kettle and plugged it in. Then I knocked on the door of Jordan's room.

"Do you want a cup of tea?"

The most definite "no" I had ever heard thundered back at me. I filled my own cup and went to the window.

The hotel was one of the tallest buildings in the old part of town, which wasn't saying much. I could see roofs below, slate and tile and an occasional quaint bit of thatching, and beyond them the clustered little boxes of recent development. They looked as if they were huddled together for protection against the green folds of the hills that closed in around them.

Giles was probably already on his way to Brighton. Alone, sick with anticipation and dread. Even if the dead child wasn't his, it would be a horrible experience. Someone should have gone with him. I would have offered, but I knew he wouldn't have let me.

At least he didn't have Lindsay with him, keening and wringing her hands and fainting in coils. She really must be in bad shape or she'd have showed up before this, to offer tea and sympathy to the victims. Physical collapse seemed an excessive reaction to the news; no one had been killed, and Jordan, the only one she really gave a damn about, wasn't even hurt.

I could think of one reason why she might have fallen apart. Maybe Sean wasn't the only one who suspected the fire might have been deliberately set. The same grisly possibility must have occurred to Giles; it would ride with him, like a skeletal shape in the passenger seat, all the way to Brighton. Which was worse—to know your son was dead, or to wonder if he was guilty of attempted murder?

iii

Jordan emerged from his lair shortly before seven to find me watching television, or at least staring at the screen. The phone had rung several times. I had not answered it. He must have, for I had heard his voice droning on at considerable length.

"Do you want a drink?" he inquired.

"I've already had one." I indicated the minibar. "Yes."

"You mean you want another one?"

"Yes. I don't care what."

"Getting drunk doesn't help, you know."

"I *don't* know. I figured it was worth a try."

"I guess one more won't hurt you." He handed me a glass and sat down next to me. Reaching for the remote he turned off the TV.

"I was watching that."

"No, you weren't. Pay attention, there are a few things you need to know. Dad's office is handling the publicity. There has been, as you should know, quite a lot. You will refer inquiries to me, I will refer them to the office. Neither of us has any comment. Any comment at all, got that?" He didn't wait for an answer or a question. "Certain members of the administrative staff are on their way here. You don't need to know their names. They will stay in Preston to be near the hospital. As soon as Dad can be moved—most probably day after tomorrow—

he'll be transported to a private hospital near London to recuperate. You will accompany him. You will—"

"Wait just a damned minute!" I put down my glass. "Where do you get this 'you will' stuff? Why should I accompany him anywhere?"

"Because he wants you. He's been asking to see you all day. At the top of his lungs."

That shuttered face of his gave nothing away, but there was a note in his voice that deflated me like a pricked balloon. I went on the defensive.

"Why didn't you say so? I'd have gone, I thought he wasn't allowed visitors."

"He wasn't. We'll visit him tomorrow and you can argue with him about your future plans. It's between the two of you, I'm just passing on orders."

"Right," I muttered. "Obviously."

"What's that supposed to mean?"

"Nothing." Why should he care about my future plans? And why should I care whether he cared? Frank was concerned about me; that should have been enough.

"I'm sorry about your dissertation," I said. "Is everything gone?"

He looked at me in surprise. "What? Oh, that. Yes, it's gone."

"Didn't you back up your files?"

"Of course. The backup files were in my study too. Not very smart, was it?"

"Can you do it again?"

"Nice of you to take an interest," Jordan said. I couldn't tell whether he was being sarcastic. He went on in the same calm voice, "I intend to try, at any rate. I'll have to ask for an extension, and hope a major conflagration will be considered a reasonable excuse. Luckily I still have the material I found in Nottingham; I was too tired last night to take it out of the car, so it survived."

"That's where you were—in Nottingham. I meant to ask, but there hasn't been time. And it didn't seem very important."

"It isn't important—not compared with other things. I found what I hoped to find, though. Had no trouble locating the old gent, or extracting his family papers from him; he was delighted at my interest. That's why I was able to come back sooner than I expected. I haven't had a chance to examine the material yet, but from what he told me—"

A knock at the door interrupted him. He got up, stiffly and slowly. "As you said, it isn't important. That must be room service."

It was. Jennet followed the waiter and his cart; she told him we'd serve ourselves and then handed me a couple of parcels.

"It occurred to me that you didn't have a nightgown," she explained. "The proprieties must be observed."

"They certainly will be," I said, holding the garment out at arm's length. Long sleeved, high necked, pin tucked and ruffled and dripping with crochet, it was white with little flowers embroidered on the yoke. I could see Queen Victoria in that nightgown, tiptoeing shyly into Albert's room.

"That's all there was in stock," Jennet said with one of her enigmatic smiles. "Do you mind if I join you for dinner? And I wouldn't say no to a drink if anyone were kind enough to offer."

I tossed the nightgown over a chair and investigated the other parcel, while Jordan opened the bottle of wine that had come with the food. My thanks, this time, were sincere and heartfelt.

"Books! God bless you, Jennet."

"I wasn't sure what you'd like, so I brought a selection."

"Just so long as it isn't witches. I'll even settle for angels."

"Is Giles coming?" Jordan asked.

"No." The reminder cast a cold shadow over my pleasure. "He's on his way to Brighton. The police found a body."

"Poor devil," Jordan said. "You knew, Jennet?"

"Yes. I wanted to go with him, but he refused. It may not be Bob, the body was . . . Oh, Lord, I don't want to think about it. Let's eat, shall we?"

"And drink," I said, helping myself to the wine. Nobody had offered me any.

"Yes, why not? None of us has to drive, and it's been a long day. Jordan, you look done in."

"It's the result of dealing with my father's business associates," Jordan said dryly.

I had not had a long day, but I was still tired,

and I had missed at least one meal. I ate too much and I probably drank too much and I let the others do most of the talking. I tried not to think about Giles. It wasn't until I was morosely polishing off a piece of cake that I remembered someone else.

"How is Sean doing? Is he here, or still at the hospital?"

"I wondered when you'd ask," Jordan said. "The fickleness of women! He's gone back to the house."

"What?" I dropped my fork. "What house? It's gone, surely. There can't be anything left of it."

"The cottage wasn't damaged."

"But he shouldn't be there alone! How did he get there? He can't drive, with his hands."

"He'll be touched to know that you were concerned," Jordan said. "Perhaps you'd like someone to run you out there so you can tuck him into bed and open beer cans for him."

"Stop that, Jordan," Jennet ordered. She sounded like his mother. Not his father; Frank would not have been amused. "He'll be all right, Heather. Someone's looking after him."

"Ah," I said. "Doreen?"

"Mrs. Greenspan."

I had picked up my fork. I dropped it again. "I thought she was afraid to stay there at night."

"Whatever gave you that idea?" Jennet asked smoothly. "She has a home of her own, and a husband. She prefers to be with him, but this was an emergency. Sean felt the place shouldn't be left unguarded."

"That's not why Sean is there," I said. "He could have found someone else to keep an eye on the place. He's looking for evidence of arson."

"I hope he's not," Jordan said coolly. "If he interferes with the official investigation they'll arrest him."

"The police?" I stared at him. "I thought you thought—"

"Reading minds is not your forte. I said Sean was drunk last night. He'd certainly been drinking, and it's understandable that he would want to find a scapegoat. What more obvious scapegoat than that miserable child? However, in a case like this there will be an investigation. Dad's own security people would insist on it even if there were no other— Jennet? Grab her, Heather, she's going to—"

She didn't fall; she caught herself, hands gripping the arm of the chair, and straightened up. She had gone pale, but when she spoke her voice was steady.

"I don't understand. Are you saying the fire wasn't an accident? That Bob . . ."

"I'm saying we don't know. Are you sure you're all right?"

"Yes, quite. Tell me."

"Well." Jordan rubbed his forehead. "I didn't take the idea seriously at first. I've been thinking about it, though, and there are a few odd indications. The wiring in the house was new; Dad had the entire system replaced. I got home a little after twelve and went in through the kitchen door. There wasn't the slightest sign of anything wrong then, not even the smell of smoke, yet two hours later that side of the house was an inferno. There are certainly grounds for an investigation."

"Yes, all right," Jennet muttered. "I see. But why Bob?"

"His record," Jordan said bluntly. "I'm not accusing him, Jennet, but I can't think of anyone else who'd be likely to do such a thing. My father's enemies prefer more subtle methods."

"It wasn't Bobby," Jennet said. "It can't have been."

She didn't elaborate, and neither of us asked her to; it was obvious to me that her denial and distress were on Giles's account. She couldn't seem to leave the subject of the fire, though; she kept asking questions and demanding details. Most of those details were ones only I could supply; I went over the whole thing, from the cat prodding me awake to the splintery descent from the roof of the veranda. By the time I finished I was practically babbling; I hadn't realized how much it would bother me to relive those memories. Jordan listened with an air of patient boredom, though he hadn't heard all the facts either. When my voice started to wobble he interrupted.

"Enough already. Have another piece of cake."

"Bastard," I said gratefully.

"Leave my mother out of this. Why don't you go to bed?"

Jennet took the hint. I took my proper Victorian nightie and my books and retired to my room, leaving Jordan tête-à-tête with the television set. I fell asleep in the middle of a lovely story about werewolves, but I came awake instantly when the phone rang.

He said, as I had known he would, "I'm sorry to have waked you."

"For God's sake, Giles!"

"No," he said quickly. "It wasn't."

"Thank heaven."

"Yes."

"I'm so glad you let me know. Get some rest now."

"You too, love. I'll ring you tomorrow."

He didn't hang up right away. I sat with the phone to my ear, listening to his quiet breathing, until he broke the connection.

We didn't leave for the hospital until late the following morning. Jordan was in an even fouler mood than usual; he had spent several hours on the phone, and from time to time, when I went to the sitting room to get another nibble of breakfast, I would hear him shouting at whoever was on the other end.

I had a few calls too. One was from Jennet. She wanted to see me—alone.

For one of those little chats, or was she going

to propose another expedition into a place I didn't want to explore? Either way, I wasn't sorry I had a legitimate excuse to postpone the pleasure. "We're leaving for the hospital as soon as Jordan gets off the phone, and then he's going to take me to buy some clothes. At least I hope so."

She must have been at the shop; I heard someone's voice, and Jennet's response: "I'll be there in a minute." Then she said, "You'll be with Jordan today? Good. Stay with him. Call me as soon as you get back."

More orders, even more annoying than Jordan's because they made no sense. "Why don't you just tell me what this is all about?" I demanded.

"It's about . . ." She hesitated, and then went on, "About your future plans. Are you going to London with Frank?"

"For heaven's sake, Jennet, I haven't had time to think, much less make plans. If Frank wants me I probably will go to London; he's a sick man and deserves—"

"All right, all right, I'm coming," Jennet yelled. In a slightly lower voice she said, addressing me this time, "I've got to go. Just stay with Jordan. You're safe with him."

She hung up and so did I. In addition to being annoyed, I was a little hurt. She didn't have to be so obvious about getting rid of me, or insult my intelligence with hints of imminent danger. She had seen it in her crystal ball, no doubt, and would tell me all about it when we met. "Safe with Jordan" implied I wasn't safe with other people. Like, for instance, Giles.

He had been the first to call. He had asked me to have dinner with him that evening. Jennet needn't have been so unsubtle. I would probably never see Giles again. There was no reason for me to come back to the area.

The third telephone call was the most surprising. As soon as Lindsay identified herself I said, "Jordan is on the other phone."

She said that was quite all right, she wanted to talk with me anyhow. How was I? How was Frank getting on? Were we comfortable at the hotel? Was there anything she could do for any of us?

I said all the proper things and asked how she was. Big mistake. She told me, at length, about how shocked she had been to hear of the fire. She wanted to know all about it. She wanted to know all about everything—especially my future plans. I had to admit she was more polite than Jennet. She said she was sorry I was leaving so soon and asked if we could get together before I went. Tea, lunch, dinner, whatever?

Praying that Jordan would bang on my door and announce it was time for us to go, I made excuses, some true, some not. Finally I said, "I've got to hang up, Lindsay, Jordan is yelling for me. You know how he is when he's in a hurry."

She said, yes, she did.

When Jordan finally emerged I was making a shopping list. It was depressingly long. "Ready?" he asked.

"I've been ready for over an hour."

He glanced at the breakfast tray. "You haven't eaten all the rolls."

We went out through a back entrance and skulked through alleys to reach the car—a rental, I assumed, since it wasn't his.

"Is all this necessary?" I inquired, as we headed out of town.

"No, I'm doing it because I enjoy playing hide and seek. This," said Jordan, slamming his foot down and roaring past a van, "is my father's normal lifestyle."

"And you hate it. You don't have to take it out on me."

He slackened speed a little. "I've made arrangements for your name to be added to one of the corporate accounts. You'll get the card today. You will be picked up at the hotel tomorrow and driven to London. You've a reservation at the Savoy. The car and driver will be at your disposal while you're there, and someone from the office will accompany you to the embassy to help with arrangements for a new passport."

After a moment I said temperately, "Is that all?"

"No. But that's all you need to know now. One of Dad's people will be in touch as soon as you arrive in London; he or she will help you with the other arrangements."

"Have you bought my plane ticket back to the States?"

His hands tightened on the wheel. "I just

want to get you out of here. Once you're in London you can do as you like."

"I will."

Neither of us spoke again until we reached the hospital. Taking my arm, Jordan hurried me into the elevator. We got quite a few curious looks, and no wonder. My outfit wasn't any more eccentric than others I had seen, but if I had been a security guard I would have stopped Jordan before he crossed the lobby. In the same wrinkled ill-fitting garments he had worn the day before, darkly scowling, he looked like a gangster.

As soon as we got out of the elevator he was pounced on by several people—some of the ones whose names I didn't need to know, I gathered, because he didn't introduce us. One of the men, who looked like a prosperous banker, exclaimed, "Miss Tradescant? Thank goodness you're here, he's been asking for you."

"I'll bet he has," Jordan said. "Go ahead, Heather. That's his room, the second on the right."

"Aren't you coming?"

"No."

The nameless ones—two men and a woman, all carrying briefcases, all dressed like bankers—surrounded him and escorted him toward the waiting room.

The room looked like a flower shop—or a funeral home. Frank looked very pathetic, flat on his back, hands motionless on the white spread—until he opened his eyes. They were dim and dark at first, but when he recognized me a ghost of the good old wicked sparkle appeared.

"Finally!" he muttered. "Where have you been?"

I was only allowed ten minutes, and he spent most of it telling me what he wanted me to do. He had it all worked out; Jordan might have been stuck with making the arrangements, but I didn't doubt the overall plan was Frank's. I argued about some of the details, because I thought it would amuse him and liven him up, but I didn't try to change the subject. It was safer than some of the topics he might have asked about. When the nurse poked her head in and made gestures at me, he told her to go to hell in almost his old bellow.

"Shame on you," I said. "Such language! I'll see you tomorrow, Frank."

I was holding his hand. His fingers tightened. "You will, won't you? You'll stay with me?"

"As long as you need me." Gently I withdrew my hand. "Now get some rest and stop bullying the nurses."

I didn't get to meet the nameless ones at all that day. Jordan was in the waiting room with them, looking beleaguered; as soon as I appeared he jumped up, took my hand, and towed me out, leaving them waving folders at him.

"That wasn't very nice," I said.

"You don't know anything about it, so kindly refrain from comment." He thrust an envelope at me. "Here's your credit card and travel confirmation."

"What am I supposed to do with it? I don't have a purse and there are no pockets in this skirt."

"Oh. Yes, that had better be the next project. I suppose you expect to be fed, too."

I waited until we were in the car and he had backed out of the parking space before I answered. "Just take me back to Troytan."

"Why, in God's name?"

"So I can get my car. I'm sure Frank ordered you not to let me out of your sight, but I'm sick of being treated like a two year old and I won't have you standing around sighing and looking patient while I shop, and I can feed myself." I opened the envelope. The card was silver. Or was it platinum? "I'm going to pay it back," I growled. "You're going the wrong way. Turn around."

"Don't be childish. We're practically there." Which we were; the hospital was on the outskirts of the town. Jordan continued, "I have no intention of standing around watching you buy clothes, I'd rather be manually strangled. I'll meet you in an hour—there, at that restaurant. If you don't want to eat you can watch me. I missed breakfast."

He had almost finished his lunch by the time I joined him. "I'm only twenty minutes late," I announced, before he could complain. "And I'm not finished, either."

In silence Jordan appraised me and I returned the compliment. He had acquired slacks, shirt and jacket, and, I presumed, the accompanying underpinnings, and one smallish suitcase. I was wearing one of my new outfits—slacks, shirt and jacket—and carrying my new purse. I piled my parcels on and under and around the vacant chairs and sat down. He handed me a menu.

"No comment?" I inquired.

"You look fine."

"Thank you." I had had time to think about what I wanted to say, and I proceeded to say it. "I don't want to start a fight, Jordan, I just want to get a few things straight. I'll hang around until Frank is better, if that's what he wants. He's got some goofy notion that I'm a mascot or good-luck charm, though why he should cling to that idea after he almost got killed—"

"The key word is almost," Jordan said, impassive as a toad. "If you hadn't been there he would have died."

"Who knows what would have happened? Frank thinks I was sent here, by God or fate or something, as part of some eternal pattern. I don't, but my opinion is irrelevant. Right now he needs me or thinks he does, which is the same thing, so I'll stick. When he doesn't need me anymore I'll be on my way."

"Where?"

"I don't know yet. But I'm closer to knowing than I was a week ago. What you said that night, about hating and blaming . . . You had a hell of a nerve saying it, but you were right. I think I'm on the road to recovery now. It will take a while, but I've made a start. No, don't interrupt me, if I lose track of what I want to say I'll never get through this. There's one more thing. I don't know exactly how to put it. . . ." I gestured irritably at a man who was standing next to my chair. "What does he want?"

"He's the waiter," Jordan said in a stifled voice. "If I were to hazard a guess, I'd suspect he wants to take your order."

"Oh. I don't care. Coffee and a sandwich. Cheese or ham or something."

"You must have something serious on your mind if you can't concentrate on food." Waving the waiter away Jordan studied me intently. There was the queerest look on his face. "Maybe this isn't the time or the place—"

"No, I have to say it now." I took a deep breath. "You're jealous. Oh, I don't blame you, I would be too if my father took a fancy to some unknown nobody just to spite me. You needn't worry. I don't want Frank's money, I'm going to repay every penny, and I don't want . . ." The words I had meant to say wouldn't come out. They weren't true. I tried again. "I don't want anything of his that is rightfully yours. You don't have to be so all-fired anxious to get rid of me. You and everybody else! I thought . . . Damn it! What does he want now?"

I glared at the unfortunate waiter. He deposited a plate on the table and fled.

Jordan's face had undergone an alarming series of transformations. It was now darkly flushed. "Who wants to get rid of you?" he asked in a strangled voice.

"Besides you? Lindsay, of course. That didn't hurt my feelings much, but I thought Jennet was beginning to like me."

"What makes you think she doesn't?"

I repeated the conversation I had had with Jennet that morning. His color gradually subsided and when I wound down he said mildly, "Eat your sandwich. You're doing Jennet an injustice. You may not believe in her powers, but she does, genuinely and sincerely."

"Do you?"

"No, of course not. Feelings, hunches, whatever you call them, are prompted by subconscious worries or desires. I think it's concern for you, not dislike, that prompted this one."

I had my own opinion about that. Subconscious maybe, but Jennet had one reason to want me out of town, and it came under the heading of desires, not concern.

"No comment?" Jordan inquired.

"No."

"Have you finished what you wanted to say?"

"Yes."

"Do you want to hear what else I think?"

"No."

"Damn it," Jordan said savagely.

He wasn't talking to me. The waiter started to back away. Jordan plucked the check out of his hand and the man retreated. I doubted he would return.

"Let's get out of here," Jordan said.

Jordan graciously allowed me another hour

to finish my shopping. He even carried my packages to the car. No reason why he shouldn't be gracious, now that I was doing what he wanted. He seemed abstracted. Once or twice he started to speak, glanced at me, and fell silent. If it had been anybody but Jordan I would have said he was embarrassed about something, though I couldn't imagine what.

I insisted on one thing, and that was the retrieval of my rental car. He gave in with poor grace, and as we turned into the familiar lane I asked, "Have you been there since the fire?"

"No, and I'm not keen on viewing the ruins. You won't like it either."

"We ought to see how Sean is making out."

Jordan made a rude noise.

"Surely not with Mrs. Greenspan," I said.

We found her in the kitchen of the cottage, having a cup of tea. She greeted me with a rumble of pleasure, produced a plate of cookies, and invited us to have a cup with her. Jordan said we didn't have time. "I told Jenkins I'd meet her at the hotel at five."

I deduced that Jenkins was the woman who had been at the hospital—the only female among the nameless. "What for?" I asked.

It was none of my business, and the look Jordan gave me said as much. "Signing things. They give 'em to me, I sign 'em. Let's get your car."

"Go on back to the hotel. There's no point in your staying."

"When are you . . ." He glanced at Mrs.

Greenspan and started again. "I may as well have a word with Sean while I'm here. You said he was at the garage, Mrs. Greenspan?"

Sean wasn't in the garage. He was standing by the blackened rubble that had been the kitchen. I had a feeling he had spent a good many hours in that same position.

Jordan had been right. I didn't like it. Two of the chimneys and a section of the wall of the north wing still stood, but everything else was gone—a pile of burned, broken fragments as high as my head. The most horrible things were the bits and pieces that were still identifiable—a cast-iron frying pan, the oven door, the lower part of an aluminum ladder. It must have been the one Sean had used. The top half had melted into a fused shapeless mass.

Sean greeted Jordan with a nod. With me he was more forthcoming. "Hi, Heather. Have you seen the old man yet?"

"Yes, this morning. He's doing okay. How are you?"

"Not bad." He certainly looked a lot better than he had. Except for the bandages on his hands and the blistered skin on his wrists and forearms, he was relatively undamaged. The skin on his forehead was peeling and someone had trimmed his beard. Without that impressive black bush the resemblance to John the Younger was gone.

The portrait was gone too. The rare books, the letter from Roger Fallon, all the treasures

Frank had collected—I would regret their loss for a long time, but they were inconsequential compared to the things that had survived.

I headed for the garage, leaving Sean and Jordan talking. The doors were open. Everything looked so normal it seemed abnormal, after the total ruin of the house—except that the Bentley was covered with a faint film of dust. Poor Sean. It must drive him crazy to see that dust on his beloved and not be able to use his hands.

I started toward my car and then remembered something I had unaccountably overlooked. "Damn it!" I exclaimed.

"Now what?" Jordan asked. He and Sean had followed me.

"The keys. I don't have the damn keys, they were in my purse."

"You should have thought of that before you dragged me all the way out here."

"You didn't think of it either!"

"You don't need the car anyway. You're leaving tomorrow."

"Yes, I . . . No, I'm not! They won't be moving Frank tomorrow, he's not well enough yet." It was only a guess, but his eyes shifted and I knew I was right. He was so frantic to get me out of his life he had made arrangements to send me to London ahead of Frank.

"You couldn't stand it for another twenty-four hours?" I demanded furiously. "You can just cancel your damned car and driver for tomor-

row. I'll go when I'm good and ready, and I'll figure out some way—"

"How about the extra key?" Sean inquired.

"What extra . . . Do you have it?"

"Uh-huh. I took it off your keyring before I
returned it. Figured you wouldn't notice one
was missing. It was the old man's idea," he
added quickly.

"And a good idea, as it turned out. Hadn't
you better get going, Jordan? You don't want to
keep Jenkins waiting."

Jordan turned on his heel and stalked away.
"What was that all about?" Sean asked.

"Oh, just one of Jordan's little games. Never
mind. Are you managing all right? I'd have
come out before this if I hadn't known Mrs.
Greenspan was here."

"Thanks. I inquired about you too, in case no
one mentioned it." His smile stretched the
cracked skin of his lips. They were shiny with
ointment of some kind. "Are you in a hurry?
Come and sit for a few minutes."

"Okay."

I thought he intended to go back to the cottage, but instead he led the way toward the table
and chairs under the oak tree. I turned my chair
so I wouldn't have to look at the blackened
wreckage. The sun shone bright and warm on
the green grass, and the old terrace wall was
outlined in shadow.

"I wonder if Frank intends to go ahead with
the garden work," I said.

Sean lifted his left foot onto his right knee. "Sure. He'll be back. You couldn't kill the old man with a blowtorch." He waited for a moment, watching me. Then he said, "It was arson, Heather. A team was out here this morning."

"That was quick."

"You can get anything you want as quick as you want if you're working for Franklin Karim," Sean said. "They'll locate the kid before long. Not the cops, they aren't worth shit. Our people."

"Sean, you can't be certain—"

"Who else could it have been?" He uncrossed his legs and leaned toward me. The doctor must have given him something for pain; his eyes were blackly dilated. "It was an amateur job, Heather. Gasoline and kerosene splashed all over the kitchen. Whoever did it knew how and where to short the alarm. It didn't go off. I was asleep—yes, and I'd been drinking, I admit that—but I'd have heard it."

"I didn't hear anything either. But how would a child—"

He waved this objection away. "He's thirteen. Boys that age build pipe bombs and hot-wire cars and strip down automatic weapons. He's been here a number of times, poking and prying and asking questions. They found one of his secret hiding places this afternoon—a tumble-down shed, not far from his grandmother's house. He had stockpiled jerricans of gas, there were a couple still there."

It was a damning indictment, and given the boy's past record, horribly convincing. "Where do you think he is now?"

"There." Sean's bandaged hand indicated the jungle. "Maybe not all the time, but he'll be back."

And Sean would be waiting for him. The look on Sean's face, the way he sat, senses alert and muscles flexed, like a fighter ready to attack, turned me cold. Such a passion for revenge against a boy—still a child, for all Sean had said, for all Bobby had done—was exaggerated, unnatural. The slight figure in the neat school uniform of blue sweater and gray slacks had looked so harmless.

I wondered if Sean had spent the night here under the big tree, ears alert for the slightest sound, eyes fixed on the looming dark mass. That strange unnatural growth had become a symbol of everything wrong, the source and the focus of all the danger. I knew that was silly and superstitious, but if I had had a chain saw in my hands at that moment I'd have attacked it, hacking and slashing.

Then I saw the creature walking slowly across the grass. My cry of surprise brought Sean out of his chair in a single spring.

"It's just the cat," I said quickly. "Or is it the same one? Tibb—Tibb, is that you?"

His tail flipped up and he broke into a trot. People were sitting under the tree, the same people who had fed him salmon sandwiches. It was Tibb, all right. I was so glad to see him I forgot I was nervous of cats. I scooped him up into my arms and hugged him.

Sean dropped back into his chair. "You weren't that happy to see me," he said, with a good imitation of his old grin. "What do I have to do to get a hug?"

Tibb had indicated in no uncertain terms that he wished to be put down. I lowered him to the ground. "You don't understand. I thought he was dead—trapped in the house. How did he get out? If he hadn't waked me none of us would have gotten out. Oh, Tibb, you're a hero, and I did try to find you, and I'm sorry I don't have any salmon. I'll bring you some tomorrow."

Tibb rubbed against my leg, unable to believe he wasn't going to be fed. Sean reached down as if to scratch his ears, but withdrew his bandaged hand, wincing. "He's entitled to free salmon for the rest of his life, all right. I guess we'll never know now how he got in and out of the house. The old servants' stairs maybe; they're blocked up, but a cat can find holes people don't see."

It had finally dawned on Tibb that there were no sandwiches. A hero he might be, but his manners left a great deal to be desired. He spat at Sean and stalked off, tail switching. I went after him, burbling apologies and promises— and then I stopped. He was heading straight for the jungle. He didn't hesitate or cast around.

One second he was there, the next second he was gone.

Sean brushed past me. His eyes were fixed on the spot where the cat had vanished. He looked like a sleepwalker. When his bandaged hands reached out I caught at his sleeve.

"Sean, what are you doing?"

"That's where he went," Sean said. "Right there." He tried to flex his hands, grimaced, and swore. For a second I thought he was going to rip off the bandages with his teeth. "Damn! I can't hold onto anything. Heather, go get a hoe or rake from the shed. And some stakes."

Arguing with him would have been as pointless as debating with Tibb. If I didn't do as he asked he'd do it himself, somehow, no matter how much it hurt him. I ran toward the garden shed, leaving him standing like a pillar, marking the spot. When I got back he hadn't moved, not even his eyes.

I tried to ram the heavy metal stake into the ground, but it wouldn't penetrate the mat of roots and grass, so I poked it into the brambles. So thick was the tangle the stake protruded at right angles, held firmly in place. "There, that will mark the spot. Tomorrow—"

"The hell with tomorrow. Shove it in farther. No—wait. Pull it out and try again, lower down."

I was tempted to cheat. The crucial area was only five feet high and a couple of feet wide. One glance at his inflexible face told me he would keep me at it until I found what he wanted. It was there, where Jennet had told me it was—a single narrow space where the barrier was thinner.

The stake was thirty-six inches long. Two feet of its length still protruded when I felt the resistance lessen. The far end had broken through into empty space.

After a period of prodding and pushing I found the edge of the thorny curtain with the hoe handle, but I wasn't strong enough to lift it out of the way.

"That's it." My breath was coming hard, and not from effort. I didn't want to go in there. I was trying to talk myself, and Sean, out of it. I had a nasty feeling I wouldn't succeed. "That's it, Sean. No more. I'm not dressed for this and you're not fit."

He covered his face with his arms, turned his back, ducked his head and pushed through.

I had borrowed a pair of Will's gardening gloves; I knew I'd need them when I used the stake. Had I also known this was the inevitable end, that I would be no more able than Sean to resist the need to learn the truth? We wouldn't find the boy. He would run from pursuit and he knew the pathways as we did not. But there was something there, something waiting.

I picked up the stake and followed Sean's example, backing in and bowing my head. His arm stopped me when I broke through. There was enough light for me to see his face, shiny with sweat as well as salve, and the trickle of blood that ran down from under his scorched hair.

"Do you know where we are?" he asked.

The place where we were couldn't be called a side passage, it was more like an alcove. Beyond I saw green walls curving off in both directions and sunlight—golden now, as the sun sank lower—filtering through the roof. I didn't know where we were, it all looked the same, but I said, "Let me go first," and edged past him.

Within five feet we hit a dead end, and it took several minutes of poking with the stake to find the veiled continuation of the passage. Our progress was slow—stooping, testing the uneven ground for fear a stumble would throw us against the thorny wall. As we went on I became conscious of a strange, sickly smell. It faded and then suddenly grew stronger.

"Stop," Sean said.

I had to stop. We had entered another false passage. Directly ahead it ended in a rougher, more tangled barrier than the others we had seen. It resembled a pile of brush, the foliage wilted and withering.

"Back up," I gasped. "I can't turn around, it's too narrow."

"You'll have to. Let me past."

"No, it's a dead end. I'll have to find the . . ." I stopped and swallowed the bile that threatened to choke me. "God! Let's get out of here. What's that awful smell?"

Sean said very softly, "Back up, Heather. Two steps. Now another one. Here you go."

He had found the veil of thornless vines that hid the continuation of the passage and was holding it aside with his arm. It might have been the stench, and my suspicion of what it was, that provoked me; it might have been frustration, the need to do something violent and forceful after those long minutes of slow, painstaking progress. I grabbed the vines with gloved hands and yanked as hard as I could, ripping them free and tossing them aside. The passage ran straight for another ten feet. At its end I saw sunlight and the glimmer of something solid and white.

"I know where we are now," I exclaimed. "Sean? What are you doing? It's this way."

He had gone on, dropping to his knees in front of the barrier at the end of the dead end. I was about to call out to him when he jerked upright with a choked exclamation. Then he edged back, still on his knees, and slowly, carefully, stood up. Now I could see what his stooped body had hidden before. In the sun-speckled shadows it resembled an oddly shaped fungus, pale white against the tangled stems, spreading out into protrusions that looked like . . . They were fingers. The fingers of a small human hand.

Sean came to me. "Go on," he said.

"Is it—"

"I didn't uncover the face. But he's got on a blue sweater. Can you hang on? There's no room to faint here, and I don't think I can drag you out."

I would like to think it was fortitude that kept me calm, but it was probably shock. I wanted out of that place so badly I couldn't think about anything else. "Right," I said. "Which way?"

"This way."

Sean hadn't spoken. The voice had come from behind me, from the end of the passage, the heart of the maze, where the goddess awaited her worshippers. I turned my head. Someone was there—a slight slim figure wearing a blue sweater and gray slacks.

THIRTEEN

*There is but one path that leads to the centre
and that is attended with some difficulties and
a good many steps.*

STEPHEN SWITZER, *ICHNOGRAPHIA RUSTICA*, 1742

At that time and in that place anything seemed possible. That's what it was all about, after all—rebirth, resurrection.

Sean let out the sound a man might make after he's been punched hard in the pit of the stomach. It wasn't until later that I realized what had prompted it. The consequences of what he had found hadn't sunk in until that moment.

It took me even longer. After the first instant of shock I had recognized her, but I didn't know what Sean knew. When she said, "Come here, both of you," I still didn't understand—until she added, in the same gentle voice, "Or run, if you like. It won't matter."

I couldn't retreat, much less run. Sean was close behind me, barring the way. "Go ahead," he muttered.

Lindsay stood in front of the statue, so slight and childish in the boy's clothes that the shotgun looked like a toy—an ugly, authentic toy. "It was my daddy's," she explained, seeing me stare. "He taught me how to use it. Mummy's kept it all these years."

Sean emerged from the passage and straightened up. "You don't want to do this, Lindsay. Someone will hear the shot."

"Shots," she corrected, with a dimpled smile. "I'd prefer some other way, but I don't suppose it will matter. There's no one here except Mrs. Greenspan and she'll assume someone is hunting rabbits. I'm sorry, Sean, but you leave me no choice. You'd tell them about Bobby, and he mustn't be found yet. They would know he couldn't have set the fire."

"You killed him?" I gasped. "Your own son?"

"You don't suppose I wanted to do it!" Her voice rose in genuine outrage. "It wasn't easy for me."

"Harder for him," I said, swallowing.

"I wouldn't hurt him. It was quick and painless—well, almost painless. The last thing he said was, 'Mummy.'" Her voice broke.

The most horrible thing was that her emotions were absolutely sincere. She wasn't protesting too much, in order to cover an underlying awareness of guilt. She felt none.

"It was your fault," she went on angrily. "If you hadn't come here—"

"Mine?"

"Shut up," Sean said. "Lindsay, I'm not going to tell anyone. You can trust me. You know how I feel about you. I'll help you. There are easier ways."

Lips pursed, she considered the idea. Then she shook her head. "Sean, I'd like to believe you, but I can't take the chance. You must see that."

"I haven't told anyone you were with me the night of the fire. What can I do to prove I love you—that I'd do anything for you?"

Her eyes brightened. "Kill her."

That should do it, I thought crazily. Sean hadn't known she had set the fire. She could have managed the whole thing quite easily while he slept, drugged or drunk and worn out with making love. Now that he knew, there was only one way out for him if he wanted to stay alive.

Sean turned slightly. I backed away. I was still holding the stake but I couldn't bring myself to strike at him. What could he do with those painful, bandaged hands?

I soon found out. Sean kicked the stake out of my hand. His arm caught me across the chest and knocked me down. I went sprawling across the carpet of moss, tearing ugly holes in the pristine surface. I heard Lindsay laugh, and Sean call out, and another sound, the ugly sodden sound of a blow that must have missed because I didn't feel it. I knew I was as good as dead though. Sean didn't need his hands. I curled up like a worm, trying to protect my face.

It wasn't his booted foot that smashed into the ground a few inches from my head. It was the butt of the gun. Reflexively I scrambled away from it. Lindsay swung the shotgun again, not at me this time, at Sean. The other blow, the one I had heard but had not felt, must have been aimed at him. And it had struck him; his face was distorted with pain. He got his arm up in time to save his face, but the impact sent him staggering back against the white slenderness of the statue. He fell to his knees and Lindsay spun around to face me. Her face was luminous with laughter and she held the heavy weapon as lightly as if it had been a fan.

I stumbled to my feet. I wanted the stake, but there was no way I could get it, it was behind her and she was coming at me, swinging the shotgun. She wouldn't fire unless she had to, and she didn't have to now; Sean was bent over, unable to rise, and one of those swinging blows was bound to connect sooner or later, on my head or my shoulder or my knee. Once I was down, I was done for.

I ducked behind the statue and heard the crash as the gun struck it.

It cracked clean across the slender ankles and fell, straight and hard.

ii

Jennet was waiting for me when I came out of the hospital room.

"What are you doing here?" I asked, though I didn't really care very much. "I thought you'd be with Giles."

"He wouldn't let me stay with him. Can I talk to you for a minute?"

I thought of shrugging, but it was too much effort. "Okay. I'm not going anyplace in particular."

"You've talked with the police?"

"Some. They want me to come in tomorrow and give them a more detailed statement."

I balked, though, when she started toward the waiting room. I had spent too many terrible hours in that dismal little room. "Not there. I'm really not in the mood for a prolonged conversation, Jennet. Jordan is downstairs, dealing with insurance and admissions and the rest; he's pretty mad at me, but if I don't keep him waiting he may be willing to give me a lift back to the hotel. What did you want to say?"

She leaned against the wall and folded her arms. "First, to thank you for calling me. Giles wouldn't have."

I managed a slight shrug. "Second?"

I expected an apology, or at least a show of embarrassment. Instead she fixed a furious glare on me and snapped, "I warned you. Why didn't you stay with Jordan?"

I glared back. I had just come from saying good night and a few other things to Sean, wrapped in bandages and groggy with painkillers, and I was in no mood to be bullied. "Because you didn't give me a reason, that's why. You must have suspected Lindsay was the arsonist. That's why you told me I'd be safe with Jordan; you knew she wouldn't do anything to endanger him. So why the hell didn't you say so or go to the police, instead of giving me mysterious occult hints? They almost got me and Sean killed!"

"It's not that simple." She leaned toward me; her eyes held mine as effectively as her hands might have done. "Why should you have believed me? You knew I had a simple, selfish motive for wanting you away from . . . Oh, hell, why not admit it? Away from Giles. I've loved him for years, and I was so jealous of you I began to wonder whether I was unconsciously inventing reasons why you should get away from this place—and him.

"Well, now it's finished, and I've lost, and it doesn't matter whether you believe me or not.

"I knew Bob was dead, Heather. That was what I felt that night, what I described—darkness, nothingness, and the barrier between the dead and the living. I didn't say so; how could I, with all of you thinking I was putting on an act and poor Giles still hoping? It wasn't until last night, when Jordan admitted the fire was deliberate, that the possibility of Lindsay's guilt occurred to me. I lay awake all night putting the pieces together.

"Someone had set that fire, and it was not Bobby. I started with that assumption—that fact, as I knew it to be—and other facts began to make a horrible sort of sense. Your illness, and the image in your bed, after Lindsay had spent some time alone in your room; the fact that Jordan had been away from the house that day and had returned unexpectedly, unbeknownst even to you; the fact that one consequence of the fire would be postponement of work on the garden—and the maze. I had an advantage over you; I knew I hadn't done any of those things, and that no other member of our group had done them. Lindsay had been one of us. Not for long; when I learned she was dabbling in black magic for her own selfish purposes I took steps to expel her. But she knew about the maze. I was afraid she had profaned the place by showing it to Bobby and letting him hide there. I swear, Heather, I never suspected she had profaned it in another way. She must have gone back the night Jordan saw the light there, and tried to conceal the body by cutting and piling brush over it.

"But that was all I had this morning—theories, feelings, hunches. The police would have laughed at me. You would have laughed at me. I didn't know Lindsay had been with Sean that night, or that she would follow you today. I didn't realize how much she hated and feared you—or why. I did try to warn you, but I thought you'd be safe, for a while at least. I . . ."

The flood of words stopped. Face drawn, body sagging, she looked drained of emotion and feeling. But she hadn't quite finished. "I may as well make a clean breast of it. Early this morning, just at dawn, I tried to foresee. I had taken your scorched, torn nightgown away with me, so you wouldn't have to see it and be reminded of what had happened. I used that; and after I had held it a while and focused my mind as I have learned to do, I saw. You and Jordan, smiling, holding one another's hands."

Jordan was waiting downstairs, glancing at his watch and looking like a Gorgon. I deduced he was still mad at me. He offered Jennet a lift, but she declined; she had driven herself and could get home all right.

As she turned away I said impulsively, "Go to him."

"He told me—"

"The hell with that. He won't ask for what he needs and wants. You're his friend, aren't you? Kick the door and yell till he lets you in."

Her lined face broke into a smile. "All right. I will if you will."

I didn't have to ask what she meant. I shook my head. "I don't think—"

"Try it. You might be surprised."

She didn't say good night. Straightening her

shoulders, she walked briskly and with purpose toward the door.

Jordan cleared his throat. "Finished?"

"It sure looks that way," I said.

In ominous silence he led the way to where he had parked the car. He let me open my own door. "Buckle up," he said shortly.

Stars shone in the dark vault of the sky. Jordan drove slowly, without speaking. He didn't look at me.

No living person had been the instrument of Lindsay's death. Her end had been quick and merciful—more merciful, some might say, than she deserved—but it had also spared the innocent. Giles wouldn't have to endure a prolonged painful trial, long drawn-out arguments between psychiatrists and mental health experts, public probing into private torments. The goddess had judged and condemned, and carried out the sentence with what some might consider supernatural accuracy.

Jordan broke into my musings. "Roger Fallon was a member of the coven."

It took me a minute to remember who Roger Fallon was.

"What the hell does that have to do with anything?" I demanded. "How can you think about your damned dissertation at a time like this?"

"It all goes back to that." Jordan slowed for a turn. "If you believe in the twisting and turning of the labyrinth of fate, his involvement was the start. He betrayed the other Pendle 'witches' to save his own skin. His testimony was kept secret, so his name never appeared in the official records of the trial, but it was he who built the maze and placed the statue there. Over three hundred years later the belief was still alive. Lindsay was a member of the coven—"

"Oh, so you figured that out, did you? But they kicked her out when they discovered she was playing around with black magic. Their fundamental rule is 'Do no harm.' Lindsay would have found some other way of doing harm if she'd never heard of Wicca."

"Obviously. She didn't need black magic to get to Sean."

"That's not fair. He didn't know Bobby was dead. The case against the boy was overwhelming. It wasn't until we found the body that Sean realized Lindsay must have drugged him that night and stolen his keys. She'd have shot both of us if he hadn't pretended to go along with her plan. The way he handled her was absolutely brilliant. He even had me believing for a minute or two that he was so madly in love with her he was willing to dispose of me."

"Quite the hero," Jordan said sourly.

"Well, he was. Two cracked ribs and a concussion on top of his other injuries—at least he's in the hospital, where he'll be properly cared for. It's Giles I'm worried about. His son and his wife, both dead, and the scandal . . ."

"He'll make out all right. He's better off without them."

"You are a cold-blooded bastard," I said angrily.

"Do you want something to eat?"

"Yes."

Jordan slammed on the brake and pulled off the road. "This isn't a restaurant," I said. "It's a shop, and it's closed."

"I can read." He wrapped his arms around the steering wheel and stared straight ahead, out the window. The small parking lot was empty and the lighted sign of the shop was some distance away. I could only see his profile in outline. "The one thing you haven't mentioned is motive."

"The police didn't ask me about that."

"Tactful of them. Surely you have a theory."

"I was trying to spare your feelings," I said.

"That would be a first. Well?"

"She wanted to marry money. Simple as that, to a mind as warped and selfish as hers. She did make advances to Frank, didn't she? Well, maybe you didn't know about that, but I'll bet she did. He laughed at her. So . . ." Jordan lowered his head onto his arms and I said, in some annoyance, "I don't know why men always have to take these things personally. She didn't care about anybody, she wasn't capable of caring. She got rid of the boy because he had become an impediment and an embarrassment and a damned nuisance—that's how she would put it, anyhow. When she started the fire she didn't know you had come back—she was genuinely shocked when she found out she had almost killed you, that was never part of the plan. She would have been quite happy to get rid of Frank and me, but her primary motive was to stop him from proceeding with the garden restoration. She couldn't risk having the body found too soon; an autopsy might have determined when Bobby died and how he died—not of exposure or some other natural cause, but violently. She wrote that note herself. It stopped us from investigating the maze, and directed the search farther afield. Jennet—"

But I couldn't tell him what Jennet had said. He wouldn't believe it—any of it.

"Jennet suspected the truth, she knew about Lindsay's proclivities and she—uh—she noticed that the note was printed, not written by hand. She was suspicious, but she wasn't sure. She was going to tell me tonight. Now can I have something to eat? I haven't had any dinner, you know."

His voice muffled, Jordan said, "Where do you want to go?"

"Anyplace. Except The Witches' Cauldron."

"I thought . . . What about Giles? Don't you want to be with him?"

"Jennet is with him." I was beginning to get ideas that had nothing to do with witches or murder or tragedy; my stomach felt funny, and it wasn't because I was hungry. "Giles is a dear sweet man. Just like my father. Too much like my father. I don't want another sweet, kind man who puts up with a miserable life because he hasn't got guts enough to break free. I'm not blaming my dad; I loved him and I don't regret those years, but . . . um . . ."

Jordan didn't move. I said hopefully, "I don't want a hero either."

"A characteristic compliment." Jordan raised his head. "Unfasten your seat belt."

"What?"

"I said, unbuckle the damned seat belt!"

He had to do it, my hands were too unsteady, but when he reached for me they moved smoothly into place around his shoulders, as if we had rehearsed it a dozen times.

"I suspected as much," he said, after a long, breathless interval.

"So did I."

"I might have known you'd say that. You're always right, aren't you?"

"No. Kiss me again."

"Why not?"

It was even better than the first time. Giddy with disbelief, I leaned against him. "When did you know you . . . Come to think of it, you haven't mentioned that word yet."

"When did I know I was in love with you? I can't remember exactly. It grew on me. How about you?"

"The night of the fire, of course. When I realized I almost left you there . . . I can't think about it."

"Then don't. And I'll try not to think about

you nearly getting yourself killed this afternoon. How could you have been such an idiot?"

"You're so romantic," I murmured.

"I haven't even begun to be romantic," Jordan said, and kissed me again. "The only negative aspect of this situation is that the old man is going to take the credit for it."

"Who cares what he thinks?"

"Not me. Not now."

"I think that's a policeman," I remarked, as a car turned into the parking area and headlights glared accusingly at us. "We'd better get moving."

"Oh, right." He let me go and slid back behind the wheel. "You're probably starved. You know, I love the way you eat. You do it with such enthusiasm."

I said, "I'm not hungry."

"What?" He gave me a startled look.

"I can wait till later. Breakfast, even."

"Then let's go home," Jordan said, and put his foot down on the gas.

New from **Barbara Michaels**—a tale of terror only she could tell.

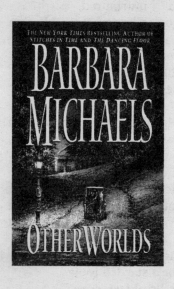
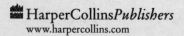